W9-BWB-981

THE
ONES
WE
BURN

THE
ONES
WE
BURN

Rebecca Mix

MARGARET K. MCELDERRY BOOKS

NEW YORK LONDON TORONTO SYDNEY NEW DELHI

MARGARET K. McELDERRY BOOKS

An imprint of Simon & Schuster Children's Publishing Division

1230 Avenue of the Americas, New York, New York 10020

Text © 2022 by Rebecca Mix

Jacket illustration © 2022 by Eliot Baum

Jacket design by Karyn Lee © 2022 by Simon & Schuster, Inc.

MARGARET K. McELDERRY BOOKS is a trademark of Simon & Schuster, Inc.

For information about special discounts for bulk purchases, please contact Simon & Schuster Special Sales at 1-866-506-1949 or business@simonandschuster.com. The Simon & Schuster Speakers Bureau can bring authors to your live event. For more information or to book an event, contact the Simon & Schuster Speakers Bureau at 1-866-248-3049 or visit our website at www.simonspeakers.com.

Interior design by Karyn Lee

The text for this book was set in ITC Galliard.

Manufactured in the United States of America

First Edition

10 9 8 7 6 5 4 3 2 1

Library of Congress Cataloging-in-Publication Data

Names: Mix, Rebecca, author.

Title: The ones we burn / Rebecca Mix.

Description: First edition. | New York City : Margaret K. McElderry Books, [2022] | Audience: Ages 14+. | Audience: Grades 10–12. | Summary: A blood-witch's mission to assassinate the prince she is betrothed to is compromised by the discovery of a deadly plague—and the beautiful princess intent on stopping it.

Identifiers: LCCN 2021055951 (print) | LCCN 2021055952 (ebook)

ISBN 9781534493513 (hardcover) | ISBN 9781534493537 (ebook)

Subjects: CYAC: Witches—Fiction. | Princesses—Fiction. | Diseases—Fiction. | Lesbians—Fiction. | LCGFT: Novels. Classification: LCC PZ7.1.M6348 On 2022 (print) | LCC PZ7.1.M6348 (ebook) | DDC [Fic]—dc23

LC record available at https://lccn.loc.gov/2021055951

LC ebook record available at https://lccn.loc.gov/2021055952

for the kids who survived.
may your lives be filled with nothing but light, healing, and love.
so much love.

PART ONE

SKRA

SIXTY DAYS REMAIN

1

THE WORLD BURNED GRAY.

Ranka knelt among the conifers, a scrap of bloodied cloth pinched between her black-nailed fingers. She'd picked up the scent of something dying at sunrise. Broken twigs oozed sap around her, the pine needle carpet churned raw where someone had sprinted through, not bothering to hide their trail. The earthy tang of witch blood filled her world, tinged with echoes of pain, of death edging near. But was it the blood of an enemy coven—or the blood of her own?

Whoever it was didn't have long. Still, it didn't hurt to investigate. Even corpses held answers.

Ranka latched on to the scent of decay and slipped through the trees, looking for clues of the ones they'd lost.

Five witches, vanished in under a month. The number was a punch to the chest. Word had come up from the southern covens—of witches disappearing one by one, leaving no notes, no bloody trails or footprints in the half-melted snow. It was as if the sky had opened up and swallowed them whole.

This is all my fault.

Ranka flinched. Surely, she was just being paranoid. She had no way of knowing if the disappearances had anything to do with her. At least—not yet.

The wind shifted; the reek was stronger now. Ranka shoved her guilt away, focusing instead on that scent, the world of clues unfolding around her, the hungry pulse under her skin and whatever lay dying ahead.

Guilt would get her nowhere. As the only blood-witch left in the north, she was far more valuable here, in her *home*, than as some political prisoner in the south. And once she found answers, her coven would have no choice but to believe that, too. She hoped.

Ranka drew her axe and broke into a run.

The land unfurled around her, sprawling into a wild tangle of boreal forest unsullied by human hands, brilliant even when rendered in blacks, whites, and soft grays. She could have run for days like this, her blood-magic a hum beneath her skin, her only concern the target ahead. This was what she'd been born for—the solitude of the hunt, tracking in the shadows of mountains with nothing but a weapon and the drumbeat of her heart for company.

Out here, she was no one. Out here, she was *free*.

Younger witches always thought they wanted adventure. They dreamed of bloody battles, secret missions, and noble sacrifices. They were never prepared for what came after—injuries that ached more every year, nightmares that never ended, and the guilt, festering like a wound, fed by memories of friends killed in an act of mercy because the healers always arrived too late or never at all.

Ranka gulped in clean air, tearing over a bend, sunlight warming her back even as her cheeks grew numb. Wind whipped at her face, snatching her straw-colored hair from its braids. The world could shove its glory. Here, in the north, far from the border and the whims of cruel princes, her coven could build a life away from bloodshed. They could rest.

And maybe, someday, they could even be happy.

Ranka stepped through the trees and froze.

A fangwolf lay on its side.

Incisors curled from its lips, longer than the span of her hand, their points dripping poison that Ranka knew was the soft hue of a robin's egg. Memories flashed behind her eyes: witches lowered into the earth, skin broken by puncture wounds ringed blue. Her hand twitched to her weapon—but no. This beast could barely move. Gashes carved its flanks, revealing glimpses of bone. Bite marks mangled its neck. She frowned. Cougars didn't come down from the mountains once the north shifted into summer, and even the greenest witchlings knew to stay far away from a predator as deadly as a fangwolf. What, then, had attacked this beast so viciously?

Not my target. I should move on.

Instead, beneath her skin, her blood-magic began to hum.

Even after five years under its grip, Ranka was startled every time the power rose. Her vision was the first to go—colors melting away, rendering the world in burning gray. Power rushed in like adrenaline tenfold, filing her nails into claws, swelling her muscles. Her hearing sharpened, suddenly capable of picking up the soft scuttle of mice beneath the snow, the nervous snort of a whitetail deer picking its way through the pines. She could break bone with her bare hands and run for miles without growing winded.

It made her an excellent hunter; it made her a better killer.

But with it came a hunger satiated only by taking a life. With it came the death sentence that was blood-magic.

All witches were stronger than humans, but blood-witches were the rare extreme. Regular witchery could be detected in toddlers, but blood-magic didn't erupt until puberty. It was always born of bloodshed, demanding more death each year. Once a blood-witch rose, the clock began its countdown. At seventeen, Ranka had ten, maybe fifteen, years before her magic killed her—if her coven didn't put her out of her misery first.

After her power had surfaced, Ranka had begged to be free of it. Instead, her leader had knelt and taken Ranka's tearstained face in her hands.

Blood-magic is not a curse—it is a gift. You carry death in your veins, Ranka. You carry the power of a god.

But what good was the power of a god if it made her the very monster humans sought to burn?

The fangwolf panted, jerking Ranka back to reality.

For two weeks she'd patrolled, passing up easy kills, keeping her power starved and primed to hunt, searching for missing witches, for any clue as to who or what had taken them. For two weeks she'd starved.

It'd be a waste, to give up such an easy life.

She'd done her due diligence, hadn't she? Two weeks in the cold, following the trails of ghosts, her dreams filled with blood and her world drained of color, wandering as far as her coven permitted and farther still. The fangwolf wouldn't make it regardless; it could either die now, ended mercifully by her hand—or slowly, suffering over the course of days.

That witch probably passed through weeks ago.

The wolf lurched. The warm, coppery tang of blood flooded the air.

The faces of the missing vanished, replaced by the thrum of the wolf's weakening heartbeat, the scent of infection in its blood. The birds fell silent. The stench of decay thickened, burning the back of Ranka's throat.

And finally, her blood-magic rose—and took control.

Ranka forgot why she'd come here. She forgot the coven she fought for, the sister she'd lost long ago, the faces of the missing and the ones left behind. She forgot her own name. Somehow her weapon appeared in her hand. Somehow she ended up kneeling over the wolf. It panted, eyes rolling. One of its fangs was cracked down the middle, the hairline fracture stretching to the gums.

Ranka killed it with a single stroke.

Its life flared through her in flashes of blue-edged white, in the taste of the wind and the memory of cubs waiting back in the den, their milky fangs soft and harmless. It swelled, filling her veins, and then disappeared, swallowed by a power that always wanted more.

Ranka gasped and doubled over. Minutes crept by as she crouched on her hands and knees, heart pounding, skin dripping sweat as the itch under her skin vanished and her senses dulled, rendering her more girl than predator once more.

Slowly the colors returned. The wolf's body steamed in front of her. Its fur was chalky brown, and the blood splattering the snow was the most beautiful red she'd ever seen. A sob choked out of her. How had she forgotten the vibrancy of the forest's green, the way it filled her mouth with the taste of sunlight, the blue of a northern summer sky, so bright it nearly burned? She pried the wolf's jaws open, marveling at salmon gums, ivory fangs, a yellow-spotted tongue. If colors were wine, she'd have gathered their hues in her palms and drunk until she burst.

But instead she'd take her prize.

Ranka hummed as she worked, sawing through bone. Fangwolf incisors were worth their weight in gold to the humans who dared trek this far north for trade—but they'd make a better gift to Yeva, who could trade them for some precious human good. A scarf, a dress, maybe one of those glitzy necklaces crows always tried to steal.

Ranka's eyes flicked to her wrist, to the faded scrap of leather and sun-bleached beads that circled it; Yeva wore its twin. She'd woven it for Ranka five years ago.

Forget her, Yeva had pleaded. *For all of us.*

Ranka had certainly tried.

The birds remained silent. The death-drunk feeling swirled through Ranka, rendering her warm and off-balance as she pocketed the fangs. Ranka wiped her hands clean and paused, regarding the wolf with a clear head for the first time.

The wounds were all wrong; the slashes along its flanks were long, jagged lines—but the bite marks on its neck were oval and messy. As though they'd come from blunt teeth.

Ranka breathed in—and gagged.

The scent of rot was overpowering. Had it gotten *worse*? Unless her nose was lying to her, the rotten scent wasn't coming from the wolf—it was coming from the trees. It was coming from behind her.

And behind her, something moaned.

Slowly, Ranka turned.

A person swayed at the clearing's edge.

"Hello?"

A familiar, earthy scent curled in the air. *A witch.* Her fingernails were coal black, ending in fine, sharp points. Ranka would have wagered her life that this witch's eyes were a solid, milky white.

"You're a blood-witch," Ranka breathed. "I . . . I thought I was the only one left. Where have you *been?* I have so many questions; I thought I was alone—I thought—"

Ranka looked closer and froze.

The witch's nails dimmed and returned to blunt edges—and then darkened again, the edges morphing to fine points once more. The witch's power was . . . flickering. That wasn't right. Blood-magic didn't flicker. It rose and faded only once a life had been taken. But this witch seemed caught in a cycle, her power sputtering in and out like a candle that wouldn't stay lit.

The witch shuffled forward, and the light hit her in full.

Purple, pus-scabbed sores covered her body. Her pale skin had the pallor of someone three days dead. Her clothes were of the southern human style, reduced to bloodied tatters. Blood crusted her face, and blue-ringed puncture marks marred her arms.

Ranka went cold. Only a handful of blood-witches were born every generation. She should have rushed to the witch's help, overjoyed to meet someone like her at long last. Someone who *understood.*

Instead, she remained rooted in place.

Instead, something inside her whispered: *Run.*

"Are you all right?"

The witch panted. A beetle crawled from her left nostril and skittered down the hollow of her throat.

"Do you need a healer—"

A horrible gurgle crawled out of the witch's throat—and she lunged.

Ranka scrambled away. Her heel snagged on a root and down she went, tumbling backward to land awkwardly on her wrist. Pain lanced up her arm. The witch ran straight through a briar patch. Nothing registered in her eyes but hunger. Ranka scrambled for her blood-magic, but it hovered out of reach, satiated by her recent kill.

The witch leapt on top of her, slammed a hand to Ranka's throat, and pinned her to the earth.

Ranka clawed at her fingers. "*Wait.* I can help you."

The witch licked her lips, her rotting teeth flashing. Her all-white eyes rolled.

"Please."

Ranka's vision swam. After everything she'd fought for, here she was again—weaponless, terrified, alone.

At least if she was going to die, it was here in the north where she belonged. Not in some distant human kingdom.

Please, let it be painless, let it be quick, it's more than I deserve, but please, give me this.

The witch raised her other hand—and her eyes cleared.

A gasp left her. The witch snatched her fingers away from Ranka's throat, face contorting, and *keened*. She jerked away from Ranka and collapsed to her hands and knees, retching violently, tears dripping from her cheeks, her entire body rocking with convulsions. Finally, the witch raised her head. When her eyes met Ranka's, they were a clear forest green.

"From the poison," she croaked, "comes the cure."

And then she collapsed.

Once, when Ranka was a witchling, she'd held a piece of glass above an ant and angled a beam of light onto it. The sun had fried it instantly. The ant had twitched in a horrible dance before it finally curled up and went still. That was what that witch's body did on the ground, body convulsing, fingers spasming, blood leaking from her nose as she writhed. It was a mercy when she stopped moving. The witch died with her eyes open—one eye a blank, blood-witch white, the other shining green.

Ranka remained where she was for a long time. Tentatively, the birds began to sing again. Still she didn't move, her eyes frozen on the witch.

I ought to bury her.

It was what she would have asked of any other witch—to bury her deep, far enough a fangwolf wouldn't dig her back up, where her flesh could melt into the earth and the roots of pines might tangle through her bones.

But Ranka couldn't stomach touching her. She rose to leave—and paused.

Something gleamed in the witch's fist.

The witch's fingernails were ragged, the nail beds packed with dirt and rotting bits of flesh. Ranka used her axe to nudge the fingers apart. A small, golden object slipped free, twinkling in the sun. It was a pin, no bigger than a coin, framed in a spiral of human writing.

Why was she in a human city? Her clothes were the southern human style, but the wooden beads in her ears marked her as a Kerth witch. Could she be one of the missing? Why not just return home? Why flee farther north, into Skra lands?

The witch's empty eyes stared up at the sky. Any answers had died with her.

Ranka watched the witch for a long time before she reached forward to close her eyes. She hesitated, then picked up the pin. A fist wreathed in flame gleamed from its face. The symbol meant nothing to her. Hopefully, it never would.

Ranka tucked the pin in her pocket and began the long trek home.

2

WITCHIK WAS CHANGING.

Ranka moved north, deeper into the mountainous, witch-ruled lands, the memory of the rotting witch lingering like a bad dream. A boom ripped through the air. Behind her, a flock of crows startled and took flight.

This land had once been brilliant for hunting elk—until two springs past, when the humans crossed the border to blast open illegal copper mines. The herds fled, leaving fields overgrown and the covens starving. The Bloodwinn treaty, born three generations before, was supposed to prevent this—divvy up the land, establish trade, protect the border. But humans crept farther north every year, craving metal for their weapons, and weapons for their wars.

If it was war the humans wanted, the north would be ready.

The sky burned with sunset by the time Ranka was north enough that the thunder of the mines couldn't reach her. The land shifted to towering, old-growth forest. Berry-dyed banners snapped from the trees' highest boughs. Above her, a lone cardinal sang.

Ranka whistled, and the world rustled to life.

Five Skra witches dropped from the canopy, landing with muffled thuds. Ranka looked at them and saw herself—scarred bodies cloaked in Northlander furs, hardened by a wild life in Witchik's far north. The only difference was their hands; on brown and pale fingers alike, their nails ranged from deep gray to the barest tint. None were coal dark like Ranka's own. None carried blood-magic in their veins.

The witches recognized her and lowered their weapons. "Find anything?" one asked.

"Best if I report in first." Just picturing the sickness made her heart stutter. Ranka spun her bracelet. "How is Yeva?"

The witch's lips thinned. "Best if you report in first."

Before Ranka could respond, they turned away, breath fogging in the air as they left her behind.

When she'd been named Bloodwinn—and the human prince's future bride—a month ago, her coven had been thrilled. The Bloodwinn treaty had promised to protect Witchik from the pillaging of humans. Instead it had simply continued without the official blessing of the Crown. Witches were barred from retaliating, lest they be cut off from meager shipments of medicine funneled through the human-ruled south.

In only three generations a treaty meant to foster peace had come to promise death by suffocation.

Then Ranka had been named Bloodwinn. The Skra's plan was simple: send her south under the guise of accepting the prince's proposal—and kill him. End the line, break his kingdom from within, and destroy the Bloodwin treaty for good. It was perfect. It was all the Skra had ever dreamed of. It would set them *free*.

But Ranka refused.

No one dared accuse her of cowardice to her face, but she saw it in their eyes, in the turn of their mouths when their sick waited on shipments of antiseptics that would not come and more hunting lands were ripped apart by mines. The Skra looked at her and saw the future she'd denied them.

You were offered a new world, their stares accused. *And you said no.*

Ranka took in the century-old pines that towered high above, the coal-pit smoke coiling in the air. She pictured Yeva's timid smile, Ongrum's proud gaze, and thought, *This is the only world I want.*

Ranka tightened her grip on the fangwolf incisors and stepped into camp.

All around her, witches worked. The hunters were gone, tracking prey that grew scarcer every year, while middling witches felled trees for lumber exports or monitored the few humans granted access to the rich copper veins that snaked through Skra land. Weaker witches like Yeva remained at camp on farm duty, harvesting the garlic, kale, and potatoes planted in winter-proofed cabins. Others stoked low-burning beds of coals, carefully stacking wood so that the pits would stay lit without erupting into flames. A few witches leaned against cabin walls, plucking steaming venison from bowls with bare fingers, their laughter tinkling through the trees like Arlani sleigh bells.

Every ache and pain of the past two weeks melted away. This was her family. They'd forgive her, in time. They'd understand why she could never give them up.

The camp fell quiet. A few witches glanced toward Ranka, frowned, and looked away.

Her heart twinged.

They have to.

She spied Asyil, Yeva's sister, and Ranka's fingers flew to her pocket. Asyil hadn't inherited her sister's gentle heart, but unlike the other Skra, she'd never judged Ranka for rejecting her role as the Bloodwinn. That alone was a gift. Ranka waved—but instead of acknowledging her, Asyil went rigid and looked away.

"Witchling," someone said. "Welcome back."

Ranka turned toward that voice like a flower to the rising sun.

The woman approaching was pale and stocky, with a harsh mouth and a body honed by fifty years of hardship. When Ranka had first met Ongrum, the Skra leader's hair had been a deep, rich brown. Now it was mostly gray, threaded with silver, contrasting the wicked burn scars that warped her neck and arms, mirroring Ranka's own.

Ongrum clapped a hand to Ranka's shoulder and frowned. "You lost your gloves."

Ranka leaned into her touch. Thirteen years Ranka had been a Skra, yet in Ongrum's presence she still felt like the weeping four-year-old Ongrum had carried through the snow.

Behind Ongrum, Asyil finally turned. Even from across the camp Ranka could see that her eyes were full of tears.

Finally Ranka realized what—and *who*—was missing. Every part of her went cold. "Ongrum, where's Yeva?"

"Right." Ongrum's hand dropped. "We need to talk."

3

WHEN ONGRUM CALLED THE SKRA TOGETHER, THE coal-pits remained cold.

Typically, coven meetings had a celebratory air, filled with food, liquor, and laughter. They were a meeting of family bonded deeper than blood, thriving in spite of a world that hated them. But tonight there were no embers wrapping the camp in an orange, smoky haze, no slow-roasting venison that dripped sizzling fat into tiny, carefully controlled flames. There was only darkness, and a chill to the air despite the late summer night.

Ongrum had called the coven together in this manner only three times in Ranka's life—the first was when several of their own had been slaughtered in a raid. The second was when they'd been called south to aid the Kerth coven in a fight against some human poachers.

The third time was five years ago, after Ranka's blood-magic had woken in Belren.

Now Ongrum stood in front of the sixty-odd witches that made up the Skra, her face a mask of stone. Ranka stood to her immediate right. She wanted nothing more than to sink into the ground. Not a single witch met her eye. For most of Ranka's life, they'd treated her with a cautious distance, but ever since she rejected the

Bloodwinn treaty, that caution had morphed into resentment.

For five years they'd tolerated the volatile blood-witch in their midst, flinging Ranka into battles, skirting her hungry outbursts. But if she was too weak to head south? Then she was deadweight. *Useless.* And there was no room for deadweight in the Skra.

Ongrum stepped forward.

"As many of you already know, three days ago Yeva and I went out to scout." She closed her eyes. "We were ambushed by humans. We split ways, and she has not returned. I fear the worst—I fear she's been taken."

Ice crept through Ranka's veins.

She'd already lost one sister. She couldn't survive it again.

Everyone began shouting at once.

"We knew this would happen!"

"It's the prince's bounty hunters, it has to be! How many more are going to disappear?"

Ongrum raised a hand for silence, but the fervor kept swelling. And could Ranka blame them? When Ranka had declined to go south to marry the prince, a price had been put on her head. Now bounty hunters cut their way north every few weeks, kidnapping any girl even remotely similar to Ranka. Save for their height and their nails, Ranka and Yeva could have been twins.

"Enough," Ongrum boomed. "I know you're scared. I know you're grieving. But a few missing witches proves nothing." Ongrum spoke slowly, her raspy contralto carrying over the camp. "The men wore no province colors. For all we know, they could have been northerners, eager to act out their revenge on two stray witches."

The pin dug into Ranka's thigh.

"Besides," Ongrum continued. "Say it *was* a bounty hunter. Say Yeva is being delivered to the palace as we speak. We have no recourse. Not without someone on the inside."

"We *had* someone on the inside," someone muttered.

The blood drained from Ranka's face. Suddenly it was only a

month ago, and she was just a nameless blood-witch handed the title of Bloodwinn, telling them she wouldn't—*couldn't*—go south and start a war that might kill them all. She'd expected her coven to support her, to understand that after so many years of fighting, she just wanted to *rest*.

Instead, they'd marked her a coward.

"They'll kill her," someone called. "When they realize she's not who they want."

Ongrum closed her eyes. "I can't lead us into chaos on the chance the prince *might* be involved. Unless anyone else has information, we stand down."

Yeva. The pin. The rotting witch.

Ranka swallowed. The Skra were her family. They'd raised her after the world rejected her for the witchery in her bones. They'd protected her, had sworn to die for her, and she for them.

Now a question seemed to rise from the sixty hearts beating around her.

Would she fail them—or would she fight?

I'm tired, she wanted to say. *I've spent my whole life fighting. I've had enough.*

Ranka's hand drifted to her bracelet.

Had it been anyone else, she could have turned away. But all Ranka could see was Yeva.

Yeva, washing Ranka's wounds after Belren, teaching her to sew, sneaking her meals when Ongrum cut her rations. Calming her when Ranka woke screaming in the night for a sister who was never coming back. Yeva, always gentle, always kind, long after Ranka no longer deserved it.

Yeva, alone.

So Ranka said, "Wait."

The attention of the coven snapped to her.

Ranka's hands trembled, but she stepped forward. "I found something, earlier. In the woods."

Her stomach turned. From her pocket she drew the pin. In the half-light of late evening, it was barely visible against her palm, a splash of dull gold winking in the air.

"Light," Ongrum ordered.

Someone prodded a coal-pit to life, alighting the camp in an orange glow. It took everything in Ranka not to flinch. Just the sight of the flames made her stomach turn.

She ground her teeth, and slowly, softly, Ranka told her coven of the witch in the woods.

Ongrum was silent for several minutes after. "You're certain of what you saw? There have been no rumors of deaths in the south."

She had a point. If there *were* a new plague, surely they'd have heard of bodies piling up in the southern cities? All witches came from humans, and the lines between them were blurry at best. The marked difference was their power: human magic manifested externally, granting the ability to stir a breeze with the twitch of a hand or bend the mind of an animal with a whisper. But witchery was in the bones, the blood, the breath. With it came a tougher body, a longer life, sharper senses, and a turn of the nails. No plague could have attacked the covens without filling death wagons in human cities first.

"She was in southern clothes," Ranka said slowly. "Human clothes, but she wore Kerth beads. It seemed like she was . . . running from something. She was carrying this."

She held the pin aloft and watched as it dawned on them. The witch she'd met had been running from humans. One group of humans this far north was rare enough. The chances there'd been *two* separate groups pressing into Skra land within the same day, with no connection to each other?

Ranka knew better than to believe in coincidences. Whoever that witch had fled from—they had taken Yeva. Ranka could feel it in her bones. And from the looks on the faces of the witches around her, they felt the same.

Ongrum leaned forward to look at the pin but didn't touch it, pausing as though it might leap out and bite her. Her face was carefully blank, but Ranka knew that hesitation. It had stayed her own hand many times. Like so many of the witches rescued as children, Ongrum could not read.

"I can read it." Asyil stepped forward, looking everywhere but at Ranka. She and Yeva had come to the Skra late, and Ranka had often wondered if it was not their witchery that had kept them weak, but their former lives, clinging after all these years like a stubborn second skin. Asyil took the pin, held it up to the light, and read. "'We are Solomei's light. We are her Hand in the night.'"

Solomei. The sun goddess humans prayed to.

Ongrum had gone terribly pale. When she spoke, her voice was ragged. "When I was a witchling, a trader brought a collection of prayer plates north, each from a different city within Isodal. He said every city had a different mantra, to mark the temple sect there. They were useless to us, but beautiful, and obsessive in that odd human way. But only one carried this line."

Ongrum closed her eyes. "This pin is from Seaswept."

The royal city.

The home of the prince Ranka had rejected.

The Skra began to shout again, crying for bloodshed, for the very coup they'd cast aside when Ranka wasn't brave enough to play the role of assassin. Ongrum stepped toward Ranka. Ranka flinched—but all Ongrum did was settle a callused hand on her cheek. Her thumb traced the scar that wound from Ranka's left eye to the corner of her mouth. Yeva always said the scar made Ranka look like a fish that'd escaped being hooked. The truth of how she'd earned it was a lot less charming.

"I know that look on your face," Ongrum murmured. "Careful, witchling, before you start a fire you cannot put out. It could just be a coincidence—she could have stolen that pin. Or the humans could have no connection at all."

"You know as well as I do that's not true," Ranka whispered. "Could it still work? Your plan?"

Ongrum's face grew grave. "We couldn't go south with you. Until the coronation you'd be on your own. If this goes wrong, I wouldn't just lose the coven's only blood-witch. I'd lose the only person I ever considered a daughter."

"I am no one's daughter," Ranka whispered. "I am a weapon. Use me."

Ranka thought she saw Ongrum smile, but then it was gone. A trick of the light.

Ongrum raised her voice. "You chose, as Bloodwinn, to deny the treaty—and deny the coup. I respected that. I stood down, even with freedom within our grasp. But now one of our own has been taken. If you want this fight, I will not stand in your way. If you want the prince's blood, it is yours to spill. Every witch here would be honored to fight with you."

"It would be war. If we killed their prince—"

"War among the *humans*." Ongrum smiled wryly. "There are no other male heirs. His sister was deemed unfit to rule. Kill the boy, and the humans turn on one another in their scramble for power. And Witchik will be free."

A rumble of approval went through the coven. A second fire was lit, and then another. Someone broke a bottle of pine liquor with a whoop and sent a gout of blue-green flame roaring into the sky, and in the presence of so much flame, it was pride the Skra witches summoned, not fear. Now the entire camp was aglow. Now they were painted in burning light. The coven pressed closer, their faces alight, their eyes eager.

When was the last time she'd had their attention like this?

When was the last time she'd mattered at all?

Ranka could nearly see it—a boy in a crown crumpling to the floor, blood spilling down his chest, her stag-bone knife buried between the delicate gaps of his ribs. A lifetime of freedom as the humans ripped one another apart over the throne instead of ripping Witchik apart.

A treaty ended by the will of a girl.

A country freed with the stroke of a blade.

And Yeva—alive and well, bright eyed, rosy cheeked, and *home*.

Ranka waited for Ongrum to tell her it was the wrong choice. To remind her that her place was here, in the north, that she'd taken enough lives. It was another witch's turn to bleed, another coven's turn to suffer. Now it was Ranka's turn to rest.

Instead, Ongrum looked at Ranka like she was the beginning of something.

"You could do it, child," Ongrum said softly. "With you, we would win."

The coven pressed closer. Hands brushed her shoulders, her back, her hair. She leaned into the weight of their palms, skin burning from the heat of their touch, drunk on the caress of their acceptance, lost in the pride shimmering in Ongrum's eyes, bright as the days post-Belren. It'd been dimming for years. Now she could bring it back. She could make Ongrum proud forever.

And yet.

"I'm a fighter, not a spy," Ranka whispered. "I haven't trained for this—I haven't—"

"Look at me, child. Weapon you may be," Ongrum said. "But you *are* my daughter, by right if not blood. And no daughter of mine could fail."

Behind her, the coven rumbled with approval. Ranka's head spun, her leader's words ringing in her ears, her blood humming with the collective hope of the witches who surrounded her.

She could still say no. She could live out her days safe but alone. Ignored but alive.

But if she said yes?

If she pulled this off?

"You really think it was him?" Ranka whispered, her voice far away. "The pin could just be a coincidence. . . ."

Tell me no, a part of Ranka begged. *Tell me there isn't a chance. Tell me everything or nothing at all, but that it's my fault she's gone.*

"You know I don't believe in coincidences," Ongrum said slowly.

"And it was only Yeva they went after. The witch who died in front of you, child—was she blonde like you?"

"Yes," Ranka croaked, her voice weak.

Her legs threatened to buckle. It was her fault, then, truly. After all this time—after everything Yeva and the Skra and Ongrum had done for her—her sister had been right. She was a threat to everyone around her. A monster, even when she tried so hard to be anything but. And now Yeva would pay the price.

"It's your choice," Ongrum said finally. "I backed you before when the prince wanted you to head south; I'll back you now if you wish to remain hiding from him still."

"Just tell me this," Ranka whispered. "Is there a chance—even a small one—that I can save her?"

"Oh, witchling." Ongrum touched her cheek. "You'll save them all."

Ranka touched her bracelet—and drew her axe. "Tell me what I have to do."

4

"HANDS OUT!"

Ranka sank into her cloak, sweating in the relentless heat, and tightened her grip on the poster she'd stolen. Six guards swathed in mourner's black manned the checkpoint ahead, armed with buckets of soapy water and instant-click torches. Behind them, the royal city of Seaswept rose up before the sea, a behemoth of light, sound, and life. Seabirds whirled over a bay choked with dozens of ships, some Isodalian, some bearing flags and cargo from nations across the Broken Sea. Envy coated Ranka's tongue. Unlike Witchik's shoreline of harsh cliffs and storm-plagued seas, Isodal's sloping beaches and gentle waves had allowed the humans to open hundreds of trading ports, and it had made them strong.

If it were reversed, Ranka thought bitterly, eyes tracking the ships, *if it were Witchik connected to the rest of the world, it would be us who grew rich on your resources. It would be us who lived like gods while you starved.*

"Next!"

A child stumbled to the front of the line. A pale human guard seized his wrists and shoved his hands into an old wash pail, scrubbed his nails with a brush, and yanked his hands back up. Sunlight hit his fingers—pink against brown skin. *Human.*

"Clear," the guard drawled. He stamped the child's checkpoint card and waved him through. The boy whimpered and stumbled past, waiting for the rest of his family to be processed.

Ranka's line moved at a crawl. In the line to her left were more strangers, most of them single travelers, a few parents with children—but to her right was the merchant line, travelers with wagons and carts, tugging along produce and pricey raw exports from Witchik's north.

To her right, poised atop a wagon, was a witch.

At first glance she was just another a farmer's daughter, a gangly girl with dirty clothes and tired eyes, sitting awkwardly astride an old mare whose better years were behind her. Ranka had sniffed her out immediately. Her witchery was weak, a pulse that was barely there, and had she been closer, Ranka wagered her nails would have been like Yeva's or Asyil's, holding only the barest tint of gray.

Ranka's own sister had possessed nails like that—so barely tinted, one might wonder if the label of "witch" was a mistake. Had Ranka not been sniffed out by a Skra patrol, her sister might have lived out her days among humans, never knowing of the weak thread of witchery pulsing within. Maybe that's where Vivna was now, eking out a life in some tiny Isodal town, happy as a lark away from the witches who had raised her. From the little sister who was willing to die for her.

Stop it.

Vivna was gone. Dead or alive, she was gone, and she wasn't coming back.

But Yeva—*Yeva* still had a chance.

"Clear," the guard said. An old man dressed in green ambled forward, tugging along a tiny cart of cabbages, and dutifully plunged his hands into the water.

Ranka swallowed, her eyes on the lone witch. How many had tried to sneak through, nails carefully painted, only to end up ablaze? It seemed foolish to risk being burned alive, all to enter a city.

But what a city it was. The heartbeat of a country, a chance to start anew, big enough for a lesser witch to get lost among the crowds and make a life. The Sunra palace was a distant glimmer atop the cliffs, poised over the city like a silent guardian. From here it looked fragile, as if the smallest gust of wind could send the entire thing careening into the waves. Ranka's eyes tracked the city walls, the buildings that stretched east and west and curved around the bay in both directions. Three hundred thousand, Ongrum had estimated. Three hundred thousand lives within those walls.

If you're in there, Yeva, I'll find you. And I'll bring you home.

"Clear," the guard said, waving the cabbage merchant through.

It was the witch's turn. She hesitated, hands shaking on the reins of what must have been a stolen horse.

Not my coven. Ranka set her jaw. *Not my problem.*

And yet.

"I said *clear*," the guard snapped.

Ranka's legs tensed. The poster nearly slipped from her hands.

The witch slid down on wobbly legs, flinching as she dipped her hands into the bucket. The second guard held the stamp, pale fingers stained with red ink, his turnip-shaped head shining with sweat. "What's your business in Seaswept?"

"Hey," someone said. "Hey, girl. The line's moved."

The guard jerked the witch's hands out of the water, and the world went quiet. Paint ran in rivulets down the witch's palms and her brown wrists, dripping her own death sentence into the dust. The guards' faces fell as they processed what they were seeing.

They'd burn her for trying to sneak into the royal city.

They'd burn her alive.

You won't just save her. You'll save them all.

Ranka watched the witch, and all she saw was Yeva, Vivna, Ongrum, and so many others, so many people born on the wrong side of the border. How many had burned? How many more, until the prince fell?

The guard raised his hand.

The witch flinched.

And Ranka broke into a run.

She shoved the person in front of her and barreled forward, beckoning with her free hand at the guards, black nails flashing in the sun. Their bewildered faces morphed to fury. The witch watched Ranka with her mouth hanging open.

"*A witch!* Lock the line down—*stop her!*"

Her feet slammed against the earth. The wall loomed closer. Ranka made it ten feet, twenty, thirty feet.

"Stop!" Behind her came six clicks, the acrid scent of oil igniting—and the creak of a bow being drawn. "Unless you want to burn."

Ranka skidded to a halt, crinkling her stolen poster.

"Turn around, witch."

Slowly Ranka turned. Six flaming arrows were pointed at her chest. The guards' eyes flicked to her nails. Behind them, people stirred, watching Ranka with naked fear. A baby screamed somewhere down the line, its howls broken by *Shh, shh, shh*. Ranka looked past them to the anonymous witch, inching forward, fingers stretched for the wet stamp lying in the dust.

"You lot get more desperate every year, don't you?"

We don't have enough food, Ranka wanted to snap. *You hoard it all. You shirk trade regulations and ruin our land. So yes, we're desperate. Starving.*

Stall. Ranka swung her attention back to the guards. "Shoot me, and you'll regret it."

"The more of you we burn," Turnip Head said slowly, "the better."

Ranka rocked back on her heels, watching the witch from her periphery. She was close to the stamp. Once she had her pass marked, she'd be in the clear. Free to live out her days in the city so long as she remained within the walls. *Safe.*

Ranka dove.

She shoved the cabbage merchant out of her way and vaulted over his cart. Six arrows flew. The produce went up in a whoosh of flame, spitting sparks into the air.

The cabbage merchant slumped to the ground in defeat and put his head in his hands. "Every time," he moaned. "Every *single* time."

Ranka danced away from the heat. The witch snatched up the stamp, marked her card, and dropped it into her pocket.

Six more arrows were lit.

"Okay! I surrender!" Ranka blurted. She dropped to her knees, and her voice emerged in a nervous chatter. "Sorry for the commotion—I was sick of waiting in line. Not built for the heat and all that. Can't blame a girl for wanting a dramatic entrance."

The guards paused, plainly confused.

"I mean, you *have* been looking for me—haven't you?"

And before they could move—before they could look back at the witch slipping through the gates—Ranka tossed back her hood, still kneeling, and unfurled the poster.

The guards froze, their faces slackening. A murmur went up from the crowd. They'd all seen the poster before. It'd been printed in their very city, identical to the thousands plastered across Isodal, covered in a rough sketch and garish text.

<u>WANTED ALIVE</u>
RANKA OF THE SKRA
NAMED BLOODWINN
APPROX. 6′2″, BLONDE OF HAIR,
LEFT CHEEK SCARRED
APPROACH WITH CAUTION.
HIGHLY DANGEROUS & KNOWN KILLER.
REWARD: 80,000 G &
AUDIENCE WITH PRINCE GALEN

She hated those damned posters. The humans made her sound like some kind of criminal eager to see a war break out, when all she'd ever wanted was to be left alone.

Five years she'd hidden. In the end, whoever had given up Ranka's identity to the palace knew her well enough to describe her down to her scar.

"Lights above." A burning arrow clattered to the dirt. The lead guard's legs twitched, as if he wasn't certain if he should chase her or kneel. "I—I almost *shot* you."

"I don't suppose you could put the fire out?" Her voice came out higher than usual.

The first rule little witchlings learned was that if you smelled smoke, if you heard that crackle of flame, you ran.

Humans burned witches for a reason. When witchery manifested in a human child, tinting their nails and sharpening their senses, something in them changed, altering the chemical makeup of their very cells. Witches burned brighter, faster, *hotter*. Their strength faltered in the presence of flame. The more powerful the witch, the more susceptible they were.

Flame was a nuisance to a witch like Yeva. To Ranka, it might as well have been poison.

Memories wormed free—charred bodies in the snow; ribbons of red, orange, and cruel blue flame licking over homes, echoed by her sister's screams.

Ranka didn't open her eyes until the fire was out.

Guards hauled her to her feet, their touch hesitant but firm, as if not quite certain how to handle her. They frog-marched her toward the city, hollering for replacements, for the prince to be notified. Ranka twisted as they passed under the gates of Seaswept.

The witch was gone, and the stamp with her. A new guard manned the checkpoint. He'd look for it later and probably chalk it up to carelessness. Maybe the witch would throw the stamp into the sea. Maybe she'd send it north to help others sneak through.

It didn't matter. She was safe.

Ranka tilted her head back, eyeing the bronze-edged cliffs, the pale towers against a cloudless sky, the streets that all curved down toward the sea so that when the king called hurricanes, he didn't drown his own people by accident. Languages from all over the world blurred around her and fell into a hushed silence as eyes caught the witch marching through their streets. How different might her life have been if she'd grown up among travelers from Drakhara, Bouvan, Limeria, the Star Isles, or any of the countries from across the Broken Sea? Ahead, gold-wrought gates reared up before the cliffs, the Sunra palace crouching behind them like a sleeping giant.

Had the last Bloodwinn felt fear when she'd come here? Had she trembled like Ranka now wanted to, or had she strode forward with certainty, brown face serene, Arlani robes a swirl at her feet as she accepted the pale hand of a boy-king who carried hurricanes in his blood?

Had she been happy?

Vivna would have loved this place. She would have wanted to make a life here. Yeva might have loved it too, had she come here willingly and not as a prisoner, paying for Ranka's crimes.

But all that Seaswept stirred in Ranka was a sense of freedom stolen, of missing girls and a gold pin delivered in the fist of a dying witch.

"Welcome home, Bloodwinn," the guard to her left sneered, gripping her bicep tight enough to bruise. He tied her hands behind her back and shoved a blindfold over her eyes, his touch quick and rough. "Or should I say *Butcher*?"

Ranka narrowed her eyes. Belren would have been blamed on any blood-witch. It was only a stroke of irony that this man was right.

A deadly calm swept over her.

These people had hunted her. They'd pillaged her home, taken her family, ruined what little peace she'd had left.

But they were right to look at her with fear.

And in forty-six days she'd show them why.

5

THE BLINDFOLD CAME OFF, AND ALL RANKA SAW WAS wealth.

White halls sprawled in every direction, broken up by hand-tiled murals of pale storm mages surrounded by hurricanes, their robes adorned with gemstones, commanding clouds rendered in glittering gray quartz. Guards flanked her, dressed in crisp blue, gold-trimmed uniforms broken only by the black silk mourning bands encircling their biceps. They wouldn't meet her eyes. One guard flinched when she looked at him, and drew a prayer circle on his chest, whispering about the curses of witch-women.

Ranka rolled her eyes. Witchery largely favored women, but there were witches of every gender. A male witch had led the Kerth; a nonbinary witch piloted the Oori coven's fleet. Even if a witch was given the wrong gender at birth, the power remained.

"Bloodwinn," a voice said. "It's nice to finally meet you."

The guard approaching looked to be in his midforties, pale and lean with a shock of red hair. His uniform gleamed with medals, and the sword at his side was simple, lightweight, and well worn.

The other guards dipped their heads, stepped back, and mumbled, "Sir."

The man looked her over. He had more freckles than anyone she'd ever met. "I'm Captain Wolfe, though you're welcome to call me Foldrey." His eyes were wary but kind. There was a harsh lilt to his words, one that felt like home. This man had been a northerner once. "I know you must be terrified, but no harm will come to you here. The Sunra family has always honored the treaty."

Ranka swallowed, her head spinning. The captain of the guard—good. If anyone knew where Yeva was, it was him. "You can let her go now."

Foldrey smiled awkwardly. "I'm sorry?"

"The witch you mistook for me. That you kidnapped, to bring me here. Yeva. You can release her."

They stared at each other. Ranka kept her face carefully blank, though her heart threatened to beat out of her chest.

"I—I'm sorry," Foldrey said finally, looking more uncomfortable with each passing second. "I don't know what you mean, child. We're not in the business of kidnapping girls."

Disappointment clouded her.

He had to be lying. No one else had reason to take Yeva. He had no reason to be honest with her. For all she knew, Yeva was rotting in a dungeon cell right below her feet, held prisoner to ensure Ranka's compliance.

No matter. Ranka would find her one way or another.

Foldrey cleared his throat. "Right, well . . . if you'll follow me, Prince Galen is very eager to meet you."

Galen. The guard said the name so softly, like the wretched Skybreaker prince were his own child and not a monster of a boy who sought to force her into marriage for some treaty that'd done more harm than good.

Ranka swallowed the bile rising in her throat and followed Foldrey across the palace grounds.

The grounds unfolded as they walked. Gardens swollen with pale irises and dark vines gleamed between arguing diplomats and opulent statues. Boardwalks stretched over shallow ponds, where sunset-colored carp swam in lazy circles, bobbing to the surface to compete for the bread crumbs a squealing little girl was tossing over the lilies. Even in the shade, the heat of the midsummer sun pressed down with suffocating weight. Vivna would have loved it. Yeva would have melted at the sight of the beauty shimmering across the grounds.

Ranka sank into her coat, sweating in the unrelenting heat, and wished she were home.

Servants blanched at the sight of her, their whispers trailing like smoke as they fled to spread the news.

"The Bloodwinn. They've found her, at last."

Their emotions swirled over her tongue—acrid fear, bitter loathing, the nectar sweetness of relief. The guard that had sneered and called her Butcher walked only a few paces back. She was a necessary evil to these people. Her body secured the treaty and the resources that allowed Isodal to triple its exports and thrive. Even the farthest reaches of the human kingdom felt the ripple effects of expanding wealth.

They would tolerate her, if they must. What was one witch for the prosperity of a kingdom?

More guards stepped around the corner. Like the others', the neat pastels of their uniforms were broken by the black silk mourning bands on their arms.

Foldrey kept talking, but Ranka was too tired to listen. She heard the words *prince* and *dinner* and *meeting*. Someone darted forward with a wet rag and wiped her face and arms. Hands wove into her hair without permission to fix her braids.

Her skin crawled.

"Foldrey, do you want her in new clothes?" a maid asked, freckled nose wrinkling. "Or . . . a bath?"

I want to go home. The words rose to Ranka's lips. *I just want to find my friend and go home.*

But what she wanted—who she *was*—didn't matter anymore. Not here, not to these people who saw her only as a means to an end. Ranka remained silent and swallowed the bitter words back down.

Foldrey waved the maid away. "Later. He should meet her now."

The scent of seafood, garlic, lemon, and some strange, sugary herb wafted forward as they turned a corner. Glass balls holding heatless white mage-fire flickered overhead in a gray-tiled veranda. Above them, wooden wind chimes swayed in a low, mournful harmony. Loaves of dark bread waited on the table, still steaming from the oven.

Ranka's stomach lurched. She hadn't eaten all day.

She reached for the bread—and a throat cleared.

"Traditionally," a young voice said, "we wait for the ones who actually *run* the place before we inhale their food."

Ranka froze.

A boy lounged at the end of the table. He was about her age, dark haired and dark eyed, dressed in purple nobleman's silks that made his pale skin glow. The servants fanning along the walls tittered behind their hands.

"New here?" He looked her up and down and grinned. "New to civilization in general?"

Ranka curled her lip, breathing in for a retort, and froze.

His scent was all wrong. The boy looked human, but his scent was touched by old snakeskin.

Ranka narrowed her eyes. "Galen, I presume?"

Shock flashed across the boy's face, and then he threw his head back and laughed, exposing a long, elegant neck faintly ringed with scars. "*Me?* How on earth could you mistake me for . . ." He looked closely at her for the first time, and recognition lit his face. "Oh, Scala's scales. You're *her*. It must be my birthday. This is going to be a *riot*."

Ranka gaped, but before she could question him, the breeze vanished with the swiftness of someone pinching out a candle flame. *Magic.*

Every servant snapped to attention. The irritating noble boy rose with a rustle of silk.

The hair on Ranka's arms stood on end. The air was suddenly dead, without the slightest stir of a breeze.

New scents hit her: wind and storms, metal and paper, new summer rain on old rust and well-loved books. Swirling over it all, growing stronger by the second, was the scent of fear.

Ranka turned—and met the eyes of the prince she'd come here to kill.

6

PRINCE GALEN WAS SMALL.

He was at least a head shorter than Ranka, slender, with rich brown skin, a kind face, and curly black hair cut close to his skull. Silver thread circled his cuffs and swept down his lapels, woven in the image of gusts of wind. Like the others, a mourning band gleamed on his bicep. Galen's gaze swung over Ranka, and his smile cracked. He looked . . . disappointed to see her.

If Ranka hadn't known better, she'd have thought he looked scared.

Galen shook himself and turned to the nearest servant. "Rhyla, how's your daughter?"

"Better," the woman breathed. "Thank you again, Your Highness. If it weren't for you—"

Galen waved her off, his nose wrinkling as though he was embarrassed. "It's nothing. Truly. I'm glad she's well." He moved down the table, greeting each servant by name, asking after family members, neighbors, and even one man's pet cat. Ranka blinked. The Skra didn't dare to even look Ongrum in the eye. These people met their prince's gaze and stood with ease. Where was their respect for their leader? Where was their fear?

Galen took his seat and refused to look at her.

Ranka could only stare.

This was the boy who'd sent bounty hunters into her land. He was the Skybreaker heir, a boy with hurricanes in his blood, and he was a monster.

Wasn't he?

Another stepped onto the veranda, and Ranka's thoughts were torn from Galen entirely.

Princess Aramis was the same height as her brother, with a delicate, yet athletic frame and thick black curls framing her face. Deep navy silks rippled like water as she walked, blazing with the gold-threaded image of a bursting sun. The princess met Ranka's gaze with an intensity and tucked a curl behind her ear with ink-stained fingers.

As the first girl ever born to a Bloodwinn marriage, Princess Aramis was famous long before her wind-wielding brother. She'd been groomed for power, trained in matters of state and war, poised to be the first woman ever to take the Sunra throne. The first true witch queen.

But her witchery never rose. Galen developed his father's devastating wind magic, and when the twins entered puberty, it became clear Aramis didn't have a grain of magic—no internal witchery, nor a shred of external human magic. The Sunras had kept an iron grip on Isodal thanks to the power that flowed through their veins. Without it, Aramis could never be allowed to make a legitimate bid for the throne.

Her parents took her crown, and then a year ago death took her parents. The public story said fever. But staring at this girl, at the bright fire in her eyes and the way she regarded the world with cool indifference, Ranka wondered if the rumors of poison might hold weight.

Aramis locked eyes with Ranka and tilted her head to the side. "She's so . . . underwhelming."

"Aramis," Galen said, his voice clipped. "Be nice."

The princess lifted a brow. "This *is* me being nice."

She plopped down beside the noble boy, crossed one petite leg over the other, and the two exchanged a meaningful smirk.

The room lapsed into an uneasy silence. There were only three other guests—palace officials, by their dress. They stared at their empty plates and didn't say a word. Aramis fished a piece of bread from the bowl and tore it into smaller and smaller pieces, eyeing everyone with a challenge in her eyes. Galen sat immobile, looking for all the world like he wanted to disappear. The noble boy watched it all with an ill-concealed grin.

Ranka waited for someone to speak to her. The minutes ticked by. She stared at her empty plate. Did they . . . not want her here? That couldn't be right. Why would Yeva have been kidnapped, then? Why the posters?

What was going on?

After another beat of silence, she couldn't take it anymore.

"It's hot," she blurted.

Everyone lifted their heads to stare at her. Heat crept to her cheeks. Perhaps silence had been better.

"The weather," she clarified lamely. "It's, um, warm. Warm-*er*. We still have snow in parts of the Northlands. In the mountains. Although I suppose the mountain snow never really melts. . . ."

More stares.

"Do you have mountains here?" she chattered. "I didn't see any— you have cliffs, but obviously those aren't very high, and, um." *Good Goddess, strike me with lightning, make me stop talking.* "Your clothes are different, you don't even wear boots, you've got those funny strappy things on your feet—"

"Yes," the noble boy said slowly, "because it's hot."

Ranka willed the floor to open and swallow her whole. Instead the doors swung open and a servant stepped through, bearing trays that sagged under the weight of food.

"Oh, thank the sun," Galen breathed.

Ranka agreed.

In seconds the table was covered—bowls overflowed with mixed greens, and trays sagged under mounds of garlic roasted potatoes, green beans, carrots, and buttered snapper. Acid climbed in her throat. Three months ago Isodal had raised the tariffs on their agriculture and medicine exports to Witchik, claiming a shortage of food in the face of the drought. Yet this table alone could have fed her entire coven for a week.

It wasn't like Witchik had other options. The Kithraki mountain range cradled Witchik's far north in a crown of frozen rock, but past that was nothing but miles of barren sea ice. Anyone who wanted to trade with Witchik needed access to Isodal's ports. If the covens wanted anything from the outside world, it had to go through the south first.

"Still," some witches said. "It's better than before, when we got nothing at all."

Ranka took in the surplus of food and wasn't so sure.

The hour crept by in silence, everyone picking at their plates, the sound of chewing broken only by murmured conversations between Aramis and the noble boy that often ended in laughter Ranka was certain was directed at her.

Finally, whether out of desperation or pity, Galen swiveled toward her. "Did you have a long journey, Bloodwinn?"

"Ranka, please. Just—call me Ranka." She cringed. "Two weeks. Not bad, really. I've taken longer patrols, scouting out Murknen lands."

The blank look on his face told her that meant nothing to him.

This was going incredibly well.

"Two weeks," Aramis said. She twirled her fork in a slow, lazy circle. "And yet you were named Bloodwinn a month and a half ago. Where were you, exactly?"

Hiding from you. "It took me . . . time to come to terms with my duty."

"Yes, it certainly did, didn't it?"

Galen made a pained noise in his throat. "Aramis."

"Galen," she mimicked.

He glared at her, and she stuck her tongue out at him. They were definitely siblings.

A stone-faced servant bearing a pitcher of wine approached Ranka. She shook her head, stomach turning. Six years ago her sister had gotten roaring drunk on blackberry wine she'd flirted away from a merchant. Ranka remembered the sickly sweet smell on her breath, the way her head had lolled as though her neck had been snapped. Ranka had carried her home. Right before they'd stepped back into camp, Vivna had looked up at Ranka with cloudy eyes and slurred, "You ruined my life by being born."

The memory made nausea roll through her. Ranka shoved it away, a cold sweat breaking across her skin.

She's gone. She left you. Focus on the ones who stayed. Focus on the ones you need to save.

Pastries and pale-pink wedges of cake were whisked forward. Ranka reached for the nearest and someone made a disapproving *tsk* to her right. Two silver forks gleamed in front of her, one slightly smaller than the other, their handles carved into the shape of a bird in flight. She hesitated, hand hovering over the forks. They looked the same. Why would anyone in their right mind have rules about forks that looked the same?

Galen nudged her foot beneath the table. "Second one."

Ranka snatched the second fork, face burning, and finally, blessedly, they seemed to forget about her, switching the conversation away. It was easier to focus on her food and listen, methodically cutting her cake into smaller and smaller pieces as the twins discussed the weather, an upcoming parade, and apparently endless Council meetings.

"Once I'm named king, I'm never going to another one of those meetings again," Galen grumbled.

Aramis poked him in the ribs with the end of her butter knife. "Once you're king, you need to *lead* the meetings."

"Once I'm king, I'm banishing you."

"Finally, a good idea," the noble boy said. "She's a pain in the a—ow." He rubbed his forehead where Aramis had flicked him.

Galen may have been prince, but it was Aramis who led the conversation, steering the adults to whatever topic she pleased, inquiring about food shortages, the border conflicts, the silence from the Kerth coven.

Ranka froze midbite.

Had she heard that correctly?

"Still no word," a palace official said, cutting into a honey-glazed pastry.

Aramis pressed her lips into a thin line. "Strange. They came for the funeral when Mother died. Send more scouts, would you?"

Ranka stared at the table. The scouts would do them no good. Ranka knew, because on the way here she'd passed right through Kerth territory, hoping they'd know something about the rotting witch in the woods. Instead she'd found cold firepits, unlocked cabins, and dishes of maggot-infested venison still set out on tables, as though they had vanished midbite. There were no bodies, no bloodshed. They were just gone.

But why? And how could the palace not *know*?

Aramis's head snapped toward her. "Excuse me?"

Ranka blanched. She'd spoken the last part out loud.

"I . . . ," she said. "Um . . ."

Aramis's eyes narrowed. "What don't we know?"

Ranka hesitated, grasping for a way to change the subject.

The door banged open.

Foldrey hurried toward the dining table. Sweat gleamed at his temples. But instead of turning to Galen, it was Aramis he knelt beside with a whisper.

All Ranka caught was *found* and *tunnels* and a word she didn't understand: *winalin*.

It was nonsense to her—but Aramis's fingers curled around her knife until they were bloodless.

"You should wait," Foldrey said. "I can arrange an escort—"

"We'll leave now." Aramis rose, ink-stained fingers tapping a rhythm against her thigh. She looked at the noble boy. "I hope you're done."

"I wasn't," he said mournfully. But he didn't argue, just stuffed a roll in his mouth and leapt up, trailing at the princess's heels, that unsettling scent of snakeskin curling in the air long after he'd left.

Galen watched them go with a funny expression on his face, his fork frozen in midair. There was a look there that Ranka didn't understand—frustration maybe? Betrayal? It faded, and Galen turned to Ranka with a smile that didn't reach his eyes.

"I apologize for my sister's rudeness," he said with a tired edge to his voice. "She and Percy are always running off toward trouble."

Ranka nodded, her eyes lingering on the space Aramis had just occupied. Galen turned back to the other guests, inquiring politely about their lives and poking half-heartedly at his food. Cold crept over her. Aramis had just left the room in a dash—and it seemed for all the world like Galen didn't care.

Wasn't he their leader? Their future king?

Disdain curdled in her mouth. If he was this uninvolved in the affairs of his own palace, she was doing his people a favor by killing him. Here was a boy raised with a kingdom at his fingertips—and he squandered it. He would be useless in finding Yeva and the other missing witches.

She would start, then, with the ones who *did* seem to have a keen eye fixed on the happenings within the palace walls—the noble boy and the princess.

And she would start with winalin.

7

FOR TWO DAYS NO ONE CAME FOR RANKA. SHE SPENT her time in her room, watching the sea, straining for the whispers floating down the hall. At night she ghosted the palace halls for signs of Yeva—and found nothing. No mention of a stray witch, no trace of her scent on the clothes of guards or wafting down corridors that surely led to concealed dungeons.

And no gold pins.

It didn't make sense. Even if Yeva wasn't *here*, if someone in the palace had ordered her kidnapping, surely there would be mention of her?

Unless they didn't take her. Her throat tightened. *Unless Foldrey was telling the truth, and the palace had nothing to do with her disappearance at all.*

No. Ongrum said they'd targeted Yeva because she looked like Ranka. It *had* to be the palace. If not the twins, then someone working for them. They couldn't lie to her forever.

Still—it disturbed her that they left her alone. Her only visitors were the servants bringing her meals. On the third day, as a woman set a plate of greens and sea bass by her door, Ranka leapt up. "Where is everyone?"

The servant blinked. "I'm sorry?"

"The twins! Foldrey! *Someone.* Shouldn't I be attending meetings?" Her voice faltered. "Or receiving tutors? Or . . . doing . . . *something*?"

The woman paled. "You *are* doing something, miss. You're here."

A different servant brought her food the next day. When Ranka tried to question her, the woman practically ran from the room.

You'll be a figurehead, Ongrum had warned. *No more, no less.*

She'd ceased being Ranka. Now she was just a nameless witch, here to keep the treaty alive. If she was breathing, she served her purpose. Nothing mattered beyond that to these people.

So Ranka wandered.

She crossed the grounds at a turtle's pace, arms swinging, face curated into the picture of boredom as she mapped out the palace. Any time a guard passed her, she yawned. The only entrance she'd found so far was the main gate, a hideous beast of gilded metal, guarded day and night by men with swords and instant-click torches. She left the palace behind, aiming for the fields that sprawled across the back of the property. No one stopped her. No one seemed to care. Only the blur of sandstone walls on the horizon was a reminder of her status as prisoner.

But everywhere she went, she felt their eyes.

A small crop of stables and weather-beaten fences loomed into view. Several overfed horses grazed in the fields, tails lazily flicking away flies biting at their flanks. Ranka's blood-magic rolled through her veins, flickering her vision to black and white. Her palms ached. Her power demanded death every few weeks to keep it under control; judging by her hunger, she had six, maybe seven, days before she needed to find a way out of the palace to feed her blood-magic.

Ranka hopped the fence and kicked off her strange shoes—sandals, the maid had called them. She wiggled her toes in the grass, relishing its softness, the way it held the sun's warmth but remained cooler than the air. One of the horses lifted its head, snorted, and went back to grazing. She closed her eyes, drinking in the scent of the sea, the sun radiating down on her skin. The heat was still a weight, but not nearly as bad dressed in the human's flowing robes.

Laughter rippled nearby.

"Come on. No one is out here. I'll be fine, and *you* need the practice."

Ranka flattened herself against the stable wall. Voices rumbled. There'd been no one here seconds before. She inched backward, concealing herself as Aramis and Galen Sunra stepped out of the stables, the noble boy from dinner trailing at their heels.

"Why couldn't we stay in the tunnels?" Galen demanded. "I don't . . ." He lowered his voice. "I don't want people to *see* me."

"Too dark," Aramis said. "No good for practice."

"Also, we don't want to bash Percy's head in," the noble boy, Percy, added.

Aramis shrugged. "That might be an improvement, actually."

Percy threw her a wounded look. He pulled his shirt off with one smooth movement, revealing a sheen of sweat gleaming over dozens of thin scars that wrapped his body in a wicked lace. *Odd.* He dressed and spoke like a nobleman's child—but those were the scars of a soldier.

Percy crooked a finger at Galen. "Come on, princeling. I'm hard to break, I promise."

Galen looked slightly disturbed. "Is everyone from the Star Isles as insane as you?"

"We're not insane. You people are just *boring*."

"Aren't ambassadors supposed to be polite?"

"Aren't princes supposed to be *charming*?"

"Father always said the Star Isles bred madness," Galen deadpanned. "I thought he was being dramatic. Now I'm inclined to think he was right."

Percy gave Galen a grim smile. "You don't know the half of it, princeling."

Ranka's eyes narrowed. There was a hitch to Percy's tone she didn't trust. A hint of something deeper, an echo of a secret held back. She knew painfully little of the Star Isles—Ongrum had said the island kingdom had once been a powerhouse of trade, but a decade ago a bloody coup had forced them to abruptly close their ports. A rebel queen had taken the throne after slaughtering the royal family, much of the noble class, and many civilians. After that the island went dark.

Or so they thought.

Yet here was Percy—who seemed to be wildly unfit for the role of ambassador, even to Ranka's untrained eye—now residing within the palace walls, lingering close to the princess. Was he an honored guest? A spy? And why send him *now*?

Maybe Queen Ilia had sent him as an insult. Or maybe they really *were* all madder than a bag of cats.

Galen crossed his arms. "This is ridiculous. I know you guys want to help, but I have teachers for that— "

"Teachers you keep *firing*," Aramis interjected.

"But what if I hurt Percy?"

"I'll consider it a perk." Percy winked dramatically. "I like a little pain."

Galen made an interesting noise. "You are the most—Percy, if I break your spine, the Crown is not paying your healer fee."

"You rule justly, young prince." Percy gravely dipped into a bow. "If you break my spine, cast my body to the sea. Let the mermaids cradle my tragically beautiful face and drown Seaswept in their mourning cries—"

"Solomei's light, Galen," Aramis called. "Shut him up or I'll do it myself."

Ranka's skin crawled. Undone and laughing, sweating and smiling in the sun, Aramis and Galen seemed less like polished royals and more like the witchlings she'd grown up alongside—innocent and energetic, drunk on how eternal the rest of their lives felt.

They didn't seem like the heads of a country. They just seemed like kids.

"Come *on*, Galen. You've got to try." Percy waggled his fingers. "Do the sparky thing."

"The *sparky* thing?"

"Hurricanes and lightning, terrible floods! Like your dad, the feared, uh . . . cloud . . . bender."

"Skybreaker," Galen snapped. "And I told you before—I can only summon wind. I'm not like him. Which everyone loves to remind me of, at all times."

"Galen." Percy's face grew soft. "Just try. For me?"

Galen looked away and then back at Percy with a frown. His eyes were wide and vulnerable, searching the other boy's expression, and then he sighed. "Oh, fine. You win. Back up, you absolute nut."

A massive smile broke across Percy's face. He skipped a few steps backward, bouncing on his toes, and patted his chest. "Do your worst, princeling."

"That is not the proper title," Galen muttered.

Aramis sat upright, watching her brother with interest. Even Ranka couldn't help herself from perking up.

It was a hot, still day. The sky was cloudless. Any ship that tried to leave the bay would have been dead in the water. Most wind mages would have been hard-pressed to muster little more than a breeze.

Galen merely raised a hand.

Wind leapt forward, howling with the ferocity of a Northlander storm, flattening palm trees with distressing creaks until one snapped clean in half. Dust flew into the air in billows, and with it, Percy. He laughed with mad delight as Galen's wind carried him ten, twenty, thirty feet into the sky. And despite his protest, Galen laughed too. He held Percy aloft effortlessly, as if hefting a whole person into the air were nothing.

Goddess help her, he was using only one hand.

Ranka stood stock-still, the feeling draining from her limbs.

The wind vanished. Percy landed on his feet with the neatness of a cat and crowed, "Again!" Galen waved him off, staring at the sky. It was an endless, bright blue. Disappointment clouded Galen's face.

Ranka stayed hidden long after they left, her skin clammy despite the late-summer heat. She'd always relied on being the deadliest one in any room she entered. She was the monster, the blood-witch, the Butcher of Belren.

But as Ranka eyed the sap dripping from the splintered palm tree, recalling the boy who'd laughed as though his gale winds were a party trick, a new truth unfolded before her.

Someday, Galen Sunra would grow up. If he *did* learn to command entire storms, if he became a Skybreaker like his father, his winds would stop being a toy and become a tool of war.

And when that happened, there wouldn't be enough blood-magic in the world to stop him.

8

FOR TWO MORE NIGHTS AND TWO MORE DAYS, RANKA was left alone. No summons came from the Sunra twins. No whisper of Yeva emerged. Ongrum had been so certain they'd targeted Yeva because she looked like Ranka, so where was she? Why weren't there any clues? Why wasn't there any hint of her at all?

On the third night it was not a yearning for Yeva that woke her—it was hunger.

Ranka jerked upright, an all-too-familiar knifepoint pain twisting in her gut, accompanied by the telltale slickness between her thighs.

"No," she whispered. "No, no, *no*. Please, not now."

The scents of the palace flooded her. She tasted every living body within these walls, from the guards in the hallway to the serving girls in the kitchens to the prince asleep in his bed. All of them vulnerable, all of them a life burning, thrumming, and hers to take—

Ranka clapped her hands over her nose.

It'd been three, four months since she'd last bled. Skra life made her menstrual cycles blessedly irregular. It was safer for everyone else that way.

A memory stirred of the first time—the blood, pain, and embarrassment. In those days there was no wave of bloodthirst accompanying her cycle. Only Vivna, laughing quietly, washing her bedclothes in snowmelt rivers fed by the Kithraki Mountains.

"It's nothing to be ashamed of." She'd wrung the fabric until the water ran from red to pink to clear. "Plenty of witches bleed, little sister. Plenty of witches don't. Bodies are strange, changing, beautiful things. Now look, this is how you get the blood out. Let's find some herbs to help the pain."

After Belren, Ranka carried her clothes to the river alone.

Another throb rolled through her lower abdomen. The scent of the guard outside her door flooded through her—musk, rose soap, and sweat.

If she were in the Skra camp, she would head to the mountains for a week. Glut herself on hare, whitetail deer, whatever she could get her desperate, starving hands on until the hunger faded.

But she was stuck in this goddess-cursed palace. And there certainly weren't any deer for her to slaughter.

The stables.

Percy, Aramis, and Galen had said something of tunnels. That had to be the way out. If she could make it out of the palace, she could settle for killing rats, something, *anything.*

Ranka drifted to the window. It was only a six-foot drop to the manicured lawn below. She held her breath and set out across the grounds.

Ranka stared at the horses, her hands over her mouth and nose. She'd searched for several minutes and found nothing. No way out, no hint of any secret tunnels, no indication of where the twins and Percy had come from.

And now she had a choice to make.

The horses stomped, bumping against the backs of their pens. It wasn't fair, and it wasn't right. But she could feel it now—the whisper of what was to come. When her blood-magic demanded death, she didn't feel the hunger that people who grew up with full bellies felt if they missed a meal.

Real hunger burned.

It clawed its way up from her stomach, burning her throat, her eyes, pounding headaches through her forehead and temples and the space where her jawbone hung below her ears. The world became blurred. And after came the pain—cramps in her stomach, weakness and fire in her limbs, as if her very cells were crying out in protest. The hunger for death became a part of her, as constant as the need for air, until it shifted from desperation to sheer pain. When it reached its crux, she'd do anything—hurt anyone—to make it go away. To feel whole again, if only for a moment.

It was in these moments she had been the object of Vivna's disgust, and Ongrum's pride.

Two voices broke the night.

"Tell me the truth, Percy. Are you *certain* you destroyed it?"

"I burned everything. And then I ran."

Shit.

Ranka dove into one of the empty pens right as Aramis and Percy turned the corner. Instead of their palace finery, they wore drab cloaks. Their emotions spiked in the air—worry, fear, grief. And from Percy, guilt. Ranka recoiled.

Hunger throbbed in her head, her limbs, her bones. Her vision flickered gray. Percy and Aramis were alone. They'd be so easy to attack. Wouldn't even see her coming. She'd hit them from behind, cut their delicate throats—

Ranka raised her hands to her cheeks and dug her fingernails in until it hurt.

Her eyes darted around the stable, tracing pockets of shadow and hay-dusted walls. She'd have to come back later. Find a way into the city, hunt something easy and small. A rat, a stray dog, or some lost drunk with bruised fists made bolder by whiskey. Anything to curb this endless, pulsing need.

"Have you considered," Percy said slowly, "asking your brother for help?"

"Absolutely *not*."

"You can't lie to him forever."

"What? You *are* here to help him train. He doesn't need to know the rest."

Ranka slunk toward the exit. The stable was a palette of gray, and hunger burned in her veins. Her sweat-slick hands trembled with the effort of keeping her magic at bay.

"Now, the witch—how long has she been dead?"

Ranka hesitated.

"A day, maybe two." Percy sounded resigned. "Just like the others. Oh, good—right on time."

Footsteps echoed, coupled with the rub of leather against cloth, the sharp scent of a well-oiled blade. The skin beneath Foldrey's eyes was the color of a day-old bruise as he stepped into the warm light of the stable, his face lined with weary resignation. "The morgue is paid off. You have two hours."

Ranka was going to be ill. One dead witch didn't seem important enough to involve the captain of the palace guard—unless that witch was someone special. Someone they wanted to keep hidden.

Someone they'd kidnapped.

"We'll only need an hour." Aramis strode across the stable and threw her shoulder against a barrel of hay. It slid free, revealing a hatch in the stable floor. Aramis yanked it open, and the scent of salt flooded the air.

Foldrey stepped forward. "Princess, let me go instead. I'm failing you, letting you chase trouble like this."

Aramis softened and patted his shoulder. "No, you're following orders. Here's a new one for you: go home and sleep, Foldrey."

He looked down at her, and only her, as if Percy weren't even in the room. For the first time Ranka wondered who had raised the twins while their parents had been running a kingdom. It had to be a complicated thing—to love a child, knowing someday you'd have to take her orders and step aside as she barreled toward harm. His jaw worked.

Before Foldrey could argue, the princess hiked her skirts and leapt into the tunnel. A dull thud sounded below, and Percy followed.

Foldrey remained for a while after. He closed the hatch and knelt there, his expression troubled, his eyes fixed on something only he could see. "I'm doing what I can for them, Alus. Even if they won't— even if it doesn't seem right. But lately . . . I don't know. I just don't know."

He blew out the lamp and left.

There was a witch. A dead witch, important enough for the princess to investigate, for the captain of the royal guard to pay for silence.

What if . . .

Ongrum would tell her to remain in the palace. But Ranka had made the mistake of not putting Vivna first when it mattered. She would not repeat that mistake with Yeva.

Ranka opened the hatch and leapt into the dark.

9

THE TUNNELS GLOWED.

Seaswept's salt mines had been abandoned centuries ago, leaving vermin to make their home where the humans had once walked. An endless stretch of stained white walls and unlit offshoots yawned around Ranka. The tunnels were narrower than the copper mines humans had carved through Witchik—cramped, wet, and sloping—but they were built to last.

But swirling through the tunnels, so faint she nearly missed it, was the reek of decay.

Something else was down here. Something not quite dead, but close.

Something that felt like it was waiting for her.

Ranka shook herself and switched her focus on to the tunnels.

Light flickered ahead. Ranka hadn't seen Percy or Aramis with a torch, but it was definitely fire lighting their way, casting garish shapes that twisted and danced on the walls as they hurried along. Aramis moved like a noble even in disguise, her head up, shoulders straight, but Percy walked with a rolling gait, footsteps soundless, fingers hovering over his hip, ready to draw out a hidden weapon.

He moved like a predator.

No matter. Percy could play at being a predator all he wanted; Ranka had been born one.

She scented the morgue long before she saw it; death and decay blanketed the sharp bite of chemicals, bodies preserved just long enough for their families to mourn. The flame vanished, and light spilled into the tunnel as a hatch creaked and Percy and Aramis climbed out. Ranka counted to twenty, then scaled the grime-slick ladder after them.

"Cremated tomorrow . . . matches the rest . . ."

Their voices were too far away.

Leave, a voice in her head whispered.

Ranka grit her teeth and climbed through the hatch.

A layer of dust covered the floor. Mold grew along the walls, and the windows were streaked with black paint. This morgue hadn't seen proper use in years. And yet the glow of firelight came from a far room.

Aramis's voice broke the air. "Lights above, Percy. What—what *is* this?"

"I'm sorry. I never thought it'd get this far."

Ranka breathed in. Her knees buckled under the sharp scent of pure, naked fear. She stole across the room, slid behind the open door—and time ground to a halt.

A dead witch lay in the morgue. She radiated the same rot Ranka had encountered back in Witchik. Fist-sized purple cysts had destroyed her skin, erupting across her body, leaving it raw, broken, and weeping. The fingernails on her right hand were sharpened to coal-black points, and though Ranka couldn't see the others, she wagered they were a pale gray.

She had died with her eyes open—one a blood-witch white, the other a pale brown.

It wasn't possible. Not this far south.

Aramis stared at the corpse. "How many?"

Percy winced. "This makes seven."

"How is that even possible?"

"I don't know, okay? The strain shouldn't be able to replicate." A shudder rolled through him. "But that's why I'm here. To fix it."

Aramis trailed her fingers over the face of the dead witch. There was no revulsion in her eyes, only a desire to understand. Her fingers skimmed over the wooden prayer beads studded through the witch's ears. "She's Kerth. The bracelet isn't witch craft, though."

Aramis lifted the witch's other hand—the one that had lain out of Ranka's sight, clawed and curled in death. A pale leather bracelet flashed in the light. It was a worn, unremarkable piece of jewelry, the once-vivid orange beads bleached by sun and time.

Ranka would have known it anywhere, because there were only three in this world, and one encircled Ranka's wrist.

Her knees buckled.

No.

Yeva would never have willingly taken that bracelet off. It had to have been stolen.

But how had it ended up here?

From the look on Aramis's face, the dead witch was a mystery to her. Maybe it was a coincidence, or maybe the palace wasn't involved at all. Maybe the path to finding Yeva was not the royals—but whatever had killed this witch.

Footsteps, deliberately light, broke her from her thoughts.

A stranger entered the morgue.

He was young, dressed in threadbare clothes, with a shaved head and pockmarked pale skin. The boy stalked across the room, quieter than a prayer, his attention focused solely on the princess ahead. In his palm gleamed a knife.

He wasn't alone. Outside, Ranka scented three more.

The boy stepped into a shaft of moonlight.

And on his chest—something gleamed.

It was so small, she'd nearly missed it: a gold pin no bigger than a coin, with an all-too-familiar engraving on its face. Ranka couldn't read the words circling the edges, but she would have recognized it anywhere.

It was identical to the one clenched in the sick witch's fist as she died.

10

THE BOY CROSSED THE ROOM, SO CLOSE TO RANKA SHE could see the gaping pores on his pale cheeks, the delicate blond hairs dusting his upper lip. He was still a child, teetering on the precipice of adulthood. And yet, like her, he was already a killer.

The boy leaned against the doorframe, masking his terror with arrogance. "Curious hobby for a princess."

Percy's head snapped up. A knife appeared in his hand, and in a blink he was in front of Aramis, body tense and blade poised. In the murky light Ranka could have sworn his eyes flashed a melted gold. That beneath his skin, a faint outline of scales rippled. She blinked and the image vanished.

"Aramis," Percy said, his voice hard. "Go. Now."

"Don't bother," the boy said. "I've got three more outside."

Ranka tensed. Percy was a warrior, but could he take on four men at once? She doubted it. It wasn't her place to interfere. The last thing she needed was for the princess to be on high alert because her brother's new fiancée was tailing her.

But if they die, Yeva whispered, *how will you find me?*

The pin. The bracelet. The sickness. Somehow they were connected.

"Come now, Princess," the boy crooned. "Let's make this easy. Step away from the body."

Aramis's throat bobbed, but her face was blank. "We can resolve this peacefully, surely." Her eyes darted to the exit. "You know the Sunra name. Our coffers have never been fuller, and the Hands have never been shy about taking bribes in the past. Name a price."

"We have plenty of gold." The boy jerked his chin at Percy. "We want him, and the corpse."

"What do you want with Ambassador Stone?"

From the look on Percy's face, he was wondering the same. Ranka's eyes narrowed.

A muscle feathered in the boy's jaw. "You tell me, Princess. An ambassador from the Star Isles lands on our shores for the first time in decades—and suddenly the Bloodwinn is found. Suddenly there are blood-witches in our streets, killing our livestock, snatching our dogs."

Percy raised a hand in caution. "I seek the same as you—an end to this nightmare."

"Liar. Your people *wanted* this nightmare." He jerked his chin at Aramis. "And *you*—you and that brother. You don't care. You just let us die. You witch-loving Sunras deserve to burn with them—"

"Enough," a new voice snapped. It had the lilt of Yaris, an eastern city that teetered on the edge of swamplands ruled by the Murknen coven. "Let her highness go, Edon."

Three more humans entered. All wore gold pins.

What is going on?

A woman with terra-cotta skin marred by burn scars stepped forward. She was older and, from the confident cruelty in her eyes, the leader. "Take his advice, princess. Leave the boy and the corpse with us, and keep your life while you still can."

Percy's throat bobbed. "Go, Aramis. I'll be fine."

"Percy," Aramis grated. "Shut up."

The Yaris woman snapped her fingers. White-blue sparks puffed into the air, and electricity threaded down her wrist. "Do as he says, Princess."

Let Percy die, Ranka willed Aramis. *If you have any sense, you'll let him die.*

Percy was expendable—but Galen was Aramis's blood. They needed each other, and he needed *her*, that much was already clear. Surely Aramis knew this. Surely she would do anything to protect her brother who was set to inherit a cruel, wide world.

Ranka knew better than anyone what it meant to love a sibling so much that reason and right no longer mattered, so long as they were safe.

Aramis lifted her chin. "Percy, hand me a knife."

You proud fool.

The blond boy raised his weapon—and Ranka lunged.

She leapt from behind the door and seized the boy by the back of his neck, jerking him off his feet. He cried out, flailing, but Ranka wrapped her forearm over his mouth, used her free hand to catch his wrist, and jerked it in the wrong direction. The bones broke with a crunch. He screamed against her arm, and Ranka pressed his blade to the soft hollow of his throat.

She could feel Aramis's and Percy's stares, but her eyes were only for the Yaris woman.

"That sick witch," Ranka said slowly. "What happened to her?"

The Yaris woman raised a dark brow. Though she wore an air of calm, Ranka could scent the fear spiking in her. "We're as clueless as you are."

"Don't lie to me."

"I'm not—"

"You *are.*" Ranka pushed the knife in, just hard enough to break skin, until blood welled on the moon-bright blade. The boy whimpered, and Ranka kept talking. "I'm going to ask you one more time, and if you want him to live, you're going to tell me the truth. Who are you? And what did you do to that witch?"

The Yaris woman glared. Ranka stood there with her hostage, her breath coming quickly, her body still, a barrier of muscle and starved blood-magic. Somehow these people were connected to the first witch's death. To Yeva's disappearance. Logic demanded restraint, but the power in her veins wanted something far darker.

"Tala," one of the others said softly. "We were told not to hurt the girl—"

Anger flashed in the Yaris woman's eyes. "Accidents happen."

Time slowed. Ranka's blood-magic rose, pinpointing the way the woman's hands flew upward, sensing the charge building at her fingers, predicting the bolt of sheer power about to light up the room.

Ranka drove the knife home.

It'd been so long since she'd killed a person. She'd forgotten how easy it was—like putting out a candle with a pinch of damp fingers. The boy sagged, and her blood-magic roared in triumph as his eighteen years unfolded before her.

This is what she saw:

A blue sky broken by a red kite and a brother's laugh.

A mother's feverish eyes, shot through with yellow. *You must look after each other.*

A brother, facedown in a pool of blood, a blood-witch panting over him.

And finally, them.

They were a sea of threadbare clothes and gold pins and eyes that burst with righteous purpose, a throng of humans who claimed to have the blessing of a sun goddess. *Sweet child,* they said. *Our world is plagued, but you can be the cure.* A pale woman streaked oil over his cheeks and dipped him in the ocean as sunrise lit the water on fire. The strangers gave the boy a knife, and he named it revenge.

And then he was gone.

Ranka staggered. Her blood-magic swelled, latching on to the rest of the lives in the room. In that moment there was no corpse, no meddling royals or missing witches. There was only blood, the fragile thrum of heartbeats, and the power in her veins demanding *more.* She teetered on the edge of it, barely aware of the way her nails were sharpening, her muscles swelling, every part of her hardening, expanding, morphing from girl to predator.

A monster, Vivna had accused her once. *You are a monster dressed as a girl, and it's all you'll ever be.*

"Princess," Ranka whispered. "Run."

And then Ranka gave in.

She killed the next person with a twist of his neck, the second a slash to her throat. Their lives flashed through her too—the melody of a wife's laugh, a sister's weary sigh, a ringed hand offering a gold pin, a ticket to Seaswept, and a promise. Her magic devoured it all. Blood sprayed the walls, coating her skin, painting her hair rust. The morgue was a museum of death; Ranka was its curator.

Lightning arced toward her.

Ranka threw herself sideways. She leapt, seized the Yaris woman's tunic, and slammed her to the ground. "Who are you?" Ranka knelt on her chest and pressed the knife to her throat. *Where is Yeva?*

The Yaris woman looked at Ranka with hateful eyes as blood dripped from her nose. "We are Solomei's light. We are her Hand in the night. From the poison, we bring the cure."

She seized the knife from Ranka—and drove it into her own heart.

"No!" Ranka cried, but the woman was dead by her own hand. Her secrets vanished with her. Ranka knelt there, heart pounding, grief and rage whiplashing through her as blood cooled on her skin; she had been so *close*. And she'd failed.

Slowly the colors returned—the red on her hands, the silver of the knife, the lilacs someone had once set on an end table, now dust-covered and withered by time. Ranka's blood-magic hummed pleasantly, sated and calm. But all Ranka could hear were those words.

From the poison, we bring the cure.

Ranka turned.

Aramis pointed a knife at her. "Don't move."

Behind her, the wooden hatch in the floor stood open. Percy and the corpse were gone.

Ranka swayed. It was as though she'd chugged an entire bottle of wine and her skin were two sizes too small. She held up her bloody hands. "It's okay. I won't hurt you."

She waited for the horror, the screams. But instead, Aramis moved

across the room toward Ranka, her steps deliberate. Silent. Her eyes never left Ranka's face. Ranka didn't dare move. Finally, Aramis Sunra came to stand over her, lashes casting shadows over her cheeks—and offered her hand.

"Get up."

Ranka took her hand, and the princess jerked her upright. When Ranka staggered, Aramis caught her arm, her fingers surprisingly warm against Ranka's skin.

Ranka swayed, head spinning, blood-magic still roiling in her veins.

Even Ongrum had shown fear when Ranka was in the throes of her power. Even Yeva had balked. She'd grown so used to the hatred that came after, the disgust that she'd more than earned. But Aramis looked at her like she was familiar.

Aramis looked at Ranka like she was the beginning of something.

This close, Ranka could see the fine scars on Aramis's hands, the faint rivulets of sweat that glazed her temple. The ink stains on her fingers. Her eyes—a deep, rich brown—drank up all the color in the room. The princess tilted her face up to Ranka's.

She really was beautiful.

Aramis tilted her head to the side. "My mother was like you, at the end of her life—completely at her blood-magic's mercy. It's getting worse, isn't it?"

Ranka swayed. She knew she ought to lie. But here was this girl, looking at her like she was a person instead of a monster, touching her without a shred of disgust—and so the truth slipped free. "Yes."

"Good." A shadow flitted across Aramis's face. "That makes you easier to control."

Metal flashed. Pain pricked Ranka's neck, and she lurched back, fingers flying to her throat, watching as Aramis tossed a syringe aside.

The princess folded her arms and waited.

Numbness crashed over Ranka in a muddy wave, spiraling from her neck to her chest, her arms, her legs. She reached, but it was as if a wall of glass had descended between her and her power. She staggered, no longer in control of her legs, and Aramis caught her, lowering her to the floor.

"What—" Ranka wheezed.

"Shhh." Aramis shifted Ranka's head into her lap. "You're fine. It's a tranquilizer my mother developed for blood-witches. For herself, actually. Works wonderfully, doesn't it?"

I should have let her die. The thought cut through the haze with blistering clarity.

Another syringe poked into Ranka's neck, and her thoughts turned liquid.

"Do you think we're stupid? Do you think we didn't know you left your room at night, that you've been poking around, following us?"

Aramis bent down so that her lips brushed the shell of Ranka's ear, featherlight, her curls forming a curtain around the two of them. To someone passing by, they might have been lovers, embracing in the quiet hours of night.

Aramis trailed her knife over Ranka's throat.

"We never would have been friends, but we might have been allies. I would have helped you with your blood-magic, if only to keep you from endangering Galen—but if this is how you want to spend your time here? So be it. I don't care if you're the Bloodwinn. I don't care if you're the most powerful blood-witch on the goddess-damned continent. I will not let you hurt Galen. And I will not let you get in my way."

Ranka could no longer feel Aramis's hands. Could barely register her voice.

She didn't know whether to laugh or cry.

She'd come so close, had found Yeva's bracelet, the sickness, the pins. This princess was the key. Ranka *needed* her. And now Aramis hated her.

When the darkness finally took her, it was a relief.

11

THE MONTHS THAT FOLLOWED BELREN HAD BEEN unbearable.

For three months Ranka did not rise from bed. Her world was a fog of pain and nightmares, of days spent swathed in bandages while her body burned with a new, furious power and a never-ending hunger. With sleep came the nightmares—bodies in the snow, houses collapsing under the weight of flames, and a sister's voice screaming *what have you done?*

"Ranka?" a familiar voice whispered. "Are you awake?"

Ranka's eyes cracked open.

"There are those pretty gray eyes," Yeva murmured. "You had me worried, sleeping for three days straight again. Are you hurting?"

Yeva leaned over her, her narrow face pinched with concern. At sixteen, she was training to be a healer. Her witchery was too weak for her to scout or fight, but her sharpened sense of smell, like Ranka's, gave her a penchant for sniffing out disease or festering wounds. Asyil sat in the corner, grinding a poultice she balanced on her thigh. Asyil was no healer like Yeva, had no desire to be one. But she would go wherever her sister did.

Ranka understood that more than anything.

She'd been dreaming again—not of Belren, but of Vivna, holding her hand, leading her through the snow, her cheeks rosy, scarf snapping in the winter wind. These days, it was always Vivna she dreamed of.

"I'm going to change your bandages—can you sit up for me?"

This was their routine. Yeva came every morning, to change Ranka's bandages, clean her wounds, hunt for any sign of gangrene or a warning that a burn was about to turn necrotic. She was gentle in a way Ranka had never known, and she was kind. It was those gray winter mornings that made the nights bearable, that precious hour as Yeva cared for Ranka and Asyil rattled off updates on the latest camp drama that helped Ranka forget, if only briefly, that she was only a girl of twelve and she'd already lost everything that mattered.

Until the hunger came.

It was always there, that ache in her veins, the twitch in her hands. Even now bits of gray spotted her vision. She could hear Yeva's heartbeat, quick and nervous in the watery light of dawn. She could scent the witches beyond the cabin walls. At night she heard their whispers.

"The first blood-witch in twenty years . . ."

"Did you see what she did to that town?"

"If she could do that at twelve, imagine once she's an adult. . . ."

"I think our mornings together may end soon." Yeva's smile didn't quite reach her eyes. "I brought you something." From her pocket she pulled a bracelet. It was beautiful—a delicate leather band adorned with shimmering, iridescent orange beads. Human craft, by the look of it.

Ranka stared. She had nothing to trade in return. She started to shake her head, and Yeva's eyes flashed with grief.

"It's a gift, Ranka." Yeva tied the bracelet around Ranka's wrist and held up her own. "See? We match. Asyil has one too."

Ranka knew she ought to thank Yeva, that this was extraordinarily kind, more than she deserved. But she felt nothing. She didn't know what to say to her, this witch who had already given her more kindness in three months than most had in her lifetime. Ranka searched for something, anything—and the door swung open.

Bitter winter air and sunlight rushed in. A familiar shadow leaned against the frame. "You've done good work on her."

Ranka went still.

She'd not seen Ongrum since Belren. Ranka had betrayed the Skra by fleeing, and thanks to her actions in Belren, the rapidly disintegrating cease-fire between humans and witches was surely doomed. Ongrum was probably furious. Ongrum probably wanted her dead.

"Leave us," Ongrum said, her voice soft. "Both of you."

Anger flashed across Yeva's face, so brief that Ranka might have missed it, had she blinked. Yeva wrapped her hands around Ranka's, her face suddenly raw, and dropped her voice to a whisper. "Look at me, Ranka. You're a good girl, with a good heart. You can still protect it. You can survive. But you have to move on. You have to let her go."

There was only one *her* Yeva could be referencing. But why would Ranka ever want to let go of Vivna? Vivna, who had been her entire world, her hope and her prayer, the one god she believed in and the joy her heart spun around? Vivna, the only family she'd ever had?

Yeva exhaled through her nose and rose. She dipped her head in deference to Ongrum, careful not to meet her eyes, and slipped from the cabin, Asyil trailing on her heels.

And then they were alone.

Ranka swallowed. If Ongrum asked her if she regretted what she'd done, she wouldn't be able to lie. She'd have followed Vivna to the end of the world, every time.

But instead, Ongrum crossed the room and knelt beside her. "How are you feeling?" She lifted a brow. "Did you think I'd forgotten you? For two weeks you lay asleep. For two weeks I was here. Three months ago, when I found you half-dead in the snow, a village burning around you . . ." Her voice caught. "Tell me this, witchling. The power that woke in Belren. Is it with you now?"

"Yes," Ranka rasped.

Ongrum looked almost reverent. "How does it feel?"

When Ranka spoke, her voice sounded far away, as though someone else were piloting her body for her.

"Hungry," she whispered. "It's always hungry."

It was there in every moment. That—that *thing* that had woken in Belren, lurking in her veins, painting her dreams with blood. Some days Ranka wished she could cut herself open and pry it loose, rip free whatever demon had spawned inside her amid the flames. She'd hoped it would fade. Instead it seemed only to settle, to sink deeper inside of her, until Ranka didn't know where the hunger began and she ended.

Ongrum watched her with an odd look on her face. She cast her eyes skyward, scanning the old cedar ceiling. Kneeling there, face concealed in shadow, the burn scars warping Ongrum's body had never been more pronounced.

The older witches often whispered stories about her over the coalpits. They said Ongrum had been born among humans, but they'd tried to burn her. She'd lost three sisters and her mother to the flames and barely escaped with her life. The Skra had found her half-dead in the snow and had taken her in. Six years later, at twenty-two, she killed their leader, assumed control, and spent the next three decades transforming them from a coven on the brink of extinction into a force. She'd raised an entire generation of warriors. She'd made them *conquerors*.

And now—now she was looking at Ranka like there was something she could make of her, too.

"Stand up, child," Ongrum said abruptly. "You've rested long enough. You will walk."

And though Ranka's body ached, though her burn wounds cracked and bled from the movement, though every part of her screamed out in pain, she swung her feet from the bed. She'd not made it more than a few steps since Belren, but Ongrum's words were not a suggestion.

And so she rose.

Step by painful step, Ongrum guided Ranka from the cabin, propelling her out into the bright winter light. Her eyes watered. The witches working in the camp stopped to stare openly. She'd not bathed since Belren. Her lips swelled with cold sores, and her still-healing burns formed a warped patchwork of peeling skin and bruises across her body.

But it was not disgust the other Skra regarded her with.

It was fear.

She'd heard them at night, when they thought she slept. Most of them had visited Belren. They whispered about what she'd done there, about what she'd become, what she might yet be. Ranka couldn't recall what had happened, not really—but the looks on their faces told her whatever she'd done was bad enough.

From the edge of the camp, Yeva watched Ranka with a strained expression, her arms folded tightly in front of her. Asyil glared at the ground, spinning the bracelet on her wrist.

You have to let her go.

Ongrum led Ranka to the center of the camp. She turned, looking at her expectantly, as if she was waiting for Ranka to say something. But it was all Ranka could do to stay on her feet. She'd not seen the Skra camp since she fled that night with Vivna, what little belongings they had tucked into a knapsack, Vivna whispering, *Come on, quickly, before someone notices we've gone.*

Now she was back—and everything and nothing had changed.

One cabin had a new roof. The coal-pits had been cleaned recently. At the far end of their settlement, the carcasses of two stags hung from the boughs of a stripped-down sycamore to dry-age out of reach from fangwolves, bears, and wandering witches. But the winter gardens were still dead and empty, the river that snaked along the east side of camp still half-frozen. The pale and brown faces staring back at her remained the same.

It was as if she and Vivna had never left at all.

In her veins, her power twitched, spinning ribbons of gray through her periphery. It was barely a flicker—a warning, and a promise of what was to come.

"She's not coming back, is she?" Ranka whispered.

Ongrum gave her a long look. Dully, Ranka thought Ongrum might hit her. She'd seen Skra punished for less. Once, when Ongrum learned one of the witches was sleeping through watch duty, she kicked her with metal-tipped snowshoes and forbade the others from treating her cracked ribs. The girl had never healed properly.

But instead of a slap, arms encircled Ranka. Ongrum's chin settled on top of her head.

Ranka didn't dare move.

"Listen to me," Ongrum said. "Vivna didn't understand you. Vivna was selfish. She didn't understand how powerful you are—how *brilliant* you are." A snow-crusted glove stroked her hair. "She didn't love you, Ranka—not the way we do."

When Ranka was seven, she'd cut Vivna by accident, a deep slice along her forearm. The blood had been bright against her sister's pale skin, and Ranka had wept as Vivna cried out in pain and shoved her away. That night, she'd crawled into Vivna's bed and whispered, "Do you still love me?"

Vivna had rolled over in the dark and taken Ranka's face into her hands. "You're my sister. My blood. I'll always love you. Nothing will change that."

A well opened up inside Ranka. She had the sense she was collapsing, as if her ribs had been removed from one side and her body could no longer support itself. A strange keening left her throat, and she knew she was crying, but she was too far away from her body to care.

Ongrum held her all the while. When her sobs slowed, Ongrum stepped back and gripped Ranka's shoulders. Were it not for her hold, Ranka would have sunk to the ground.

"Your life is never going to be the same—you understand that, don't you? You are a blood-witch now, Ranka. You are the hope of every witch alive. You are the nightmare of the humans. You are a cause. And you are the most powerful weapon we've ever had."

"I am not a weapon." Tears welled in Ranka's eyes. "I'm just a girl."

"You are so much more now. You were sent to us by the Goddess herself, witchling. Let me train you. Let me hone the gift you've been given." Ongrum caressed her cheek. "I cannot promise you love, nor safety. But I can promise you something better."

Ranka looked up at her. "What?"

"Purpose." Ongrum unbuckled the top half of her coat and drew out an ice axe. It was a slender, heavy tool, Kerth craft by the aged pine handle, made to slice through frozen underbrush and sleet-crusted snowbanks alike. But in Ranka's hands, it would cut through bone. "The witch who trained me gave me this, when I was not much older than you."

Ranka swayed. She had the sense that she was standing on the edge of a cliff, one foot still on solid ground, one dangling over endless, empty air. The thing inside her shivered. Maybe if she never fed it, it would wither and die, shriveling like a flower on an unwatered vine. Maybe Belren could be a fluke, an accident, a scar on her life that would cease to ache as she aged.

There was hunger in Ongrum's eyes, but something else, too. Pride, maybe? Love? When was the last time someone had looked at Ranka like that? Like she was someone to be proud of—someone to be protected?

The coven stared at Ranka.

Ranka stared at the weapon. "You can make me strong?"

"Strong?" Ongrum's voice was a thing of hunger and thorns. "Oh, witchling. I'll make you a legend."

Ranka took the axe, and she never let go.

12

RANKA'S EYES FLEW OPEN. SUNBEAMS FILTERED through open windows, heralding the cries of gulls, the roar of the sea, the low melody of distant prayer bells. Pain throbbed deep in her abdomen, but no hunger accompanied it. The dream hung all around her. She'd been such a fool then, hoping she might be better. Thinking Vivna might come back. She'd taken Yeva for granted, even at the beginning.

She knew better now. Dead or alive, Ranka would never see her sister again.

But Yeva was still out there. And Yeva needed her.

"Good morning. Did you sleep well? I certainly didn't."

Aramis Sunra leaned against the wall. Sunlight outlined her in gold, rendering her the very image of the goddess her people worshipped. Percy lounged at the threshold.

Memory rushed in—the Hands of Solomei with their golden pins, the corpse, the sick witch, and *Aramis*. Knocking her out, handling a blood-witch with expertise, not a glimmer of fear in those dark eyes as she whispered that her mother had sought a way to control her blood-magic and nearly found it.

This was it. They'd come to punish her for stepping out of line.

Ranka braced herself, rallying a thousand excuses, pleas, and even threats. She would do whatever it took to stay in the palace, even if it meant groveling—

Aramis tilted her head to the side. "Who is Yeva?"

Ranka's mind blanked. "What?"

Aramis spun a syringe of tranquilizer between her fingers, the glass flashing each time it made a circle around her thumb, her expression unreadable. "You snoop, you lie, you follow us—and then you save us, even though you knew we'd find out you'd been spying." The syringe stopped. "When you killed that woman, you asked her about someone named Yeva. Foldrey said you asked him about someone by the same name, your first day here. Said you thought we kidnapped her. Who is she?"

Another memory stirred—of Yeva, only a few weeks after Ranka had taken that axe from Ongrum, stopping her outside of camp as Ranka returned from training.

Yeva, staring at Ranka in horror, taking in the blood that coated her hands, her hair, her face. It wasn't human blood—not yet—but Yeva had known the path Ranka would walk down. Had known what she'd become.

She'd tried to save her anyway.

"*Look at me*," Yeva had demanded, shaking her bracelet in Ranka's face. "You're not alone, okay? Not if you have me. And not because you owe me, or because we share a coven name, but because you're my *friend*, and I love you because I choose to. Because you're worth it. And I'm not going anywhere. Let that be enough, Ranka. Walk away from this, before it's too late. I'm begging you."

Ranka's eyes burned, and she looked away. The weight of Aramis's stare pressed down on her. She was on fragile ground here. If the palace had taken Yeva, it wasn't likely Aramis would suddenly admit to it in an act of goodwill. Ranka was a warrior, trained to kill, to head straight for a problem and fight until it wasn't a threat anymore—but Aramis was raised to rule. She had no weapons, no combat training, only a sharp tongue and a sharper mind. This girl would see through Ranka's lies before she could finish them. In a game of deceit, Ranka would lose every time.

So instead, she told the truth.

"Yeva was Skra," she said finally, her voice catching, rough. "She was family. The humans kidnapped her. I suppose I have your wanted posters to thank for that."

Aramis's expression faltered, and for a beat, she looked genuinely disturbed.

Ranka lifted her wrist, the sun-bleached beads rattling, and Aramis blanched as she recognized them. "Your dead witch had Yeva's brace-let. And she wasn't the first I've seen. One attacked me in the North-lands, well into Skra territory, carrying one of those pins with her. She was in southern clothes, but she was in my lands, Princess. So put yourself in my boots. I turn myself in—travel all the way south, desperate to find my friend—and then I see her bracelet on the wrist of a witch with the disease I saw in the north." Ranka licked her lips. "Why did I save you? Because letting you die meant losing my chance at getting her back."

Percy and Aramis cast each other an uneasy glance.

"We're not in the business of kidnapping girls," Aramis said, her expression troubled. "Whoever took your friend—it was no one that serves my family. I can assure you of that."

"If you didn't," Ranka said bitterly, "then who did?"

"I don't know, witch girl. I'm sorry."

And though Ranka loathed it—she believed her. An ache pulsed low in her. She was back at the beginning, then. Someone had wanted her here badly enough to steal Yeva. There were still answers in this city, she could feel it in her bones.

Aramis turned away and drummed her fingers against the window-sill, her voice sharp with anger. "You've put us in an impossible posi-tion here. I was ready to tolerate your wandering. Prepared to help you with your blood-magic, the way Mother was ready to help me.

But after last night?" She shook her head. "You have meddled too far. You cannot remain in the palace."

"Wait, what?" Ranka blurted. "But you *need* me. Without me, the treaty—"

"Continues, so long as you're alive." Aramis watched her through half-lidded eyes. "Do you really think you'd be the first difficult royal shipped off to some distant isle to live her days in private captivity? Do you think you're the first Bloodwinn who's come here with a prison cell waiting for her, should you prove to be too volatile? An appearance at the wedding, the occasional public visit once every few years . . . so long as you're breathing, you serve your purpose."

"You're bluffing," Ranka said.

"Try me."

Panic thrummed through Ranka. She couldn't be exiled, not when she'd finally found a clue. The memory of that sick witch lingered. Something bigger was happening in this city. Something deadly that would put every witch at risk, coup or no coup.

And if Aramis was telling the truth—if the palace truly hadn't taken Yeva—then the sickness was now her only lead.

Ranka's mind spun. Aramis and Percy had come with their guard up, ready for things to turn nasty, but even with Aramis's threat of exile lingering in the air, they were waiting for something.

"Your mother," Ranka said. "You said she thought blood-magic could be controlled? That you had planned to help me?"

Aramis's nostrils flared.

There it is.

"It was a theory," Aramis said reluctantly. "My grandmother had hoped the same—blood-magic gets stronger every year. It's harder on the body, more difficult to keep under control. Mother thought it might be . . . managed, the same way a long-term illness would." Her voice softened. "Her hope was that if she could save herself, then she could save me, too."

It was a hope Ranka had never dared to entertain. Blood-magic was a death sentence, a guarantee that any who inherited it were suddenly living their life on a shortened clock.

Ongrum had called it a blessing of the gods—and what if it truly could be? What if it could be a gift instead of a curse? A tool to be wielded at will, a power so unstoppable, so brilliant, that even a Skybreaker couldn't stand against her. The Skra would be unstoppable.

And maybe—finally—they would think Ranka worthy. She could see the pride that would light Ongrum's eyes, the shock of the Skra, and then the relief of knowing that at last they wouldn't have to fear her. That she could protect them.

"Exiling me gets me nowhere," Ranka said slowly. "Not when we could benefit each other."

Aramis's eyes narrowed.

"Train me," Ranka breathed. "Carry on your mother's work, and help me the way she would have helped you. In return I'll give you whatever you need—no questions asked." She didn't say what she suspected—that somehow they needed her, and that was the only real reason she wasn't already chained onto a ship and bound for some distant isle.

The temptation glimmering in Aramis's eyes told her she was right.

They glared at each other—the northern warrior, a wall of muscle and scars, and the delicate southern princess who carried secrets in her ink-stained fingers.

Aramis stepped forward.

She closed the distance between them, tilting her head to meet Ranka's eyes. Ranka could feel the heat of her skin and make out the individual lashes of her eyes. It took everything in her not to step back.

"I will help you—but we do it my way," Aramis said. "There will be no more spying. No more lies. And if you step out of line—if you give me a single reason to think you might hurt Galen?" Aramis reached up as if to cradle Ranka's cheek and settled her fingers on Ranka's jugular instead, exerting just enough pressure that her touch teetered on the border of pleasure and pain. "I'll make you wish I'd merely exiled you."

"Is that a threat?"

Aramis's lips curved. "Would you like it in writing?"

An odd thrill bubbled through Ranka. She was the Butcher, the blood-witch, the monster. But here was this—this *girl* who looked at Ranka with half-lidded eyes and arrogant confidence, who threatened her without blinking. It was maddening. It was unacceptable.

And if Ranka was being honest, it was a little bit thrilling.

There was a light to Aramis's eyes, a flush to her cheeks, and a part of Ranka wondered if maybe—just maybe—some small part of Aramis was enjoying this too.

"Um," said Percy. "Are you guys okay?"

The charged air between them vanished. Aramis dropped her hand and stepped back, fixing her attention on the doorway, making a grand show of picking at her cuticles. Ranka tried to ignore the dizziness rushing through her, the weakness of her legs, and the strange, lonely ache at her throat where the princess's fingers had been only a moment before.

"We start tomorrow," said Aramis. "Congratulations, witch girl. You're involved now. Let's see if you survive it."

And then Aramis was gone, Percy on her heels, leaving Ranka alone with the roar of the sea, the chill in her bones, and the unsettling feeling that somehow, she'd given Aramis Sunra exactly what she wanted.

13

ARAMIS MADE GOOD ON HER THREAT. FOR TWO WEEKS
Ranka was summoned at dawn and didn't return to her room until
midnight, bones aching and brain threatening to leak out of her ears.
In the mornings she was woken by tutors, who dragged her off to
teach her a litany of useless things.

In the evenings, they trained.

"Come on," Percy goaded. "Hurt me."

The evening sun beat down on them, gilding the cliffs in gold
and casting the world into sepia. The grass that had been a soft green
when Ranka first arrived had fried to sad brown as a relentless summer
rolled toward a dry, rainless fall. For the past week all of southern
Isodal had been gripped by yet another heat wave. Water mages were
called out to farmlands to try to save wilting crops, leaving only a
skeleton rank of guards within the palace. The whole city buzzed with
restless energy. Even the palace had the sense of something swelling,
like a storm on the horizon, gathering strength before it hit land.
Ranka didn't know what was brewing in Seaswept's heart, only that it
was nothing good.

Now she stood weaponless across from Percy, a battered sparring
sword in each hand, sweat dripping from her sunburned skin. Her

vision sputtered to gray, and her palms itched with that familiar ache.

She was trying to kill him, and the unhinged bastard was *enjoying* it.

Focus, Aramis's voice rang through her mind. *And breathe.*

Ranka exhaled through her nose. She tried to imagine her magic as a river inside her, like Aramis had instructed—flowing through her heart, her limbs, her legs. Spreading out in shallow ripples, instead of roaring in a tidal wave that blocked out the world. A force to be controlled and directed, instead of one that swept her along, taking her and anything in its path with it.

"Sometime today, Bloodwinn," Percy yawned. "Or are you tired? Do you fancy a nap? Shall I fetch you some tea, maybe? A pillow, for your delicate head?"

When Ranka trained with the Skra, she'd always held back for fear of hurting them. But Percy was another story. Percy, with his snakeskin scent and gold eyes, was a challenge, egging her on, prodding her to fight harder, better, and stronger.

And Percy was *fast.*

He was a blur against the hard-packed earth, a whirlwind of flying limbs and flashing scars. Witches fought dirty and in close quarters, while humans were slow footed and favored distance—but Percy danced, circling and sidestepping, weaving and twirling, never staying in one place for more than a breath. He was beautiful to watch and infuriating to fight.

The practice swords snapped against her ribs, her stomach, her shins. Ranka lunged for him but snagged only fabric. A sword cracked against her cheek. Ranka spat out a mouthful of blood, her jaw smarting. "What the *hell?*"

"Percy!" Aramis shouted. "*No* head shots!"

"So sorry," Percy said. "I can't hear you, must be the wind!"

Ranka struggled to quell the rage spiking in her.

Think of your power like a rush of adrenaline, Aramis had instructed. *A chemical in your system, boosting you up. Harness that rush, and breathe through it—make it last, instead of letting it overpower you in one great wave.*

Percy swung directly at Ranka's head, and she threw herself to the ground to avoid the blow. Her hands curled into fists. Percy's eyes locked on hers, blazing that strange, ethereal gold as he skipped backward, his torso gleaming with sweat, and raised his sword at Ranka. "Catch me if you can, witch."

Ranka rose—and gave in.

The colors faded. Ranka could *feel* the thrum of Percy's major arteries, could hear the creak in his left ankle that had broken years ago and never healed quite right. Her power expanded, filling her up, testing its limits. She'd spent her life trying to keep this power, this part of her, tamped down and locked away. *Trapped*, lest she leave another scar on this world. But here, sparring atop cliffs beside the sea, a boy made of fire before her and a princess carved of ice at her back, for the first time in a long time, Ranka almost felt . . . free.

Percy flew at her again. He swung both practice swords for her head in a brilliant arc—and this time, she caught them.

"Um," said Percy.

Ranka sank her nails into the swords and ripped them free of his grasp, flinging them to either side. Her thoughts were gone. Her pain was gone. All that mattered was this moment, this boy, this *life*.

All that mattered was winning.

"All right, Aramis. I think she's gone murder-happy again. Take her out."

Percy leapt away, his heel dragging by a tenth of a second—and she lunged.

She slammed into him, and the world tipped sideways as Ranka locked her arm around Percy's throat. Now instead of a river flowing through her, her blood-magic roared upward, blocking out the world, erasing everything except the life beneath her hands, the life that was hers for taking. Pain and fear swirled off Percy.

Ranka drank it in, and squeezed.

Percy's hands scrabbled against Ranka's, his fingers forge hot. "Aramis! *Aramis!*"

Why was she here? She didn't remember. Ranka tightened her grip, her blood-magic swelling her muscles, lending an impossible strength to her hands. She would break his neck with a twist and be done with it, relish in the way death rendered him limp, and then—

A tiny starburst of pain broke through the fog.

Ranka turned, eyed the syringe quivering in her calf and collapsed.

A pleasant numbness swept through her, turning her limbs to water. After two weeks of sparring, she'd come to expect it. Her blood-magic faded, retreating behind the glass wall the tranquilizer created as the colors leaked back in. Beneath her, Percy lay gasping, rubbing the skin around his neck where her fingers had left red marks. He gently maneuvered Ranka off him, and Ranka tried to say *sorry* but all that came out was a garbled *aaghh* and some drool.

This was how it had happened every day. Every time she was close to winning, her blood-magic rushed out of her control, overwhelming her mind, rendering her a monster once more—and then Aramis tranquilized her like a runaway horse.

It was becoming infuriating.

She was losing time and learning *nothing*. Every day her chances of finding Yeva grew slimmer. Half their training sessions ended with Aramis and Percy scurrying away, heads together, voices too low for her to make anything out. If Ranka tried to follow, Aramis would roll her eyes, give Ranka a look that made her feel two inches tall, and sigh, *Sit down, witch girl. This is a matter of the mind. When we need you to come break things, we'll let you know.*

Ranka was really, *really* beginning to hate her.

Now she lay sprawled on her back, waiting for the numbness to fade. From her position on the sidelines, Aramis picked up her skirts and made her way toward them, her eyes on the book that she'd propped against her forearm. She was always scribbling in that damned thing, muttering to herself, filling pages with lines of looping, messy text that intersected with numbers.

She knelt down and took Ranka's pulse, scribbled more nonsense in that little book of hers, and squinted. "You lost control faster this time. Sloppier at the end, too."

Ranka braced herself, waiting for a sharp rebuke. She'd failed again.

Instead, Aramis frowned. "Is she okay, Percy? You shouldn't let her face-plant like that."

"She's fine," Percy said. "I don't think I could break Ranka if I wanted to."

He rubbed his neck, where bruises had already bloomed in the shape of Ranka's fingers. An older yellow mark cradled his left eye. Three days ago, she'd clocked him right in the face.

It had been incredibly satisfying.

"It's definitely tied to emotion and pain," Percy said, tilting his head to look at Aramis. "She does good until I piss her off. Then it's all brawn and no skill. She might as well be a bear on a rampage."

"Hey," Ranka slurred.

Percy ignored her and hopped to his feet to peer over Aramis's shoulder, his lanky frame dwarfing the princess as he read her notes. "Wait, didn't we already try that?"

Aramis waved him off. "Yes, with old blood. Did you notice this time it took longer for her eyes to shift?"

"I hate that part." Percy shuddered. "She looks like a corpse."

"Hey!" Ranka said. "I am *literally* right here."

"You get used to that," a new voice sighed. "When Percy and Aramis get going, there's no breaking into their bubble."

Galen approached them, an uneasy smile on his face. Ranka struggled to sit upright. She'd barely seen the prince—he never came to the sparring sessions and missed half of their meals. He stood awkwardly, fingers twitching, tiny funnels of dust racing around his ankles. Yet even now he was beautiful, limber and gleaming under the late-summer sun.

"What are you doing here?" Aramis asked, a slight edge to her voice. She angled herself between Ranka and her brother.

"I live here." Galen's brows knitted together. "Also, I'm bored.

What are you lot even doing? Are you and Ranka finally getting along now, then?"

"No," Ranka and Aramis said at the same time. They glared at each other.

Percy added, unhelpfully, "They are not."

"Ah." Galen quirked an eyebrow. "Aramis is punishing you by making you train with Percy?"

"Something like that." Ranka looked up at Galen, still trying to wiggle feeling into her hands. "Why don't you train with us?"

"Oh, um. I don't really . . . train."

Liar. Had she not seen him only two weeks ago, summoning gale winds with the lift of a hand? "You've mastered your magic, then?"

"It's not really—"

"Galen has other priorities," Aramis said coldly, her eyes holding a clear warning.

"Right." Ranka looked pointedly at the drought-burned grass. Seven months without rain. The summer crops had long withered, and without a break in the weather, the fall ones would fail, too. "Been a minute without rain, hasn't it, Galen?"

Everyone went still.

Galen recoiled, and Ranka had the odd feeling that she'd hurt him far deeper than she'd meant to.

Even Percy looked at Ranka with a flash of anger. He settled a gentle hand on Galen's shoulder. "I promise Ranka's utter lack of manners becomes charming eventually."

Galen took a long breath and then plastered on a polite smile, his voice holding the barest of quivers as he angled his attention away from her, speaking to the air instead. "Well—I suppose I shouldn't have intruded. Come on, Percy. I think we should leave Ranka and my sister to their games."

He left and Percy followed, walking so closely to the young prince their shoulders brushed, murmuring something only for his ears, Galen's posture slowly growing less rigid with each step.

Aramis waited until they were blurs against the grand Sunra estate before whipping around to glare at Ranka, fury vibrating in every line of her body. "What is *wrong* with you? You hardly *know* him—"

"And shouldn't I?" Ranka snapped. "He *is* going to be my husband—isn't he?"

Aramis's mouth clicked shut.

Frustration mounted in Ranka. Ever since she'd arrived, not a word had been breathed of what they all knew—that the Bloodwinn treaty had to be sealed with marriage. Once Galen was eighteen and held the crown, they would wed, as the two Bloodwinns before her had. At first Ranka'd thought they'd avoided the subject to ease her into the idea.

Now she was beginning to suspect it was because Galen was dreading it, too.

It made this all the more confusing. Were they not her enemies? The powerful Sunra children, the precious, privileged heirs who had never wanted for food, water, or shelter. They'd never known hunger. Not the way she had.

And yet. They were prisoners in a way—to their name, their status—the same way Ranka was to the power in her veins, the title she'd been handed. What would it be like to be raised by the most powerful storm mage and blood-witch in the world? To know your hopes, your dreams, your fears, mattered so little with a country at your feet, and only a fragile treaty preventing an age-old war from starting once more?

Aramis and Galen had been raised to be political tools, but they were still children, orphaned in a world content to devour them. It was almost a shame they were her enemies. In another life they might have understood each other. They might have even been friends.

"I'm sorry," Ranka said quietly. "I know he doesn't want to marry me. I don't want to marry him, either. I never wanted any of this."

After a long pause Aramis said, "What is it you want, then?"

A dozen truths rose to Ranka's lips: *I want to find Yeva. I want to go home. I want control of my blood-magic. I want it to go away completely. I want Ongrum to be proud of me. I want Vivna to come home, though I know she never will.*

But now, staring at the princess, framed in the golden light as the sea crashed around them, all Ranka could see were the sores that had ruined that witch's body—and the bracelet on her wrist.

"I want to help."

Aramis rolled her eyes. "We've been over this. You *are* helping. Percy and I have the rest handled."

"Do you?" Ranka pressed.

"You are beginning to wear on my patience, witch girl. I don't want your help because I don't trust you. I don't even particularly *like* you."

"Trust me, Princess. The feeling is mutual."

They were so determined to keep her at bay, yet it was clear Percy and Aramis had linked her to the sickness somehow. Aramis was always taking Ranka's pulse, analyzing the way her power rose, questioning Percy on its ebbs and flows. Once, Ranka had returned to find Percy in her bedroom, plucking a strand of her hair from the pillow.

They were up to *something*—but Ranka couldn't figure out what. Any bid she made for information received a sharp rebuttal; any attempt at closeness was shut down. How was she supposed to find out anything that could help Yeva at this rate? How could she learn anything at all?

There had to be another way through to her.

"The people who attacked us in the morgue—" Ranka began.

"The sickness is none of your business—"

"I'm *not*," Ranka snapped, "*asking* about the sickness, for the *love of* . . ." She pinched the bridge of her nose. "The sick witch I told you about—she had one of their pins with her. I thought—well, I thought they might secretly work for the palace. But that night they were ready to kill you. Why?"

Aramis looked faintly troubled. Ranka half expected her to deflect—

but instead, the princess knotted her hands into fists and lowered her voice. "The Hands of Solomei are . . . hardly fans of me or my brother. Or anyone associated with the Bloodwinn treaty." She chewed on her lip. "I never thought they'd be so bold as to attack me directly, though."

"So remove them. You have the guards, and the power—"

"It's not that simple. You have to understand—before the treaty it was the Hands who turned Solomei temples into shelters during witch raids. It was the Hands who were willing to wield torches against rampaging blood-witches when the city guards cowered." The princess fixed her attention on some distant point of the sea. "And though they've grown bolder, their methods more questionable, they are still protectors in the eyes of many."

"And what about you, Princess? Is that why you hate me? Do you think witch-burners are noble protectors, too?"

As soon as Ranka said it, she regretted it. Aramis stood abruptly, snapping shut the book she was always scribbling in. She looked down at Ranka, contempt lining her face.

"Let me make something clear," Aramis said. "I *do* hate you, Ranka. More than I've hated most. But not because you're a witch." Aramis's voice grew quieter, each word cutting like a blade. "I hate you because you are a miserable, lonely, selfish girl, and because you're a liar. I hate you because I believe if you get whatever it is you truly came here for, I'll lose everything I love. But my country needs the treaty, so I tolerate you. And my mother was the Bloodwinn, so I help you—loathsome as you are."

Ranka reeled, thrown by the vehemence in Aramis's eyes. The princess had never lost her patience with Ranka when she failed during training. She didn't shout the way Ongrum did or cut her rations in punishment. Even now Aramis Sunra was trying to rein herself in—and somehow that was far worse.

"You think you're so noble," said Aramis. "The poor Skra witch, forced to head south and become the Bloodwinn. You can feign innocence all you want, but I saw you in that morgue. You're a killer, Ranka. You are a murderer and a monster, with blood on your hands and death in your heart. Think what you will of me—but I am trying to save lives, not end them."

Ranka stared after Aramis long after she'd left. She'd grown so used to people not looking her in the eye that she found it far worse when they seemed to peer right into her soul. Only Vivna had ever been able to see her so clearly.

Hurt threatened to bloom in the cracks Aramis's words had opened.

Ranka latched on to anger instead.

Who was this spoiled, privileged girl, who'd grown up behind gilded walls, to lecture *her*? Who was Aramis to judge Ranka, when her very existence was only possible because of everything Witchik had lost?

If training Ranka was about honoring Aramis's mother, then why hadn't it started the day Ranka stepped foot in the palace? Why had it taken her stumbling upon the sick witch—and revealing to Aramis and Percy she'd met one before?

Aramis and Percy were lying to her. She would never find Yeva at this rate. She'd never find answers about the sickness. And she'd have nothing to offer the Skra.

Aramis didn't want to involve her? Fine.

Ranka would simply force her hand.

14

THE NEXT MORNING RANKA SLIPPED FROM HER ROOM and dragged the scents of the palace over her tongue, seeking a familiar signature. Percy and Aramis were never going to be honest. But perhaps someone close to the twins could give her what she wanted.

Ranka followed the signature she sought to a tall oak door engraved with sweeps of intricate gold along the frame. Voices rumbled on the other side. Ranka raised her hand to knock, hesitated, and shoved the door open instead.

Foldrey Wolfe stood against the far wall. His hair was wet, slicked back against his skull. Instead of his regular uniform, he was in polished military dress, completed by the ornamental sword at his hip.

At the center of the room, his narrow chest bare, was Galen.

Maids flurried around him like birds, folding him into a sleeveless, flowing tunic, polishing the circlet he typically wore. The prince looked bored to tears, and more vulnerable than she was used to—like he was just a doll, a toy to be dressed up and trotted around. He caught Ranka's eyes, surprise flickering over his features, and held up a hand.

Everyone turned to stare.

Foldrey frowned at her, a wariness in his eyes. Gone was the warmth he'd greeted her with before. No doubt Aramis had told him of what had happened in the morgue. "Good morning, Bloodwinn."

"It's Ranka," she corrected.

"Apologies." His frown deepened. "To what do we owe the plea-sure?"

"I had a—I'm sorry, what's going on?"

"Oh," Galen said dully, wrinkling his nose as a servant stretched a measuring tape across his chest. "There's a parade today. Aramis didn't tell you? Of course not. She manages to get out of them. I, however, get to spend an hour in the middle of Seaswept in the sun, waving until my hand falls off."

"Can I come?" Ranka blurted.

If it had been awkward before, the silence that filled the room now was so deafening, she could have heard a pin drop. The maids openly gaped. Foldrey's mouth turned downward at the corners. Ranka turned to Galen with what she hoped was a somewhat friendly smile. "I've barely seen the city. And this is meant to be my home, is it not? I'd like to go—if you don't mind the company, of course."

She'd been coming to speak to Foldrey—but maybe Galen wasn't a completely lost cause. Perhaps there were answers to be found here yet.

At the very least, if he proved to be insufferable, she'd feel better about sticking a knife in his ribs in a few months.

"I'm good company," Ranka added awkwardly. "And I've never been to a parade before."

Foldrey was already shaking his head. "Perhaps next quarter. Unfortunately, we'd have to prepare another carriage—"

"She can ride with me," Galen interrupted. He lifted a brow, a ghost of a smile on his lips. "I wouldn't mind the company. Ranka, how soon can you be ready?"

A slow smile spread across Ranka's face. "I already am."

Parades, it turned out, were awful.

Ranka sweated like a sinner in a Solomei temple. They'd been out for only an hour, and her leg bounced incessantly. Every few minutes her fingers twitched to her hip, seeking the comforting weight of her axe. Humans gathered along the streets, waving tattered flags and tossing hibiscus petals already wilted by the heat. All Ranka saw was the shine of their rings, the fine cut of their clothes, the soft, clean hands. Guards walked among the crowd in civilian dress, handing out bouquets of flowers. In the alleys, others lingered—citizens with gaunt cheeks, dirty faces, and glassy eyes. When they pushed forward, hoping to catch the eye of their prince, they were shoved back by the city patrol.

The farther they went, the more her unease built.

She tried to focus on the world around her—the perfume clinging to the women waving from the streets, the sweet rolls rising around the corner, the sickly saccharine scent of petals crushed under carriage wheels.

But above all, she scented rot.

It was that same undercurrent of wrongness she'd noted in the Northlands, a stronger echo of what she'd sensed in the mines. Now it swirled around her as if sickness were stamped into the very cobblestones, slicing through the marrow and flesh of Seaswept, burrowing into its heart.

If the humans noticed, they didn't care.

Foldrey strolled ahead, his posture relaxed. There were no scouts. The palace escort watched Galen, not the route. Barriers were erected on both sides, sealing off the alleys, yet the guards strolled at a languid pace, weapons sheathed.

But everything in Ranka pulsed with warning.

Beside her, Galen half dozed, waving lazily to the people they passed but not really seeing them. He'd barely spoken to her. And why would he? All he likely knew was what he'd heard from his sister, and with a height that easily cleared six feet, broad-shouldered and bulky with so many scars she'd long given up trying to count them, Ranka was hardly the friendliest-looking witch on this side of the border or the next. Yet she recalled the brightness in his eyes, that hint of something more behind the soft, shy prince. Had she Percy's charm or Aramis's sharp tongue, breaking through might have been easier. It wasn't like she could brandish her axe at Galen and demand he open up to her.

So instead Ranka lowered her voice and said, "I'm sorry about yesterday."

Galen jerked. "Pardon?"

"What I said about the drought. It was cruel." She dug her nails into her palm. "I hurt you, and I'm sorry."

Galen looked out at the street. A wrinkle appeared between his brows, and his fingers twirled. A breeze leapt to life, catching a few of the flower petals tossed their way, swirling them overhead before winding down an alley.

"All I've ever been able to summon is wind," Galen said finally. "It's no secret. You weren't the first to poke at me about training. You won't be the last."

A little girl tossed a bouquet of lilies their way, and the carriage crushed them under the back wheel, filling the air with their sickly sweet scent.

"My father, my grandfather, all the Sunra men before me, they all mastered the Skybreaker magic—they could call rain to save parched fields, summon wind to launch ships dead in the water, redirect lightning and quell entire hurricanes." He hesitated. "But that wasn't all they did."

Memory flashed behind Ranka's eyes—scarred, scorched earth from a lightning strike Galen's father had called against the Murknen. Ghostly remnants of a town whose leaders he'd drowned when the residents refused to pay their taxes.

"No," she agreed quietly. "It wasn't."

What had Galen thought of his father in those moments? Had he watched his father's pale hands call down storms and prayed his own would never do the same? Had the late king's power weighed on him the way it clearly did on Galen, or had he merely accepted it, embraced it as a tool to serve his kingdom, drumming dissidents with hail and suffocating wildfires to save their neighbors in the same breath?

What would it be like to be raised with a legacy of that power? She had never asked for blood-magic, certainly, but it'd been a surprise the day her power erupted in Belren. Galen had known from the time he could walk he might someday command hurricanes with a twist of his hand.

From his first breath, Galen Sunra's magic had never been anything more than a tool of war. It made him a protector to some—a monster to many more.

They had that in common, at least.

The rot swirled thicker.

Ranka fixed Galen with a square look. "You know I don't want to marry you, right?"

Relief washed across his face. "I had a feeling."

"What," she deadpanned. "You mean you weren't dying to make me your wife? I'm heartbroken."

"You're not exactly my type."

Ranka recalled the way Percy had been so attentive to the prince's mood, the closeness with which they'd walked. The softness Percy seemed to reserve for Galen alone.

She wondered if Galen was thinking of him, too.

"What a miserable pair we make," Galen muttered. "The prince desperate to avoid the throne. The witch desperate to avoid the prince."

Ahead of them, a guard broke from the crowd and hurried toward Foldrey. He whispered something that made the captain jerk—and then Foldrey waved him away. The guard shook his head and disappeared back into the crowd.

Was it her imagination—or had that been blood speckling the front of his coat?

"So why bother with any of this?" Ranka asked slowly, her eyes now glued to Foldrey, who was walking a little more rigidly than before. "Why not just walk away?"

"And . . . what? Let the treaty fail? Return to war, soak the earth with blood again? Flee, so some tyrant can fill the vacuum I'd leave behind?" Galen laughed, low and bitter. "There's no escape. Trust me. I've spent a lifetime looking for one."

Galen's throat bobbed. He looked at her, a flicker of doubt in his eyes, and then back at the route ahead of them, as if seeing it for the first time. "I've . . . studied the maps. Why?"

"I think something is broken in this city. Something they don't want you or Aramis to know. I think you feel it too."

Galen had gone carefully still.

"You say you'd like to be friends. Then let me do something a friend would. Get us out of here—and let us see your city for real."

Galen's eyes darted from her to Foldrey to the streets he had clearly seen a dozen times before. She could feel the fight between the boy who'd never wanted any of this, who shirked any and all responsibility, and the boy with bright eyes who noticed far more than he let on.

"Galen," Ranka said. "Please."

A light of defiance flashed there.

Galen raised a hand—and the air erupted.

Suddenly the street was impassable. Sand, dirt, and garbage formed a thick haze of swirling brown. The crowd shrieked. Somewhere ahead of them, Foldrey shouted for everyone to remain in place.

Grit filled Ranka's mouth, and then a slender hand was on her arm, tugging her out of the carriage. He tightened his grip, weaving through the crowd, blanketed by dust. They slipped down a side alley, then a second, a third—and then they were free.

Galen exhaled, his eyes wide, his entire body vibrating with an unwieldy, nervous energy.

Ranka latched on to the scent of rot. Something had happened that Foldrey didn't want Galen to know about. Something that ended in blood. So much in Seaswept had been hidden or carefully curated, not just for the sake of Galen's ignorance, but hers, too.

But Foldrey wasn't here. It was just the witch and her prince, with a maze of alleys between them—and death on the wind ahead of them.

"Come on," Ranka murmured. "We'll need to be quick."

It was time they both met this city for real.

15

SEASWEPT FELL APART AS THEY WALKED. THE WIND carried not just the reek of old blood, but the aftermath of true horror, clinging to the very bones of the city. Galen's eyes widened as they passed houses missing doors, windows, chunks of their roofs, all of them still clearly lived in. A man sprawled facedown in the street, piss drunk though it was barely noon, a halo of vomit spread around his head. He groaned as they passed. Ranka put a firm hand on Galen's shoulder and propelled him forward.

They stepped around the carcass of a horse that had to be at least a week old, its body bloated with maggots, bridle gone and eye sockets long picked clean by gulls. In the wealthy districts they'd ridden through, a dead animal would have been moved in hours. But here, where the poor and the sick worked, where the healers always arrived far too late and the guards usually never arrived at all, decay was a permanent fixture.

Galen shrank into himself with every step.

The streets were silent save for the soft crackling of palace announcements that flapped from noticeboards, their ends curled by heat. They were all gibberish to her—but Galen stopped short, reading the same one over and over again, his eyes growing wider with each line. Ranka tried to make sense of the letters, but it was useless.

Education had hardly been high on the Skra's priority list.

Not that she was going to admit that to Aramis. She'd rather the princess think her openly defiant and failing her language lessons on purpose than know of another weakness.

"It's an order from the Grand Council," Galen finally said. "I guess they, uh, revoked civil protection of witches indefinitely when you were found." He pointed, his fingers tracing sloppy handwriting that looped over the original announcement. "But this—this isn't from the Council."

In the center of the poster, a single gold pin gleamed.

"What does it say?"

Galen gave her a long, uneasy look. "I don't think—"

"Read it."

Galen licked his lips. "It just says: 'Now we burn.'"

Ranka turned before he could see the panic on her face. Her arrival had done this. *Surely, they won't actually burn witches, right?* Not here, with a Bloodwinn poised to rule. It had to be an empty threat.

Except they already tried to kill Aramis. And they tried to kill you, too.

The princess's voice floated through her mind.

They are still protectors, in the eyes of many.

The scent of death swirled around her, and Ranka forced herself to zero in on the problem ahead. There was nothing she could do about the Hands, the Council, or the laws Galen clearly let them pass without knowing what he was signing off on.

But answers lay ahead—and she could find them.

The city held its breath, and they turned the corner.

Double-woven ropes with hastily tied palace flags blocked off the end of the street. An old street sign lay crooked and broken on the ground. Galen picked it up, his brow wrinkling, his voice barely audible as he read, "Bell's Corridor."

Ranka ducked under the ropes and stopped.

Galen came to stand beside her. "Solomei's light."

Bell's Corridor was painted in death.

Corpses lay in the street, their throats ripped open, their panicked stares wide and unseeing. Shattered windows gaped like broken teeth. Doors hung open on their hinges—the occupants had left in a hurry. Fresh blood streaked the fronts of buildings, swept across cobblestones where bodies had been thrown and dragged. Overhead, a lone cloud passed over the sun.

Galen's eyes had a glassy, unfocused look to them. Gone was the prince, replaced by a child not yet eighteen, seeing the horror of his kingdom for the first time. He braced a hand against one of the buildings and immediately cringed away. Flecks of still-drying blood clung to his fingertips. "What happened here?"

"I don't know." Ranka scanned the street. A few of the homes had golden pins pressed into the doors, as if the mark of the Hands was a mark of pride.

Galen worked one free, turning it between his fingers with an uneasy frown. "Foldrey said the head priest was murdered the other day—found dead in an alley, with his throat slit, pins pressed into his eyes." His next words were weak. "Maybe this is where it happened? And they retaliated?"

Ranka shook her head. The pins on the other doors were covered in a layer of grime—these people had believed in the Hands long before death visited their street. Aramis's words rippled through her.

They are still protectors in the eyes of many.

So why a massacre? And why *now*?

A child's shoe lay in the road, the once-white ribbon laces now stained crimson. Ranka knelt and picked it up, turning it over in her hand. That scent was familiar. It was not the reek of a blood-soaked, still-smoking battlefield, or the festering rot of sick bodies dying in the dank bowels of a prison.

It was the scent of terror—and of blood-magic, newly born, as brilliant and burning as the power now lurking in her veins.

It was the scent of Belren.

Ranka dropped the shoe as though it'd burned her. Belren was gone. Erased. The memory couldn't touch her. She was safe and she needed to focus. Something about this wasn't right. Where were the city guards? Why wasn't Seaswept on lockdown? These bodies were fresh—whoever had killed them was still loose.

So why were they alone?

"Princeling, I think . . . I think there's something you need to know," Ranka said slowly. "I was hoping to find answers on my own. But if the sickness is getting worse, then your sister's plan clearly isn't—"

"What does Aramis have to do with this?"

She raised her head—and in the window behind him, something moved.

"Ranka?"

She put her finger to her lips.

The broken window gazed back, its jagged, blood-flecked glass winking in the afternoon light. From inside, a floorboard creaked.

"Princeling," Ranka whispered, "get behind me."

Her blood-magic begged to flood her muscles, her heart, her breath. Ranka heard Aramis's voice, crystal clear in her mind, a balm to the power desperate to overwhelm her.

Breathe, the princess whispered. *And control it.*

Ranka inched toward the house. She tried the handle. The door swung open without protest, the lock long broken. A few flies zipped out, carrying the scent of fresh bodies already beginning to turn in the heat. She hesitated and breathed in. There it was—a flicker of life amid the carrion, a panicked heart, beating fast.

"Someone is here," she whispered.

Galen blanched. "We should wait. I'll get Foldrey, or—"

Something crashed inside the house.

"Stay outside," Ranka warned. "And if you see anything—run."

Ranka stepped across the threshold.

The house was dark. The first floor was a disaster—the kitchen table was cracked in half, chairs lying at awkward angles. A line of blood splashed over the wall, across the floor, and up the stairs. Childish drawings depicting parents and two children had been torn down from the wall and ripped in two. Ranka stepped over them and picked up one of the chair legs, snapping it over her knee to form a jagged edge. What she wouldn't have given for her axe.

Something trembled behind torn curtains. She pulled them aside. A cat cowered on the floor, its white fur flecked with blood.

"You poor thing." She poked it with her foot to break it from its shock.

The cat hissed, leapt up, and streaked out the door.

At least someone in this house would make it out all right.

A door slammed overhead.

"Hello?" Ranka called. "Is someone there?"

A sharp intake of breath, followed by a pause—and then a hoarse voice, filtering through the floorboards, weak with fear. "Go away."

Ranka took the stairs carefully, eyeing the fingernail gouges on the wooden steps where someone had fought with everything in them not to be dragged upstairs. Sunlight filtered through a skylight, casting the house in an ethereal golden glow. The buzzing grew louder.

She stepped onto the second floor.

A long, narrow hallway greeted her. Bed frames, chairs, and book-shelves had been toppled over one another in a kind of barricade. Three bodies were strewn across the floor, eyes open, mouths already covered in flies. Ranka crouched in front of them. Their skin was covered in bite marks. She closed their terror-bright eyes and wiped her fingers clean.

None of the furniture was bloody. The witch must have barricaded herself *after* her blood-magic had risen.

Ranka couldn't help herself. Excitement mixed with the ache of loneliness. Maybe this witch could be reasoned with. Maybe she could be saved.

Death was all around, but it was concentrated in the room at the end of the hall, and it was there she scented warm blood. She moved forward, shifting broken furniture out of her way, sidestepping glass.

"I'm not here to hurt you," Ranka called. "It's okay. I'm a blood-witch too. I'm here to help."

Belren flashed behind her eyes. What she wouldn't have given for another blood-witch that day. Someone to pluck her out of the snow and explain how to keep living once your humanity had been ripped away.

She would have given anything, for anyone at all.

"Please," the voice begged. *"Go away."*

Ranka pushed open the door.

A girl of around fourteen cowered in the corner of her bedroom, a piece of jagged glass held out in front of her. Blood matted her yellow hair. She was scrawny, covered in scratches, and where her left thumb should have been there was only a sad knob of bone. But it was the sores on her pale skin that took Ranka's breath away. The blisters were tiny, no bigger than nailheads, and instead of black this girl's fingernails were a dull gray. She had Vivna's eyes—a soft, washed-out blue.

Disappointment flashed through Ranka. Not a real blood-witch. Another sick one—and recently infected, at that.

The girl cringed backward. "You can't be here. You *can't*. You need to *go*."

Down the hall, the floorboards creaked.

Ranka crouched and held out a hand. "I can help you. I'm Ra—I'm the Bloodwinn." The title still felt wrong, but the flicker of recognition in the girl's eyes pushed her forward. "Come to the palace with me, and you'll be under my protection."

Was that even true? She didn't know. The humans would probably sneer at her. Who was she to think anyone would listen to her? To think after a lifetime of killing, she could save someone instead?

Ranka kept her voice soft. "What's your name?"

"Talis." Tears streamed down the girl's face.

"Nice to meet you, Talis. I'm Ranka."

"You need to *leave*."

"I won't hurt you. Making the barricade to keep yourself in was smart, but—"

"I didn't make it to keep myself in," the girl sobbed. "I made it to keep *her* out."

The girl pointed behind Ranka.

And behind Ranka, something breathed.

Pain exploded across the back of her head. Ranka pitched forward, her jaw hitting the floor with a painful *crack*. The door slammed on the first floor.

Talis sobbed harder. Ranka lay there, head throbbing, blood dripping from her ear. Her mind spun sluggishly, aching from the blow, struggling to make sense of what had just happened. Her blood-magic yanked at her senses, trying to drag her to her feet.

"What are you doing?" a familiar voice shouted from the street below. "Stay away!"

A guttural scream sounded, followed by howling wind and the stench of rot.

Oh no.

Galen.

16

RANKA POINTED AT TALIS. "RUN FOR THE PALACE. TELL them you're under my protection. *Go!*"

She descended the stairs two at a time.

From the street came a cry, a blast of wind, and the thud of flesh slamming into something hard. Ranka tore through the living room, heart pounding, and burst out the door. Afternoon sun slanted into her eyes. She stumbled, shading her brow—and found the street empty. Only the dust swirling in lazy particles was any indication of a struggle at all.

"Galen?" Ranka shouted. *"Galen?"*

Silence.

Bell's Corridor looked back at her. Panic bubbled up in her chest. This wasn't the plan. If she lost him now—if he *died* on her watch—

Enough.

Ranka forced herself to straighten.

She was not some green witchling. She was Skra. She was the Bloodwinn, and before she'd been named Bloodwinn, she'd been a hunter.

Ranka closed her eyes and inhaled.

She tasted the sea, the carrion of the street, and the horror baked into the very stone of this city. She tasted decades—centuries—of pain. Of not just witches burned alive, witches who'd only wanted a life among the humans they'd been born from, but the pain of humans, too. Humans who woke to find their streets soaked in blood, who starved under careless kings and mourned children sent away to die in a needless border war. All of them trapped in a cycle of pain, and for what? It'd changed nothing. Saved no one. This city was a living graveyard, and its citizens were already ghosts made flesh.

She pushed past it all, seeking something living, seeking something new, tasting rot and ruin and hatred, and *there*—metal polish, an ocean breeze, and an ever-present blanket anxiety. *Galen.* He was alive—for now.

Ranka ran.

She sprinted down a side alley, counting ten, fifteen bodies in the street, abandoned to the rats. Galen's scent grew stronger, and so did that reek of a body turned septic. Beneath it, something familiar squirmed. Something that reminded her of home.

Ranka turned the corner.

Galen slumped against an alley wall. Blood crusted his temple. He looked at her, dazed, blinking sluggishly. "Ranka?"

"Goddess, Galen, you scared me." She hurried forward to pick him up. "I thought—"

"Ranka," Galen whimpered. "She's behind you."

The scent of rot spiked.

Ranka turned—and the world ground to a halt.

A sick witch stood in the alley.

Her skin hung from her bones, fist-sized sores weeping watery blood where the scabs curled free of rotting skin. The girl's eyes were a soulless, blood-witch white. She scented the air, tongue lolling, head cocked at an unnatural angle as she panted.

And Ranka couldn't move, couldn't think, because she *knew* this witch.

She would have known her anywhere.

"Yeva?" she whispered.

It wasn't possible.

Yeva had only just gone missing.

And Yeva was not a blood-witch.

Yet here she stood, eyes white, nails sharpened to wicked black claws. Her left arm hung at the wrong angle. Glistening bone poked through the skin.

"Yeva," Ranka tried, her voice wobbling. "It's me, Ranka. I came here to find you. I came to bring you home."

This couldn't be real. It couldn't be happening—couldn't be *her*. Not Yeva, who had rubbed poultice on Ranka's burn wounds after Belren. Yeva, who remembered Ranka loved dried strawberries and managed to acquire some every year for her birthday. Who'd nursed her back to health, held her hand through countless nightmares, and woven her a bracelet on a gray winter day.

Yeva, who had loved her long after Ranka no longer deserved it.

Not her.

Anyone but her.

"I'm sorry," Ranka whispered. "I was too late."

Yeva panted. Half of her teeth were missing. The ones that remained were stained red. One nostril was swollen shut by blisters, and most of her hair had fallen out, leaving only stringy, blood-soaked clumps. She had been a beautiful girl, once.

Tears rolled down Ranka's cheeks. "What happened to you?"

Yeva gurgled—and hurtled forward.

17

RANKA WAS LOSING.

She lurched backward, scrambling out of Yeva's way, and tripped, ramming her shoulder into the alley wall with a painful *crunch*. Her head spun. She was faster than Yeva—but not by much. And she couldn't keep this up forever.

"Please," Ranka wheezed, twisting out of the way of Yeva's claws. "I don't want to hurt you."

Galen cowered against the wall, his eyes dazed.

Yeva moved forward.

Ranka moved back.

"Yeva," she tried again. "We're *family*."

Yeva licked her lips.

Tears cut tracks through the grime on Ranka's cheeks. Her blood-magic tugged at her senses. She shoved it back down. If she let it take over, Yeva didn't stand a chance.

Yeva flung herself at Ranka—and this time, Ranka didn't move.

They collided in a crunch of bone. Pain exploded across Ranka's vision as Yeva slammed her into the alley wall. Ranka forced her knee into Yeva's stomach, attempting to drive the witch back, sobbing as she tried to hold her off. This was wrong, all wrong. Ranka had come here to save her. Ranka had come here to bring her home.

Yeva screamed and lurched, snapping her teeth at the hollow of Ranka's neck and biting deep into her shoulder instead. Ranka howled as agony turned her shoulder into a crackling black void.

I can't fight her.

"Yeva," Ranka half sobbed, her body trembling. "Yeva, please, it's *me.*"

I won't.

Yeva slammed her shoulder into Ranka's chest and took them both to the ground. Ranka's blood-magic was a flood inside her, yanking desperately against the reins, but if she let it free, there'd be no controlling it. This was no battle or harmless Skra training. This was no sick witch in the forest.

This was Yeva. This was her coven. Her family.

And if Ranka fought her for real, she would die.

"Ranka!"

She jerked backward, trying to break free of Yeva's grip, but her regular strength was nothing against that of a blood-witch—even a rotting mimicry of one. Yeva wrapped her hands around Ranka's throat. She wheezed, thrashing, clawing at Yeva's fingers, but Yeva just kept squeezing. Spots swam in the corner of Ranka's vision.

I'm going to die.

The thought cut through her with blistering clarity. Ranka gasped, writhing on the ground, trying to pry Yeva's fingers free.

Wind roared down the alley.

It slammed into them with the force of a hurricane. Yeva went flying with a howl, her mouth contorting as she let loose a guttural scream.

Galen slumped against the wall. He flung his hand forward, and another blast of wind ripped past Ranka, pinning Yeva against the stones. Galen swirled his tongue over his teeth and spat out a mouthful of blood. He shrank against the alley wall, and Ranka cowered beside him, dread forming a stone in her throat.

Yeva had protected her. Fed her, healed her, guided her when no one else had. Yeva had been a force of light and love and warmth when Ranka had thought she deserved none of it. Ranka had given up everything to save her and bring her home.

And Ranka had failed.

Galen trembled beside her.

"I'm sorry," Ranka said faintly. All her training, all her pain, and now she was useless. Frozen. Unable to strike back against someone she ought to, rooted in place by love—and fear. She'd come to kill him for Yeva—now Yeva would end them instead.

"Just. . . ." Galen started, his voice faltering. "Just don't leave me, okay?"

Tears rolled down her cheeks. She didn't know what to say to him, didn't know what to *do*, so Ranka did the only thing she could—she took his hand, and she didn't let go.

Galen locked his fingers around hers, trembling worse than before, and squeezed so hard it hurt.

Footsteps scraped ahead of them.

Ranka opened her eyes—but Yeva was gone.

In her place was a girl who could have been Ranka's twin save for her dark, curled hair. She was older, leaner, with watery blue eyes, a bitter mouth, and slender fingers covered in a patchwork of old scars. Smoke writhed around her ankles.

Behind her, Belren burned.

"Vivna," Ranka whispered.

She was just a little girl again, bleeding in the snow, and the one meant to protect her looked at her with contempt.

Vivna looked down at her. "You ruined my life. You ruin everything."

Maybe Ranka was dying—maybe she was already dead. But after five years, this—even under the circumstances—was a gift.

"Where are you?" Ranka whispered. "Where did you go?"

Are you alive? Do you miss me? Do you regret it—any of it, at all? Even a little?

"You loved me once—right?"

Vivna's lips peeled back. She locked her eyes on Ranka—and a spear flashed in the dark.

"Cut her down!"

Reality crashed back in. Vivna vanished—and red bloomed across the front of Yeva's chest as a spearhead impaled her from behind.

Blood bubbled from her lips, and she sagged. A second punctured her thigh, pinning her to the ground.

"No!"

Yeva moaned, twisting against the spears to face the newcomers.

A fifth guard entered the alley and Yeva went still.

Hatred warped her face. She jerked, a strangled noise leaving her— and then a blade sliced the air, arcing faster than Ranka's eye could follow. A line of red appeared across Yeva's throat. She collapsed, and distantly Ranka realized someone was screaming, that the scream was coming from *her*. She didn't care. She closed the distance between them and caught her, pulled the bleeding, broken witch she loved into her lap. The guards rushed past, hurrying toward their prince. No one cast a backward glance at the witch in the alley, cradling the sister she'd failed. Tears dripped from Ranka's cheeks, mixing with the blood coating Yeva's.

"I'm sorry," Ranka sobbed. "I was too late, and I love you, and *I am so sorry.*"

The fifth guard stepped forward, a wild light to his eyes, red hair plastered to his forehead with sweat, his sword dripping blood from that fatal blow.

"Hi, Foldrey," Galen said weakly. "Thanks for coming."

Foldrey scowled. "You two are in so much trouble."

18

THE GUARDS BLINDFOLDED RANKA.

The others broke off, leaving only Foldrey to guide her. Anger crackled off him, brittle and burning in the early evening air as he steered her forward with a rough grip, but Ranka was too numb to care.

Yeva.

She hadn't said goodbye.

Yeva.

She hadn't even gotten the chance to close her eyes.

Ranka had given up everything—and she'd failed.

They led her underground, back into the tunnels she'd first followed Aramis through, where the air was so damp with seawater, it stung. A door closed behind them, followed by the hiss of a seal locking in place. Someone bound her wrists, tight enough to keep her captive but not enough to hurt, and left. Voices from the hallway beyond pitched higher and higher; Ranka could hear Foldrey shouting that Galen could have been killed, Galen shouting back that he had no right to keep secrets, shouting that Foldrey was his guard, not his father, and that by hiding the truth, he'd put everyone in danger.

You're lucky, she wanted to tell Galen, *to have someone love you the way he does.*

The door clicked open, and cool fingers slipped her blindfold free.

"You just can't mind your own business, can you?"

Gone was Percy Stone's arrogant smile. Walls of salt glowed behind him, illuminated by the white light of mage lamps. Clean bandages and vials of distilled alcohol stood on a tray in the corner. They were in a chamber with a single, curious door—heavy oak, sporting multiple locks, the frame lined with rubber seals. Chalkboards covered in hundreds of numbers filled the far wall.

"The others will be here soon." Percy tilted Ranka's chin up. "We need to come to an agreement before they arrive."

Pain throbbed through her.

Yeva.

"No more agreements," she mumbled. "No more deals."

His eyes snapped to her shoulder, ruined by the blunt edges of Yeva's teeth. He picked up a scalpel. She flinched—but all he did was peel her ruined skin away from the wound, angle the scalpel, and slice away some of her masticated flesh. He poured a cleaning agent over the wound that hissed and foamed white on her shoulder.

"The witch," Percy said. "You knew her?"

"She was family."

The scalpel slipped a hair.

"I'm sorry." He kept cutting. "Let me ask you this—after what you've seen, are you afraid?"

Her voice was small. "Yes."

"Good. Because in two minutes Aramis and Galen are going to walk in and exile you. You need to convince them to let you stay."

His words flowed over her like water. None of that mattered anymore.

Percy's fingers found her chin. They were cool and firm, rough at the pads. Working hands, not the pampered touch of a noble boy. He tilted Ranka's face back up to his.

"Look at me, Ranka. The disease that killed your friend is no accident. It's just getting started—and it's coming for every single coven. You want to honor your friend? Don't let her death be meaningless. Don't let what happened become the fate of every witch on the continent."

"Why do you care? What stake does an ambassador from the Star Isles have in a disease killing witches?"

Percy's voice was carefully monotone. "Because I helped create it."

Ranka's vision went red.

She jerked forward and slammed her forehead into Percy's nose, straining against the bonds, trying to work her hands free so she could throttle him where he stood. *Yeva. Talis.* The nameless witch in the north, the one in the morgue. How many had died? How many more would? She'd kill him. By the grace of the Goddess, she would *kill* him—

Percy didn't move.

He just stood there, nose dripping blood, scalpel dangling from his fingers.

"You're a *monster*—"

"We have that in common." Percy's eyes flicked to the door. "One minute."

A sob died in her throat. If Ongrum were here, she'd order Ranka to glean whatever information she could from her enemy. *"Why?"*

"Do you know your history, Bloodwinn? Do you know that before Witchik and Isodal fought each other, they came to our shores with warships and mage-fire?" He gripped the edge of the table until his knuckles went white. "Did you know your people nearly wiped mine from existence?"

"That was hundreds of years ago."

"My people have a long memory." His eyes flicked to her, and in the half-light they shifted from brown to molten gold. Ranka tasted smoke, recalling stories whispered over dying campfires of a time when the world teemed with magic, when merfolk sang sailors from their ships, and dragons shed their wings to walk among men and whisper in the ears of kings.

They'd all been hunted to extinction. Progress took its casualties one way or another.

Then the moment was gone, and the person standing in front of her was only a boy incredibly far from home.

"Winalin was never supposed to be a disease, it was supposed to be a defense. A shield." Percy's lips trembled. "We were supposed to be protecting ourselves. Fight fire with fire, so to speak. Even the playing field, so we finally had the weapon the humans feared most."

The horror of it dawned on her. "The Star Isles were trying to make blood-witches."

Percy looked like he wanted to be ill. "Yes."

"But Yeva—the sick witches I've seen—"

"Test strands," Percy said softly. "When I fled, a winalin-sickened witch could only survive for a few days, and it wasn't infectious. But eventually the strain has to mutate. Eventually—"

"The new blood-witches will live." The room swam.

"And if they don't? Then our work is done for us." His mouth twisted. "Either way, it removes the threat. We get our blood-witches, or you go extinct."

Her head pounded. If what he was saying was true, if they could make it last longer—if they could make it *infectious*—

How could the covens fight when their own bodies acted as invader and weapon all in one?

"The coronation," Ranka said thickly. "In a few weeks witches from every coven will be coming here. . . ."

Ongrum was about to lead the entire Skra coven into a trap. If Ranka didn't find a way to protect them against winalin, the coup wouldn't matter. The Skra could be wiped out entirely.

Ranka glared at Percy, trying to swallow the nausea roiling in her. "Why should I trust you?"

Percy inclined his head to the side. "What other choice do you have?"

The door swung open.

Foldrey entered. Galen followed, looking sullen and thoroughly chewed out. He wouldn't meet Ranka's eyes. Aramis slammed the door behind them.

The princess had traded her palace finery for formfitting commoner's clothes, her curls pulled away from her beautiful, naked face. She carried a single, delicate knife, and she glared at Ranka like she wanted nothing more than to jam the blade into the hollow space of Ranka's throat.

"I'm *done*," Aramis snarled. "I warned you. You didn't listen to me—and nearly got my brother *killed*. You leave on a ship first thing tomorrow."

Her words swirled around Ranka. Something about a well-guarded royal estate half a world away.

They meant to exile her for real this time.

The sickness, winalin, was poised to wipe out every witch on the continent. And if Ranka was exiled—if she was sent away for being too reckless, too sloppy—Ongrum would never forgive her.

And Yeva was dead. Yeva, who had been her only reason for coming here, had been murdered by that sickness, the same one Aramis was investigating.

Ranka struggled to keep her voice steady. "You can't just ship me off."

"I can, and I will."

"Do you think I wanted us to get attacked?" Ranka demanded. "I caught a strange scent, so I followed it, because no one has told me a damned thing about a disease killing *my* people. This never would have happened if you'd just involved me from the beginning."

Percy made a pained noise and covered his face with his hands. Aramis's eye twitched.

"Galen," Ranka appealed, twisting to look at him instead. "You were there. I protected you. I *defended* you—"

"You're a stranger," Galen said. "I like you, Ranka, but I don't know you. I'm sorry."

He looked away. The others stared at her, tight lipped and angry. And a part of her understood. She would have done the same in their position. She was a risk, a liability, and it was easier to get rid of her.

Percy looked at Aramis, an appeal in his eyes. "Can we speak in private?"

Galen glared at him. "Oh, no. You two have done enough damage on your own—"

"You're not my prince," Percy said coolly. "I don't answer to you."

"Watch your tongue," Foldrey warned. "He's not your prince, but this is his city."

Percy smiled. "Try me, ginger dad."

How was she supposed to convince people who knew more than she did? People who'd been studying a disease she'd learned of only a month ago? There had to be something—anything—she could offer them.

Of course.

"I can help," Ranka blurted. "With your research."

Foldrey grimaced. "I think you've done enough."

But Percy said, "Wait."

"Use me." Ranka leaned forward as far as her restraints would allow and looked straight at Aramis. "You're studying my blood-magic, right? That's why Percy keeps stealing my hair, why you take my pulse and analyze every little thing I do when we fight. But what if I could give you more? Those witches, they're dying of a fake blood-magic, right? What better than a real blood-witch to look for a cure?"

Aramis and Percy looked at each other, something unreadable passing between them. Foldrey stared at the ceiling, probably wondering what he'd done to be cursed with a problem so far outside of his duties. But Galen—patient, quiet, never-wanted-the-crown Galen— was looking at Ranka.

"We should do it," Galen said, his voice soft.

Aramis whipped her head around. *"What?"*

He straightened, making a point to lock eyes with Percy, Foldrey, and Aramis individually. "Ranka's not the only one you've been lying to." He paused. "Our city is under attack from a plague that mimics blood-magic. There are only a few real blood-witches alive every generation. We have one in front of us that wants to help, and we're going to say *no*?"

They all glared back at him, but Galen held his ground.

"Seaswept is my home," Galen said, his voice deadly soft. "This is my city. My burden. You've all been so desperate for me to step up, to take responsibility and act like a leader. Well—now I lead. We *need* Ranka."

They glared back at him, but what could they say? Galen was right.

Percy kept his voice carefully disinterested. "If she ends up betraying us, there's a lot of fun tests I can run on her corpse."

Foldrey glanced quickly at her. Was that a flash of anger in his eyes, or something deeper? He rubbed his face with his hands and inclined his head toward Galen. "I follow you, always. If this is what you think is right—I'll stand by you."

Aramis remained silent. She sat with her arms folded, legs crossed and foot bouncing, watching only Ranka.

Galen turned. "Aramis?"

Her chair scraped the floor.

Aramis crossed the room. She leaned over Ranka, a stray curl clinging to her forehead, and locked eyes with her. Sweat gleamed on her skin, and the gold flecks of her irises were liquid in the half-light of the salt mines.

For a wild, foolish moment Ranka thought Aramis was going to kiss her.

Aramis pressed her knife to Ranka's jugular.

"If you betray us, I will make you disappear, piece by piece. There won't be anywhere in the world for you to run where I can't find you. Am I clear?"

Ranka held carefully still. "Crystal."

Aramis cut her free, and Ranka's head spun as she rubbed the feeling back into her wrists.

"If you're going to be a part of this team, there can be no secrets. No lies. Is there anything you need to tell us, witch girl?" Aramis's gaze lingered. "Anything at all?"

It would be so easy to let it slip free—she could tell them about Ongrum, the Skra, their mission, Galen's impending death. But this girl, these people, were not her responsibility. They were a means to an end. Once the winalin was dealt with—once her coven was safe— she owed them nothing.

"No," Ranka lied, meeting their eyes one by one. "I'm with you, until the very end."

PART TWO

———————————

MONSTER

TWENTY-FIVE DAYS REMAIN

19

FOR NEARLY TWO WEEKS THEY HEARD NOTHING OF winalin witches. The only rumors that filtered into the palace were those spread by the Hands. Ranka tried not to listen as the twins read off the accounts of monsters roaming the streets at night. Whispers had begun to trickle in—of the freshly dead dug up from their graves, only to be found miles away, half gnawed and dismembered. Of missing pets snatched at dusk, and at night, from the mines beneath the city—rumors of screams.

The rumors weren't limited just to the winalin witches. They claimed the Bloodwinn was actually a demon, that she'd bewitched Galen, and he was dooming them all. Reports came in that the ranks of the Hands were swelling. Every morning new doorways were marked with gold pins as the citizens of Seaswept turned to zealots in their streets to protect them from the monster in their palace.

If Seaswept had been unwelcoming before, now it was outright hostile.

And yet—a strange peace had settled within the palace walls. Ranka spent her mornings beside the sea, running and stretching and lifting in the heat. Fall was nearly two weeks away, and Yeva's death hung over her like a shadow, touching everything. No word came from the Skra.

Every morning Ranka trained, and every morning she reminded herself that Percy and Aramis were a means to an end. Sure, Percy was a lot friendlier, and even Aramis had traded open threats for glares and frosty silence, but they could never be her allies. She was only using them for information. She was a prisoner, she hated them, and she wanted nothing more than to see them ruined.

Except sometimes—she didn't.

"Hey, Ranka," Percy said. "How many of these do you think I can balance?"

Ranka reclined on a wooden chair, the needle Percy had inserted into her forearm itching something terrible. She watched with an increasingly unsettled stomach as tubing dark with her blood wound into the vial below. Blood from a wound was one thing, but watching it drain out of her, drip by drip, gathering slowly, slicking up the glass walls—

"Hey. Don't look at it, look at me," Percy said.

He'd stacked five empty vials on top of one another. He added a sixth, waggling an eyebrow, turning slowly to make the glass wink in the light. The tower wobbled precariously in his palm. Percy reached for a seventh.

"Aramis is going to kill you if you break those."

"She'd have to catch me first." He winked. "I'm quite fast."

A smile tugged at the corner of Ranka's mouth.

"Who am I killing?" Aramis walked into the room, eyes trained on the notebook splayed open on her hand. A smudge of ink marked her cheek. She looked up and nearly dropped the notebook. "Percy, *again*? No, don't skip away from me—you're going to drop them! Seriously, it's not funny. Percy, *get back here*!"

Ranka sat back, her smile fading as Percy spun and sidestepped Aramis's hands with fluid grace. Percy laughed, and Aramis swore at him with a ferocity that even a Skra would admire.

There would be no more of these mornings when Ranka killed Galen. She tried to push the thought away, but it lingered like a sour taste.

Percy finally stopped his whirling to swap the vial full of Ranka's blood for an empty one. Aramis moved to the table and held it up to a white beam of mage-light, turning it this way and that, her lips pursed.

Ranka couldn't help herself. "Any progress?"

Aramis's eyes slid to her, bright with suspicion, ringed by more dark circles than usual. Ranka half expected the princess to tell her to piss off. Instead Aramis's brows knitted together. "We don't have a cure, if that's what you're asking."

"Better than before," Percy said. "Before you, we were practicing on samples from corpses and pieces of hair I stole from your pillow."

"That was creepy, by the way," Ranka pointed out.

"It *felt* creepy. This is much better."

"How does it work?" Ranka had never been trained as a healer, and she liked the funny words Percy had for his craft—*doctors* and *science* and *vaccinations*. She liked even more the soft light that bloomed in Aramis's eyes whenever she spoke of the puzzles she saw in Ranka's blood and the winalin they sought to cure with it.

"We're building off of my mother's research," Aramis said softly, her face distant, as though she recalled the years she'd spent as a little girl, clutching at her mother's robe while the past Bloodwinn hunted for a cure to the power that had plagued her, too. "We know witches and humans are one and the same; no one had even known my grand-mother was a witch until her blood-magic rose. Mother always believed there was something within blood-witches that changed when their power manifested. Some chemical switch, a shift in the body and the hormones already reshaping it during puberty, when all other defenses had failed. If trauma can alter our cells, why not magic, too? No blood-witch lives to see old age. The condition is never steady. It worsens each year, taking more and more, like a parasite blooming in the blood."

That was how it had always felt to her—like her blood-magic had not been something inherent, but a morphing of the witchery she'd carried. A curse, a sickness in her body, in her blood, born from pain and always demanding more in turn.

"Congrats, Ranka," Percy said cheerfully. "You've got the plague. Or you . . . are . . . the plague? That part is still unclear."

Aramis rolled her eyes and continued.

"We believe winalin is changing their blood," Aramis said finally. "Different magics have different anchors—wind magic is tied to breath. Infect Galen's lungs, and his magic would weaken. We know blood-magic resides in your veins—that's why it moves in waves, why it floods you and spikes with your anger. It's a biological defense mechanism. Somehow winalin is triggering that in non-blood-witches. But it's getting it wrong. It's killing them, because their bodies aren't designed for it. We're hoping to inoculate them." Her cheeks were flushed when she finished, and Aramis looked a touch embarrassed.

Ranka wondered what this all might have been like had the past Bloodwinn still lived. Had she felt her body weaken, like Ranka already did? Had the hunger come sharper, crueler, faster? What horror had caused her witchery to change in those vulnerable years of puberty when a blood-witch could be born—what nightmares from childhood had she, too, run from years after she'd become Queen and had children of her own? She knew little of the Arlani blood-witch, had seen her only once from a distance years ago, black nails flashing on her brown hands as she met with Ongrum to mitigate a border dispute with the Kerth.

She had been beautiful, like Aramis, her words soft like Galen's but her chin lifted with the confidence of a queen. Ranka had not known her, had never even spoken to her, but as she watched Aramis now, she thought the past Bloodwinn would have been proud of her daughter.

She hoped Aramis thought so, too.

It was normally Percy who unhooked Ranka, but now Aramis leaned over her, hand braced against Ranka's bicep. Her fingers were warm, softer than Ranka expected, gentle yet firm. A stray curl hung across her forehead, damp with the sweat. This close, Ranka could smell the ink clinging to her skin, mingled with the mint oil Aramis dotted across her wrists to mask any whisper of winalin.

It was strange, to see Aramis like this—focused but at peace. There was a lightness to her that was never there within the palace walls.

"Hold still," Aramis murmured. She pulled the needle free and pressed a wad of cotton in its place. Blood welled up through the cloth, cherry bright. Aramis wrapped Ranka's arm with the quick confidence of someone who'd bound a thousand wounds.

"You're good at that," Ranka said, and then her cheeks heated. She hadn't meant to say that out loud. *You're good at that?* What was wrong with her?

Aramis's eyes flicked to Ranka's, and the corner of her mouth twitched. "Thanks. I've had a lot of practice."

A strange flutter rushed through Ranka. She actually felt faintly dizzy. Aramis must have taken more blood than usual. When had the mines become so warm?

Percy turned back to Ranka, his eyes bright. "I know Aramis says you're not supposed to exercise on blood-giving days—"

"For good reason," Aramis said dryly.

"—but I'm going to train by the cliffs later, so when Aramis is done tormenting you, do you want to join me?"

"I don't *torment* Ranka."

Percy patted the top of Aramis's head. "Just being around you is torment."

"You know I can have you executed, right?"

Percy fanned himself. "Don't tease me, Princess."

They carried on, sniping at each other even as they returned to their work, Aramis using syringes to carefully drip Ranka's blood into a dozen and a half tiny, flat dishes, Percy chattering in her ear as he recorded measurements on the chalkboards lining the room. A stone formed in Ranka's throat. Aramis drove her absolutely nuts, and Percy was entirely unhinged, yet in moments like these, she almost liked them. More than she'd ever expected to.

And in a matter of weeks she would betray them.

It's war, she reminded herself. *They'd do the same to me. It's not personal.*

So why was it starting to feel that way?

20

"BLOODWINN?"

Ranka sat in the palace gardens, dozing beneath the greenery and the lullaby of afternoon birdsong. *The Basics of Witchery* sat open on her lap. The letters before her were still largely a confused jumble that took forever to understand—but some were beginning to make sense.

A guard approached, sweat already beading on his upper lip in the early day heat. "Bloodwinn? Captain Wolfe would like to see you."

"Am I in trouble?" Ranka joked.

The guard frowned. "He'd like to see you now, miss."

The hair on the back of Ranka's neck stood on end. She rose and followed the guard out of the garden, toward the back of the palace, where intricate mosaics faded to plain white tile and the air buzzed with the murmur of servants. Barracks loomed ahead, an outcrop of squat brown buildings. One bore the sigil of an exploding sun with a sword behind it.

Foldrey's office.

Ranka's heartbeat quickened as she stepped inside. She looked around, half expecting to see the blade of a sword pointed at her—and met the eyes of a little girl.

The child couldn't have been older than eight. She sat with her pale legs stretched out on the floor, a book open on her lap, red curls hanging over her face.

"Um," said Ranka. "Hi."

The little girl looked up and scrunched her nose in a way that made her freckles dance. *"Daaaaaad!"* the girl called, eyeing Ranka suspiciously. "There's some lady here. She's tall."

"I'll be right there! Ranka, make yourself comfortable. Moira, be nice."

Moira narrowed her eyes at Ranka and went back to her book.

Ranka waited, shifting her weight from foot to foot, eyes sweeping Foldrey's office. Everything was worn and well loved, polished by time and the captains who had come before. Framed battle stars sat in a velvet case amid books with cracked spines. The only portraits in the room were several different pictures of the twins.

Ranka attempted a smile at Moira. "What are you reading?"

"The Star Isles: From World Traders to Isolationist Foreign Policy," Moira recited in a monotone.

"Isn't that a little dense for a kid?"

The little girl looked up at her, plainly annoyed. "I wouldn't know. I keep getting interrupted."

"Moira, what did we say about manners?" Foldrey entered the room, buttoning his uniform over a threadbare white undershirt. He pressed a kiss to the top of Moira's head and swung her up to her feet. "Go get a practice sword and terrorize Damon. His ego needs bruising."

Moira leapt to her feet and tore from the room. Foldrey closed the door after her, his expression soft and melted. He glanced at Ranka, and the warmth left his eyes. "Please, sit."

From his desk he pulled out two glasses and a slender bottle filled with dark liquor.

Ranka blinked. "It's not even noon."

Foldrey raised an eyebrow and poured them both a drink. The gray threaded through his hair and beard seemed more abundant in the bright light of day.

Ranka sat, every muscle in her body rigid.

"I miss it still," Foldrey said finally. "The north. All these years, and I still dream of snow."

Ranka eyed him. Surely, he hadn't called her all the way here to reminiscence. "Where are you from?"

"Kravist—do you know it?"

"Not well. But we traded there once."

She could see it now: Ongrum, Nadya, and Sigrid, returning from a trading expedition, laden down with medicine and weapons they couldn't forge in the north. The sweet, smoky scent of human had clung to everything. The traders had sent gifts, eager to keep a relationship that brought them elk meat and rare furs. Ongrum had plucked a doll made of old corn husks from the pile and handed it to Ranka. She'd been just a witchling then, only a few years into her life with the Skra, and yet it'd seemed so distant—that scent, those gifts, those people. A world to which she no longer belonged.

After Belren, Ongrum sent two witches to Kravist to trade. They never came back. The villagers stole their goods and burned them alive.

Ongrum never sent the Skra south again.

"I went north once a few years ago," Foldrey said slowly. "But everything had changed. That land, those people—the Bloodwinn treaty isn't just a concept to them. It's a promise, one we didn't keep. I'm sure you feel the same."

Ranka froze. She searched his face to see if he was joking, but the guard's pale eyes were steady. "The Bloodwinn treaty has brought us peace," Ranka said hesitantly. "I am grateful to continue its legacy."

Something like sadness touched his features. "You're learning fast."

The truth burned behind her teeth. Ongrum always said the covens knew the treaty wasn't a fair deal, but it seemed like the only option. Give the humans a share of the resources, and maybe they'd be left in peace.

They'd been wrong.

In recent years alone entire forests had been felled for illegal logging. Miles of thicket burned, hillsides where rare trilliums blossomed blasted flat, entire wetlands drained to make way for farmlands north of the border. Witchik was being gnawed from the edges, and the prince who was supposed to enforce the border wasn't even reading the laws he signed.

There will never be enough for them, Ongrum had warned. *The humans have tasted Witchik—and unless we stop them, they'll suck her dry.*

"The Council loves the treaty," Ranka said carefully.

"The Council is chosen from noble families," Foldrey snorted. "Most of them have never been north. Other than the last Bloodwinn, most of them have never even *spoken* to a witch. I know the north in a way they don't. I was twenty-seven when King Alus—Solomei rest his soul—gave me this office. We swore we'd change the world." He took a drink. "That was twenty years ago."

Again her attention caught on the battle stars. There were an awful lot of them.

"I was prepared to die for him. Prepared to do terrible, brutal things in the name of serving him." He paused, tracing one of the scratches carved into his desk. "You know what I wasn't prepared for? The flies. Clouds of them, buzzing so loudly, you felt it in your bones. No one prepares you for that sound. Or the smell of bodies lost to fire. I couldn't get it off me. I dream about it, two decades later."

Ranka closed her eyes. After Belren, the stench of burned flesh had clung to her hair for weeks. "I dream about it too."

His laugh was flat. Humorless. "What a world we've wrought. A child dreaming of those flies."

"I'm not a child," Ranka said. "I'm a warrior."

"Is that what they told you?" He sighed. "Plenty young folk are handed a weapon and told they're a soldier. It doesn't make them any less a child."

The look he gave Ranka made her skin crawl. Like she was just some lost little girl—one he'd been too late to save. Like he was sad for her.

Ongrum had never looked at her like that.

"Forgive me, Captain," Ranka said. "But why am I here?"

Foldrey held his drink up to eye level, turning it this way and that. Reddish-brown liquid beaded on the lip of the glass. In that golden light of midday, it looked like blood. "I can't imagine how terrified you were to come here. I know the stories your people tell, of the wicked Skybreaker king and his treaty wife. Of the bloodthirsty, witch-burning humans they ruled." He ran a thumb over the grain of his desk. "Alus and Lyra were not perfect—but they were not storybook monsters, either. They loved each other. They loved their children and their people even more. And most of the time we loved them back."

"If you've called me here to change my mind about dead rulers—"

"I haven't. Let me be blunt." Foldrey laced his fingers together. "Galen is too soft to rule alone—oh, don't look at me like that. We all know it. His gentle heart is a blessing, but this country would eat him alive. And Aramis cannot rule while a male heir lives. But together? They might just be enough."

Dread stirred in her. He was still dancing around why he'd called her here.

"I've spent my life trying to protect them. To be their shield." He paused. "I have loved them, more than I ever had a right to. But I don't know if I can protect them from what I saw in that alley."

She nearly went limp with relief. This was about winalin, then. Not her, or the coup. He suspected nothing. She was in the clear.

Foldrey traced his thumb along the edge of the desk, his attention fixated on some distant point. "When Aramis proved to be human, she was devastated. I felt nothing but relief. At least she would be safe, and Galen safe from her." A grim smile flickered over his face. "Now, thanks to winalin, the twins have never been more at risk—and I am terrified. Because if we lose them, we lose all of Isodal."

"I agree," Ranka said easily. "The sooner we can cure winalin and protect everyone, the better."

Foldrey smiled as if she'd said something funny. "Your parents," he said lightly. "Were they northerners?"

"I don't remember them. The Skra are the only family I've ever known."

"The family you choose are the ones who leave the deepest mark." He took a sip of his drink. "I think it may be time you return to yours."

Shock jolted through every nerve in her body. Foldrey paused, glass hovering at his lips, pale eyes trained on her as he let what he was suggesting hit her in full.

"C-Captain," she began. "What—"

"You'll find an address in your room," he said slowly, each word clearly, painfully enunciated. "There's a change of clothes there for you and a false passport granting you transport north."

The dread returned, drip by terrible drip. "What you're suggesting—"

"Suggesting? I'm simply giving you an address." He leaned forward, his gaze unblinking. Some warmth returned to his voice. "I don't think you're a bad person, Ranka. Truly. I think you're a scared kid in an impossible position who never asked for any of this. I think you're in over your head, and your loyalties are confused. And I think, more than anything, you want to go home."

Every part of her was locked in place. He could be lying, but she didn't think so. It wasn't hatred he regarded her with, but sadness. Like he saw a piece of Ranka he recognized—and was trying to do her a favor.

And isn't he?

A passport, a change of clothes, a guaranteed ticket home. She could leave this cursed city behind, bring evidence of winalin back to the Skra and push them north, into the Kithraki Mountains or beyond to wait winalin out. Ongrum would be furious—but anger faded over time. What good was a kingdom riddled by disease? An angry coven was better than a dead one.

She should have jumped at the chance. She had every reason in the world to. Thanks to winalin, bringing the Skra here was a death sentence.

So why did the prospect of abandoning Seaswept now feel like one, too?

"Tell me, Bloodwinn—do you know what the role of a guard is?"

"To protect," Ranka said slowly, still reeling from his words.

"To *shield*," he corrected. "That is my job, Ranka. To be their shield, their knife in the dark. Stain my soul, to keep theirs clean. If I do my job right—because by the Goddess, they're our best hope, and this country is worth it, though you may not be inclined to agree—history will forget me, but it won't forget them." Foldrey steepled his fingers together, and all his warmth vanished. For the first time she saw him for who he was: a man who loved the twins he served, yes, but a soldier first.

Ranka had become a killer to survive. Foldrey Wolfe had trained to be one by choice.

"I will not let anything jeopardize those twins or the future they represent," Foldrey said. "Do you understand me, child?"

"Perfectly," Ranka whispered.

"You're a smart girl, Ranka," Foldrey said softly. "What you lack in social skills and political tact, you make up for in sheer survival instincts, that much is clear. You may not be built for court politics—but you know when to pick a fight, and when to back down. I trust those instincts to protect you. You have it in you to make the right choice. I see it, even if you can't."

Outside, Moira's shrill laughter rang in the air as she played with one of the guards. A sunbeam filtered through the window, catching dust motes as they danced over Foldrey's desk.

"I hope I'm wrong about you," Foldrey admitted. There was real regret in his eyes. "I hope I'm just a paranoid old man and I've just made a terrible mistake, terrifying an innocent bride over nothing. I hope I've misread everything, truly." He tipped his empty glass in her direction, his smile strained and sad. "But I wouldn't have the job I do if I made a habit of being wrong."

Ranka's throat was completely dry. She didn't dare speak. Didn't dare breathe.

He leaned back with a tired smile, and the tense air evaporated. "Forgive me, I've taken enough of your time already. Enjoy your day."

She couldn't get up fast enough. Ranka beelined toward the door, trying to keep her heart calm.

"Ranka."

She froze, her dread a stone in her throat. "Yes?"

"I followed Alus to war because I believed loyalty demanded it. It took me twenty years to learn no one is owed your loyalty. Someone worthy will earn it." The chair creaked. "I pray you learn faster than I did."

Finally, she turned to look at him—but he stared past her, lost in some memory only he could see. Ranka left his office in a hurry, the echo of flies buzzing in her ears long after she had left.

21

FOR THREE DAYS RANKA STARED AT THE SLIP OF PARCH-
ment she'd found beneath her pillow. For three days she ago-
nized, turning the address between her fingers, memorizing the
instructions—*small single-story house, two blocks north of Druid's Mark
center, on the corner of Fellhaven and Draine*. Day and night she toyed
with the thought of freedom, drifting off during her lessons to dream
of the Northlands. Of home.

On the third night, Ranka broke.

I'll just go look.

She was committing to nothing. Perhaps it was a trap and she'd
walk into an ambush—or worse, there'd be nothing there at all, and
Foldrey was simply offering her false hope to humiliate her.

Just a look.

Ranka slipped from her window and crept across the grounds.

The moon hung low and swollen in Seaswept's night sky. The grounds
were abandoned, and nearly everyone ought to have been asleep. Only
two guards manned the eastern gate. In a few minutes the watch would
change, leaving a precious gap—one Ranka was counting on.

But Aramis Sunra had already beaten her there.

The princess crouched with her head low, tucked in the shadows stretching beneath the palace's inner wall, invisible to the guards stationed above. And she was alone.

No Percy?

The two did everything together. Winalin was a burden they shared, and they were inseparable. But here was Aramis entering the city alone and without the knowledge of her guards.

I think, more than anything, you want to go home.

Foldrey clearly wanted her gone. If she didn't take him up on his offer soon, she had no doubt he'd try to find another way to remove her. She needed to use tonight to explore her options. Come up with a plan, decide if she was staying or fleeing, and prepare accordingly.

The guards posted above the wall descended the stairs. Aramis slipped out the gate with an ease that hinted she'd done this many times before, her steps quick and sure.

Ranka crumpled the address into her palm and followed.

The signs of drought were everywhere. Flowers wilted in their windows, the sprigs of basil that shared their plots shriveled to a fragile crisp. Dockworkers and maids relaxed from a long day of labor against scorched brick walls and fanned themselves half-heartedly, picking at their heat-chapped lips and sunburned skin, calling out to neighbors and passing cheap liquor between porch stoops. Posters snapped overhead, their edges curled with heat, offering charms to stave off thirst or help parched gardens grow.

But worse were the leaflets, scattered across cobblestones with no signature, no namesake. Easy to distribute and impossible to trace.

Ranka's own face stared out from them, warped by blood-magic. The words swam in front of her eyes.

A MONSTER AMONG US

She couldn't read all of it, but the general gist was that the treaty had invited demons into the city, the Star Isles were killing their country from the inside, the drought was a punishment from Solomei for not purging the unclean witches from their land, and the only way to reclaim their country was to join the Hands and fight back. Galen was hardly even mentioned. The leaflet made it seem like everything was *her* fault.

She tossed it aside. Let the Hands sow their zealotry all they wanted. They were as doomed as the rest of the city if winalin wasn't stopped.

Ranka scented the sickness before she saw it.

A small, squat building, mashed between two crumbling town-homes, loomed into view. A sigil of two open hands marked the door. Warm light and the bitter scent of antiseptic spilled into the street. Even at this late hour, there was a steady murmur of voices, a thrum of bodies, some ill, some in pain, all of them seeking care, comfort, or answers. The outside was abandoned. Only a fat little gray-and-white cat lay curled in front of the door. It cracked open one green eye to glare at Ranka, gave a pitiful, high-pitched meow, and went back to sleep.

What would a princess want with some crowded, shoddy clinic? The palace infirmary had its own healers. No doubt the palace clinic was the best in the city, if not all of Isodal—not to mention clean, quiet, and private.

Ranka waited. A few fishermen shambled past, picking scales from their forearms and mopping the sweat from their brows. Ten minutes crept by, then twenty. People trickled in and out of the clinic, but Aramis never emerged.

Before Ranka could lose her nerve, she crossed the street and stepped through the door.

Light washed over her.

The building was smaller than she'd expected—bright, clean, a little too warm. A woman glided past, her dark hair slicked tight against her scalp, the lower half of her face concealed by a sanitary cloth. She knelt in front of a dockworker whose pale cheeks were peeling and tilted his face up to hers.

"I think you're just dehydrated." Her voice was older, all warm brass. "But I can give you something for the sunburn."

"Take a seat," a familiar voice chimed. "We'll be right there."

Ranka turned, and her mind ground to a halt.

Aramis Sunra stood before her.

The fine silks she wore within the palace were gone, replaced by dull brown robes and slippers. Her mass of curls was twisted up on top of her head, save for a few that'd wormed loose and were now plastered against her forehead by a thin layer of sweat. A sanitary cloth concealed the lower half of her face, but Ranka would have recognized those dark brown eyes anywhere.

They gawked at each other.

Ranka blinked. "Hi."

"If you have a question for Lanna," Aramis said tensely, "you can wait over there."

Please, her eyes begged. *Don't ruin this for me.*

"Miss," a patient said, rising to move toward Aramis. "Apologies, but we've been waiting, and my son really needs someone to look at his wrist." The boy in question held his hand against his chest, wrist bent at a terrible angle as he fought back tears.

"I'm sorry, I have two patients ahead of you, and Lanna's busy with—"

"I can take him," Ranka blurted.

Aramis whipped around to look at her.

"I trained in basic aid." Her face burned. "We all do."

It was mostly true. Knowing how to stitch a wound or set a broken leg could be the difference between your coven mate making it back to camp or not. It had always brought Ranka some comfort, knowing that despite everything, even her hands could be good for something besides hurting.

The other healer, Lanna, paused to glance back at Ranka. She was older, probably in her midforties, with bronze skin, gray-dusted hair, and dark, intelligent eyes. She glanced at Aramis with a raised eyebrow, smiling beneath her mask. "How helpful of you to bring an extra hand."

Let me stay, Ranka willed. *Let me help.*

It was only because she wanted to find out what Aramis was up to. If there was one thing she knew about Aramis Sunra, it was that every action she took was calculated. Even if she *was* doing good here, she was playing a larger game.

And yet.

Take a girl, hand her a crown, and watch her become anyone. Behind a wall of silks and guards and gold, it was easy to change faces, to don and shed versions of herself with the nonchalance of a girl discarding a new dress.

But *this* girl, who stood in rough-spun healer's robes, sweat flecked across her brow and someone else's blood crusted on her sleeve, could be nothing but herself.

And this girl was someone Ranka wanted to know.

Aramis rolled her eyes to the ceiling in a silent prayer. "There are spare robes in the back. Go get dressed."

22

THE HOURS PASSED IN A BLUR.

Cut, clean, soothe. Ranka saw everything from minor scrapes to a leg that was little more than mangled flesh and snapped bone. She spoke only in orders: *ready on three, don't look, hold your breath*. Anyone in need of medicine was passed to Aramis or Lanna, while Ranka handled basic care. The three of them quickly settled in a comforting rhythm—Aramis sewing closed wounds, Ranka setting bones and wrapping sprained wrists, Lanna administering herbs, medicine, and advice with the confidence earned from a lifetime of prescribing them.

It was strange how at home Ranka felt. These human bodies were far more fragile than hers, but their bones broke the same.

In the early hours of dawn, the trickle of patients finally slowed and stopped altogether. After Ranka finished wrapping the ankle of a florist who had toppled from a ladder, she remained on her knees, fingertips aching from handling dozens of rough-textured bandages.

Her stomach turned. What was she doing here, giving care to the very humans who would be all too happy to see her burned if they saw the nails under her gloves? How many of the people she'd treated tonight supported the Hands? How many more would?

Behind her, Lanna rose with a groan and stepped into one of the back rooms.

As soon as the door shut, Ranka turned to Aramis. They'd not spoken all night, save for hurried orders and directives while funneling patients back and forth, but now curiosity tugged at her. "Does she know . . . ?"

"Yes." Aramis laughed. "She figured it out the first day. No one else knows, but Lanna's too smart for her own good."

"Why not tell them? It's not every day you get to meet a princess."

Aramis wrung out one of the linens, twisting it until the water ran from pink to clear. "If I were here as Aramis Sunra, these walls would be packed with nobles preening for attention. The people who need care wouldn't be able to make it through the door—and even if they did, no one would get treated. No one would say what they actually needed." She squinted. "Galen can't leave the palace. But when I'm here, I can be his eyes and ears and heart."

Ranka's hands slowed. It had to be a lie, right? Just another clever tactic of a calculating princess? Another deception from an enemy?

Except it felt genuine. And right now, Aramis felt like anything but her enemy.

The shadow of a smile touched Aramis's lips. "It's also not a terrible place to do research. And Percy hardly has the best bedside manner."

Ranka hid a smile. *That* felt more like the princess she knew. If you were a sick witch, what better place to seek treatment than an under-funded clinic, where the healers would be too busy to notice the tint of someone's nails or the way their body handled pain better than the average patient's? "Have you found anything yet?"

"Not yet, but we will." Aramis's eyes glittered. "We have to."

They were alone now, and the air felt fragile, as if anything more than a whisper would upend their peace. For a while they worked in silence, Ranka cleaning, Aramis resetting the clinic back to some shadow of normalcy before the next rush. The watery pink light of early dawn crept in under the door, casting the clinic's gray walls into delicate blush. And slowly, softly, seabirds began to sing in the new day.

Aramis looked over at her. "Who taught you to heal?"

"A human." Why did it feel so good to see that light of interest in her eyes? "Things were . . . different when I was younger. There were no border soldiers. Barely any raids. The humans up there, they had more in common with us than they do with you southerners."

She'd been just a witchling then, only five years into living with the Skra, not understanding why Vivna, with her pale nails and barest shred of witchery, hated it so. Before her blood-magic had risen, Ongrum had always expected Ranka to become a hunter.

And to be a hunter, in those days, meant to trade.

"The town was called Orvist." She could see it even now, a small outpost town so close to the border, it was more Witchik than Isodal. A few witches had lived there openly, working alongside townsfolk during long winters and longer nights to fend off wandering fang-wolves or bandits that came to terrorize a village too far north to depend on the protection of the palace. Without the influence of the nobles, they'd made their own kind of treaty. Their own peace.

It had felt normal. And it had felt right.

In those days, the differences between humans and witches had felt as arbitrary as the border itself. It was hard to ignore the question everyone knew not to ask: What if witchery really *was* just a kind of human magic, one that manifested in strange nails and strength and a sharpening of a particular sense, the same way Galen's magic manifested into wind? Witches were born from humans, after all, and witches could birth humans in turn.

Ranka cleared her throat. "On one of the trips, I fell through the ice and twisted my ankle. One of the men we traded with was married to a healer."

If Ranka closed her eyes, she could still see the snow clinging to the man's pale eyelashes, his breath fogging in the cool air as he showed Ranka how to wrap the bandage.

"We?" Aramis asked lightly. She was prying, Ranka knew that, yet still the truth slipped free.

"Vivna," she said, the name barely audible. "My sister. She was always the one who wanted to head to the villages—I tagged along after her because I couldn't bear for Vivna to be anywhere I wasn't."

Aramis softened. "Galen used to be like that. We were inseparable. Mother used to tease us for it—called us each other's little shadows. But I liked it. We were a team. I never felt alone, not if I had him."

"You still do."

Ranka pictured Vivna's annoyed face, the way she puckered her lips whenever she realized Ranka had followed her again. And later, Yeva and Asyil—a perfect pair, until Ranka intruded. Guilt bloomed in her chest. Yeva had welcomed Ranka and paid with her life.

"Do you remember your life before the Skra?" Aramis asked. Her face looked so open, so curious. It was disarming, to meet her eyes and receive anything but a scowl. "Surely, there must be something— your parents' faces, your human name."

"No," Ranka lied. She closed her eyes. Witches left their human names behind for a reason—that way lay only pain. "I don't remember any of it at all."

From the look on Aramis's face, she didn't believe her. But she also didn't pry further.

Ranka laid the wet linens out on a table, smoothing away the wrinkles with the heel of her hand. "The last time we tried to visit Orvist, it was filled with southern soldiers."

She recalled the men even now, how they'd stood bright against the bleak winter sky, shuddering in brilliant blue uniforms far too thin for northern cold. The villagers had smiled apologetically, as though it was an inconvenience they all had to bear.

"I remember when Father sent the soldiers north," Aramis said, her voice distant. "Belren was the tipping point. All those people. Even our southernmost provinces were terrified. He said the soldiers were only temporary—and he believed it at the time, I think. But that was the change, wasn't it? After Belren—we could never go back."

Ranka's hands slipped on the jar she was holding. "Yes. It was."

The floor threatened to open up and swallow her whole. After Belren most traders stopped coming north. Villages grew hostile, and the covens suddenly had to scramble to rescue children whose witchery manifested south of the border. Humans pressed north with weapons to cultivate new farmland or blast open new mining sites. Even Ongrum had been stunned to see everything fall to pieces so quickly. The tentative peace had been far more fragile than any of them realized.

Aramis kept watching her. There was a strange rawness to her face—an openness Ranka wasn't used to. An interest she feared. Something had softened between them in the hours they'd spent healing together, tending to strangers, too busy mending wounds to inflict them on each other for once.

"I never thanked you," Aramis said. "For saving Galen, that day in the alley."

"Foldrey saved us," Ranka said cautiously. They'd not spoken of Bell's Corridor since the night in the mines, and though Aramis had stopped threatening her, the princess clearly still didn't *like* her. If Aramis was about to pick another fight, Ranka would let her win it. She was simply too tired.

"Galen told me about the attack. The witch had thrown him against a wall. He'd struck his head, and he was so out of it, he was too dizzy to flee." Aramis's throat bobbed. "You could have left him, but you didn't. He said you tried to protect him—and when you couldn't, you didn't abandon him. He said you stayed, and you held his hand."

She had taken Galen's hand out of instinct and guilt, had been shocked by the way he gripped it back. But if Aramis thought she'd done it to comfort the prince, she was wrong. Ranka wasn't that noble.

She had been just as terrified as Galen was—and too weak to fight back against a girl she loved.

"Galen told me something else." Now Aramis had the grace to

look away. "The witch that attacked you—the one they killed. He said you called her Yeva."

All the air left Ranka's lungs. Her eyes burned, and she gritted her teeth.

"I know it doesn't mean much," Aramis said softly. "But Ranka—I am sorry."

Ranka's eyes blurred. "Thank you."

Aramis nodded. She didn't push the subject further. This grief was Ranka's alone, and the princess knew better than to wade into it.

Still, her attention wandered back to Ranka.

"I don't trust you. And I don't quite like you," Aramis said, but she sounded unsure, as though she had trouble believing the words. "You lie, and you follow us. You reject the treaty—and then appear out of nowhere. But you cooperate with winalin. You try to help, even after Percy and I make your life unbearable. And then, when your moment comes, instead of killing my brother—you hold his hand." Aramis's eyes searched her face. "But you don't love him. You don't want to marry him at all."

Ranka chose her words carefully. "I am . . . trying to do the right thing. But I'm less sure of what that is every day." She hesitated. "I thought you would all be awful, truly. I came here prepared to hate everyone in this palace—but Galen is kind. Foldrey is honorable. Percy is . . . Percy. And you . . ."

You infuriate me. You impress me, and amaze me, and drive me utterly mad, and every day I hate you a little bit less, and it's making all this far, far worse.

"You," Ranka said finally, "are not what I expected."

Aramis suddenly seemed very focused on the bandages she was cleaning. "You confuse me, witch girl."

"Trust me, Princess. The feeling is mutual."

A low warning hummed in the back of Ranka's head. This was dangerous territory, and the rawness in her would become a bleeding wound if she prodded any further.

"You don't have to love Galen to be queen, you know." Aramis's voice was strained. "My mother and father were lucky. But my grandmother—she already loved another when she was asked to come south and end the war. You would still have a good life. You could take a lover in secret, if you wanted to. Galen wouldn't care. He's never hoped for a marriage built on love."

"And you, Princess?" Ranka found herself asking, though she shouldn't have, though she knew this way only lay pain. "Do you hope for love?"

Aramis's fingers jerked. Ranka caught the movement, though Aramis redirected the slip of her hands into folding a bandage. "My hopes don't get to matter."

Her tone made it clear further questions were not welcome. Ranka's cheeks burned. Why had she asked that? It was none of her business. Had no impact on her mission or her role here. Still, she found herself watching the princess. Found herself aching to ask not just if she hoped for love, but what kind of love that would be—and what kind of person she'd find it with, when she did.

"I think about her sometimes," Aramis said. "The blood-witch of Belren."

Ranka willed her face into a blank mask. "Why?"

"I saw the way my mother's blood-magic weighed on her. She spent her life trying to find the answer to it, to ensure no one would have to endure what she did. Belren to her was evidence of her failure." Aramis twisted a roll of bandages together, her voice soft, careful. "People always say the Butcher acted out of revenge or bloodlust. But if Belren was intentional—why didn't it happen again?"

Ranka forced herself to take several slow breaths, to quell the panic threatening to pull her under. "I think whoever that witch was, she probably never wanted to hurt anyone. I think she'd take it all back if she could."

Aramis looked at Ranka, a question in her eyes—a question Ranka desperately hoped she wouldn't ask. "I bet she would."

"It doesn't excuse what she did."

"No, it doesn't. Still—I wish Mother had found her. I wish anyone had. She should have never come into that power alone."

Ranka pressed her hands against the table to keep them from trembling. Memories of fire and blood on the snow lingered behind her eyes. "No one should."

Aramis looked exhausted all of a sudden, her attention trained out the window, where morning light was beginning to wake Seaswept with a gentle, golden glow. "Do you think we could fix what Belren broke? If the right changes were made? If we had enough time? Do you think the Bloodwinn treaty could work?"

Ranka closed her eyes. She saw Vivna's dark curls bobbing down the streets of Orvist, the warm blue eyes of the human who had taught her to heal. The blankets she'd sheltered under, woven by southern hands. And she saw the *after*, when witches learned to take instead of ask, when her wounds from Belren hardened into scars and she learned fear could be a tool as sharp as any knife when wielded right.

"I don't know," Ranka said, and it was the truth.

Could the world ever become what the Bloodwinn treaty was meant to create—a haven for both humans and witches, where they learned to at least tolerate one another, if not thrive?

Did she want it to?

She didn't know that, either.

23

RANKA DREAMED OF YEVA.

In her dreams they were children again, rosy cheeked, tromping their way through thick snows in pursuit of a herd of elk that a scout had spied earlier that morning. Bundled in furs, with hair plaited away from her face, Yeva looked a little like Vivna. Sounded like her too.

But unlike Vivna, she waited for Ranka when she lagged behind.

Ranka's breath fogged in front of her. They were silent, but it was a warm silence. Vivna always whined, and Ongrum barked orders, but with Yeva the world was quiet, and safe. They turned the bend, blinded by a flash of sun on snow.

On the winter breeze came a familiar scent—sweat and smoke, and veins that bled too easily.

Humans.

Ranka and Yeva were down in the snow in a blink, belly-crawling to a patch of bushes. One of Ranka's gloves worked itself loose, and her bare hand struck snow. The cold burned. Ranka reached back—and Yeva grabbed her hood, tugging her forward, eyes wild with fear.

Better a glove than a limb. Better a glove than a life.

Only two weeks before, they had stumbled into a copse of trees and found two witchlings hanging from their ankles, both younger than Ranka herself. They had been burned alive.

They came from the west: five men, beards flecked with ice and cheeks pink with winterburn. On sleds they towed carcasses dismembered into hunks of meat, bundles of antlers, and thick, fatty hides.

"Well," Ranka whispered. "Guess Tafa was right—there *were* elk out here."

Before Belren, Ranka and Yeva would have called out and approached the hunters with tentative smiles. Even if their gloves hid their dark nails, any human would have known a child emerging from the northern woods could only be a witch. The humans would have been wary—but polite. They'd have inquired after their coven, maybe offered them meat in hopes the witches would grant them access to their lands.

And they would not have carried so many weapons.

It was funny, how quickly things changed.

Take a girl and hand her a knife. Take a village and make it bleed.

Take a country, tear it in half, and see who is the first to burn.

Ranka's blood-magic stirred, slipping the world into that tantalizing gray.

Them, it promised. *It will always be them.*

Ranka woke to the scent of smoke.

The golden light of late afternoon filtered through the window. She'd dozed off. The heat was too oppressive to train in, and Percy and Aramis had declared her free of both them and her lessons. Ranka blinked groggily. She could still feel the burn of winter on her cheek, feel Yeva's hand shaking in hers. She could scent the blood in the veins of the men, whom she knew, even at fifteen, she could kill if she needed to.

But she was not fifteen anymore. She was far from home, and the smoke was real.

Her eyes flew open.

Ranka was out of bed and moving in a flash. There was no guard outside her door, and the hall was empty. Warm afternoon air hit her. Smoke curled in heavy swaths, clinging to the plants, slipping over the walls, hanging so thick it concealed the ponds of fat, lazy carp.

Rippling through the air, pulsing from the city like a sick heartbeat, was the putrid stench of anger.

What is going on? Where is everyone?

Ranka broke for the stables—but when she got there and stepped into the scent of hay, of horses and heat and sweat, something else greeted her: snakeskin.

"Going somewhere?" she called.

"You just love to meddle, don't you?"

Percy Stone stepped out from one of the pens. Instead of his usually elaborate robes, he was dressed in shabby clothes. Every line of his body was tense.

Ranka met his eyes. "You're headed into the city?"

Percy nodded.

"Take me with you."

And to her surprise, Percy sighed and said, "Okay."

Percy was fast, navigating Seaswept with the familiarity of someone who knew it well. The smoke grew thicker, itching her eyes, burning her lungs. But instead of heading toward the source, Percy took a sharp left, striding west. They dove into a side alley as a patrol of guards passed, waiting several long beats before continuing.

Something cracked to their left and Ranka spun, her hand flying to her hip. She'd brought her axe with her this time. Percy put a hand on her shoulder, his eyes gentle.

She flushed, embarrassed by her overreaction. "Sorry. I just—"

I'm smelling smoke. I'm thinking about what we're walking toward.

"I know," Percy said. They sidestepped a pool of vomit baking in the heat, and Percy shook his head, forcing a lightness into his tone to distract them both. "This city is disgusting."

"Aren't you also a city rat?"

"The Star Isles was nothing like this," he snorted. "The capital city was carved into the face of cliffs. Our houses were limestone, packed together so tightly you could walk from roof to roof, all glittering and white." He closed his eyes, his lashes fluttering. "Every year, there was a parade, and we'd sit on the roof, splitting moon fruit we'd picked that morning. My sisters made a terrible mess every time."

Ranka heard the love in his voice, and she thought of her own home, of the snowcapped Kithraki Mountains, which fed the rivers yearlong, the miles of conifer forests that never relinquished their shade, the apple trees that grew heavy and swollen in the fall, and the raspberry thickets that bristled over swamps in the summer, tempting witchlings and black bears alike. They passed yet another empty street. "It sounds beautiful."

"It was."

"Do you miss it?"

Percy closed his eyes. "Every day."

"You said 'was.' What happened to the city?"

Percy flashed her a humorless smile. "Why, it's gone, of course. Queen Ilia burned it to the ground."

The silence of Seaswept pressed in around them.

"We didn't expect her to kill so many," Percy continued, his voice soft. "Or maybe we did, but we were so desperate for change, and she was so convincing that hers was the only way to reach it. She spoke of a Star Isles where everyone was equal." He grimaced. "Did we know it was wrong? Maybe. But we were starving for someone to believe in. And my father—he'd come from nothing. Can I really blame him for believing in her new world? For trying to include me in that dream?"

Bile rose in Ranka's throat, dark and bitter, because instead of a distant queen, all she saw was Ongrum's face, the light in her eyes as she spoke of freeing witches forever.

"Is it worth it?" Ranka whispered.

"Is what?"

"Rebellion. All the horror, bloodshed, and death. You had to have lost friends. People you loved. But you did it to make something new—something *better*. Was it worth it? The new world?"

Percy turned his attention to the heavens. "There's never a new world, Ranka. There's only fixing the one we've got."

He might as well have punched her in the stomach.

"Don't get me wrong," Percy said quietly, his eyes tracking the smoke billowing overhead. "Sometimes drastic measures are needed. Governments topple. A war is won, a people revolt. But it's never because of just one person." Percy licked his lips. "People like Ilia . . . they'll call themselves heroes and convince you they're gods. They'll make everything look so painfully simple, so black and white. But the gods are dead or ignoring us, and there are no heroes coming to save us. There's just regular, messy people. A good leader knows that. But people like Ilia? They don't want anything new at all, just the power they'll get from pretending they delivered you to it."

Ranka reeled. There was nothing she could ask him without giving herself away.

But oh, how she *ached* to—to ask him how it felt to realize the new world had been a lie, that he'd only been a pawn in bringing in a new evil from the same old horrors. She wanted to know if there was a way to gauge whether a leader was one of those messy, imperfect people he spoke of, or a beautiful liar spinning hopes built on falsehoods and smoke. She wanted to ask if it was worth trying anyway, on the off chance that *some* change was better than what had come before. She wanted to know when he'd realized he was wrong—and how he'd lived with himself after.

She wanted to tell him everything.

There's never a new world.

But what if there could be?

The question rose to her lips—and a scream shattered the air.

On the wind they smelled it: smoke, blood, and the earthy scent of a girl who had only just come into her witchery.

The scream came again, and then they were running, pounding toward a richer district of the city.

All Ranka could see was the smoke, curling in the air, shifting from the pale clouds of regular bonfire to the black plumes of people burning wet wood and whatever they could get their hands on. The streets teemed with people, jostling at one another to move forward, packing sweaty bodies in the narrow alleys.

Something familiar lingered in the air, something that didn't belong. Ranka forced her way forward.

In front of her was a pile of kindling. A slip of a girl knelt before it, hands tied behind her back.

And across the crowd, dressed in commoner's clothes, was Foldrey Wolfe.

24

FOLDREY STOOD IMMOBILE, ONE HAND ON THE SWORD he'd concealed beneath his cloak, his face carefully blank as he stared at the girl who was aboout to be burned.

And she *was* just a girl, maybe a few months shy of fourteen, still narrow hipped and full cheeked with youth. She had Vivna's eyes—a pale, watery blue. Tear tracks cut through the layers of grime on her cheeks.

A woman stood over her, cradling a small dog that dripped red onto the cobblestones.

"Please," the girl begged. "Mama, I didn't mean to. I'm sorry. I don't know what *happened*." Her fingernails were already beginning to blacken.

She was a blood-witch. A real one.

Ranka's eyes blurred. How many years had she followed Ongrum through northern forests, tracking the scent of a new witch, hoping against hope it was someone like her? How many years had she prayed to meet someone with this power, this curse, so Ranka might take their hands and help them to survive it? Vivna had never understood her magic, Yeva and Asyil had tolerated it as kindly as they could.

But to be seen by another blood-witch, to be mentored and *known*, instead of feared . . .

Percy finally caught up with her. The blood drained from his face. "Ranka—"

"I know," she said, her voice low. "I see him."

Ranka cut through the crowd. What was Foldrey doing here? And out of his palace uniform, no less? She wove her way toward him, Percy on her heels, fingers curled into her palms to conceal her nails.

She'd prayed in Belren for someone, anyone, to save her. Had vowed she'd never be a bystander.

What a pathetic liar she was.

Ranka touched Foldrey's shoulder, and he spun, eyes widening as he recognized her. "Oh, thank the light. You're here."

"What are you doing—"

"Shhh." Foldrey wrapped a hand around her bicep, pulling her to the side, and beckoned for Percy to step closer. "Listen to me very carefully, both of you. We found one—a winalin witch, alive. And we caught her."

Percy's eyes widened. *"How—"*

"A message arrived about an hour ago. They're holding her in the iron district. I looked for you in the palace, but you were already gone. I assumed you'd seen the smoke and came here as quickly as I could." He turned to Ranka. "I see you haven't taken me up on the opportunity I offered you—well, here's a better one. Find her, Bloodwinn. And help us save her."

Behind him, the girl continued to weep. A man darted forward and threw oil on her. The crowd roared in approval and the girl sobbed harder, her bony shoulders trembling. The mother clutched their dead dog and stood terribly still.

Treacherous, fragile hope took root in Ranka's chest. With a live winalin witch, they could gather samples. They could *treat* her, and maybe even find a cure.

They could be *saved*.

Why did she even want that so badly? If she returned home and kept the Skra safe, winalin would do their work for them. So why did her eyes now burn with the prospect of a cure? Hadn't Ongrum trained her better than this? If she knew of the weakness Ranka felt right now—of the way she cowered before these humans and hid her nails—she'd be disgusted.

And yet. A cure gave her options. It gave her a choice.

She tried not to think about the fact that there shouldn't have been a choice to make to begin with.

Another man stepped forward. On his chest gleamed a single gold pin.

"For too long we've lived in fear," the man called. The crowd quieted. "Bell's Corridor is still wet with blood. Our own neighbors are dead. We starve as fields burn from a seven-month drought. And what has the prince done? *Nothing*."

A murmur rose among the humans. A pale blond woman broke away, and from a satchel at her hip she began to draw out fistfuls of gold pins. To Ranka's horror, she began offering them to the people gathered around her. No one turned her down.

"The Skybreaker prince feasts while we starve," the man said. "He throws parades but won't call the rains. The Council raises taxes and nobles cut our pay. They ignore our pleas and murder our priests for protecting the streets *they* neglect. They don't care about us! They never have!"

The woman worked her way through the crowd, weaving through throngs of adults and children alike. They donned the pins one by one, until a dozen, two dozen, three dozen chests gleamed gold. A part of Ranka supposed it was brilliant—something as small as a gold pin could be donned and cast aside in a heartbeat. It allowed the Hands to materialize one second and disappear the next.

Ranka turned to Foldrey. "I'm in."

Percy's eyes widened and he caught her arm. "Hold on. You can't mean for us to go there alone."

"Who said anything about us? I'll bring her back myself."

"Do you have a death wish?" Percy gave her a light shake. "*Think*, you big oaf. I want a cure as badly as you do—but we're about to be in the middle of a witch-burning frenzy. Even if you *can* subdue the witch, how are you going to contain her? How are you going to bring her back?"

"I'll figure it out—"

"That's not good enough," Percy snapped, his voice breaking. "You tried that before, and you nearly got you and Galen both *killed*. This isn't just about you anymore, Ranka! Maybe you don't care if you throw your life away, but some of us do, okay? You don't get to be reckless anymore. You need to *think*, because you need to come *back*."

Ranka stared at him, stunned. Percy's chest rose and fell. Spots of color touched his cheeks, and for some reason her eyes were stinging. An awkward silence lapsed between them as they stood there, Percy in his anger, Ranka in her shock. She wanted to tell him she didn't know the last time someone had cared that she came back from a fight. That she came back at all.

She wanted to tell him *thank you*.

Foldrey cut in. "I can send word for extra soldiers. By the time Ranka has the witch restrained, they'd be there, with chains and a cart to bring her back safely—but I don't know how much longer my men can hold her until then."

Percy gave Foldrey a long, strange look, then glared at Ranka. "Fine. If you insist on getting yourself killed, I guess I'm dying with you."

Gratitude rushed through her, so overwhelming it threatened to make her knees buckle. They'd never been direct enemies before—but they'd certainly not been friends. Something had changed in their days of sparring and bloodletting and quiet conversations in the mines.

Something was changing still, and it terrified her.

"Quit looking at me like that," Percy said half-heartedly. "I'm just protecting Aramis's science experiment."

"Right." Ranka cleared her throat. "Let's go. We don't need to watch this."

She turned to leave—and stopped short.

Oh no.

"Ranka?" Galen asked, his voice small. "What's going on?"

The Sunra twins were so poorly disguised, it was nearly comical. Their faces were too clean, their clothes too new, their posture proud and wildly out of place. Horror dawned on Foldrey's and Percy's faces as they recognized them.

"It's smoky," Aramis said, her voice edging toward hysteria. "Why is there so much smoke?"

"Princess—"

Aramis shoved her way forward. Foldrey stumbled to stop her, to block her view, but she shoved past him, forcing a path through the crowd until she could see what had worked them all into a fever pitch. Every line in her body went rigid.

Ranka came to stand beside her. Behind them, Foldrey and Galen whisper-argued, Foldrey demanding to know what they were doing there, Galen saying he'd heard Foldrey mention something to a guard about dealing with a witch problem in the city. Ranka didn't know whether to laugh or cry. Could she even be surprised? Aramis had spent day and night working toward a cure, trying to use Ranka's blood to bridge the gap between a healthy witch and the winalin that killed them. Not even a hurricane could have kept the princess out of the city. All she had to do was follow the smoke.

Ranka put a hand on Aramis's shoulder. "Princess, we need to leave."

Aramis twisted to look at her, wild eyed and furious. "*Leave?* Ranka, they're—they're going to burn her alive."

Ranka looked away. She couldn't bear to look at Aramis, but she couldn't look at the girl, either, because if she looked at the girl, she would see herself, her sister, her coven, and then she would have to *do* something. Bodies pressed around them, vibrating with anger, with eagerness to see someone, anyone, pay. Could she even blame them? They'd suffered too, cowering in their homes while blood-witches roamed their streets, starving while their prince was tucked away in a palace whose tables overflowed with food.

Humans came forward, hauling chair legs and scrap wood to toss onto the kindling pile. It was good lumber, old-growth cedar and oak. It had probably been culled by witches themselves, packaged and shipped south before the sap had even finished bleeding. A little boy tossed a small wooden soldier on the pile.

"The royals have failed us," the man said. "The Hands have always been the true protectors of this country. This city is shrouded in darkness; we will burn it clean."

From his pocket the man drew a match.

"The Hands of Solomei reject the Bloodwinn treaty." The man's face was red, flushed with rage or excitement, Ranka wasn't sure. He ripped the pin from his shirt and held it aloft. The humans who had just donned them touched their own as if bespelled, their faces alight. "*We* will purge the sickness from this land. *We* reject the demons so the Goddess might bring the rains again. If the prince will not protect us from terror, we will protect ourselves."

He lit the match.

"We are Solomei's light. We are her Hand in the night."

"Mama," the little girl screamed. *"Please."*

"And by her Hand—we burn."

The match fell.

And the world caught fire.

Red, orange, and blue swirled up, building to an inferno in seconds. The girl howled as the flames spread to her cotton dress. Ranka jerked forward—and two strong arms locked around her waist, hauling her back.

"I'm sorry," Percy whispered, his voice breaking. "But if you try to save her, they'll know—and they'll burn you, too."

Ranka thrashed, but Percy held fast. He drew blood and she kept fighting, because by the Goddess, she'd been that girl and no one had helped and she wanted to be *better*. She'd not saved Yeva or Vivna, not saved so many others, and it felt like cowardice to be idle now.

The crowd roared, and all Ranka could see were those little, dark-nailed hands curling in pain. The smell of burning wood shifted to charring flesh. The girl kept screaming. Ranka gagged. The scent was all around her, the scent was inside her, burrowing into the marrow of her bones. The twins backed away until they collided with Foldrey. He put a hand on each of their shoulders.

Galen turned away, but Aramis stood witness the entire time.

Ranka sagged against Percy's chest. He kept muttering something over and over again. Ranka realized he was saying: *I'm sorry.*

Only a handful of blood-witches were born every generation. Winalin had felt like a cruel trick, a twist of her hopes. Now, after all these years, here was another blood-witch. A real one. Here was a girl like *her.*

And Ranka could not save her.

She was a child again, kneeling in the snow, screaming as they dragged her toward the pyre. Behind her, Vivna wailed with pain.

They're going to burn us, she realized. *They're going to burn us alive.*

The girl screamed in front of her and another screamed in her memories. It all blurred together—the crowd, the flames, the girl who was dying but not fast enough.

Ranka went slack. She dropped like a stone, slipped through Percy's arms, and seized the knife from his belt. Fourteen years of Skra precision guided her hand. Ranka pivoted and threw.

The blade hit the witch in the center of her heart.

The screams ended abruptly. Ranka turned away, shivering despite the heat. She could no longer tell whether the taste of smoke in her mouth was from this pyre or one set five years ago.

Aramis and Galen stood as still as stone, tears streaming down their cheeks. Seventeen years in this city, and this was the first time they'd met its heart. They were the most powerful children in all of Isodal—and yet even in the face of this, they could do nothing. Foldrey stood behind them, the muscles in his jaw twitching, still gripping their shoulders.

"Come on," Ranka said, her voice low. "We have a witch to catch."

25

FOLDREY AND THE TWINS WHISPER-FOUGHT THE whole way.

Ranka's right hand skimmed her axe, her other on the knife tucked into her waistband. A warning thrummed through her. Something wasn't right.

"Please, both of you, listen to me . . . ," Foldrey whispered. "I never would have left if I'd known you were going to *follow* me—"

"Winalin is my burden too," Aramis said firmly. Her voice shook, but the princess held fast, her short legs moving quickly to keep up. "If we can't take the witch alive, we'll need samples. Percy can't do it alone."

Foldrey looked like he wanted to tear his hair out.

Galen's voice trembled, but the prince lifted his chin. "Where Aramis goes, I go."

Red swept up Foldrey's neck, but what could he do? He was their guard. He answered to them, in the end. Yet when he spoke, it was not in the tone of a guard, but that of a worried father. "This is an extraction *only*. We go in, subdue the witch, and smuggle it out through the tunnels. Look at me, both of you. Your lives are the top priority. If something goes wrong, you do not look back. You *run*. Promise me."

The twins made a face.

"Promise. Me."

"We promise," both muttered.

Ranka looked between them, Foldrey's words ringing through her ears.

I have loved them, more than I ever had a right to.

Ongrum said she loved her, but she'd never looked at her like that.

The guard closed his eyes, made a prayer circle on his chest, and drew his sword.

Foldrey had said they'd secured the winalin witch in an abandoned house. As Seaswept sank into late evening, it loomed into view. In a past life this home had been beautiful—whorls of peeling yellow paint depicted flowers across the siding and tattered cloth that used to be a mat was stretched across the cement porch. Now it, like this city, was rotting.

The faintest trace of blood lingered in the air, nearly lost amid the reek of the fish canneries. Ranka stepped inside—and saw only dry-rotted walls.

Foldrey approached warily. "She's gone?"

She nodded, eyes tracking the room. There were no scuff marks—no blood, no signs of a struggle.

Relief washed across his face as he turned to the twins. "My men wouldn't just abandon their post. They must have taken her to the palace. We should head back."

Percy gave Foldrey that funny look again.

But if they'd gone back to the palace, why not leave a note or some kind of sign? She stepped deeper into the abandoned home, scanning the cobwebbed walls and dusted floors.

Ranka dropped into a crouch and inhaled.

For a precious beat she was back in the Northlands, tracking a wounded stag through knee-deep snow. She was home. Scent had always been her map to make sense of the world. It told her not only where people died, but how, and *why*.

And if they lived—where they went.

There.

Ranka followed her nose, moving to the far wall, ghosting her hand over a boarded window. It creaked under her touch. Her fingers came away wet. Ranka pushed, and the board fell to the street with a dull clatter. Evening light lanced through, revealing where other boards had been broken and carefully replaced. Blood gleamed on the street alongside upturned stones and scuff marks. She rubbed it between her fingers. Iron and earth. Human and witch.

Found you.

"Back here," Ranka called softly. "Foldrey, one of your men is bleeding. There was a fight—and it looks like he lost."

The color drained from Foldrey's face.

Percy stepped forward, his expression grim. "Can you follow the trail, Ranka?"

She met his eyes, trying to understand why he was looking at her like that—like he was worried for her. Doubt flickered, but Ranka nodded.

"Then let's go," Aramis said. "And don't even start, Foldrey—we're seeing this through."

Foldrey gritted his teeth, looking for all the world like he regretted ever stepping foot in the city at all.

Ranka followed the blood.

For nearly an hour they followed the trail. The city unrolled around them, eerily quiet despite it being late evening, when laborers should have been returning from work. If she hadn't known better, she'd have thought this district was abandoned—or evacuated. Percy walked behind her, Foldrey at the rear, the twins sandwiched protectively in the middle. At one point Ranka glanced back and realized she was leading them. No one had told her to, but no one had questioned it either. Her eyes stung, and she blinked to clear them.

Aramis looked at her, clearly alarmed by the wetness of her eyes. "What's wrong?"

"Nothing," Ranka said roughly, turning back to the trail. "It stinks here."

With her heart in her mouth, Ranka caught the scent and tried to shake the feeling she was leading them toward death.

26

SEASWEPT WAS DYING.

Decay flourished like mold in every corner of the iron district. Here, where city guards didn't bother to patrol, even the stones bled fear. Piles of trash flowed from alleys and clogged gutters. Gold pins gleamed on every corner, shoved into wooden light posts and the faces of noticeboards. Some homes even had them pressed into their doors. Aramis touched the wall of a burned-out townhouse. It was a husk, the windows gone, the sills lined with ash, but the footprints on the stoop made it clear someone was still living there. They turned the corner, and vomit rose in Ranka's throat.

The charred corpses of three witches lay in the street, a gold pin pressed into each of their chests.

The first was little more than a pile of sinew-wrapped bones to fester in the late-summer sun. Their eyes had been pecked away by wandering crows long before Ranka had entered this city. The second was weeks old—little more than a bag of rotting, loose flesh, long bloated with decay. A colony of maggots now teemed where a person had once been.

But the third was fresh, and the third was a child.

And the child was missing their left thumb.

Ranka's knees buckled. It couldn't be Talis. It was just a coincidence, surely. Just another witch. And yet—she'd forgotten Talis. Her throat bobbed.

How had she forgotten her so easily?

Ranka staggered forward. She couldn't bear to look at them any longer, left to rot in the sun with those goddess-cursed pins gleaming among their bones like some badge of conquest. Witches were supposed to be buried in the earth, so their souls could return to the soil from which they'd been formed. At the very least, buried at sea. The Oori coven believed the first witches had crawled from the belly of the ocean and walked north even as their skin blistered and cracked, lungs burning and lips bleeding, knowing anywhere was better than here.

Seaswept's ocean wasn't Witchik, it wasn't home, but it was better than this.

Aramis caught her arm. "If you move them, the Hands will know."

"You don't understand."

"I was raised by a witch, Ranka." Aramis touched her wrist. "We'll fix this. And we'll come with swords."

"That doesn't help them." Ranka jerked away and pretended not to see the hurt on Aramis's face.

The blood trail was thicker here, winding around the bend until it led them to an old, broken-down mine entrance. Ranka slammed her elbow into the rotten boards covering it and they collapsed inward, sending up a plume of dust and grit. Four different tunnels yawned before them. The path split in two. Human down one, witch down the other.

Percy broke the silence. "You guys don't seriously want to *follow* those things?"

"The witch is down there," Aramis said. "And so are our men."

Foldrey turned to the twins. "For once, I agree with Percy. I'm begging you both—let us handle this. Stay here. Head back to the palace—"

"We do this together," Galen said.

"Galen." Foldrey's voice cracked. "Please, son, if anything happened to you—"

"That's an order, Captain Wolfe."

The air turned frigid, and Foldrey closed his eyes. "Very well, Your Highness." He cast a long, loathing look at the mines. "Percy and the twins will come with me. Ranka—you take the left tunnel."

"I'll go with Ranka," Aramis said. She crossed her arms when both Ranka and Foldrey whipped to look at her. "What? If she finds anything in there, she won't know what to bring back."

"If something happens—" Foldrey began.

"She'll protect me—won't you, Ranka?"

Ranka hesitated, completely and utterly thrown. Ever since their night in the infirmary, something had shifted. They were hardly friends, but the thorn of animosity had dulled, replaced by some kind of understanding. Aramis was making a bid toward peace, in her own way. Now the princess waited for her answer, looking frail and vulnerable against the derelict city sprawling around her. She had no weapons, no training, not even a bit of armor on her. And now, when it mattered, it was Ranka she was putting her faith in.

It was Ranka she trusted to lead her through the dark.

Ranka couldn't afford to think about why that terrified her.

"Of course I will," Ranka said roughly. "I'll protect you with my life, Princess."

Aramis held her stare, a strange spark in her eyes, and nodded.

Panic flashed in Foldrey's eyes, but he reined it in. He'd never looked more miserable. He opened his mouth as if to appeal to the twins one last time before shaking his head. "One hour. Then we meet back here. What's our signal if something goes wrong?"

Percy pretended to consider this. "I think the horrified screaming will probably suffice." Everyone glared at him. "What? I'm right. We're all going to die."

Aramis punched him in the arm, and together, they descended into the mines.

27

THE TUNNELS REEKED.

The bay was higher here.

Seawater had long permeated the mines, leaving stagnant pools along the walls. Ranka led the way, squinting against the dark.

"How much longer?" Aramis whispered. "We've been walking for ages—"

"Quiet." Ranka ran her fingers over the wet walls. "Voices carry. We don't want whatever's down here to know we're coming."

That shut her up.

The tunnel curved south, sloping downward. The blood scent grew thicker. The only sign that Aramis was still with her was the whisper of her breath. She and Aramis traded positions every quarter mile. The princess led now, shoulders trembling through her shirt. She turned the corner—and screamed.

A guard sprawled across the tunnel floor. He was missing his head.

"Solomei help us," Aramis gasped. She braced a hand against the wall and gagged, her shoulders trembling from the effort of swallowing down bile. Ranka waited for her to recover and crept forward to investigate the dead man.

Ranka knelt and read the name on his uniform. Lieutenant Sorhee.

Yeva flashed through her mind's eye, and she swallowed her grief. At least this man's death had been fast.

If they weren't able to get a team to recover his body, at least his family would have closure. She ripped the patch free, tucked it into her pocket, and rose. "Come on. Lieutenant Forthis may still be alive."

They kept walking.

There had to be hundreds of miles of tunnels down here. Openings yawned on either side of them, and it took everything in Ranka not to flinch every time they passed one. Her axe kept slipping in her hand. She counted under her breath to keep calm—it was a trick Ongrum had taught her years ago, when the nerves before a raid left her bouncing and unable to sit still. The rhythm of the numbers always brought her back down.

"Ranka," Aramis whispered, lifting a trembling hand. "Look."

Bloody footprints formed a haphazard path in front of them, tracing forward and back, shooting ahead and back through side tunnels, as if whoever had been down here had been running in laps to make the trail unreadable. The slashes of rust were small and round, not the steady tread of a booted guardsman. Whoever had been down here was barefoot, and in bad shape.

Behind them, somewhere deep in the tunnels, something moaned.

The hair on Ranka's arms stood on end. Aramis looked at Ranka, her pupils blown wide in the dark. Ranka swallowed her bolt of terror and reached for her. "Take my hand, Princess. And don't let go."

They walked faster, increasing their speed until she and Aramis were half jogging. A breeze caressed their cheeks. Salt water and open air beckoned ahead. They burst from the mine entrance, spilling into a section of Seaswept Ranka didn't recognize, the palace on the cliffs nothing more than a distant glimmer. A crescent moon gleamed above. Just how long had they been down there?

Something flashed in her periphery. A foot scraped stone. Ranka twisted—and Percy froze, a second away from driving a knife into her throat.

"Oh," he said awkwardly. "Hi."

Ranka placed her hands on his narrow chest and shoved him. "What are you *doing*? You were supposed to be following the other trail!"

"We were," Foldrey said.

"No, *we* were following this trail."

"Ranka," Aramis said quietly. "Look."

The bloody footprints Aramis and Ranka had followed were indeed there, slashes of rust against brown and gray—but a second pair met them only several yards away, coming from another direction.

Foldrey's face turned dead white. "We need to leave. Now."

"What?" Ranka demanded. "But we just got here—"

Foldrey grabbed her shoulder. He was scared, his eyes stretched wide, his grip so tight it hurt. "*Think*, Bloodwinn. Sorhee, Forthis? Both dead. There are *two* sets of prints. There shouldn't be *two* of them. Something is wr—"

From the far end of the alley came a moan.

The stench of rotting flesh and fresh blood pulsed forward, so overwhelming it made Ranka's eyes water.

Two winalin witches limped from the shadows.

Like the others, they were covered in sores, caught between varying cycles of decay. Blood coated their faces. By the sharp, iron tang in the air, it was human. In their hands, they carried small knives, blades gleaming with a strange, oily substance.

The first witch had been sick for quite some time. Her skin drooped from her bones as if it were stretched two sizes too big, and maggots twitched in sores festering along her arms. What was left of her hair hung in filthy clumps, and her green eyes were now dead white. Wooden beads curved the shell of her left ear. She was Kerth, just like the witch in the morgue.

The second witch was younger, maybe twelve or thirteen. A child. Her clothes were little more than tattered, soiled rags made filthy by layers of old blood. Tattoos of cypress roots encircled her wrists. Murknen coven, then. Her sores were smaller, but she was dying all the same.

"Whatever you do," Foldrey said slowly, "don't let the knives touch you."

Ranka, Foldrey, and Percy formed a wall in front of the Sunra twins. The winalin witches raised their knives—and lunged.

28

SIDE BY SIDE, FOLDREY AND RANKA BATTLED THE witches.

The guard captain moved in perfect sync with her, his sword cutting a deadly arc through the air, Ranka's long arms slicing her axe in great sweeps whenever the witches drew too close. Behind them, Percy guarded the twins. Foldrey took the Murknen, and Ranka spun to face the Kerth, seized the witch's hair, and dragged her back. Metal sliced Ranka's arm. She barely registered it. Her blood-magic rose and she shoved it down, struggling to remain in control. She didn't want to kill this witch. There had to be a way to save her. It had to be different this time. *It had to.*

To her left, Foldrey battled the Murknen. He was a wonder, a blur of movement in the dark, a testament to what a lifetime of training could hone—but he was tiring. The Murknen planted a foot on Foldrey's chest and kicked him backward, sending him sprawling. Percy leapt forward. The twins cowered against the wall, exposed and unprotected.

The Kerth slammed her elbow into Ranka's stomach. She twisted, slashing one knife across the backs of Ranka's calves—and drove the other into her stomach.

Pain blistered through her. She gasped, staggering backward, and the Kerth twisted, barreling toward Percy instead. Foldrey and Percy turned, fighting in tandem, moving like two halves of the same whole as they formed a shield in front of the Sunra heirs.

Ranka swayed. The Murknen was distracted. Ranka rose, creeping toward her, her heart pounding. With the Murknen taken out, it'd be three against one. They could win.

The Murknen turned, her nostrils flaring. Ranka tensed her legs. She'd sidestep her at the last minute—let the witch's own momentum carry her right into a wall. The Murknen barreled toward her. Ranka braced herself—and a gust of wind slammed directly into her, sweeping her clean off her feet.

"Shit!" a familiar voice squeaked. "Ranka, shit, oh no, I'm so sorry!"

"Galen," Foldrey bellowed. "Stay out of this!"

Ranka sprawled on her back, ears ringing.

The Murknen headed toward her.

"I'm sorry!" Galen cried. "I—I was trying to help, I'm sorry! *Ranka, look out!*"

The Murknen stood over her. Ranka's head spun. The witch snarled and brought her foot down on Ranka's wrist. Pain turned the space of her hand to a void of crackling black.

The Murknen flipped her knife and slammed the hilt into Ranka's temple.

The last thing Ranka felt was a flicker of surprise.

It'd been ages since someone had bested her.

The first time Ranka had kissed death, it'd been with Tafa.

On the morning of Ranka's ninth birthday, they snuck out of camp and crept across fresh snow, stolen axes in hand, determined to learn the throws the older Skra had mastered. Ranka was tall for her age, and if she pitched her shoulder just right, she could throw the axe hard enough to sink the entire blade into a pine trunk.

It filled her with a thrill like no other to hear the *thwump* of that blade slamming into wood. To envision what it'd sound like for a blade to hit a body.

What a fool she'd been.

"Let me try," Tafa begged. "Please."

"You're too small."

Tafa kept missing the tree. The axe skittered across the hard-packed snow until it vanished into the underbrush. Her face grew redder. Her throws grew wilder.

On the tenth throw the axe slipped—but instead of forward, it flew back.

The blade hit Ranka in the middle of her stomach.

The pain startled her. So much blood everywhere—down her legs, across the snow. Tafa kept screaming, and Ranka's vision swam in and out, her head feeling five pounds too light. She stumbled back to camp, leaving a trail of red behind her.

The blood loss should have killed a witch twice her size. Ranka remembered a burning cold, bone-deep exhaustion, the urge to sink into sleep and never rise. But above all, she remembered voices.

Get up, a voice like Yeva's whispered.

Fight back, one like Ongrum's snarled.

And her own, hard and determined, filling her mind, her veins, her world.

I am not done.

29

EVERYTHING HURT.

Waves of pain rolled through Ranka's stomach and pulsed down her temple where the Murknen had struck her. Her mouth filled with blood—she'd bitten her tongue.

"Please," Foldrey whispered. The guard was on his knees, his sword gleaming uselessly several feet away. "Please, just let them go. They're *children*—"

The Murknen made a low, guttural noise. Her words emerged strangled, as though speaking required a terrible effort. "So were we."

Ranka's blood-magic rose—and this time she welcomed it.

Her nails elongated, and power flooded her muscles, her heart, her breath. Ranka heard Aramis's voice, crystal clear in her mind, a balm to the anger churning through her.

Breathe, the princess whispered. *And control it.*

Seaswept faded into a world of gray, the monotone broken only by the warm glow of bodies, but her stomach was free of cramps, her mind clear. And for a precious breath, all Ranka felt was pure, unbridled awe as her blood-magic coursed through her and she didn't hunger for death.

Was this what it would be like, if she learned control?

Could her power be a gift instead of a curse?

Aramis curled over Percy, bleeding from a dozen shallow cuts. He stretched across the alley floor, unconscious, bleeding heavily from a deep slash in his thigh. Jagged claw marks curved down his cheek, weeping the black substance that coated the witches' knives. Galen cowered against the wall, frozen in place.

The Murknen took a step toward them.

"Don't touch them," Ranka slurred. Blood dripped down her chest. "They're mine."

The Kerth and Foldrey both turned. The Kerth bared her teeth—but Foldrey froze, a strange expression sweeping his face. It was the first time he had seen Ranka truly transformed, and when Foldrey looked at her, it wasn't with horror, but with weary regret. As though Ranka had given him an answer to something. He looked at her like he was sorry.

I will not let anything jeopardize those twins or the future they represent.

At least he saw her fully now. A monster made, if not born.

A girl made weapon, whose only purpose was to kill.

Ranka recalled the day Ongrum had given her her axe. She'd known, in that moment, she was starting down a path she could never walk back on. That was how Foldrey looked at her now, with something like grief flickering in his eyes, fading to a grim resolve. Like he'd just made a choice.

She could only hope that choice involved fighting alongside her.

Ranka held his stare and bent slowly. She placed her axe on the cobblestones and put her toes against it. Understanding brightened Foldrey's eyes.

The Murknen raised her knife.

Foldrey's legs tensed.

Ranka kicked her axe across the ground.

Foldrey lunged. His fingers closed around the handle and he turned, swinging his arm in a great, sweeping arc. The axe blade slammed into the Murknen's calf, and she screamed. Ranka darted forward, snatching up Foldrey's sword, slashing it toward the Kerth.

And finally—blessedly—her blood-magic took over.

Every ache, scrape, and worry vanished. She was no longer Ranka. She was just a vessel made to kill, a heartbeat piloting flesh and bones. The Kerth howled, clawing at Ranka's arms and face and neck, pressing the black substance deep into the fibers of her torn muscles, but Ranka's blood-magic ate the pain, just as it had every time she'd stepped onto the battlefield. It was like pulling on a second skin, so familiar in that haze of chaos.

Monster. Butcher. Murderer.

Ongrum was right. This was who she was, all she'd ever be—and it was glorious.

Behind her, Foldrey kept fighting.

Numbness crept up Ranka's legs, her body growing stiff and cold as it lost more blood. Her skin burned as though someone had lanced open her veins and filled them with hot metal. Her blood-magic propped her up, but she was so tired. The alley swam.

Behind her, Galen's voice: "Aramis? Aramis, wake up."

Foldrey buried Ranka's axe in the Murknen. She collapsed with a scream, dead before she hit the ground. He bent down to pull the weapon free, but it was stuck.

Ranka turned her attention back to the Kerth. She'd come south to kill humans, not witches. She was so tired of failing. Of letting the ones she was meant to save burn or die. But the Kerth was too far gone—there was only one way this could end.

The Kerth hissed. Tears cut through the grime on Ranka's cheeks. She would kill her with the weapon, not her hand, to avoid seeing the flashes of her life.

"I'm sorry," Ranka whispered.

The Kerth lunged for the Sunra twins, and Ranka swung. The sword blade arced, cleaving one of the Kerth's hands away. The witch barreled forward as if she hadn't even felt it. She kicked out at Ranka and knocked the sword from her hand. Ranka staggered, lost her balance, and fell.

The Kerth stood over her. She stared down at Ranka with nothing but hatred and hunger registering in her gaze. But she looked so frail—a girl of sixteen, maybe seventeen, her entire body ruined by a man-made plague.

Maybe it was fitting that winalin would end Ranka, when its makers had sought to re-create her. Ranka took a breath and readied herself for the blow.

The Kerth raised Foldrey's sword.

A hand grabbed her by the hair and yanked her back.

Ranka saw the Kerth, face warped with bloodlust, skin broken by sores, hands shifted into claws—and Foldrey, dragging her so hard that her feet left the ground. Weaponless, bloody, and alone. He pulled her away from Ranka, bloody fingers buried in her shaggy mess of hair, chest heaving, a wild, desperate light in his eyes.

He saved me, Ranka realized numbly. All his threats, all her fears, all his reasons, but he'd saved her all the same.

The Kerth twisted and drove Foldrey's sword into his stomach.

Time slowed. They stared at each other, witch and guard, the Kerth holding the sword, Foldrey holding her hair, each looking bewildered by how easily the weapon had gone in. A gasp rattled out of Foldrey. His face softened. Tenderly, he reached up and cradled the Kerth's face in his hands. She looked so small in front of him. So young. Blood spread across Foldrey's stomach in a slow red wave, staining the linen of his uniform.

Foldrey broke her neck with a crack.

The Kerth crumpled. Foldrey swayed, his hand going to the sword protruding from his abdomen. From down the street a familiar scent rippled forward—smoke-stained robes, oil-streaked skin, and torches, ready for burning.

It was only a matter of time before someone heard the commotion. And only one group would respond to a fight here, deep in the city, where the palace had long since left its own people to die.

In the distance, gold flashed.

Foldrey looked up and met Ranka's eyes.

"Run," he whispered.

And then he collapsed.

30

OVERHEAD, DARK CLOUDS GATHERED.

"Foldrey, *no!*" Galen staggered forward, dropped to his knees, and pressed his hands to Foldrey's stomach. "You're going to be okay. We're going to get you help and you're going to be okay."

Ranka lay in the street, losing more blood than she could afford to give. Behind her, Aramis and Percy seized, lips foaming as poison took hold. Judging by her own dizziness, Ranka didn't have much longer, either.

Again it came—that scent she'd learned to fear so quickly, one that promised death by fire. They needed to move. If the Hands found them now, they'd be easy prey. Galen and Aramis Sunra would be wiped from this world, and she along with them, with nothing but the cobblestones as witness to what had happened here.

The clouds swelled. Galen shook harder. "You're going to be okay. We're going to get you help and *you're going to be okay.*"

Foldrey cradled the prince's cheek in his hand. "You have to go."

Heat lightning flashed overhead.

"We're not leaving you." Galen's chest heaved. He looked around, wild eyed, as if still expecting someone to come to his rescue.

Ranka's skin burned as poison ate through her. She could not walk, so instead she crawled to Aramis. Reached for her. She tried to lift Aramis onto her shoulder, but her legs could no longer support the weight of her own body, let alone another. Spots swirled across Ranka's vision.

Footsteps approached.

"Look at me," said Foldrey. "Galen, my boy, *look at me*. You are special—you know that, right? You have a gentle heart, a *good* heart. But it's time to grow up. Your sister needs her brother, and Isodal needs her king."

"I'm not letting you die."

"You have the whole sky in you, Galen," Foldrey whispered. "Use it."

Cold. Ranka was growing so cold. And that scent—it was coming closer. She reached for Percy. Scales shimmered beneath the skin at his wrists; vomit crusted his lips. She hauled him onto her other shoulder. Pain ripped through her, and her vision went dark. *No.* She clawed for her blood-magic, but it was barely an exhausted flicker. Even blood-magic ran out eventually. It wouldn't be enough to carry her out of here—let alone all three of them.

"Galen," Ranka croaked. "Please."

Then, from the dark, came footsteps.

The Hands of Solomei had found them at last.

They came from all directions, sidling from the ends of alleys, slipping from vacant doorways. For a breath they were indistinguishable from other humans—they bore the same gaunt faces, tired eyes, and drought-parched lips. The image of a people run ragged by a cruel summer and careless rule.

One by one, they reached into their pockets and donned gold pins.

Ranka counted fifteen, twenty Hands, surveying the scene before them with a kind of grim satisfaction. A few turned and darted down side streets, likely to spread word more were needed. One of the Hands stepped forward and pointed at Aramis. "It's them," she laughed, as though she'd been handed an unexpected gift. "The Sunra brats."

"And the Bloodwinn," another added, pale face twisted in a sneer. "Solomei smiles upon us after all."

Galen held very, very still.

His hands were still braced on Foldrey. Save for the blood that soaked his stomach, the guard looked peaceful, as if he'd merely lain down in the road to rest. Galen stared at the Hands, who could have so easily stepped in to help, who could have carried him and his sister to safety, or tried to save the guard he loved from the gaping wound in his stomach. Who could have helped them try to cure witches and rein in winalin, instead of using it as an excuse to fill his city with fire.

Grief washed across Galen's face. He knelt there, shoulders shaking, hands wet with Foldrey's blood. The temperature dropped several degrees. The sky grew darker.

"Please," Galen said, his voice hoarse. "Please just . . . leave."

One of the Hands murmured a command.

Galen pressed his lips to Foldrey's forehead, murmuring something for only him to hear. He remained there, hovering over the guard who had raised him, eyelashes fluttering as he fought back tears.

"Please," he tried again, his voice eerily calm. "I am begging all of you . . . don't do this. Turn around. Go home. I won't ask again."

Twenty humans reached for their knives.

And Galen raised his hands.

Wind roared through the alley, peeling cobblestones up from the road, crashing into the Hands who'd collected like vultures to feed on tragedy. Thunder clapped overhead. Galen's wind kept coming, building in fury until cyclones broke away and ripped down side streets. Some of the Hands pushed forward, turning their shoulders into the wind, aiming not for Galen, but for Aramis, who lay unconscious behind Ranka.

Galen slammed his hands down, and the wind buckled *out*.

It exploded outward in one great ripple. Several Hands went flying, scattering like twigs, some of them slamming against walls with horrible thuds. The wind swirled, picking up speed and debris. Galen twisted his wrist, and a protective cyclone formed around the five of them, blocking off the Hands, building in strength as it tore down awnings and peeled shingles from roofs.

Galen grasped Ranka by the collar of her shirt and pulled her to her feet. Wind leapt to life beneath her, caressing her skin, churning up, up, *up*, keeping her aloft. Galen hauled Percy and Aramis over each shoulder, his right hand still moving in circles, somehow commanding both the winds that now held them upright and the spiral that kept the Hands at bay. He took two steps forward and crashed to his knees with a painful crack. Fury sparked in his eyes, and he stood again.

"Ranka," Galen said flatly. "I need you to take Aramis. Can you do that?"

She nodded, even as lights danced in front of her eyes. Ranka took half of Aramis's weight, gasping as her wounds tore. She was cold. So cold. Minutes. She had only minutes left.

"We need help." Galen lifted Percy onto his back and took Aramis's other arm around his neck. "I need you to find help, Ranka. Can you do that for me?"

"The city," Ranka croaked. "Bring it to me."

The winds swirled again, gentler this time, rushing over her cheeks, her lips, her tongue. She leaned into it, sorting through the blood, rot, and decay that pulsed stronger with each passing night. She breathed in, searching, and *there*—the sting of polished metal, old leather, and salt.

"Guards," she croaked.

Galen looked back at Foldrey. Beyond him, a few Hands were picking themselves up, blood dripping from their noses, their ears, their lips. Pain flashed across Galen's face. His eyes darted from Foldrey to his sister, from Foldrey to the Hands beyond. Galen sobbed, turned, and threw out a hand. A blast of wind slammed directly into an old home teetering behind some of the Hands. The building groaned and collapsed, taking out the townhouse beside it, and the one beside that, pulling down long-abandoned clotheslines strung between their windows and old, rotting verandas someone had once lovingly built when this street was a place of life. The Hands screamed as the building collapsed on top of them. Blood filled the air.

Galen turned to Ranka, sweat pouring from his face. "Which way?"

He trusted her, though he shouldn't have.

Ranka latched on to the scent and jerked her chin east.

The wind kept roaring.

Together they limped away, and left Foldrey Wolfe to die. Twice Galen sank to his knees, veins popping in his forehead. Both times he shoved himself back up. He coughed up blood as his lungs strained under the pull of his magic.

Black tunneled Ranka's vision. There was so much poison in her. She'd lost too much blood. She swayed and staggered, falling to her knees. *So tired.*

Wind lifted her back up. "Get up, Ranka."

Her hands. She couldn't feel her hands. Her skin was burning, burning, but the rest of her was so *cold.*

Galen braced a hand against an alley wall and coughed up more blood. Most mages could summon only for a few minutes. She'd never seen someone conjure so much for so long. As the prince's wind pushed them through the streets, Ranka understood why the first humans had thought the Skybreakers were gods.

"Come on, Aramis," Galen said, his voice cracking. "Stay awake. You don't get to leave me too. *You're not allowed to leave me.*"

They turned a corner, and finally, there—two guards in palace uniforms, chatting with a fishmonger, their shoulders relaxed. Beyond them, a woman sat on her porch, smoking languidly as her children played in the dark, relishing a break in the heat. One of them kicked a ball in Ranka's direction. The child stood up to chase after it—and locked eyes with Ranka.

The little girl screamed.

The guards spun, expecting a fight. One drew his sword, but the second gasped in horror as he recognized the twins. Galen finally dropped to his knees, vomiting blood on the stones. Percy slid from his back. Voices rang through the street as passersby began to notice, crying for help, crying for healers, for anyone. The guards scrambled forward to help Galen, shouting for backup. One reached for Ranka. She forced herself to meet his eyes.

"Poison," she whispered.

And then she collapsed at his feet.

31

RANKA'S WORLD WAS A HAZE OF POISON, BLOOD, AND pain. Hands washed and bound her wounds, sure fingers purging toxic substance from her veins. Poppy kept her subdued. Every time Ranka slipped back into unconsciousness, her only solace was that in her brief window of lucidity Aramis was still breathing.

Someone settled her in a bed that smelled of sweat and old lavender. A body was laid to her left, a person of snakeskin, and a smaller body to her right, smelling of ink and mint. In the Skra camp it was safer, warmer, to sleep three or four crammed to a bed. Comforting to rest wrapped in the embrace of sisters in combat, if not in blood. Some of Ranka's earliest memories involved waking up beneath layers of fur with the arms of other witchlings thrown over her, a mass heap of safety, belonging, and love.

Cool fingers brushed her forehead. "Rest, child."

Heavy, rough-spun wool blankets settled over her. Ranka willed her eyes to open, for her tongue to work, but she was so weak. So tired.

So curled between her enemies, delirious with pain, Ranka slept.

Memories returned in snippets—of palace healers clogging the room, treating them where they lay because they were too fragile to be moved; Percy screaming, his eyes turning gold, scales flickering under his skin as the poison left him; Aramis catapulting from sleep to vomit and writhe in agony. Galen vomiting into a bucket over and over again, puking blood and bile as Lanna stood over him.

"You should have died," she told him in a low voice. "You shouldn't have been able to summon that long. You're as stubborn as your parents were."

Now quiet blanked the healer's cottage. The weak light of evening sun split the room in long, warm rays that crept through the shutters. Galen dozed on the other side of the room beneath a pale blanket. Aramis was tucked against Ranka's side, her face troubled even in sleep. Poultice gleamed on her skin where the knives had cut her. Ranka's stomach did a flip. They'd never been this close to each other. For all her sharp words, Aramis seemed softer in her sleep. More vulnerable. The princess murmured something and nestled closer, tucking her face into Ranka's neck, and Ranka went rigid. Something fragile and warm fluttered to life in her chest.

And then someone snored in her ear.

On her left, Percy dozed, his jaw on Ranka's shoulder. He was heavily bandaged like the rest of them, sleeping with his head tilted up, mouth wide open. And he was drooling on her.

Ranka might have shoved him off had her entire body not felt like she'd just been flung over a waterfall.

Had it not meant waking Aramis, too.

"You're awake," a voice said. With a jolt Ranka recognized her. It was Lanna, the healer she and Aramis had worked alongside. Her fingers were quick and light as she peeled back the bandages and smeared a grassy poultice over Ranka's stomach. The burning ache didn't leave, but it eased enough that Ranka no longer felt like she might collapse in on herself. Lanna squinted at her shoulder. "That's some bite mark you've got there."

Ranka turned her face away.

"How do you feel?"

Ranka's voice emerged in a strangled croak. "Horrible."

"Good. That means you're alive." Lanna brushed her knuckles along Aramis's sweat-slicked cheek. Percy muttered something in his sleep and buried his face in Ranka's hair. "I thought I'd lost you all when the guards nearly broke down my door."

"Foldrey," Ranka gasped. "We left him. Is he—"

"*Shhh.*" Lanna put a firm hand on her shoulder and pushed her back down. "Calm yourself, little witch—oh, don't look at me like that. I know exactly who you are." Her mouth turned downward. "The guards are still searching."

They'd find nothing. If Foldrey had survived long enough for the Hands to recover his body, he wouldn't have survived the after. She didn't know why it mattered so much. Foldrey served the twins, not her. He'd made it clear he didn't trust her—but he had been kind, in his own way. He had tried to help her. He'd been a good man, doing his best to protect the ones he loved. She understood that more than anyone.

Somehow Foldrey, like all of them, had become more.

"If you hear anything—"

Lanna's eyes were warm and sad. "You'll be the first to know."

She turned away, moving toward Galen. Though she wasn't much taller than Aramis, she lifted him with ease. Galen murmured something but didn't wake as Lanna carried him across the room and settled him beside Percy. The bed creaked under his weight. And it bothered her, that she was comforted to have him within reach.

He'd been a marvel in that alley—all wind, strength, and sheer will-power. He had protected them and left Foldrey behind to save them. She'd underestimated him.

Maybe he *could* become someone strong enough to guide Isodal down the right path—or maybe she was wrong, and the throne would eat him alive.

The hours crept by. Lanna drifted in and out, checking their wounds, feeding them warm broth tasting of herbs and buckwheat honey. Ranka's wounds kept her suspended between a state of uncomfortable wakefulness and half-drugged sleep. Percy slept still as death beside her, his skin pleasantly cool against Ranka's own burning frame as he drooled. Night crept over Seaswept, easing the city into a lull, bathing the healer's cottage in cool blue shadows.

Aramis jolted, her face contorting. *"Foldrey."*

Lanna had stepped out only a few moments ago. They were alone. Aramis sobbed, lost in a nightmare, her fingers clawing and her face twisting as she fought demons only she could see.

"Hey," Ranka whispered, wriggling herself upright. Percy's chin slipped off her shoulder, and he landed facedown on the pillow with a grunt. Ranka eyed him to make sure he wasn't going to suffocate before turning to Aramis. She hesitated—and then took her hand and squeezed. "We're safe. I won't leave you."

Aramis stilled at the sound of her voice, the lines in her face easing. Only the low rumble of Ranka's voice seemed to keep the princess at ease.

Even in the realm of her nightmares, Aramis trusted her.

She'd have to talk Aramis through the night—or at least until Lanna returned.

If Yeva were here, she'd be telling fairy tales, spinning stories about far-off kingdoms and benevolent kings who granted riches to village girls. But Ranka had stopped believing in happy endings a long time ago.

"All I ever wanted to be was a warrior," Ranka whispered. "So even though it terrified me, my blood-magic felt like a calling. For the first time in my life, I was strong. I had purpose. I was inspiring instead of embarrassing. It didn't matter that I couldn't read, that I wasn't beautiful. *I* mattered. But Vivna always wanted different. She said violence made me ugly, and witches were cursed."

The crease between Aramis's eyebrows eased. Percy remained still—too still, his breathing suddenly measured and careful as he listened, feigning sleep.

Ranka kept talking.

"I don't remember my real mother, not really. The only memory I have of her is from the day we were taken."

Her mother's face was a blur. She'd caressed Ranka's face that morning, leaving only a dusting of flour behind on her cheek. That was all Ranka remembered—the smell of unbaked bread, and red kitchen tiles faded to a dusted pink.

But Vivna had been eight when the witches came for them. She remembered everything.

The Skra witches arrived in the night. For most humans, raising a witch was more trouble than it was worth. When the covens came hunting, most parents turned over their children all too willingly.

"Vivna cried the whole way back. I told myself I'd make her happy. But I didn't. I lost control when we were just girls, and I . . . I hurt people. People that mattered."

Belren. All that smoke and blood.

Hours crept by. Ranka told Aramis about Witchik's Northlands, about hunting on a cold dawn armed with only her axe and her blood-magic's deadly prayer humming in her veins. She told her of the winter snows, the lukewarm summers, the trilliums that could only grow wild on the hills, the black bears that stole their supplies, and the rainbow trout they pulled from rivers with stolen nets. She told her of the pyres that lit the southern border. How even miles away the scent of a witchling's charring flesh was unmistakable. It was the southern-trained soldiers, not the northerners, who began the burnings. They did them only on windy nights. They wanted the breeze to carry into Witchik, where the covens would catch the scent and be forced to imagine the screams. It made the violence easier: the fires Ranka set to human farmland, the arrows she fired into wagon chains pressing north, not caring who or what they hit.

Ranka told Aramis she wasn't violent because she loved it, but because she was good at it, and sometimes she wasn't certain where one began and the other ended.

Aramis nestled closer, and Ranka found herself blinking through tears.

It wasn't supposed to be like this. She wasn't supposed to care.

In ten days she would have to decide whom to fight for.

You have it in you to make the right choice.

The twins—or the Skra.

And for the first time since Ranka had entered Isodal, she didn't know who to choose.

PART THREE

BUTCHER

SIX DAYS REMAIN

32

IT WAS THREE DAYS BEFORE THE PALACE HEALERS deemed them stable enough to be moved. The last thing Ranka recalled before slipping under a blanket of poppy was the tired warmth of Lanna's face and the panic she felt when Aramis was pulled away from her side. Now they lay in the palace infirmary, still injured, but safe. Home.

No.

The palace was not her home. Could never *be* her home.

So why was it starting to feel like it?

The days passed in a blur. Galen was well enough to walk by the time they returned, and Percy—unfortunately—had recovered enough to chatter constantly from his sickbed until Aramis took to whipping pillows at his head. By their second day in the infirmary, they were doing well enough to irritate the healers and were finally released.

Ranka tried for word of Foldrey—but all the guards would say was that the search was ongoing.

She found Galen at the cliffs.

He stood with his arms limp, staring out at the sea. The sky was a muted gray, the first overcast day since Ranka had entered Isodal. Three guards were posted several feet away. Even from afar she could scent the misery rolling off Galen. In the Skra camp, it was often Ranka tasked with speaking to battle-shocked witches after their first fight. She understood the way violence stained, the blood-soaked nightmares that followed.

But grief—grief she'd never been good at.

"Galen?"

The prince didn't move.

"Can I talk to you? Alone?"

Galen raised a hand. The guards moved away, their sword buckles squeaking. Galen remained immobile, head tilted toward the sky, eyes open but unseeing.

"They haven't found him," he said finally. "They've looked every-where. Nothing."

"Do you want to talk about it?"

"No."

"Galen, I've been there. I know what it's like to—"

"But you *don't*," Galen snapped. "He's not just—he's not just *staff*, Ranka. He's family, okay? And we left him behind. *I* left him behind. And now he—" His voice hitched. "Now he's gone."

She didn't say what they both knew—that if Foldrey was dead, it was a blessing. The Hands would torture him for information before they slit his throat. Had Foldrey been a noble, they might have ran-somed him. But a guard was only as valuable as the secrets he carried.

Ranka inched forward, careful to keep her steps light, her heart pounding harder. She wanted nothing more than to give Galen space and time—but time was something they didn't have. "I'm sorry for your loss, Galen."

Silence.

"I know you love him," Ranka said gently. "I know you're terri-fied."

Galen's fingers curled into fists.

"But Foldrey wouldn't want us sitting here. Not with winalin tear-ing the city apart and the Hands growing bolder."

The prince's nostrils flared. "You don't *know* what he would want. You don't *know* him. You don't know any of us."

"I know soldiers. I know he wouldn't want you to dwell."

"Ranka, could you *please* just—"

"So if you won't talk . . ." Ranka inched closer. Her heart began to pound. "You'll train."

Galen twisted to look at her. "Pardon?"

This was either going to work or end very, very poorly.

"Lesson number one," said Ranka. "Never drop your guard."

Ranka put her hand on Galen's back—and shoved him over the cliff.

He vanished immediately, his scream swallowed by the wind. Ranka peered over the edge. Galen flipped in the air as he plummeted, flailing like a broken doll as the sea churned below, his face the picture of pure shock as he looked up at her. For a brief, terrible moment, she wondered if she'd made a horrible mistake. Just because he had wind magic didn't mean he'd be able to *fly*.

Galen howled something as he plummeted toward the sea—and then wind roared around him, launching him skyward.

Galen landed on his toes, lighter than a cat, eyes popping out of his head as he shouted, *"Did you just push me off a cliff?!"*

Ranka raised an eyebrow. "That was impressive. Have you done that before?"

"Have you lost your *mind*?" Galen shrieked. "You nearly killed me!"

"Talk to me."

"I don't want to talk to you!"

"Talk to Percy."

"Percy's *annoying*—"

"Talk to your sister."

"I don't want to talk to *anyone*!"

"Good." Her entire body jittered, bouncing under an anger that was weeks—*years*—building. Here was a boy with a kingdom at his

fingertips and a power that rivaled her own, afforded the luxury of ignoring them both in a way she could never dream. But war was coming; blood had been spilled. More would before this was all over.

It was time for Galen Sunra to grow up.

"You don't want to talk? Don't talk," Ranka said. "Fight back."

Dust swirled around Galen's ankles and wrists. The sea churned, disturbed by the gale-force winds that Galen had summoned from nothing. "Did you hit your head in that alley?"

"You're angry," Ranka said. "And you're scared of that anger. That rage you're feeling? The yawning pit of it? The jittering hopelessness? That need to lie down and do nothing—and burn down the world in the same breath, if only so it'll stop spinning? I understand more than anyone, Galen. So if you don't want to talk, don't talk. *Fight back.*"

Galen stared at her, and Ranka caught a glimpse of the boy she'd seen in the alley—the prince who could summon winds so powerful they toppled buildings, the heir who'd left behind the guard he loved to save his sister. There was understanding there, and grief, but there was also anger, the kind of anger boys like Galen spent their entire lives being told they weren't allowed to have.

It was that anger Ranka wanted to meet. "Come on, princeling."

Overhead, the skies began to darken.

"Come on, princeling," Ranka goaded. "For once in your life— fight back."

The prince's lips thinned. "I'll hurt you."

Ranka locked eyes with Galen and crooked a finger. "You can try."

The temperature dropped.

Tentatively, Galen raised his hands.

Wind whipped her skin so harshly, it hurt.

"Come on," Ranka shouted. "Your parents are gone, you're being forced into a crown you don't want, Foldrey is dead and you left him behind—what are you going to *do* about it?"

A blast of wind hit Ranka full on. It flipped her up, and she landed on her stomach, smacking her face against the hard-packed ground. The sky swelled to a deep, bruised gray. The moisture in the air clung to her skin.

"Say it, princeling," Ranka goaded. "Say you think this is my fault. Say you blame me for everything that's gone wrong in your life."

Blood dripped from Galen's nose. "That's not—"

"You hate me." Ranka picked herself up, blood running down her chin, and shoved him backward. *"Say it."*

Skybreakers were the nightmare of every witch, a weapon in their own right for the hurricanes they called. She should have wanted Galen to remain weak, celebrated him remaining afraid. And yet she wanted this . . . this *boy*, this soft-eyed, gentle boy, to reach for that power and protect himself, because while the idea of another Skybreaker terrified her in theory, the memory of Galen alone and defenseless in that alley terrified her for real. Her worry for him was a betrayal, her feelings a mockery of everything the Skra stood for. She should have just let him and that infuriating sister of his die—but she couldn't, she wouldn't, and she hated herself for it.

Galen backed away from her.

"I am the monster you fear becoming," Ranka accused, not knowing where her anger with Galen began and her fury at herself for caring about him at all ended. "I am your worst nightmare. I am everything you hate about yourself. You loathe me, and you want me dead, because all of this—every life lost, every witch burned—started when I got here, and it's my fault. You hate me because you know in another life you'd have turned out just like me. And more than anything, you hate me because you believe, down in your bones, it's my fault Foldrey is dead. *Say it.*"

Galen faltered and drew back. "No."

"Whose fault is it, then?"

"No one's."

"Who do you blame, Galen?" Wind lashed at her face, tearing at not-yet-healed wounds. "Percy?"

"No!"

"Aramis?"

"Of course not!"

Thunder clapped. "Then who?"

"I blame myself!" Power arced through him, crackling across his skin, illuminating his earth-colored eyes—and then lightning lit up the world.

It sliced through the heavens, veining through swollen rain clouds in brilliant arcs of purple, blue, and white. A bolt shot down near them and slammed into a tree, sending it up in a whoosh of flame. Clouds roiled above. It was so dark, it could have been night. Thunder exploded again, so loud it shook Ranka's bones, and still the storm built, spurred on by the grief of a prince.

Galen's hands trembled as he stared skyward with pure, unbridled awe. The clouds swelled darker, choking out the sun, casting the world in shadow. The sea frothed as the winds strengthened, churning the waves into a mass of writhing black water and whitecaps. In the bay, sailors scrambled to furl sails, to pull their boats back to dock. An entire city held its breath, watching as a hurricane brewed above it.

"Can you feel it?" Ranka said softly. "That power? So strong it aches?"

Tears welled in Galen's eyes. Lightning sparked over his fingers. "Yes."

"Are you scared?"

"Terrified," he whispered.

"Good," she said. "Now take it."

A tremor rippled through him. Galen raised his hands. The storm built. The trees groaned, their fronds tearing as the wind picked up speed. Galen's eyes widened as he stood there, palms to the sky, his entire body shaking under a terrible weight only he could feel. She wondered if he was recalling the storms his father had summoned, if he saw his father's pale face wreathed in the roiling heavens alongside the ones he'd killed and the ones he'd saved, or if it was only Galen's future he saw twisting above him—brilliant, powerful, and his to command. Lightning flashed again, snaking through the ever-darkening clouds, followed by a boom of thunder so close it made her ears ring. Galen's fingers shook as he reached for a sky that was his to break. His eyelids fluttered as his lips moved in prayer.

You have the whole sky in you, Galen.

His eyes flew open.

Use it.

Galen slammed his hands down.

And finally, after seven months of drought, the skies opened up over Isodal and poured.

33

THE RAIN POURED SO HARD, IT STUNG. RANKA STOOD there, immobile, witnessing a miracle and history wrapped in one. Rainwater plastered her hair to her forehead and her cheeks, slicking her clothes to her body. Lightning danced freely overhead, painting the world in flashes of raw energy, as if the skies were eager to make up for all the years Galen had held his power at bay. After a few minutes his legs began to tremble. When he could no longer stand, Ranka caught him, and together they sat.

For a long time they were silent. Ranka wanted to tell Galen she was proud of him. She wanted to tell him this was only the beginning. She wanted to tell him she understood.

Instead, she took his hand. "It's not your fault."

His mouth trembled.

"Foldrey made a choice to protect you because he loved you. When you love someone like that, you don't think. You act."

"I loved him, too. But I never told him."

"He knew."

"It's not the same." Water beaded on his eyelashes. "It's not enough."

The rain kept pouring. Ranka's fingers pruned, and gooseflesh rose on her skin. The trees groaned around them, bending under the force of the downpour. Far below, seabirds whirled around the cliffs, screaming their delight.

"I never wanted this," Galen whispered. He flexed his fingers again. A breeze slipped around them, playful and light, summoned by only a twist of Galen's hands. "I still don't want it—why can't they see that? Why can't anyone?"

She had no answers for him; she'd long wondered the same.

"My father was a good king," Galen said quietly. "People loved him, but they feared him too. The first time Father demonstrated storm magic, I was so excited, so ready to learn. I wanted to make him proud. He took me to a farming village—just this tiny little patch of a town, really. They'd been refusing to pay their taxes." The wind howled. "So he picked three village leaders and drowned them. And his advisors—they just stood there. They let it happen."

Ranka flexed her scarred fingers. Droplets rolled down them, pooling in her palm.

"Leaders make hard choices." How many had Ongrum hurt to secure the Skra's freedom? How many more would she? "They carry that burden so their people don't have to."

"I don't want it," Galen whispered. "None of them get it. They all just tried to talk sense into me. Father, Mother, even Aramis and Foldrey. They tried to explain the reasoning, as if I were too stupid to understand that if you let one village out of paying, the rest would follow suit. People would starve. I *know* that." Galen's mouth trembled. "But I don't want to drown people. I don't want to smash ships or call hurricanes down on witches. I don't want to rule at all. I never—I never asked for this. For any of it." His voice was so, so small. "I can't be what they need me to be. I tried, Ranka. But I can't."

Ranka's heart ached for him. They were so different—the boy groomed for his magic, the girl whose power erupted out of her. Galen had spent his entire life shying away from violence, tempering the magic in his veins, knowing the weapon they'd forge him into lest he set his power free. But Ranka had been reborn amid fire and blood. She was ruled by the death in her veins, had accepted her role of monster long ago.

She'd never been given a choice. Not really. But Galen—Galen had one yet.

"Then don't."

His laugh was humorless. "It's not that simple."

"Isn't it? If you don't want to be what they need—don't. No one forces us to wield our power, Galen. So use yours to water fields instead of drowning the villages that depend on them. Everyone will tell you otherwise, but the world needs people like you."

"And what am I, exactly?"

"Kind. *Good.*" She squeezed his shoulder. "You have a gentle heart, Galen. Protect it. *Use* it."

"Gentle hearts make dead kings."

"I think your sister more than makes up for the terrifying-ruler angle."

"That was their biggest mistake—taking the crown from her." He squinted out at the sea. "Sometimes I wish I'd had more time with them—my parents. To ask them what they were thinking. To ask if keeping with tradition was worth it, knowing they were forcing both of us into roles we didn't want."

"We really are a miserable pair," Ranka said wryly. "The gentle king and his monstrous witch queen."

Galen's eyes went to her hand. Ranka braced herself for what always came next—the nonsense reassurances she wasn't a monster, she could be a hero, she could be *good.* They were all lies. No one who'd done the things she'd done was good. Ongrum may have been cruel, but at least she was honest about what Ranka was.

"If we need gentle kings," Galen said softly, "then we need monsters, too."

Ranka looked up at him.

"My father was a beloved ruler—and a monster. I have monsters in my navy, my military, the mage academy." The prince drummed his fingers on his knee, and the storm shifted with a subtle stir of the winds. "When the heroes come back in death wagons, who do people look to? A peaceful king? A benevolent priestess?" He looked at her. "They look to the monsters. They look for someone who knows how to win."

A chill rolled over her. "Someone who can bear it."

"That's what I can't do—and what you can. Bear it. Though I wish you didn't have to either."

Ranka watched the waves, and finally she asked the question she'd wondered since the day they met. "If you had it your way, Galen—if you could give up the crown—would you?"

"Yes," Galen said instantly, softly, with every bit of conviction in the world, as though he'd been waiting a lifetime for someone to ask and she'd been the first. And maybe she was. "If you're asking me if I could step down—if I could give it to Aramis—I would, a thousand times over." He paused, his attention on her. "Would you?"

Ranka turned her hand over, her coal-black nails flashing in the murky lighting, and knew he wasn't asking her about crowns. He had seen the truth of her in that alley. They all had.

"I . . . don't know," Ranka admitted. "There are days I'm so desperate to be free of it. I think I'd *like* to be someone who would always say yes. But I—I don't know who I am without this magic. I don't know what I am if I'm not a blood-witch." It sounded pathetic even to her. Her blood-magic had ruined her life, but it had also made her valuable. It'd made Ongrum believe in her, had given the Skra an edge. And it had helped her protect the twins, in the end.

"My mother felt the same."

She looked at him, surprised.

"I never knew her the way Aramis did—the two of them were always a pair, always testing Mother's magic, always studying. Mother was obsessed; Aramis inherited that obsession, even though she didn't inherit the blood-magic." A crinkle appeared between his brows.

"Mother so desperately wanted to cure it, but I think it terrified her too. Being a blood-witch was all she was. It was why people loved her—and why they hated her. She didn't know who she'd be outside of that power."

It was comforting, in an odd, twisted way. "I wish I could have met her."

"Me too." He smiled. "She wouldn't have liked you."

"Wow. Thanks."

"You're welcome." He nudged her. "Hey, who knows? Maybe we'll both get what we want—I'll escape the crown, and Aramis will somehow make your magic disappear. And if not? I'll be the gentle king, and you'll be the monster that keeps me from getting assassinated."

Her heart ached. It was a beautiful world he was offering her—a world where someone like her, who'd done the things she had, had a place. A purpose. It didn't sound possible.

But what if it could be?

Her heart began to pick up speed, beat by treacherous beat. Galen was still talking—about his father, who used to call rainstorms in the middle of the day because the rainbows would make Aramis squeal; about his mother, who always insisted on rescuing the stray cats that managed to slip beyond the palace walls. Ranka's mind spun around his earlier words.

I'll be the gentle king, and you'll be the monster.

That was it.

All this time she'd been torn—the twins or the Skra, Isodal or Witchik. But what if she didn't have to choose? What if she could have both? The entire coup was predicated on the idea that Galen Sunra was a cruel, selfish prince who sought to punish Witchik. But Foldrey had been right—Galen had a rare heart, a gentle heart, one that promised a future she'd never dared dream of.

What if there was another way?

All Ongrum wanted was Witchik's freedom. They'd thought the only way to achieve that was with Galen's death—but Galen had no interest in war. The Skra didn't have to murder him to bring justice to Witchik; they could work with him.

They could create peace—real, *lasting* peace.

And they'd start by curing winalin.

Treacherous hope bloomed. Ongrum would be furious at first—but she was a warrior, versed in strategy, trained to minimize casualties. She would come around. Ranka would convince her. She had to.

"I'm going to be a terrible husband, you know," Galen said, bumping his shoulder against hers. "And that's going to be weird, right? Us? *Married?*"

"Ah," Ranka said, suddenly wildly uncomfortable. "Yes. It's going to be very weird."

"About that. I, uh . . . I have to tell you something."

Her heart quickened. *Don't,* she willed. He'd said once he wanted to be her friend—and they were becoming that, she thought. *Don't ruin it.*

"If we marry, I don't want to do . . . uh . . . married-people . . . things." Galen tripped over his words. It was plain he'd never been more mortified by something in his life. "I'm really sorry, I think you're great, but I don't really like girls and—"

Ranka burst out laughing. "Oh, thank the Goddess. I would sooner die."

"Hey." He wilted. "I'm relieved you're relieved."

Ranka patted his hand affectionately. "Don't worry, Galen. I would actually rather fling myself off the cliff than kiss you."

He rolled his eyes and shoved her. Warmth spread through her. This was the first time Galen had seemed like himself since the attack. She poked him in the ribs, eager to keep his mind off anything remotely related to Foldrey. "Does Aramis know?"

"We've talked about it. When they took the crown from her, the first thing she said was at least now she could just be happy and find a wife who wouldn't drive her nuts."

Ranka went still. *A wife?* She had wondered, of course. Had been curious. But it was different to hear Galen confirm it so casually. As though wanting a wife was something Aramis talked about regularly.

She'd certainly never mentioned it to Ranka.

And why would she? the sane part of her demanded. *You've both been a little busy.*

Still. It was . . . interesting. Not that it had any bearing on her. Or impacted her in any way. She was just intrigued. That was all. It was simply new information about the princess that had absolutely nothing to do with Ranka.

A wife.

Galen gave her a curious look. "Did *you* know?"

"I had a hunch. I'm sure Percy will be quite happy when you tell him."

"Percy?" he squeaked. "What does that—I'm not—"

"I didn't say anything, princeling." She grinned, and couldn't help herself. "He is handsome, though. In his own irritating way."

Galen stared at her, his mouth closing and opening as the mortified light in his eyes grew brighter. "I will push you off this cliff."

Ranka grinned. They lapsed into an easy, amicable silence, and though the rains kept coming, they were gentler now, falling in slow, warm waves. From the city, whoops could be heard in the streets, mingling with the wild laughter of a people relieved to have a break in the drought at last. Even the grass seemed brighter. All of Isodal was waking up, as if the surge of Galen's magic had reminded the land of something old and alive.

Ranka elbowed him. "My fingers are pruning. Let's go inside."

Water dripped off his nose, his eyelashes, his chin. He cast her a wary look. "If you say *anything* to Percy—"

"Oh, for the love of—it was a *joke*." She paused. "I'd like to be invited to the wedding, though. I'm very fun at parties."

"Ranka!"

She laughed, and he elbowed her, which only made her laugh harder. They made their way back to the palace, teeth chattering in the downpour, Ranka poking fun at Galen, Galen becoming more and more wound up as she teased him. It was nice to see him like this— flustered and smiling, a flicker of his old self returning. To see him finally breathe easy, a boy in love laughing in the rain, momentarily freed from the weight of a country on his shoulders.

A wave of dread dampened her ease. Because in five days, if Ranka couldn't convince Ongrum that the right course of action was mercy, not murder, Galen Sunra would cease to breathe at all.

34

ARAMIS WAS HIDING SOMETHING.

At first Ranka thought she was being paranoid, but as they moved through their lessons, it was plain the princess was distracted and on edge. But when questioned, Aramis shut her down. It was beginning to irritate Ranka. Something had shifted between them after Foldrey's death. There was a new understanding that even though she and Aramis could still hardly stand each other, they were a team.

Or so she'd thought.

Now Ranka hid in the stables, waiting for Aramis to show. Something moved in the rafters, but it was only a barn owl, its eyes gleaming like twin coins.

Maybe I'm being foolish.

Ranka was about to leave when footsteps echoed ahead and Aramis stepped inside. She glanced around and threw her shoulder against the hay bale concealing the hatch to the mines.

Ranka stepped out of the shadows. "Going somewhere?"

"*Agh!*" The princess threw her hands up and toppled backward. Aramis glared up at her and put a hand to her heart. "What are you *doing* here? You nearly gave me a heart attack!"

"What are *you* doing here?" Ranka shot back.

Aramis scowled at her, and Ranka offered her a hand.

The princess hesitated. She took it, her touch surprisingly cool, and jumped lightly to her feet. The owl in the rafters hooted, and Aramis flinched and dropped Ranka's hand as if it'd burned her. "I have my own business in the city."

"You're going *alone*?"

Aramis lifted her chin, her eyes glinting with a stubborn light. "Yes."

"Princess," Ranka said slowly, "have you absolutely lost your mind?"

One of the horses pawed at the floor and turned in its stall. Aramis folded her arms and tried to make herself look taller than her measly five feet. "I'll be fine. And obviously *you* were plotting something, since you were sneaking around too. So let's pretend this never happened. I'll go my way and you'll go yours. I don't see the issue here."

The issue is that you'll get yourself killed. A prickling heat swept through Ranka.

"Princess. You saw what those witches are like—five of us were barely enough against two. You need someone to protect y—"

Aramis rolled her eyes and pulled out one of the strangest weapons Ranka had ever seen.

It was a small board the length of Aramis's hand, fitted with thick leather straps and a firing mechanism—a tiny nock for a dart, elastic bands to fire it, a clamp to hold the dart, and a string. Like a miniature of the crossbows the Murknen favored, but without the arms. The princess buckled it to the inside of her wrist, loaded a slender, hollow dart, and looped the string around her index and her ring fingers.

"That's very cute, but I don't—"

Aramis pointed the weapon at Ranka, and flattened her hand.

Ranka threw herself to the floor just in time to avoid the dart shooting straight for her head. It slammed into the stable wall with a crack. Pale blue tranquilizer leaked down the boards, pooling on the floor.

"I know," Aramis said darkly, "how to protect myself."

Ranka pushed herself back to her feet, dusting the hay from her pants. "That would have been useful a few days ago."

"Foldrey had it made after what happened with you and Galen. I thought he was being paranoid." The princess's face crumpled, but only for a moment. She pushed her shoulders back and leveled that blistering glare that had become so familiar. "As you can see, witch, I'm perfectly capable of taking care of myself."

She brushed past Ranka with her head held high, but through the folds of her cloak, her shoulders trembled.

She needs this, Ranka realized. Aramis was the only one among them without a way to fight. She had no weapons, no power, no *training.* Even Galen, with his gentle heart, had a magic capable of toppling buildings. Even Galen had protected them in the end. *She needs this, and it's going to make her reckless.*

"Wait," Ranka blurted. "Let me come with you."

"You don't even know where I'm going."

"Does it matter? I don't want you in the city alone."

"Why do you care?"

Ranka's throat threatened to close. Why indeed? Even with her new, brilliant plan of trying to convince Ongrum to spare Galen's neck, she didn't need Aramis alive. Yet the thought of Aramis alone in the city, defenseless save for a too-small knife she'd never been taught how to wield and a tiny dart shooter she'd likely never practiced with, sent ice through Ranka's veins.

"What's the harm?" Ranka pressed. "We're a team now, right? That means we do this together."

"I'm not interested. Go back to moping in your room or whatever it is you do in your free time."

Ranka took a long, patient breath. Even after a near-death experience, Aramis Sunra was still genuinely one of the most irritating people she'd ever met. She'd hoped eventually they would simply get along, click together as allies, the way she had with Galen and Percy.

But it seemed they'd traded being outright enemies to getting on each other's nerves at every turn.

"Fine," Ranka snapped. "You want to do this the hard way? You either let me come with you, or I will *literally* carry your ass back inside and tell Galen exactly what his sister is up to."

Aramis's lip curled. "You wouldn't dare."

"You are very small," Ranka said. "And I am very strong."

"Honestly, this is so childish—"

"Fine. Have it your way."

Ranka stepped forward, picked the princess of Isodal up by her waist, and threw her over a shoulder like a cranky sack of potatoes.

"Ranka!" Aramis shrieked. *"Put me down!"*

Ranka didn't move. She stood there, holding the princess's legs firmly, face burning, heart beating harder than it had any right to. Aramis could whine all she wanted. Ranka was not going to let her die out of stubborn recklessness. Not after everything they'd been through. Aramis let loose a particularly interesting string of profanity and pounded a fist against Ranka's back, but it was no use. Even if they'd been the same size, a witch outmatched a human in strength any day—and Ranka had at least a foot of height and an extra fifty pounds of muscle on her.

"I'm coming with you," Ranka said flatly.

Aramis made a noise that could only be described as sheer rage.

"Screech all you want. You're not going by yourself."

"I don't care if you're the Bloodwinn," Aramis seethed. "I am *literally* going to have you strung up by your *toes* in the courtyard—"

"Uh-huh." Ranka started walking toward the stable doors. "Do you think Galen is in his room at this hour?"

"*Okay!* Okay, fine, you can come with me, just put me *down!*"

Ranka dropped her. Aramis toppled to the ground with a thump and leapt to her feet, looking more than a little ruffled. She smoothed her skirts and shot Ranka a look of horror. "Lights above, what do they *feed* you up north?"

Ranka bared her teeth. "Little girls who stray too far from home."

"Ha, ha. You've been spending too much time with Percy." A funny expression crossed her face as she looked Ranka up and down. "What are you, six feet of solid muscle?" She poked Ranka in the stomach, her brow furrowed, as if she expected her finger to crack against marble. She blinked, and poked her again. "Huh. You're squishy."

Ranka slapped Aramis's hand away. "Stop that."

"Well, at least if I get tired, I know you're here to carry me." The princess smirked.

Ranka's face burned. It *had* been terribly easy to lift her up. Ranka could probably carry Aramis for hours if she needed to. Not that she'd ever need to. Why was she even thinking about that? The stables were suddenly uncomfortably warm.

Ranka cleared her throat. "So I'm coming with you?"

"Yeah, yeah, teamwork, hooray," Aramis said in a resigned tone. She turned away. "Let's go, muscles."

"Don't call me that."

"Okay, grumpy."

"Grumpy?"

"Only every second of your life." Aramis swung herself down into the tunnels. Pale light flared as she activated a mage-light and wrapped the glowing beads around her fist. "Sometime tonight, witch!"

Ranka scrambled after her and yanked the hatch closed behind them with a bang, cursing herself for meddling at all. "Where are we going, exactly?"

Aramis trained her attention ahead, her earlier mirth hardening into grim resolve. "Percy found the base of the Hands of Solomei."

35

THE CITY HAD EVOLVED. THE PINS WERE EVERYWHERE, gleaming like a warning, and posters decrying the Sunra twins now flapped alongside the ones claiming Ranka was a monster. Aramis and Ranka exited the tunnels at a tiny fishing port in the western quarter of the city, navigating through winding streets, sidestepping puddles of stagnant water choked with sickly green algae blooms. The deeper they walked, the more gold they saw.

Aramis kept her head high. It wasn't until they turned a corner that her hands started to shake.

A three-story tavern glowed ahead. Six windows winked at them from old wood frames. Thick black paint streaked across the glass, creating a veil between the tavern and the world. The reek of humans came from inside, but there was a wrongness to the air, too.

A guard stood at the door. When someone approached, the guard held up a light. "Hands."

The hair on Ranka's arms stood on end.

The newcomer obliged. The guard held their hands up to the torchlight, turning them this way and that, inspecting their nails. Apparently satisfied, the guard clapped the newcomer on the shoulder and let them inside. The door swung shut, and again that sense of wrongness wafted forward, swirling around Ranka.

She rocked back on her heels. "Something is off with this place."

More humans approached, holding their hands up for inspection, many already proudly wearing gold pins on their chests. Seaswept grew quieter, but the tavern swelled. Ranka and Aramis waited in the alley, knees aching against the wet stones. Light and laughter spilled into the street each time the door opened, but so did that uncomfortable reek, a hint that within the tavern walls, something sinister brewed.

"We need to get inside," Aramis murmured.

"Not dressed like this we aren't." Everyone entering was dressed in gray. She'd thought it was a coincidence until a man approached dressed in orange, threw his hands up, exclaimed he'd forgotten the day, and returned later in gray clothing to be admitted. Smart, to have a code. Also incredibly inconvenient.

Aramis peered through the dark. "We'll have to borrow someone else's clothes."

A man and a woman stumbled out of the tavern, badges gleaming on their chests. They stunk of ale even from across the street, and they moved sluggishly, arms thrown around each other, giggling like teenagers.

Aramis nudged Ranka in the ribs. "Well? You're the muscle, right? Go, uh, be muscly."

Ranka scowled and swatted her hand away. "I hate you."

Aramis beamed. "I know."

Ranka's heart did an odd little flip, and she rose, backtracking around the building through the dark. Giggles rolled toward her. She turned the corner, one hand on her axe, but there was no need. The couple could barely stand, and they'd made her life easier by already beginning to undress each other.

Ranka leaned against the wall. "Hi."

They spun, blinking against the dark.

"I need your clothes. Seems like you don't want them anyway. If we do this the easy way, you'll save yourself a headache."

The man was still holding a mug. Its contents spilled over the lip of the container and dripped to the street, gathering in an amber puddle on the stones. He took an unsteady step forward and gave Ranka the finger. "Piss off."

It always had to be the hard way.

Thirty seconds later, both humans were stripped down to their underthings and stowed against the alley wall—unconscious, but otherwise unharmed. Ranka changed quickly into the man's clothes, rolling her shoulders against the fabric that was too tight against her shoulders. She doubled back to meet Aramis. The princess eyed Ranka and grinned.

Heat rushed to Ranka's cheeks. "What?"

"Nothing," she snorted. She held out a hand for the other set of clothes. "Don't look."

Ranka turned away. Fabric rustled behind her. When she turned, Aramis was dressed in the woman's shirt and breeches, dark curls pulled away from her face and stowed beneath the collar of her shirt. It was surprising to see her in something other than the loose, free flowing dresses she loved. In dark, form fitting clothes, she looked a different kind of dangerous. They fit her a little too well.

Aramis pulled at the leg of the breeches. "How do I look?"

"Like a drunk peasant," Ranka lied.

"So a Skra, then?"

"I think you're the one spending too much time with Percy."

Aramis's face lit up with a grin, and there came that odd little flip of Ranka's heart again. Was she ill or something?

Someone roared with laughter within the tavern. Ranka turned, narrowing her focus on the guard posted outside. She inhaled, sorting through rot, sewage, and hatred festering in the air. Dread built in her chest, a weight Ranka could barely breathe around, lining her lungs and filling her veins with lead.

Something is coming, the mist writhing in the streets sang. *And it's coming for* you.

"We need to find a way around him," Aramis murmured.

Ranka raised an eyebrow at her, straightened, and crossed the street at a stroll. The guard stiffened as she approached, his hand flicking to the instant-click torch at his hip. It took everything in her not to draw her weapon. She moved languidly, counting on the reek of ale coming off him. "Evening."

"Hands," the guard intoned.

"Right, of course." She drew closer and lifted her hands. The guard waved his torch over them. His eyes bugged. He looked up at Ranka—and she wrapped an arm around his throat.

"Good night," she murmured, tightening her grip until he could utter no more than a squeak, her other hand firmly clapped over his mouth and nose. He thrashed for a few minutes and went limp. She dragged him behind the tavern, stowed him against the wall, and tied his legs together with his bootlaces for good measure. He'd wake up with a headache and little more.

Aramis stared at her from across the street. "That was . . . aggressive."

"You told me to be the muscle. I'm being the muscle."

"Fair enough." Her eyes darted to the tavern door. "Ready?"

"If I say no, do we get to go home?"

Aramis smiled. "Nope."

They linked arms and stepped inside.

36

HEAT, LIGHT, AND LAUGHTER HIT RANKA, MINGLED with the reek of sweat and ale. There were two levels to the tavern, and the main floor was so packed there was barely room to move. Humans milled everywhere, dancing under soft white mage-light, gold pins flashing as they twirled. A few guards bearing instant-click torches wove through the crowd, separating drunks and inspecting people at random. If they checked Ranka's hands, she was dead.

Her eyes swept the crowd. Most of the recruits here were terribly drunk, but at the far end of the tavern stood four armed Hands, stone faced and frowning, fanned out in front of a hallway. *Guards.* There it was again—that reek.

Ranka tugged on Aramis's sleeve and nodded at the guards. "Something's back there."

The princess's dark eyes darted over the throng of twisting bodies, to the second floor and the closed doors leaking light under their frames. "Those rooms are positioned over the back hallway."

If they got up there, they might be able to listen. But first they'd have to weave through a crowd of witch-burners who would know what Ranka was the moment they saw her hands.

Aramis crooked her arm through Ranka's. "Dance with me."

"I'm sorry," said Ranka. "We're in a room filled with zealots who want to set me on fire. And you want to *dance*?"

"The drunk people are all dancing," Aramis said slowly, as though Ranka was particularly dull. "So, yes, I want you to *dance*. For all those muscles of yours, it seems you never bother to exercise your *brain*. Just follow my lead, okay?"

Before Ranka could argue, Aramis wrapped her arms around Ranka's waist and slumped against her, the very picture of a girl who'd had too much to drink. When Ranka didn't budge, Aramis grumbled something about having to do everything herself, took Ranka's hands, and slid them just under the hem of her shirt. Nerves fluttered through Ranka. Aramis was warm to the touch, her skin softer than she'd expected. It was to protect her, she knew—to an onlooker, they were just another pair moving amid the heat, and now her nails were concealed. But Ranka was so dizzy, she could hardly think.

"Quit stepping on my feet," Aramis muttered.

"Quit stepping on *mine*."

They danced at a languid pace, keeping distance between them and the armed Hands scattered throughout the crowd, Ranka's head bowed, Aramis's resting on her shoulder. It was all Ranka could do to keep up, her head swimming as Aramis guided her across the room, their pace languid and easy. They reached the stairs, but instead of breaking away from Ranka, Aramis hooked her arm through Ranka's and shoved Ranka's free hand into her pocket. Heat flooded Ranka's cheeks.

"Come on," Aramis muttered, tugging Ranka after her.

They reached the second level. The crowd was thinner up here, and far drunker, with most of the pairs sequestered in dark corners. All the rooms were occupied except for one. Ranka nodded toward it, and Aramis led them forward. They ought to be able to listen in to whatever was going on in the back room—if not find a way to spy through the rafters. They moved slowly, passing the first two rooms, weaving between drunken couples.

"Sorry," a voice behind them said. "Hand check."

Ranka froze in her tracks. Behind them, the guard waved a mage-light over the hands of a couple.

"Ranka," Aramis said, tugging her forward. "Come on."

Ranka couldn't move.

"Hand check." The guard was ten feet behind them now.

They'll burn me.

She needed to move—but suddenly she was back in Belren, watching as villagers brought forth ropes and matches, smoke burning her throat and a familiar scream ringing in her ears.

They'll burn me alive.

"Hand check." Five feet.

"Useless witch," Aramis breathed.

Aramis shoved Ranka against the wall. She slipped Ranka's hands under her shirt again and wound her arms around Ranka's neck, pulling her down so their lips hovered only a hair's breadth apart, her movements confident and quick, as though she'd done this before. The princess held her there in the mimickry of a lover's embrace, every line of her body taut with tension, her pupils dark with something Ranka was too scared to name.

Ranka had never been so conscious of someone's skin against hers in her life. Her heart beat so loudly it hurt. Aramis's fingers brushed her jaw, cradling Ranka's face in her palm.

"Hey," Aramis whispered. "Look at me, Ranka. Do you trust me?"

"Yes," Ranka croaked. Her legs wobbled.

"I won't let them hurt you, okay? Follow my lead."

The guard stopped beside them. "Sorry, lovebirds. Let me see your hands."

Aramis pushed herself up onto her toes and pressed her lips to Ranka's.

And Ranka froze.

Aramis's hands cradled Ranka's face, thumb trailing the line of Ranka's jaw, not an ounce of demand in her touch. Ranka's heart pounded so hard it hurt, but Aramis didn't push further, nor did she pull away. She just waited, every part of her shielding Ranka from the guard, from the humans below who would surely burn her if they knew who or what she was.

I won't let them hurt you.

Ranka's panic thawed. Aramis would not force her, would not judge her. Even now, their lips pressed against each other's, both girls unmoving, Aramis was giving her more understanding than Ranka had gotten from any of the girls before her.

Safe, she realized. *What I am—who I am—is safe with her.*

Ranka pulled Aramis against her, and kissed her for real.

Heat and light, touch and breath, give and take. It felt like eternity and only a moment all at once. Everything else fell away—the pressure of the Skra, the confines of the Bloodwinn treaty, the weight she'd long carried, knowing she'd have to marry someone she could never want.

She was just Ranka. Just one witch, and she was enough.

How many nights had she been infuriated by just the presence of this girl, by the gleam in her eyes, the lovely curve of her face, the powerful way she carried herself? How much hatred had come pulsing alongside this maddening tangle of desire that made her want to forget about her frustrations and know every inch of her instead? It had always been there, and it had made all of this so much harder—because even when Ranka had hated Aramis, she'd respected her more than she cared to admit. Had known Aramis respected her in return. They had seen a challenge in each other, a strength to be admired, a sharpness to be feared, and it had drawn them both in, like two opposing storms, destined to collide.

Aramis's hands slid down Ranka's neck and knotted in her hair. Her lips were eager, wanting, and it made Ranka's legs buckle, the way Aramis pulled her closer, the way the curves of their hips fitted so neatly together. The princess pushed her harder against the wall, their bodies molding against each other, hands and mouths exploring and seeking with an urgency, as if they were making up for lost time. Aramis kissed her, and Ranka kissed her back, and in that moment nothing else mattered.

Behind them, someone cleared their throat.

Aramis broke away. Her pupils were blown wide with desire, her lips swollen, and she looked at the guard, plainly struggling to catch her breath. Ranka couldn't help herself—she leaned down and pressed her lips to Aramis's collarbone. *Just to convince the guard,* she told herself, her hands sliding over the smooth skin of the princess's ribs. She kissed a trail down Aramis's neck and tried not to notice the way the princess's fingernails dug into her shoulders.

Aramis shuddered, and a small gasp left her.

"Hormones," the guard snorted, but he was smiling. "Oh, fine. I remember that age. I'll give you ten minutes."

"Make it fifteen," Ranka mumbled. Before she could lose her nerve, she tightened her grip on Aramis's waist and kissed her again. The guard chuckled and moved away. Aramis made a noise in her throat, and reluctantly, they broke apart, her hands still on Ranka's shoulders, Ranka's hands still gripping the bare skin of her hips. They untangled, and Aramis half staggered backward, and Ranka's skin was cold where Aramis had been touching her before.

"I'm sorry," Ranka blurted. "If it was too much, I didn't know if—"

"Don't apologize. It was my idea, and we did need to be . . . convincing." She paused, and a tiny smile flitted across her lips as she looked pointedly at the floor and tucked a curl behind her ear. "And it was hardly torture."

"I've been tortured before," Ranka confirmed uselessly. "That was not it."

Aramis grinned.

Heat rushed to Ranka's face. Why was she always saying the stupidest things to this girl?

Aramis cleared her throat several times and jerked her head to the empty room. "We can torture each other some more later. Let's go."

More? Later? Ranka tried to ignore the way her knees went weak, and followed her.

They cut through the second floor quickly. Ranka tried to focus on the task at hand instead of the wobbly feeling in her limbs. They'd spy on the Hands, she'd take Aramis home immediately after, and then she would plunge herself directly into the freezing sea. She chanted the plan in her head over and over again, and tried not to think about the softness of Aramis's lips, the pleasant burn of her fingernails digging into Ranka's shoulders.

How eager Aramis had been to kiss her. As though she meant it.

As though she'd been waiting for a chance.

"Door's locked," Aramis muttered. She dropped to her knees, pulled a pin from her hair, and twisted it into the handle with practiced ease. After a few seconds, a faint click came from the lock, and the door swung open.

"Since when do princesses pick locks?"

"Galen and I were dreadful children." She locked the door behind them. It was a cramped room, consisting of little more than a straw bed and a side table—but the boards below it glowed with light. Aramis dropped to her knees and pressed an eye to a gap in the floorboards. When she raised her head, her face was haggard.

"What?" Ranka whispered. "What is it?"

The princess gestured wordlessly, and Ranka stretched out on her stomach beside her.

The back room was below them. It was small, lit only by a fireplace and a few stray mage-lights. Twelve humans stood in the room, all armed with short swords and instant-click torches.

There was a single table, and on it lay five syringes, all of them filled with a dull gray substance. The warmth drained from Ranka's body. Even from the second floor she could smell it. It'd been in Seaswept since she first entered, had followed her into her nightmares, had lived in the veins of Yeva, Talis, and so many others.

Ranka didn't realize she was trembling until Aramis put a hand over hers.

The Hands were in possession of winalin.

How had they even *acquired* it? Before, winalin had been a curse from the Star Isles they chased through the dark, a runaway plague popping up without rhyme or reason. It had been *why* the Hands were growing so volatile.

But if the Hands had it . . .

"All right," one of the women said. The excitement in her voice made Ranka sick. "This strain is stronger, thanks to the latest samples from our friend. We should be ready for mass distribution soon."

"Will it be enough?" one asked. "The covens will be here in less than a week."

"If it's not, we'll still take out a chunk of them. Something will stick eventually. Even the most careful survivors won't last long once we begin releasing the sick ones into the Northlands again."

And horribly, finally, after so many weeks of chasing winalin and staring at the bodies of dead witches and wondering, it all clicked.

The Hands had acquired winalin—but instead of perfecting it to make blood-witches, they were using the fatal strain to kill them on purpose.

It was brilliant, in the most horrifying sense possible. The Hands had masked their hatred in the language of zealotry. Whether all of them *believed* didn't matter, not when they all had the same end goal in mind: drive the witches from Isodal—or wipe them out entirely.

That first witch. The one who had staggered so far north with a pin in her hand only to die—she'd been no accident. She'd been a test, to see if the plague she carried would catch. And then had come the leaflets about the prince, about Ranka, the rumors festering in the streets, the speeches and terror. Winalin hadn't cropped up here by accident. Of course it had to start in Seaswept, where the treaty had been born. What better way to ensure humans turned against witches than set self-destructing monsters loose among the political seat of their nation? What better way to turn them against the Bloodwinn and the treaty itself, to motivate them to take up arms? No witch would be tolerated; even the weakest of them would be a threat to any human who had lost loved ones to plague-ridden monsters.

All along they'd been chasing a cure. They'd feared someone else had sought to create blood-witches, had been comforted, in a twisted way, that someone hadn't come close. Now, as Ranka stared at the syringes on the table, terror settled in her bones. Because this was more than she, Ongrum, or any of the covens had bargained for. This was more than she could handle.

From the poison, comes the cure.

The Star Isles had sought to turn witches into weapons.

Now the Hands would wipe them out entirely.

37

"ALL RIGHT," ONE OF THE HANDS SAID. "BRING HER forward."

A witch was dragged into the room. Bruises marred her pale skin, and her dark hair had been shaved away. Kerth beads glinted in her ears.

"Our tests have gone well, but it's still hitting too fast." One of the Hands flashed two syringes in the air. "The first strain burned them out in days. We believe the second will last for weeks—long enough for them to do some serious damage."

The second witch came out fighting.

It took four Hands to pin her down, and still she fought back, screaming around her gag as they bound her. Black ink stamped her limbs, depicting whirling krakens and three-finned sea dragons. She was Oori, a seafaring coven that spent their lives navigating between the temperate Broken Sea and the harsher waters of the Trija Ocean cradling Witchik's eastern shores.

Beside Ranka, Aramis was as still as stone.

One of the women crossed the room with a predator's gait. She knelt in front of the Oori and removed her gag. "You'll make this easier on yourself if you behave."

"Monsters," the Oori spat. "When my people find you—"

"They're not coming for you. No one is." Determination gleamed in the woman's eyes, as bright as Ongrum's hatred, as deep as Ranka's fear. She grabbed a fistful of the Oori's dirty hair and jerked her head back.

No, no, please—

The Hand plunged the syringe into the Oori's neck.

The Kerth started to scream, her cries raw, broken, the scream of the mourning, the horrified cry of a witch who understood what was happening and knew it was coming for her.

The Oori's hand twitched.

Her pale gray nails darkened, like ink blossoming in deadly clouds through the nailbed. White swept over her eyes, swallowing her irises.

For a brief, beautiful moment the witch looked brilliant—all raw power and deadly magic swelling in her veins. She was the pride of every witch who had walked this earth. Witchik's history made flesh. The mirror image of the only version of herself Ranka had ever known.

Then, all at once, the blisters erupted.

They bubbled across the Oori's skin, broke free of major veins, coalescing into fist-sized, weeping cysts. Her head lolled. Her skin took on a sickly pallor. The witch decayed before Ranka's eyes, and her movements became jerking, animalistic.

"Solomei's light," Aramis whispered.

The Oori thrashed, muscles bulging, and there was a new kind of strength to her—the reckless, self-destructive power of a thing that knew no pain, no fear. Only hunger. Her skin tore and bled as she fought free of the bonds, her limbs flailing, whited-out eyes rolling. Foam frothed at the corners of her mouth.

The Kerth wept, cringing away from the newly afflicted witch.

The Hand looked back at the others. "If we set her loose, she'd drop dead in days. Useful for short-term damage—but not for winning a war." She bent down and slit the witch's throat. The Oori gurgled and slumped forward.

Bile rose in Ranka's throat.

Her entire life Ranka had faced danger head-on. She was always the strongest one in the room, the fastest, the deadliest. But the sight of winalin destroying that witch sent terror thrashing inside her, as if a thousand caged birds whirled in a panicked spiral in her heart, wings beating against her skin, talons scraping bone, all of them willing to tear her apart if it meant they could get out and *away*.

Because for the first time in her life, Ranka was not the predator.

She was the prey.

"At least it works faster now. That Skra bitch took forever to turn."

The colors vanished.

For the briefest flicker Ranka was home, standing on the frigid snows of the Northlands, bloody handprints on each cheek. The world had made more sense then. Vengeance was give and take, a constant exchange of blood, and her enemies almost always wore a human face.

A cool hand locked around Ranka's wrist. "Don't you dare."

"They killed my sisters," Ranka hissed. "My *family*."

Aramis grabbed her face with both hands and shook her. "Listen to me, witch girl. You don't get to be just a Skra anymore. You are the Bloodwinn, which means *all* the covens are yours to protect. I know you lost family, and I'm sorry, but they're gone. And that Kerth? She's your family now too. She's still alive. Honor them by saving *her*."

Ranka's throat bobbed, pain and rage and confusion tearing through her. The woman was so close. It'd be so easy—and it was what she had always done. If Ongrum were here, she'd have already slit the woman's jugular. "You don't understand."

"How *dare* you. I don't *understand*? You think I don't know how unfair it feels to be burdened with protecting them all? How the weight of it all makes it feel like every time you breathe, you suck in water instead of air?" Aramis's voice broke. "You think I don't want to go down there and kill her with my bare hands?"

Ranka had never seen her so furious before. Aramis's hands were trembling, yet in her was a glimpse of the queen she might have been—

steady and coolheaded when necessary, sharp minded and quick, with an iron will to keep her grounded. She was everything Galen was not. But there was no magic in her veins, and so they'd taken her crown all the same.

"You're a leader now, Ranka." Aramis's eyes blazed. "Start acting like it."

Even from a level above Ranka could scent the winalin in the syringe. She could scent the Kerth's fear, sweaty and sharp, with resentment burning under it. The princess kept her eyes on her, and what could Ranka say to this girl who had lost so many already? Who had every reason to turn her back on this broken, wretched country—and was risking everything to save it instead?

Ranka lifted her head.

"Tell me what I have to do."

38

WARM LIGHT SPILLED INTO THE ROOM, BUT IT DID nothing to chase the cold from Ranka's bones. The seconds ticked by in agony. The board Aramis had carefully pried loose lay beside her. The princess sat with a foot braced on either side of the new hole in the floor—and her loaded dart shooter pointed through it.

One of the Hands dragged the Kerth into an upright position.

Calm descended over Ranka like snow blanketing a field. She rose, cradling the instant-click torch Aramis had swiped from a half-drunk guard outside. The door behind her swayed on its hinges, bleeding light and laughter into the room.

The Hand uncapped the syringe.

The Kerth witch moaned out a prayer.

"Ranka," Aramis whispered. "Now."

Ranka lit the torch—and hurled it into the center of the inn.

For a breath the torch hung in the air, flames suspended in time, and then it dropped. It vanished into the crowd, swallowed by the press of bodies, winking out of sight like a single fallen star. Dread rose in Ranka.

Then someone shouted *fire*!

And flames overtook the room.

They spread from the floor to the walls, eagerly snapping up dry wood and spilled alcohol. Humans screamed, stampeding backward, and the Hands inside the back room turned toward the commotion.

Aramis fired.

The dart shot through the air—and slammed into the woman about to inject the Kerth.

She jerked, the syringe tipping in her hands. The Kerth's head swung up, nostrils flaring, and she headbutted the Hand in the stomach. The woman cried out, swung wildly, and dragged the needle across the back of the Kerth's leg.

"They got her," Ranka blurted. "*No*, they—"

Faces whipped toward her voice.

"Someone's up there!"

The Kerth staggered, her nails flickering from black to gray, black to gray, as if the winalin in her veins was at war with the witchery still ruling her body. She crashed her way through the Hands and out onto the main floor, reeling in the face of the flames and the humans who screamed at the sight of her before lurching sideways, staggering out a side door and into the street.

Ranka caught Aramis by the elbow. "We have to go."

"Find them!"

Ranka turned. The stairs were blocked. The Hands spilled onto the main floor, shouting and pointing. "Hold on."

Aramis's eyes widened. "What are you—"

Ranka hoisted Aramis onto her back, her injured muscles straining. "Don't let go."

She sprinted into the hallway right as one of the Hands crested the stairs. Aramis's arms tightened around her neck. Ranka skidded to a halt in front of a window. Behind her, someone shouted.

Ranka kicked through the window. The glass shattered, and she swung them out into the cool air of Seaswept, leaving the Hands of Solomei behind to burn.

39

THEY SEARCHED FOR TWO HOURS, BUT THEY NEVER found the Kerth. The trail of blood led them to the shore. Waves lapped against the rocks, black under the night sky, depths muddied from the downpour. Ranka searched everywhere, but the witch was gone. It was as though she'd walked right into the sea.

Now Ranka and Aramis headed back toward the palace in silence. Seaswept's murky blue night stretched between them in all its languid warmth, deceptively peaceful in the face of the horrors they'd just witnessed.

"Ranka," Aramis said finally, her voice breaking. "If they have winalin—if they mean to—"

"I know."

"It's too much," Aramis whispered. She rubbed her temples and leaned against a wall, her legs wobbling, and slid down to bury her face in her hands. "All of this is too much. I convinced myself the Hands weren't a threat. Our intelligence said the same. Even *Foldrey* believed it, and he was the most cautious of all of us. We were so sure they were just troublemaking zealots, pawing for what little power they could." She balled her fists. "It was right under our noses. We're so *stupid*."

Ranka sat, ignoring the filth of the street, and for the first time dared to speak aloud what they both knew. "They mean to use the coronation to spread it. Aramis, if they perfect winalin—if they get it right—they're going to kill us all."

"We could warn the covens. . . ." Aramis's voice trailed off. If the Sunra heirs invited the covens in only to confess a man-made plague, the covens would kill them—and everyone in Seaswept—outright.

They were trapped.

It was so painfully, utterly clear. The Hands had put them in an impossible position. If they called off the coronation, they were caving to the narrative that witches were dangerous and the treaty was broken. They'd ensure what little public faith remained in the Sunras was now solidly on the side of the zealots who sought to unseat them. Rumors of famine stirred. Fields had burned in the drought, which meant grain shortages were inevitable, and entire herds of livestock had starved as Isodal's heartland withered into a bowl of dust. Galen's rains had brought them a reprieve, but the damage was already done. Even if the fall crops came in strong, Isodal's food stores were dangerously low.

Now whispers of demons filled the streets, of pets snatched in the dark. Corpses stolen from graves, found miles away, half eaten. Troubling reports came in daily from citizens who lived near mine entrances—claiming that at night they'd begun to hear screams.

How long until the winalin witches the Hands had set loose in the tunnels began snatching people?

How long until they roved the city streets, and then the countryside at large?

"Foldrey knew," Ranka realized. "He knew this would happen, and that's why he tried to get me to leave."

Aramis whipped around to look at her. "He did what?"

So he'd truly been acting on his own, then. It felt wrong, to speak ill of the dead. Though there had been no funeral, and the official story was he was missing, they all knew with each passing day they'd never see the captain again. But Aramis deserved the truth.

"After Bell's Corridor he called me to his office. He . . . told me I was a danger to you, and to this city. And he told me to leave." She chewed on her lip. "He didn't care where I went—just that I was gone, and quickly."

And he had been right. With Ranka removed, the witches would have no reason to enter Seaswept. The Hands would have no one to infect. But fleeing was out of the question now. Border reports indicated the covens had entered Isodal a week ago. They'd be at the city gates within days.

They'd chosen this path. Now they had to find a way to survive it.

"Princess," Ranka said slowly, uneasily. "Galen needs to know."

"No. He's so fragile with Foldrey still missing—"

"You're coddling him."

"I'm keeping him *safe*."

"Are you?" Ranka pressed. The air between them was charged again, but it was no longer an aching, lovely thing. "Or are you refusing to trust him to bear the weight of the truth? This is no longer some runaway disease popping up in the streets. It's biological warfare. The Hands don't just have the Star Isles strain of winalin, they're making more. Someone gave them samples of blood-magic, samples of *me*. A guard, a noble, maybe even a goddess-damned Council member. Someone wants you both unseated. Now every coven is headed here, and the Hands are going to try their hardest to ensure they leave infected with a plague that has a hundred percent mortality rate. We need a *plan*. Extra guards, preparations in case this all goes south, safe houses set up and allies identified for the absolute worst-case scenario. And for that to happen, Galen needs to know."

Aramis's lips thinned. She balled her hands into fists and looked away, the veins of her neck pulsing as she tried to contain herself. Ranka could still scent her rage and her grief, but above all—though she did her best to keep her face blank and breathe evenly—Aramis Sunra reeked of sheer, undiluted terror.

A faint hope flickered to life inside her. If Aramis listened to her, the twins could prepare for the possible Skra coup without even realizing it. Ranka could have a backup plan, just in case it took too long for Ongrum to see reason—or in case one of the other covens arrived on their doorstep with similar designs.

Ranka put a hand on Aramis's knee. "I know you're terrified. But this goes beyond court politics, Princess. We're talking about war. We have to be ready. And we have to have every weapon in our arsenal."

"By 'every weapon,'" Aramis said softly, still not looking at her, "do you mean your blood-magic?"

Ranka stilled. She'd hit a wall in her training, and they all knew it. It took longer for her power to overtake her, but it still did in the end. If they were facing a fight for their lives, Ranka needed to be a weapon the twins could rely on, not a liability.

"I still don't have control," Ranka said softly. "I want to know why."

A vein pulsed in Aramis's throat. "No."

"Princess—"

"I said no, Ranka."

"It's not your place to say no, not when this thing has controlled me my entire *life*—"

"And if you face it, you'll *lose* it!"

Ranka stared at her, every nerve in her body suddenly alive and tuned in to the panic emanating off of Aramis. "What?"

Aramis's eyelashes fluttered. She stared at the wall, agony deepening the shadows on her face. "There were others, before you. Blood-witches Mother found that she thought she could train. *Save*." Aramis fisted her hands in her lap. "Two of them just weren't strong enough. The power took hold, and Mother ended them as mercifully as she could. But the third girl—Sorya . . ."

Darkness crept into the corners of Ranka's vision.

"She had a mental block," Aramis whispered. "She came to us when I was eleven. Mother was so sure she'd be named Bloodwinn. She was so strong, Ranka. But something was holding her back." She took a shuddering breath. "We figured it out then—blood-magic is anchored to the blood, but it's triggered by emotion. Every blood-witch manifests from death, but so few remember the events that broke their magic to the surface. It's a defense mechanism. They lock the memory away. The mind protects itself, even as that power rages. Even Mother had no recollection of the events that triggered her power. Just flashes of nightmares."

Fire, swirling everywhere. Blood on the snow.

"There was a memory Sorya couldn't face, some trauma from when her magic erupted. And when we trained, it crept back. She couldn't face it—and that denial let her power take control."

Her sister's scream, pitching higher and higher.

What have you done, Ranka? What have you done?

Panic closed around Ranka's throat. "What happened to her?"

"Ranka, please—"

"What happened?"

"She tried to face the block," Aramis whispered. "And she died."

Numbness swept over Ranka in a cold, dark wave. Aramis's voice wrapped around her, but it was as if the princess were speaking through a long, distant tunnel.

"She tried to go back, and she couldn't handle it. But she dove too deep, and it—it broke something in that girl. Her power just switched off. Balled up inside her, dormant. She said she could feel it, but it wouldn't respond. And we thought . . . I don't know. We thought maybe we'd done it. Maybe facing that trauma had just erased the power. Set her free." A horrible, ugly sob escaped Aramis. "Then one morning, we heard the screams."

Ranka put her forehead on her knees. Her heart beat harder, pounding until her whole body was shaking, as Aramis recounted in a distraught whisper what happened the morning Sorya's power woke back up. They'd feared it would turn her into a monster—set her loose in the palace, slaughtering everyone in her path. Instead, the magic simply erupted and ripped her apart from within. They found her writhing in her bed, veins rupturing as the magic burst free. The first time blood-magic awoke, it took the life of whatever was near the host.

The second time, it took the host instead.

"It took her so long to die. In the end, Father shot her," Aramis whispered. "Put her down with an arrow like a sick dog instead of a girl who'd lived under our roof, shared our meals, and played with my dolls as if she were my own sister."

Aramis fell silent, and the weight of what she'd said settled between them. Ranka didn't know if she was terrified, furious, or both. Aramis had known this the entire time and kept it from her. Had strung Ranka's hopes along, let her believe her power might be managed someday, while the memory of a girl ripped in half for attempting the same haunted her.

Yet watching her now—seeing the agony on Aramis's face, the guilt and terror in her eyes—Ranka couldn't feel anger. Only exhaustion.

"My answer is no," Aramis said flatly. She refused to look at Ranka. "You may have your death wish, but I refuse to be the one who indulges it. We'll find another way."

Ranka watched her quietly, listening to the murmur of the sleeping city around them. "And if we don't, Princess?" she asked. "If it's my life or your country—what then?"

Would you choose me, still?

Would you throw it all away, for a monster of a girl?

A muscle in Aramis's jaw feathered as Aramis stared at her. Her gaze flicked from Ranka's eyes to her lips and back again. The memory of the tavern returned—of what it had felt like to kiss her. To hold her. Suddenly the space between them was a palpable, workable thing. Suddenly Ranka wanted no space at all.

Overhead, a seabird cried. The spell broke, and they flinched, looking away from each other. Reality came crashing back in, colder than mountain water and just as clear.

There was a plague tearing through the country. Even if Ongrum listened to Ranka, she was meant to marry Galen. Maybe someday she could find someone who loved her, and they could hide it in private. But the princess?

She was not for Ranka, could never be for Ranka.

Things had been so much easier when they simply wanted each other dead.

Aramis pushed herself to her feet and wiped the snot from her nose with her sleeve. "Let's go. We've wasted too much time."

She turned away then, marching down the street without a light as though she'd walked this route a thousand times. Ranka watched her go and tried to ignore the question that lingered still. The knowledge that by not saying what she would choose—her country or Ranka's life—Aramis had given her answer, and it was the wrong one.

They made their way back in silence, the weight of everything they'd learned stretched between them. It was plain Aramis had no intention of being honest with her brother, and could Ranka truly fault her? How many lies had she told the people she loved to shield them? How many lies was she still telling now?

In only a few days witches from every coven would pour into this city, and all Ranka had was a half-baked plan to appeal to Ongrum's sensibility in a bid for peace. Her head pounded. If only Ongrum were here. She always had answers. If she'd been the one in Seaswept this entire time, she'd already have a full-blown strategy, with three backup plans in case the others failed. It would be a relief when Ongrum arrived—to pass the burden to someone smarter, someone who could make the hard, right choice. Ongrum would know how to save them. She always did.

Footsteps pounded toward them. Ranka braced herself for a fight—but it was only Percy, tearing around the corner.

"There you are," he blurted. "I need you both *now*."

"Percy, what happened?" Aramis drew back. "Where have you been? Wait—is that blood?"

"I was in the workshop running some samples when I heard something crying, so I went into the tunnels and I found a winalin witch. And she's *alive*."

"*What?* How far?"

"She's not in the city." He gulped. "I, um, caught her. She's here."

40

PERCY AND ARAMIS LED THE WAY, THEIR HEADS BOWED as she filled him in on what they'd learned. Ranka followed at their heels, humming beneath her breath to calm her nerves.

It was an old hunting tune Ongrum had taught her in the days after Belren. A rhythmic, hollow melody that sat low in the throat and reverberated through the chest. Ongrum had sung it as they tracked wounded prey across the snow, the spots of blood acting like a guiding light. The song was a ghost. Ranka barely remembered the words. And yet the melody—haunting, mourning, an echo of something lost—was buried in her bones.

"Percy." Aramis's voice startled Ranka out of her memories, bringing reality back in. "A little light?"

"With *her* here?"

A hollow thud sounded.

"Ow, okay, fine."

Gold eyes flashed in the dark, and then there were flames. Two sconces guttered to life. Percy brushed at his lips, but Ranka still caught the wisp of smoke.

The door swung open.

The Kerth lay in the chair where Percy had drawn Ranka's blood for the past weeks. Her chest rose and fell frantically, the sores on her skin weeping watery pus, sweat-slicked as though she was caught in a fever. She'd decayed dramatically in only a few hours.

"Ranka," Percy said grimly. "Hold her arms. I've got her legs."

Aramis stooped, rummaged in a cupboard, and returned with a jar filled with writhing black leeches. "If I can draw enough of the corrupted blood out, and if the leeches can keep her blood thin enough to flow, the vaccine antigens might provoke enough of an antibody response to help her body fight the winalin off. Emphasis on the 'might'." Her jaw worked. "On my count. One."

Ranka tightened her grip on the Kerth.

"Two."

Please work.

"Three."

Aramis didn't move.

Her needle hovered a hair's breadth from the witch's neck. It winked like a promise in the light, the pale fluid sloshing inside. Aramis's fingers trembled.

"Aramis," Ranka said, her voice soft.

Aramis's pupils dilated to two small, panicked points. "All we've worked on is dead witches. But she . . . if I fail . . ."

"She's already dead without you."

The Kerth's labored breaths grew more painful with each rattle. Another sore opened on her wrist.

Aramis hesitated. The panicked shudder of her chest was an uncomfortable reminder of how young she was—how young they all were. This girl, not yet eighteen, carried the fate of every witch on this side of the border and the next on her shoulders. She'd have been a fool if she *weren't* terrified.

"Aramis," Ranka said. "If anyone can save her, it's you."

And she meant it. Ranka had blood-magic, Galen his terrible Skybreaker winds, but Aramis had only ever had her mind.

Her lips thinned and the scared girl vanished, replaced by the iron will of a healer, the steady determination of a scientist with a problem to solve.

"Solomei, guide my hands," Aramis whispered, and she drove the needle home.

Aramis acted with military precision. She moved around the Kerth, fingers flying to the jar of leeches, placing them at major artery points. Throat, thighs, wrists. The leeches pulsed, and Ranka's stomach turned.

The Kerth began to seize.

"Hold her."

The Kerth thrashed. Her blisters swelled, gathering blood and pus, darkening to the color of a day-old bruise as they threatened to split across their crown. Her nails shifted from gray to black, and her eyes flew open. Her irises were gone, swallowed by a sea of eerie blood-witch white. An animal scream tore free of her throat. Ranka thought it sounded like *kill me*.

Perhaps it really would have been kinder to let her die.

"Hold. Her."

More needles, more leeches.

And then, as suddenly as she'd started fighting, the witch collapsed.

They waited for her chest to rise. Waited for her to twitch, or moan, or show any hint they had not failed. But the stillness of her body was the kind that came only with death.

"No," Aramis said. *"No."*

In seconds she was on the chair, one hand over the other, pressing on the Kerth's chest. The veins in Aramis's arms popped as she timed out her compressions. She dropped, pinched the witch's nose, and pressed her mouth to hers, forcing air into her lungs.

It did nothing.

Eventually Aramis staggered backward. "I don't understand. I did the math—numbers don't lie. We did something wrong. It should have worked."

The leeches continued pumping away, oblivious they'd failed.

"It should have worked. We tested it over and over again. We've spent months." The words left her in a panicked babble. "It should have *worked.*"

"Aramis," Percy said, and on his lips, her name sounded like an apology.

"I tested it. I studied every angle. The math was *right.* Everything we've been counting on—we're back to square one. *Damn it!*" She closed her fingers around a vial and hurled it against the wall. Glass shattered. The pieces clinked to the floor as remnants of the cure slid down the salt. She knocked the jar of leeches over, and they spilled across the chair to the floor, curling in pain when they made contact with the salt.

Ranka's heart broke for her. "Aramis."

Aramis made a choked noise and sank to the ground. She buried her head in her hands and dug her nails into her scalp.

"Aramis," Ranka repeated, softer.

Percy moved to edge of the room to clean up the glass.

Ranka knelt in front of her.

"They're all going to die because of me," Aramis whispered. "Because I wasn't smart enough. Again."

When the king and queen died, Ranka had thought little of it. Plague returned quietly every few decades, like a neighbor coming home. The late Sunras weren't the first rulers felled by disease, and they wouldn't be the last. It was a miracle, people said, their children had lived. Several healers who'd worked on the king and queen had gotten sick and died too. It'd never occurred to Ranka their daughter might have tried to *cure* them.

"Aramis, that's not fair. You are one person. One mind."

"Be quiet," Aramis said, her voice barely audible.

"You were a *child.* We all are. You can't blame yourself. Look, I understand how—"

"But you don't, do you?" Aramis's head snapped up. "How could you? Your power—your worth, Ranka—is in your blood and your bones. No one can take it from you. You, my brother, Percy, and every creature with magic was *born* with security. I was raised for a crown, and they took it because I wasn't a witch—gave it to my brother because of his inherited power. All I have is my mind. All I *am* is smart. If I can't do this one thing—if I can't fix anything—then what am I good for?"

"You tell me," Ranka said quietly. "Who are you, Princess, when everything else is taken away? What are you, after you fail? You're still resilient. You're still the most infuriatingly brilliant person I've ever met. And you still have a kind heart, though you pretend you don't. Or are all of those nothing to you too?"

Aramis stared at her, her chest heaving.

"Guys," Percy said. "You need to see this."

The leeches were dying.

Dozens of leeches, freed from the jar Aramis had tipped over in rage, now covered the Kerth. Their bodies were seizing. The first fell off with a soft, sad plop and curled into a ball—and then they dropped like flies, curling in on themselves, quivering as they died, their bodies covered in dozens of tiny blisters. Percy took a few uncertain steps forward and sliced one in half with a scalpel.

Leech blood spilled across the table, threaded with twisting gray and the pale lavender of the vaccine.

"Solomei's light," Aramis whispered. "That's it." She crawled forward, scooping the unfed leeches from the floor. Her movements were frantic.

Ranka watched her with a mix of pity and confusion. "She's gone, Princess."

Aramis ignored her. She set new leeches across the Kerth, cleared the dead ones away.

"That's what we missed," Aramis murmured, her eyes intent. "We didn't account for a living body."

It hurt to see her like this. Ranka put a hand on Aramis's shoulder. "I know you wanted to save her. But—"

A scent filled the room, like a body finding new breath. The new leeches wriggled, but there were no blisters. They were alive.

Aramis drew another vial of the vaccine and injected it carefully into the Kerth. "What did I say, witch girl? I may not be good for much—but I *am* good at this."

Ranka looked past her, to the witch, who finally looked peaceful in death, her pained snarl smoothed away.

And then the witch's finger twitched.

That's not possible.

The last of the leeches fell away—and the Kerth gasped.

Aramis looked at her the way acolytes looked at their goddess. "She's alive."

The Kerth kept breathing. Asleep or comatose, Ranka wasn't certain. But she was absolutely, impossibly alive.

Joy broke across the princess's face. She flung her arms around Ranka, hugging her in that ecstatic manner of people who were so thrilled, they didn't care whom they celebrated with, only that they did. Ranka went rigid, startled, and then relaxed and hugged her back.

"This changes everything," Aramis whispered, tilting her head back. She smelled of exhaustion, of fear, of ink and mint and a strange acidic chemical that hurt Ranka's throat but drew her in all the same. The flecks of gold in her eyes gleamed copper in the half-light.

Some foolish, self-punishing part of Ranka wanted to lean down like she had in the tavern.

Percy cleared his throat, and they leapt apart.

Aramis drifted back to the unconscious Kerth, smoothing the hair away from her face. The cure hadn't totally worked. Sores still covered her body, and the nails of her left hand still ended in sharp black claws, but she was breathing. Aramis hovered over her, drinking in the sight of the witch she had half saved, a thousand more questions flitting across her face.

"Are the sores growing?" Percy asked, coming to stand alongside her.

"No. It's like we . . . paused it." Aramis made her way around the chair, inspecting every inch of her newest patient, her dark lashes fluttering. She took her pulse and looked skyward, counting the beats. "Her heart is barely moving—but she's breathing fine." She knocked the witch on the knee, and her leg kicked up as her muscles responded. "Reflexes are still fine too."

Percy and Aramis exchanged a long, thoughtful look. It had irritated Ranka so much when she'd met them—the way they read each other at a glance, the symbiosis between their movements. Galen may have been Aramis's twin by blood, but Percy was one by choice, and they often seemed like the cruelest mirror images of each other—the boy who had unleashed a terror upon a nation, the girl who sought to stop it.

"We're close," Percy said, as if he couldn't believe the words. His eyes were bright with tears. "Extremely close. Ranka, do you have any blood to spare?"

They'd stopped taking samples after the latest witch attack to give her time to recover. She loathed blood days, dreaded the fatigue that followed her after, the overwhelming nausea and dizziness that occurred during. They would respect her wishes if she told them no.

"Of course," Ranka said, already rolling up her sleeve. "Where do you want me to—"

"Sit on the table for now, if you don't mind." Percy prepared the needle, his mind clearly half a world away. "Aramis, make sure you record the Kerth's vitals—"

The princess looked up from where she was already frantically filling the pages of yet another notebook. "One step ahead of you."

The two of them kept talking, passing numbers back and forth, and Ranka reclined on the table, only an arm's reach from the Kerth, whose life now relied on the cure they were hoping to synthesize from Ranka's blood. Now that her face was no longer twisted with feral rage, the witch looked vulnerable, almost childlike. She had Yeva's high cheekbones, Vivna's full lips. So much of her held an echo of the ones Ranka so desperately missed. The Kerth breathed so slow, her chest barely moved, unconscious and lost to the world—and lost to how much of it now relied on her.

So many had died—and so many more would. But if they could save this girl, they might save others. Ranka would have living, breathing proof for Ongrum why the Sunra twins were on their side. Why they could build a new world with them, instead of atop Galen's grave. With the Skra firmly behind the Sunras, the rest of the covens would follow. They'd be a unified front against the Hands and the Star Isles alike.

They would be *saved*.

As the morning sun rose, a new feeling swept through Ranka, so unfamiliar it stung. It was a thing she hadn't felt properly in five years.

It was hope.

41

AS WAR APPROACHED, THE PALACE PREPARED FOR A party.

Gold banners edged in navy fluttered at every corner; sugar and yeast seemed baked into the air as the kitchens worked overnight. Workers cleaned ponds, pruned gardens, and scrubbed already-gleaming tiles until the mosaics refracted rays of morning sun so sharply it hurt. Even the guard uniforms looked smarter—linens pressed, buttons polished, boots cleaned.

Soon, Isodal would watch a new king rise.

As the coronation ticked closer, Ranka hoped for a moment of peace. Instead she found herself whisked into days of fittings, last-minute etiquette lessons, more fittings, and hours of exhausting, preball drudgery. Murmurs of another event began to swirl as servants measured her wide shoulders and tutted over the state of her hair. A wedding was inevitable, everyone knew it. But when palace officials asked probing, sly questions, Ranka pretended not to understand—and as far as she could tell, Galen and Aramis had given them the same treatment. They all knew what was coming—but they were united, it seemed, in trying to survive these next few days. All the coronation would require from Ranka was a pledge of loyalty to renew the treaty. She could manage that.

They'd worry about weddings after.

Yet Ranka found herself gripped not just by nerves—but by grief, too. The coronation would be a strange kind of homecoming. After nearly two months, she'd see her coven again. But there would be a face missing from their ranks. All the covens would come with ghosts trailing on their heels, bearing losses they didn't quite understand. And Ranka couldn't help but feel like she'd failed.

She had come here to save Yeva and buried her instead.

How could she ever face Asyil again?

Now Ranka hurried from the palace and into the waning moonlight. Palace workers sweated as they scrubbed the tiles clean, others sweeping the verandas clear of leaves. She studied their faces, the calluses on their hands. A young girl whose uniform was a size too big whistled as she weeded the gardens, her arms covered in soil. A boy who didn't seem old enough to wear a uniform, let alone carry a weapon, picked at his collar as he stood guard over one of the entrances. A part of her was tempted to tell them to flee. Whatever the palace was paying them surely couldn't outweigh the cost of their lives, should she fail.

Dread weighed Ranka down. Ongrum would listen to her. She *had* to. But even her support might not be enough. Should the Hands mount a larger attack—should the other covens not come to their side—

If her word wasn't enough, they would die. Not just the twins and Percy, but witches and humans alike. If it came to a fight, she'd be a liability. A risk. She'd lost control far too many times, jeopardized their lives and nearly let Galen die because of the way her power stuttered in the face of winalin.

Fear made her heavy, but desperation pushed her forward.

Ranka stopped in front of the door she'd sought, raised her fist, and knocked.

It opened with a hiss of wood against tile. Aramis leaned against the doorframe, her hair undone, curls falling around her face, nightclothes creased with sleep. Concern brightened her eyes. "Ranka? What is it?"

The memory of their kiss returned to Ranka, the way Aramis had melted against her, the flush to her cheeks and the heavy want in her eyes. For a wild, foolish second, all Ranka wanted to do was take Aramis's face in her hands and forget the reason she'd come here.

Instead, she cleared her throat. "It's my risk to face. Not yours."

"What?"

"You said you could never live with yourself if the final step hurt me. But that's my choice, Princess. Not yours. The coronation is only a few days away. The Hands are planning something, and we need to be ready. I can't protect you and Galen if I'm out of control." Ranka took an unsteady breath. "I want to finish my training. I want—I want to clear the block. But I can't do it by myself. I need you with me. When I go back to that place. I need to know that if I fail, you'll end it, before . . ."

Before the power rips me apart piece by piece, and you have to put an arrow through me, same as your father.

Ranka looked away. Pleading and begging and speaking of death was not how she wanted to spend their final days together. A memory pricked at her, of a different day, a different promise, when she had been less sure of where she stood and whom to fight for. The words left her before she could stop them.

"I am not good for much," Ranka said softly. "But fighting— fighting I'm good at. Violence I know. And while I hope it won't come to that, I want to be able to protect you. So let me be your shield. Your knife in the dark."

Tell me, Bloodwinn—do you know what the role of a guard is?

"I am a weapon, Aramis. Let me be yours."

Grief shadowed Aramis's eyes. Foldrey's loss was still an open wound in her and Galen alike. He had been willing to give everything for them, to die for them.

It startled Ranka to think she might be willing, too.

Aramis's fingers tapped out a nervous beat against the side of her thigh, deep lines of worry settling on her face. She was beautiful, even now, even when she was exhausted and afraid. And a part of Ranka resented that this was the life they were both caught in. Somehow, they'd become allies. Friends.

A selfish part of Ranka wondered if in another life, in a better world, they could have been more.

Aramis's fingers drifted to her heart, flitted through a quick prayer sign, and fell. She closed her eyes. "All right, Ranka. All right."

Aramis led her to the gardens.

Beetles clicked from the leaves around them, their hard shells gleaming in the early dawn light. Every step Ranka took felt heavier, as if she were wading through water. Her fingers kept drifting to her cuticles, tearing at the skin until it bled. Fear turned her mouth sour. Even her blood-magic seemed afraid. It skittered and bucked beneath her skin, begging her to flee instead of fight.

Ranka kept walking.

They took a sharp turn into a small garden clearing. Petals of once-fragrant white lilies littered the ground, brown at the edges and spotted with decay. Aramis sat cross-legged in the dirt, her night-clothes rustling around her. Her eyes searched Ranka's face. "We don't need a full-fledged blood-witch to protect Galen. We have the defenses; the palace has faced insurrections before, and its walls remain standing yet."

Ranka swallowed. It was tempting. Even now she longed to flee, to tell Aramis she could survive with a lifetime of being only half in control. They'd made so much progress already. Though her blood-magic still wielded her in the end, hadn't she learned how to direct it? To stave it off and ride the waves of the power, instead of letting them crash wildly over her every time?

Couldn't that be enough?

But a coup was coming. Her coven would soon enter Seaswept. An underground coalition of religious zealots sought to upturn the twins she was now desperate to protect. A plague that would be the end of everything would burn this land to the ground.

They were about to face the fight of their lives, and they needed every weapon in their arsenal.

Besides, didn't she need every bit of evidence she could gather for Ongrum that the twins were on her side? If Ranka conquered her blood-magic, she would prove, once and for all, the Sunra princess was someone Witchik needed alive.

She could buy Aramis's safety for the rest of their lives.

And that, more than anything, made this worth it.

"I'm ready," Ranka said. "Lead me through it."

Aramis's lips wobbled. "Very well, then. Close your eyes, witch girl—and take my hands."

Ranka complied. The world became nothing but the hum of beetles around her, the bite of the stones against Ranka's thighs as she sat cross-legged in the dirt. Aramis's fingers slid into Ranka's and squeezed. Her voice wrapped around her, carrying that steady, cool confidence Ranka had hated so fiercely when she'd met Aramis and relied on now.

"You have a wound in you, Ranka, one that's festered for a long, long time." Aramis spoke slowly, her voice monotone, as though she were repeating an incantation. "Your unwillingness to face that wound has given your blood-magic free reign, to wield you as it pleases. If you want control, there can be nothing you hide from yourself. If you want freedom, the wound must be allowed to scar, once and for all."

Ranka's hands began to sweat.

"You think yourself a girl of fury, Ranka of the Skra, a monster incapable of love. But I saw you in that alley. I know what brings your blood-magic roaring back, what makes you yield, every time, because you'd sooner be a monster than face what you've been running from your entire life. It's not fury you run from. It's not rage you harbor."

Ranka's heart skipped a beat.

"You are not angry," Aramis whispered. "You are afraid."

A deep well threatened to open up inside of Ranka. Because Aramis was right—it was fear that drove her. Terror made her relinquish control every time. She'd never been strong enough. Would never *be* strong enough to stomach the horrors of the world, and so she let her blood-magic do it for her.

"What do you fear so violently that you'd let your own monstrosity consume you?"

Flames flickered behind Ranka's eyes.

"What haunts you so deeply that it's worth giving up control?"

Ranka closed her eyes. She forced herself down, willed invisible fingers to probe back to the memory she'd sealed away five years ago, the horror she'd compartmentalized so thoroughly, it existed only as fragments of memory and sound.

The memories came, and Ranka saw it: the village of her nightmares. The town where she'd earned her title of Butcher. Where she'd gained her magic—and lost her humanity. Where she'd become a blood-witch and lost the one thing she loved in this world in return.

"What is the source of your greatest shame?"

Ranka's lips formed the name.

"Belren."

42

VIVNA SAID SHE WAS CERTAIN. THIS TIME, SHE'D FOUND their parents. She felt it in her bones.

Winter wind burned Ranka's ears. Her fingers and toes were numb, but she wasn't sure if it was the cold or the harsh chemical dyes Vivna had forced her to stain her nails with. At least the cold made the blisters stop burning.

Belren was little more than a logging town clinging to Isodal's northern border. It was small enough that every villager knew one another, remote enough to have an immediate mistrust of strangers. Its people lived in squat, well-loved log houses, crouched close together like wintering beasts.

When Ranka and Vivna staggered into town, it was as if the very road felt them arrive.

Faces appeared in windows. Children cried out while mothers grabbed their best knives. This town had suffered tragedy at the hands of witches before. They braced themselves for an invading band of ruthless Skra.

But instead what they saw were two girls, red faced, delirious with cold, clinging to each other as they collapsed in the road.

For all her faults, Vivna was an excellent liar. She convinced the vil-

lagers they'd escaped the Skra. They weren't witches after all, she said, fat tears rolling down her cheeks, showing them their pale-nailed hands.

The villagers carried them aside. They rubbed warmth into their limbs and fed them hot broth, talking among themselves, eager to save two girls who'd escaped the Skra.

"Send for Hans and his family," a woman said. "Tell them to hurry."

When a tall man with broad shoulders and a sunspotted face stepped through the door, frost clinging to his pale beard, Ranka looked at him and understood. Here was the man who had given her such broad shoulders, tireless strength, and towering height. A long-legged, dark-haired woman stepped around him with a dancer's grace. She was the spitting image of Vivna.

Their parents, after eight long years.

"Solomei's light," their father whispered.

They fell to their knees and hugged them and cried. Vivna cried with them, peddling more lies, so many lies, as if she'd spent a lifetime hoarding falsehoods behind her teeth.

Ranka sat dry eyed and tense. The strange restlessness that had been plaguing her for months stirred in her veins.

The cabins creaked under the winter wind. They seemed to moan, *You don't belong here.*

Ranka agreed.

Ranka and Vivna were not the only children their parents had. When they brought them home, Ranka found herself staring at two chubby little boys.

Ranka hated that they were sweet, that they accepted her. She kept looking for flaws in their neat little life. Her mother took over braiding Ranka's hair the way Vivna always had. The small schoolhouse that crouched near a frozen apple orchard made room for both girls. When her teacher learned that Ranka could barely read or write, she spent time after hours trying to teach Ranka her letters.

It could have been perfect. It could have been home.

Except Belren was never a home for witches.

It was like everywhere Ranka looked, an echo that she didn't belong clung to the shadows. A local man laughing about a burning. The children at school playing a game called "kill the witch." Even her parents spoke in low tones over the table about the wretched Skra, and why wouldn't that useless Sunra king send troops and just wipe them all out?

These people loved them. They brought them bowls of stew and warm clothes their children had grown out of. And they would kill them if they found out what they were.

At night Ranka caught her parents whispering.

"There's something strange about that child," their mother said. "Something off. The way she stares at the boys terrifies me."

"She's had a hard life," Hans argued, his voice gentle. "She's probably still in shock. Give her time."

"I don't feel safe with her here."

"She's our blood. She's staying."

Weeks turned to months, and Ranka began to hate every inch of Belren. Vivna thrived. She was the perfect one, the smiling, doting daughter Hans and Ursa had always dreamed of. Ranka was like the feral cat that had slunk in and refused to leave.

One night Ranka overheard her father suggest that perhaps Ranka was not fit to live in Belren. Maybe one of the Solomei temples in the south would suit their wilder daughter better, where warm air would ease her temper, and the acolytes could shape her into a well-adjusted young woman. His rolling baritone whispered that he worried Ranka had been too corrupted by the Skra. Her mother agreed.

Ranka lay awake the whole night, buried beneath the scratchy wool blanket for comfort even as she sweated through her clothes. She would deal with the dyes, the pain, the pressure under her skin. She would not let them separate her from Vivna.

Vivna's cheeks grew rosy and full. She was somewhat of a star there,

the beautiful eldest daughter who had been taken by witches and valiantly escaped.

Once a month Vivna woke Ranka before dawn, a glint in her eyes and a vial in hand. "Come on. It's time."

Ranka cringed back into the layers of scratchy wool. Her nails ached just at the idea of it. "They still look human."

"If they find out you're a witch, they'll make us leave. Do you want that?"

Yes, Ranka thought. *I want to leave so badly.* But not without Vivna. Never without Vivna.

"The dyes hurt."

"Sometimes love hurts. And you love me, don't you, Ranka?"

"Of course," Ranka whispered. "You're the only person I love."

Vivna pressed her lips into a line. "Prove it."

Sweat covered Ranka's body. She pitched out the memory, her entire body shaking. She had forgotten—how had she *forgotten*? She held up her hands, eyeing the dozens of puckered scars on her fingers, echoes of trying to burn away any hint of being a witch. So much of Belren was a fog to her. But those corks of acid. The insistence in Vivna's voice.

"Ranka?" Aramis whispered. "Are you all right?"

Ranka looked up at her, her words lodged in her throat. She didn't want this—couldn't live with this. In a world of things that were broken and bad and wrong, Vivna had been her light. Vivna had been synonymous with everything good.

But Vivna had fed the monster inside her.

She'd been the first.

The change started with looks. Instead of calling out and smiling, townspeople now looked at Ranka and Vivna with tight eyes, their fingers flashing the Solomei sigil on their chest. Mothers stepped in front of their children when Ranka passed. The schoolchildren were no longer allowed to play with her. Her teacher suddenly no longer had time for tutoring.

"Vivna," Ranka whispered, her heart thumping beneath the wool blankets.

"Hmm?"

"I don't think we're safe here. I think they know."

"This again? If you don't like it here, then leave." Vivna rolled over before Ranka could respond, and tugged the blankets over her head.

Ranka lay awake long after her sister's breathing returned to normal, dread pressing down on her. Vivna wouldn't listen—but the Skra would. Ongrum would save them, just like before.

So the next morning, Ranka left.

She kept expecting their parents to see Ranka's betrayal written across her face, for the neighbor children to smell it on her skin. She waited for someone to notice the strange lumps of food in her pockets. But they barely looked at her. When Ranka set off toward the schoolhouse that morning and took a sharp turn into the woods instead, no one said a word.

Her steps grew faster and faster until she was running, tearing across the snow, sprinting like she had among the Skra. Cold burned her cheeks and yanked her hair from its plaits.

Ranka hungered for the land to shift from fields cleared by farming to the dense, unwelcoming conifer forests that marked the beginning of Witchik's Northlands. A part of her hadn't realized just how much she liked being a Skra until she'd left. Life as a witch had fit her like a second skin. She had memorized their customs, their training habits, their patrol schedules.

I'm leaving. I'm not staying.

Ranka chanted the words over and over again, but the farther she walked from Belren, the heavier her legs felt. Her fingers burned underneath her gloves, the blisters torn open by the rough wool. Ranka took one more wavering step—and froze.

Move, she willed her legs. *Go home.*

Except home was no longer one thing, a single direction she could stamp into her heart's map. Home was the Skra, their sputtering campfires that burned year-round, the hunting songs they bellowed in raucous voices emboldened by pine liquor. But home also lived in Vivna's timid smile, in the warmth of her arms on a midwinter night. It rang in the soft rasp of her voice when she whispered into Ranka's hair, *I love you, little sister.*

Somehow home had doubled, and Ranka was expected to choose only one.

A red squirrel chattered at her from the boughs of a nearby conifer, irritated by the interloper into its territory.

She closed her eyes and inhaled. Her sense of smell had gotten stronger and stronger each year. Ongrum said it was a sign of her witchery growing, filling her up. Ranka liked that idea. She pictured her witchery as a tiny, gleaming seed in the center of her chest, flowering more each year, stretching its roots until the power was twisted around the very marrow of her bones.

Scents explained the world around her: The bitter edge of winter, the promise that spring was still a distant thing. The gamey scent of the red squirrel, the bite of pine, and in the distance, the beginning of a fire.

Fire?

Ranka opened her eyes.

A plume of deep gray wound its way up from the center of Belren, twisting in the air like a dancer caught midturn.

One of Ongrum's lessons echoed in her mind.

The hotter the flame, the darker the smoke.

But why would the villagers need a fire midday?

Unless—

A scream split the air, high and shrill. Ranka went cold. She knew that scream. She'd heard it tear from the throat of the girl she loved every time the Skra dragged her kicking and howling back to camp for trying to escape.

⁓

Ranka jerked away from Aramis, her eyes wide and unseeing. She knew what came next. And she couldn't face it. "This was a mistake."

"Ranka, we're too far in—you have to see this through."

"I don't care if it kills me." Black swirled at the edges of her vision. "I can't do this."

"You're doing this, witch girl. One way or another. You opened that door—now you must walk through." Aramis gripped Ranka's hands until the bones in her fingers ground together. "What happened that day, Ranka? What woke your blood-magic?"

Ranka drew in a shuddering breath.

"What made that power rise?"

Ranka's voice sounded far away. "I tried to save her."

43

THE END BEGAN WITH A GIRL AND A FIRE.

Ranka heard the villagers before she saw them.

"I knew it! A witch!"

"But where's the other one?"

"It doesn't matter—we'll get her next."

The chemical reek of oil coiled in the air. When Ranka drew close to the village, she ducked left instead of plunging down the main street, boots skidding in the snow as she slipped between the cover of houses, inching closer to heart of the town.

Again came that strange tug in her center. It swelled behind her eyes, made her teeth ache. Her ears popped from the pressure. The conifers flickered from green to a murky gray. She blinked, and the colors returned.

Vivna, Vivna, Vivna, her heart thudded.

Help her, help her, help her, the breeze seemed to chant back.

Ranka pressed herself against the wet wood walls. She could smell and hear the humans just beyond—a whirlwind of resentment, fear, and even a tinge of regret.

Okay, Ranka. You can do this. Just take a look. It might not be her.

Heart in her mouth, Ranka peered into the village where she'd been born.

The villagers of Belren stood in a loose semicircle, the majority of them only half-dressed for the cold weather. One of her peers from the schoolhouse had forgotten her shoes. Her socks darkened as water crept up her calves.

Vivna slumped in front of them, hands tied behind her back, dark hair thrown across her face, a pyre of already-burning wood behind her.

Scattered in front of her, spilling across the snow, were the acidic dyes she'd used to burn the pigment from Ranka's nails.

One of the older children from the village had a vial in hand. His pale, freckled face creased with hatred. When Ranka had pictured the humans who would come to burn them, they'd always been adults, well settled into spiteful lives ruled by fear. Humans who carried decades like weight, haunted by memories of family they'd lost.

But this boy was only a few years older than her. He'd probably never even met a witch until now.

"We found these." The boy shook the vial. "I knew something was strange about her."

"Didn't trust her from the beginning," someone in the crowd chimed.

Liars. They had all doted on Vivna at first, drank in her attention and returned it tenfold.

Vivna didn't move from her spot on the ground. Her left ankle was twisted and bruised, her clothes disheveled and torn. They'd gagged her.

More villagers drifted forward, and more accusations flew. Suddenly Vivna was responsible for one woman's sick dog, to blame for another man's daughter running away with a miller from the town over. Their accusations rose with fury, growing more ridiculous, and then a thin, reedy voice split the air.

"There will be more."

Ranka's fingers tightened on the wood.

One of the older townswomen marched forward. Her gray hair was dusted with white, her face severe. Pale eyes flicked back and forth amid a sea of wrinkles and scars and sunspots from a hard life in the north. "I was here when that girl was taken. I was here when girls before *her* were taken. The witches come back. They always come back." She shook her head, lips thinning until they were bloodless against her liver-spotted skin. "There's only one way to show witches they're not welcome here. One way to keep them out. Do you know why they fear fire?"

Vivna tried to scream around her gag.

The old woman's suggestion seemed to give them all pause. It was one thing to accuse. It was another to kill.

But then one person murmured in agreement, and another.

I have to help her.

Pressure built under Ranka's skin, behind her eyes, pressing in her hands. Her nails ached, pulsing in time with her heartbeat.

The woman bent down and ripped out Vivna's gag. "Do you have anything to say for yourself?"

Tears streamed down her sister's cheeks. "I told you, I'm not a witch! The dyes belonged to the Skra. I *belong* here. I'm human. *Please!*" Her voice cracked. She struggled, arms flexing, but the knots held fast.

Ranka trembled. She needed to save Vivna, but she was just a child, and these people bubbling with hatred were a sea of adults.

The wood beneath her hands shifted from brown to pale gray.

"Do it," one of the villagers called. "Burn her!"

"We need to protect our families," another agreed. "If we let her stay, who's to say she won't steal my daughters?"

The boy drew the flint from his pocket. He took a step forward, and Vivna screamed again, twisting.

I have to protect her.

I have to help.

A man took the flint.

"Wait!" Ranka cried, scrambling forward.

Sunlight flashed across her eyes, and then Ranka was in front of Vivna, arms spread wide, chest heaving. Half the town milled in front of her. Could she and Vivna outrun them all? "You're looking for me."

The pressure under her skin was so bad, it *hurt*. "My sister isn't a witch. Look at her fingers—they're injured. She was dyeing *my* nails. See?" She held them up, exposing the blisters, the raw, puckered skin that always carried a lingering pain. "Punish me—but let my sister go."

The man with the flint lifted his jaw, his white cheeks reddening. "She helped you hide."

"I forced her to," Ranka lied. A headache pounded at her temples. Her skin crawled as if she were the one plunged into the fire, and the world flashed black and white, black and white. She blinked furiously, trying to clear her eyes. "Please—Vivna didn't do anything wrong."

"She forced me," Vivna babbled. "I *told* her to leave, I never wanted her here."

Ranka glanced back at her. Vivna had certainly gotten on board with that lie quickly.

The humans shifted among themselves, uncertainty breaking through the clouds of rage on their faces. They had come for a hunt, not a victim easily turned over.

Two familiar scents floated toward her.

"Vivna? Ranka?"

The crowd parted. Hans and Ursa stood with their arms brushing against each other, looking small and miserable in the cold. Their attention darted nervously from Ranka to Vivna. They looked older in the sunlight, the wisps of gray in their hair brighter, the lines in their faces deeper.

Vivna choked on a sob and sat up. "Mama, Papa, oh, thank the goddess." She struggled against the ropes. "You wouldn't believe—"

Hans held up his hand. He looked at his oldest daughter, a child stolen in a snowstorm, returned nearly a decade later, and whispered, "Did you know?"

Vivna stilled. "What?"

"Did you bring her here, knowing what she was?"

Vivna's eyes dimmed. "No."

"She knew," someone accused. "She had to have known."

"They're both guilty. Even if the oldest isn't a witch, she *knew*."

Ranka's heart slammed against her ribs.

We're going to die. These people—they had suffered too many decades, ignored by their king, preyed on by witches instead of living alongside them in a wary truce like a few other towns had. They wanted someone to blame. They needed someone to hurt.

"Stop them!"

A hot red tide swept through Ranka.

"Burn them!"

Someone lit a torch, and then another.

The pressure filled up every part of her, feeding her anger, her hurt. Fury burned her throat and swelled in her mind. Terror shivered through her blood and into her hands, her legs, her heart.

Ranka reached for the ice-covered ropes and tore at them with her teeth. They fell to the snow in frozen chunks.

Fire at her back, fire all around. It would consume them both. They were just girls, but they were witches, too, and in this wide, cruel world they would always be the ones who burned.

Vivna tilted her head up to Ranka. Her pupils shrank, as if she saw something horrifying in her little sister's face.

"Come on," Ranka begged her, tugging at her hands. "Vivna, we gotta go *now*."

Vivna crouched there in the half-melted snow, eyes wide, tears streaming down her cheeks. For Ranka, Belren had never been home. But Vivna had dreamed of it. Starved for it.

And it did not want her.

"I can't," Vivna whispered.

Ranka reached for her—and a villager grabbed Ranka by the hair, jerking her back so hard, it knocked Ranka off balance. Pain blistered through her scalp. The colors vanished.

"Burn them!"

Pressure in her skin, pressure in her eyes. She couldn't breathe. The flames were gray, the humans were gray, everything was gray. It was as though all the color had been sucked from the world. What was happening to her?

A boot kicked her ribs. Ranka gasped, curling in on herself, trying to protect her head with her hands. Nails raked down her skin.

Somewhere, on the fringe, her parents watched and did nothing.

Pain, everywhere. Exploding across her ribs, sending starbursts through her eyes. The pressure, the pressure, the pressure. Her veins felt hot. Where were the colors?

Please, no.

Vivna shrieked as someone shoved her down to the snow.

My sister. Please, someone. Help us.

Someone had their hands around Ranka's throat. Her lungs ached. She threw out a fist, an elbow, a knee. Something crunched under her hand. A woman screamed. Ranka fought back and it wasn't enough; she was never enough. She was a child fighting adults.

They were going to die.

Please. I'll do anything. I have to protect her.

Fire crackled gray just beyond them. Ash-colored blood slicked across Ranka's hands, poured down her face. Someone kicked Ranka in the stomach.

Vivna—where was Vivna?

I have to protect her.

The pressure, the pressure. It hurt to be inside her own skin. Her fingers seized and twitched on the ground. Blood dripped from her nose and lips. Something was inside her; it was burning and it was growing and it hurt and it wanted out. She wanted it *out.*

The pressure rose, swelled, expanded.

I have to protect her.

Vivna screamed. A man grabbed Ranka by her throat, and she tasted death.

Have to protect.

He drew a knife.

Protect.

And finally, Ranka gave in.

She bucked forward and sank her teeth into the man's wrist. He screamed and dropped the knife to the snow. Ranka snatched it up— it was heavier than she expected, the handle rough and warm. The man lunged for her and Ranka cried out, slashing at the air. Her arm jerked as the knife snagged on something rubbery. It was like cutting through a deer stomach but softer. Easier. Warm blood sprayed her cheek. Ranka adjusted her grip and pushed.

His life flashed through her—a field ruined by blight, a storm-wielding king drowning his family because they couldn't pay the crop tax, a witch breaking into their home to steal food. Ranka cringed backward, trembling, the colors of the world windmilling before her eyes in brilliant, saturated hues.

The man died—and the pressure exploded.

Power roared through her limbs, her veins, white hot and brilliant. It lit up her nerves, fused with the very cells of her body. Ranka screamed. Her nails darkened, shifting from gray to the deepest black, a void of color that drank in all the light. Her irises vanished.

Curled in the melting snow, in a tiny village in northern Isodal, a blood-witch was born.

Ranka opened her eyes.

The world rearranged itself. The pain was gone. Something ancient, crueler and hungrier than regular witchery, expanded inside her. Her muscles felt as if they were made of steel. She inhaled. The air tasted of pain, and nothing had ever tasted so sweet.

Something eternal and furious guided her young hands. It curled them into fists. She looked at the humans she had tried to love. The humans who had given her and her sister up once to the Skra and welcomed them back only to burn them.

A man with an axe lunged.

Ranka caught his hand with her own. She broke his fingers with a twist. He screamed, and Ranka stepped forward, prying the weapon from his ruined hand and turning it against him. Her body moved on instinct, the blade singing a terrible song as it sawed through his coat, the flannel shirt his wife had stitched him, and finally met his heart. Blood coursed down Ranka's arms as he collapsed. She felt stronger, better. His life flashed through her in images of fields, golden-haired children, a lover lost to the war—and then he was gone. The dark thing inside her swelled and demanded more.

The humans came for her.

She was unbreakable, and they were not.

I will protect her.

Ranka turned and seized the burning wood from the pyre. Fire blistered her skin, blackening her hands. Ranka hurled the burning log at the nearest house.

Fire roared up over the boards, engulfing the old cabin. Screams rose from the ones trapped inside. The flames spread to the next home and the next. Ranka limped to the barn. She set the horses free, and then she burned the barn, too.

She felt nothing.

Some villagers fled. The ones who tried to stop her didn't make it very far. She raised her nose to the wind, locking down on two scents in particular.

And then Ranka licked her lips and limped toward the parents who had failed her.

44

"I CAN'T DO IT." RANKA LURCHED UPRIGHT. SHE TOOK two steps only to fall to her knees and vomit. Black bile dripped from her lips. Memories swirled behind her eyes and a part of her yearned to dive back in—but she couldn't. She refused. That village. Those *people*.

What had happened there? How had she forgotten all of it—forgotten the way Vivna had failed her? The way Vivna had *hurt* her?

"Ranka," Aramis said, her voice low. "You can't stop now."

"I'm *done*."

The memory was bad enough. She would not relive what followed.

Vivna had refused to listen to her. Vivna had almost gotten them both killed. Everyone always made it sound like Ranka went into that village eager to kill. All this time she thought she'd been born cruel. But she'd only become a monster to save Vivna.

If only Vivna were here, if only Ranka could talk to her—

Pain shattered her world.

Ranka doubled forward, gasping. Her muscles seized and uncoiled as pain ricocheted through her. She could feel her blood-magic fighting her, pressing against her skin, like the pressure from five years ago but so much worse.

"You have to go back in. You have to see it through." Aramis crouched down in front of her, face distraught, and Ranka knew she was remembering Sorya. "Ranka, *please*."

All that power. If it hadn't been for Belren, would her blood-magic have ever manifested at all? Could she have lived a life not cloaked in death?

The pressure burned hotter than before, but it was condensing, tightening, flowing toward her heart. She could almost see it—a dark kernel of power, a miniature sun going cold. Her blood-magic shrank, twisting, retreating to the middle of her chest until it buried itself behind her heart, tightening into a tiny, jagged grain of wicked magic. One that pulsed and lived. One that no longer answered to Ranka at all.

"Ranka—"

"Leave me alone," Ranka whispered. Her ears rang and her vision swam, and all of it was worth it if she never had to see that village again. "I'm done."

All those people . . .

She'd heard stories, of course. But remembering it—feeling it—was different.

It was worse.

"Ranka, please—"

"I said leave me alone!" Ranka cried. She scrambled backward, even as Aramis reached for her, cringing away as if the princess's hands carried blades. A dozen emotions warred through her, and she latched on to anger, because anger was sharp, bright, slicing like a knife. "You were right, okay? This was a bad idea. I quit. I'm done."

"I said you weren't ready. And you demanded we do this anyway. You can't stop halfway. Please, Ranka, listen to me, let me help y—"

"Help me?" Her voice climbed higher, higher, edging into hysterics. "You never wanted to help me. You never cared about me. You wanted to crack the case of the broken blood-witch, solve the thing your mother never could. That's what I am, right? That's what the winalin witches are. Just another science experiment for the bored princess. Just another witch."

Was that even fair? Ranka didn't know, and she didn't care.

When had the lines between enemies become so blurred?

"You were never just another witch." Aramis's voice was quiet, her face a mask, and that was how Ranka knew she'd truly hurt her. "Even when I wanted you to be. I did everything I could to hate you, to think of you as nothing, to think of you as the enemy—and I failed. I think you know that. I think you feel the same." Aramis looked away, her mouth trembling, and Ranka was reminded of the day in the training arena, when Aramis had had every reason to lash out with cruelty, and held back instead. "Be angry with me all you want. But I was never the one who saw you as a weapon. I have always seen you as you are, Ranka."

Ranka lurched to her feet. She left before Aramis could tell her to stay, her steps unsteady. Her legs carried her across the grounds, through the gates. She didn't know where she was going, only that she wanted to get away.

So much in those memories didn't make sense. She had worshipped Vivna her entire life, had thought her the epitome of love and patience.

But in her memories of Belren, Vivna had not been loving and kind.

She'd been cruel.

Pain lashed through Ranka. What a pathetic fool she was, to think herself strong enough, brave enough, to dive back into Belren. To think she could conquer the blood-magic that had taken everything from her, to think she might prove to Ongrum that the princess who helped her do so was someone worth sparing, that she might be able to save anyone at all.

Ranka took an unsteady breath. She reached for her blood-magic and felt nothing. She called for it, whispered to it, even begged, but nothing happened. The kernel in her chest pulsed, sending spikes of pain through her. It swelled with the burning of a fever blister gathering pus, and it did not respond.

The next time her blood-magic surfaced, it would kill her.

45

FOR A FULL DAY RANKA HID IN HER ROOM. SHE DID not eat or sleep. Her blood-magic was gone, replaced by a useless, cold kernel nestled behind her heart. Belren filled her nightmares and crept into her daydreams. Twice a familiar scent of ink and mint came to her door, lingering outside. On the second visit, Aramis slipped a note under the door and left Ranka to her misery.

Ranka half expected an angry letter or a note rebuking her for her cowardice.

Instead, the note was just two words, written in Aramis's careful, neat script:

I'm sorry.

Somehow that was worse than anger, because in those two words was forgiveness and acknowledgment all in one—and a promise that when Ranka was ready, Aramis would help her again, if she wanted it. Ranka stared at the note for a long time, tears welling, and then carefully, delicately, folded it into a tiny square and tucked it into her pocket. Apologies were not built into the lexicon of the Skra. Ranka had thought them a weakness once—but then again, so much of what she'd thought had been upturned by this palace, this city, that girl.

She'd go back to Aramis. Apologize and admit the princess had been right, that she wasn't ready to face Belren, and maybe it was for the best that her blood-magic was temporarily removed from the equation. Maybe they could face it on a different night, in a different time, when they weren't on the brink of war.

But they were two days away from Galen's coronation—and two days away from the coup. Tomorrow witches would fill the palace, and everything would change.

She had a wound to deal with before then.

So when evening fell, Ranka slipped from her room and headed for the sea.

It drew her forward, an endless expanse of churning blue, and when she settled herself on the cliffs, she found herself shaking. The brief break in winalin-witch-induced horrors had allowed grief to open a yawning pit inside her chest. Her fingers skimmed her bracelet. So much in the Belren memories confused her. It wasn't just Yeva she'd failed; Vivna had needed Ranka to be better, smarter, and stronger.

Ranka had burned their lives down around them instead.

A shadow fell over her. "Enjoying the view, or brooding?"

"I'd like to be alone."

"Brooding, then." Percy flopped down beside her. Secretly, she was grateful. Not that she'd ever tell him that. He tilted his face into the breeze, black hair undone and flowing.

Ranka stared past him, sliding her fingers over the bracelet.

"What's that?" Percy asked, his tone uncharacteristically gentle.

"A promise." She braced herself for some kind of pity or coddling comment. If he told her he understood, so help her Goddess, she would push him off the cliffs.

Percy stretched out on his back. "Ghosts are a bitch."

"What?"

"Ghosts. The people that leave us too soon. The people we can't let go of." He paused. "You need to let her go, Ranka. May I?"

Ranka hesitated, and nodded. Her eyes blurred as Percy turned her hand over in his and slowly, gently, untied the bracelet Ranka had been wearing for five years. Her skin was paler under the leather, a thin band of stark white and free of scars. She felt terribly the same. It should have been painful to take it off. Should have been sacrilege. Where other witches had believed in a distant goddess, Ranka had only ever believed in family. Vivna, Ongrum, Yeva—they had been her prayer, her religion, the thing her heart spun around.

But her sister was gone, Yeva was dead, and this was just an ugly scrap of leather long faded by time.

"See?" Percy said gently. "No different than before. Letting someone go doesn't mean you stop loving them. It just means you're giving yourself permission to keep living."

Ranka's shoulders drooped. "How do you deal with it?"

"One day at a time. One hour at a time. One minute at a time," he said, not unkindly. "I expect I'll always be dealing with it."

Ranka blinked out at the ocean, her eyes wet.

"Do you want to talk about them?"

"I'd like to talk about literally anything else, actually."

She half expected him to crack a joke. Instead Percy closed his eyes. "When I was a boy, my father showed me what it meant to fly."

They sat there for a long time—Ranka immobile, gripping the bracelet, and Percy telling her of his ghosts, keeping her company in her grief with stories of his own. He told her about his father, who'd seen equations in the waves that crashed against their white-sand coasts, and his mother, who could mimic birdsong so well, she'd coaxed skittish petrels to settle on her wrist. He told her of the Fire Day parades, pale orchids blooming among cypress groves, of the sandstone dueling arenas and temples built into marble cliff faces that were accessible only by air. He talked until the sun sank over the horizon, and kept talking, and when he finished, his cheeks were wet with tears.

For the whole evening, Percy talked about the Star Isles. Ranka wondered if he realized he was also talking about love.

At dusk she found a rock the size of her palm, rough around the edges, colored like an overcast sky, and tied the bracelet around it. No longer against her skin, it looked like an old, worn-out piece of jewelry. Not a promise from someone she'd failed—just a piece of junk.

Percy's eyes flashed gold as he gave her the barest of nods.

Ranka looked to the sea.

She saw their faces—Yeva and Vivna, but the others, too, the winalin witches whose names she'd never learned, the lives she'd taken and the souls she'd failed. The ones she'd been too late for, the witches who'd burned because of the fear she'd sown. She carried so much guilt. Many more would die before winalin was cured. Many more would burn before they repaired the festering wound the treaty had only slapped a bandage over—if they could repair it at all.

But to do that—to really give the living a chance—she needed to let the dead go.

I'm sorry I couldn't save you. I hope you're at peace.

I hope, wherever you are, you can forgive me.

Ranka drew back her arm and threw.

The rock cut a high arc through the sky. The bracelet was barely visible, a band of brown against gray as it twirled and dropped. It hit the waves in a flash of white on blue. Ranka imagined the current snatching it up, carrying it to some foreign stretch of sand that had never known the blood of witches or the storms called by men who summoned them at will. Ranka watched the water for a long time.

Percy put an arm around her shoulders.

"Let's go," he said. "We've all had enough misery. I've got a surprise for you."

46

PERCY WOULDN'T TELL RANKA WHERE THEY WERE
going, only that, blessedly, this surprise had nothing to do with death.

The palace slumbered around them in a blur of warm shadow and
pale tile refracting moonlight. As they moved into the eastern wing,
the plain white tiles shifted to brightly colored mosaics. The steel-
eyed portraits of the Sunra royals past glared down at her. Finally they
stopped in front of a wide oak door. Percy slid a key from his pocket
and twisted to look at her, a funny grin on his face. "Do you really not
know what we're doing?"

He was beginning to irritate her.

"If I did, I wouldn't have asked you about a hundred times."

"Interesting. All those muscles really *are* stealing the blood from
your brain." Percy patted her head as though she were a cat he was
particularly fond of, and she slapped his hand away.

With a snort, Percy unlocked the door.

All she saw were wind chimes.

They hung from the ceiling and the walls, they were piled in great
silver and bronze stacks on the floor, and tiny, half-carved wooden
ones were collected in little bundles. Wooden chimes swung overhead,
making low, mournful sounds, while glittering metal ones tinkled

constantly. Even the bookshelves had wind chimes nailed onto either side of them. Ranka stepped farther into the room, swaying as melody wrapped around her. What corners of the room weren't filled with wind chimes were covered in books—piles of them, heaps of them, cast haphazardly across the floor with their bindings cracked and stacked against the walls. A single bed had been shoved into the corner, also piled with books, the sheets balled up. The only thing that seemed out of place was a table that had a white sheet messily thrown over it. Sugar lingered in the air.

"Where are we?" Ranka asked.

Percy pulled a pocket watch from the folds of his robe. "Galen's room."

"Why do you have the key to Galen's room?"

"Not important. Now, if I timed it right—"

The door slammed open. A gust of wind swirled into the room, knocking books from the shelves and setting off the wind chimes in a mad array of tinkling. Galen burst into the room and his face fell. "Oh, you *bastard*."

Aramis was only a step behind him. At the sight of her, Ranka froze—but Aramis was too busy scowling at Percy. "Percy, I thought Galen was going to *cry*."

For the first time she seemed to notice Ranka. Ranka's heart skipped a beat—but there was no anger in Aramis's eyes. Only concern.

"Will someone tell me what's going on?" Ranka asked blankly.

Aramis folded her arms. "Percy sent a guard with a note saying you set Galen's room on fire."

"What?" Ranka blurted. *"Why?"*

Galen crossed his arms, looking more than a little ruffled. "That was my reaction. Very funny, Percy. I don't see why it was nec—wait, what happened to my table?"

Percy took a long pause, as if they were all going to solve his inane plot in the few seconds he gave them, and sighed. "I have to do everything myself, don't I?"

With an overdramatic flourish, Percy ripped the sheet off the table and cast it to the side. The scent of sugar burst into the air, twice as strong as before, and the sheet fluttered to the ground, revealing a table laden down with a dozen different pastries and three little cakes he had almost certainly—very poorly—decorated himself. A few bottles of definitely stolen berry wine sat on the corner.

Percy scratched his head, and for the first time since Ranka had met him, he actually looked *nervous*.

"Um," he said. "Happy birthday."

Each pastry was different from the last, some of them drenched in a clear glaze, others coated with sugar or decorated with drizzles of honey and almond slices. And the cakes were . . . odd. One was covered in what looked like mint leaves; the second, in orange slices; and the third merely had an actual pine cone unceremoniously shoved into the frosting. It was a disaster. And it spoke of a painfully sincere effort.

He'd even remembered to bring four small plates, all of them stacked neatly together.

Aramis's eyes welled. "Percy, this is so . . . *sweet*."

"Wait," Galen said. "Why are there three cakes?"

"I figured Ranka's never celebrated her birthday, like, ever, so we might as well let her experience a shred of joy for once." He pointed to the cake with the pine cone. "That one's yours."

Now it was Ranka's turn to look at him through blurry eyes. It was a small thing—and yet it was everything. She'd been born on the last day of winter and had counted the years as they ticked by quietly, often with no celebration, only dread. Ever since her blood-magic had awoken, she'd wondered if each turn around the sun would be her last.

Until this past winter. It'd been dark when the cabin door creaked open. She'd woken with a start, half expecting to find an enemy witch in her bedroom, or a Skra needing her to dress for a fight.

Instead it was Yeva, her palms filled with strawberries.

"I'm sorry it's not more," she whispered. "But I wanted you to have something, to celebrate your last year as a witchling."

"I'm just here for the strawberries," Asyil announced loftily—though from the small smile on her lips, she was also pleased by the tears in Ranka's eyes.

Ranka still had no idea where Yeva had gotten them; in late winter strawberries were well out of season, and by then no Skra should have been trading with humans unless out of necessity. The strawberries were small and bitter, half of them covered in a white fuzz of mold they had to scrape with off their thumbnails, but it didn't matter. They could have tasted like dust, or pine needles, or nothing at all, and it still would have been one of the loveliest moments of her life as they sat in the dark, licking their fingers clean of berry juice as the sun rose and Ranka turned seventeen.

A heaviness settled in her. She'd had no way of knowing that her last birthday as a witchling would be the last one she shared with Yeva, too. That only four months later she would head south in a desperate attempt to bring her home, and fail.

"Do you not like it?" Percy asked anxiously. "Aramis loves mint, and Galen loves oranges, but I didn't really know what you like, and I know the north is full of those ugly trees. . . ."

They were all staring at her—and Ranka realized she'd been standing in total silence, tears streaming down her face, staring at the cake a boy who never should have cared about her had picked out just for her, on a day that wasn't really hers to celebrate, because he knew she'd spent a lifetime being denied the chance.

"It's perfect," she said, her voice strangled, and then, "Wait, do you think I *eat* pine cones?"

"No comment." Percy cleared his throat. "Anyway, given our luck, this may be the *last* birthday any of us see, so I figured we better celebrate."

"Oh, good," Aramis said dryly. "This was all far too sincere. I was getting worried. I'm glad you found a way to ruin it."

He beamed. "I'd say the setting is to humble you, but the truth is I didn't know where else I could trick you both into visiting last minute. And I didn't think the stables or getting attacked by winalin witches in the mines would make for a very celebratory affair."

Galen and Aramis glanced at each other, and Galen turned to Percy with a twinkle in his eye. "I might have somewhere in mind."

47

FROM THE HIGHEST POINT OF THE PALACE, IT FELT LIKE
Ranka looked down upon the entire world.

Below her, Seaswept sprawled in an endless expanse of velvet blue,
the night broken by the lonely beam of a lighthouse standing watch over
the bay, beckoning distant ships in from the safety of an endless, dark
sea. It'd been short work for Galen to bring them up. From up here, the
palace grounds were small and indistinct. Even Seaswept seemed like a
distant, breakable toy. They'd settled on a thin blanket to count down
the minutes until the twins were officially eighteen, nibbling on pastries
and huddling against the chill of the ocean-fed breeze.

And they had gotten hopelessly, irredeemably drunk.

They sprawled on their backs, pausing between bites of pastry
to giggle and pass the wine. Percy was the only one still somewhat
collected. Galen and Aramis had long since abandoned any sense of
decorum and were pointing at the stars like children, both of them
grabbing at Ranka's hands every few minutes, asking her if the stars
above Isodal were the same ones that watched over Witchik, and if
they carried the same names, too.

Percy observed them with raised brows. "You're all a *mess.*"

Ranka didn't care. She felt happy. She felt good.

"Don't worry. If we fall off the roof," Aramis slurred, "Galen might catch us."

It was a gift to finally be at ease with them. So much of Ranka's time in Isodal had been a swirl of confusion, grief, and pain. She'd arrived ready to hate the Sunra twins, to see them ended—but somewhere along the way, they'd become more. They'd become worth it.

Tomorrow, she would do everything she could to ensure the Skra saw that too.

Even now a part of her wondered if she should tell them. But telling them her plan to *stop* the coup meant telling them that she'd come here to *start* one. Ongrum would see reason. She'd choose the strategic route. She always did.

They had a brief moment of peace, and Ranka was going to revel in it.

"All right," Percy said. "It's almost time."

Aramis and Galen sat up and nestled in on either side of Ranka, cross-legged, their knees touching hers, heads bowed over the tiny, scratched watch glinting in Percy's palm. The second hand wound its way around the clockface. All Ranka could hear was the faint ticking and the murmur of the sea.

The minute hand clicked forward to twelve. In the distance, deep in the city, the midnight bells began to ring, marking the beginning of a new day.

And just like that, summer had ended, and their status as children with it.

Yet nothing about them was changed. They were still the same round-cheeked Sunra twins, still orphans, so terribly young despite all they'd endured, and what they might yet have to.

"Happy birthday," Percy whispered.

The bells kept ringing. When the sun rose, banners would unfurl in the city, celebrating the coming-of-age of a new king. Back home, the Skra typically marked the first day of fall by raking the summer fields, pruning the late crops, and preparing hunting parties to stalk the herds that'd begin grazing with an urgency in preparation for a lean winter. Fall was merely a break in the heat to Seaswept, but to the north it was a warning of the snows to come, of long days and longer nights.

Aramis hummed low in her throat. "Percy, I just realized I don't know when your birthday is."

"I defy the boundaries of time," said Percy.

She threw a pastry at his head.

"Tenth day of summer," he amended. "You know, you are the most ill-mannered princess I have ever met."

"It's my birthday," Aramis sniffed. "I can do whatever I want."

They'd brought no knives with them, so the twins ate their cakes with their fingers instead. After a moment's hesitation, Ranka followed suit. She carefully set the pine cone aside and bit deep, relishing the taste of vanilla, black currant, and strawberry. Tears sprang to her eyes, and she wiped them away, but when she looked up, the twins' eyes were watery too.

"I wish Foldrey were here," Galen whispered.

Grief lanced through Ranka's warm, drunken haze with sobering clarity. They loved him so dearly, and he'd loved them in return. They spoke of him with all the reverence with which she spoke of Ongrum, but with a warmth Ranka had never known. In another life, had she not been a threat—had she not represented everything Foldrey stood to lose—she wondered if he might have loved her, too.

Aramis closed her eyes for a moment. Pain and love shared the lines of her face in equal measure. "He'd be so pissed to know we're on the roof again."

"Oh, furious," Galen agreed. He leaned his head on Percy's shoulder and played with the cuff of his sleeve. "I miss him. I miss so many of them."

They lapsed into quiet, eating their sweets, the silence broken only by the occasional sniffle. There seemed to be a precious understanding floating between them—that this brief window of peace was only that, and there was more pain coming. More struggle. But somehow, inexplicably, they'd found one another, they'd survived together, and that was something. For a single night, instead of the heads of an empire, they were just kids who had weathered far too much, far too soon, perched on a roof after midnight, eating cake in the dark.

An hour after the bells tolled, Galen brought them back inside. But instead of going their separate ways, Galen cleared the books from his bed and pulled an extra cot from his closet. The four of them huddled together on the mattresses, and Ranka listened as Galen and Aramis took turns sharing stories of past birthdays, of when they'd awoken as children and the entire world had paused to celebrate them.

After a while Galen and Percy dozed off, slumped against each other, and only Aramis and Ranka remained awake. She knew she ought to leave; none of this was proper, and she needed every ounce of sleep she could get. But she was reluctant to end this fragile peace.

"Are you nervous about seeing them again?" Aramis asked. "Your coven?"

Ranka tensed. "Yes."

It was hard to picture the Skra here, in the palace—like her memories of them belonged to a different girl, in a different life.

"I'm sorry." Her fingers found Ranka's in the dark. "About your blood-magic . . ."

Ranka swallowed. She didn't want to talk about this, didn't want to invite everything they'd momentarily forgotten back into this brief bubble of precious calm. "We'll figure it out, Princess. I'll be fine. And—it's like you said. We have guards and defenses. Galen doesn't need a blood-witch to make it through this."

Ranka closed her eyes. She had made the decision to seal Belren away long ago, and after what she'd seen in the garden, she would not go back to it now. Not now, and never again.

Maybe Aramis knew this, because she didn't press Ranka further. Instead she sighed and lay back, resting her head on Ranka's legs, and stared at the ceiling.

Ranka didn't dare move. She lay awake in the dark, still feeling small, but no longer alone.

"What would you do?" Aramis asked slowly. "If you got to be normal?"

"Normal?"

"Invisible—an everyday person. No one. Who would you be?"

Ranka had been no one, once—just a witch, a sister, a little girl trying to survive. But she'd never been normal. Instead, she'd spent her childhood learning how to gut a deer before winter winds could freeze the meat solid, how to hunt for tubers in the spring thaw, and what barks to chew to stave off hunger pains. How to bind a broken wrist, staunch a gushing wound, or track someone through a forest who'd done everything in their power to stay hidden.

More than anything, she'd spent her childhood learning how to kill.

"I'd be a healer," Aramis continued, her voice wistful. "A real one, not just Lanna's anonymous assistant. I used to think I was so clever, sneaking out to work in the clinic. I didn't realize Mother knew. She let me pretend I was no one for a few hours a week. It kept me from losing my mind."

Ranka recalled the way Aramis had cared for the patients in the clinic, the quiet intensity with which she'd heard them, nursed their wounds, and soothed their fears. Unlike Galen or Percy or Ranka herself, Aramis had spent hours upon hours with the people of Seaswept. She'd heard their hurts and worries and taken them to heart.

"You'd make a great healer. They'd be lucky to have you."

"What would you do?"

Ranka had never had a hobby to sneak away to, a quiet passion to feed, like Aramis's love of medicine or Galen's insatiable hunger for music and books. And yet she knew what she wanted. What she'd dreamed of, every day, for the past five years, while her coven mates dreamed of glory and war and all the trappings of power that glittered for those who had not yet been cursed with it.

Her words came out soft, and slow.

"I would move to the woods, where no one could ever find me. I'd build a cabin, all by myself. I'd stay there forever, and I would rest."

It'd been her dream for her and Vivna, once. To disappear into Witchik where no war could touch them. She could see it now—a moss-dusted log cabin nestled into the hills that nearly disappeared in the midwinter snows. There'd be a river nearby that always ran clear, where deer came to drink and wood ducks taught their hatchlings to swim. They'd be easy prey, but Ranka wouldn't hunt them; for once in her life she'd exist near something delicate and simply let it be. She'd wake with the dawn, grow full on berries, and catch the trout from the river until she was absolutely sick of it. In those dreams, her blood-magic always seemed to fade like color on cloth left out in the sun—growing weaker each day, less hungry, until it was barely a flicker, and then finally nothing at all.

"I'd buy books. Dozens of them. Fat books, little books, books for adults and books for children. I'd teach myself to read and write properly." Her eyelids fluttered. "And paint. Yeva was good at that—painting. I'd learn slowly, but it wouldn't matter, because I'd have all the time in the world."

All she'd wanted was that cabin in the woods. How had she strayed so far?

Aramis yawned. "Once this is all over, I'll build you the most ridiculous cabin on the continent."

"The point is that *I* build it."

"Gross." Aramis waved a hand. "Fine, I'll buy you the books. Mountains of them. And we'll do nothing but read and paint and sing. We'll be terrible, and it'll be wonderful. Galen will have no choice but to banish us."

"Your brother would never banish you."

"You haven't heard me sing." Aramis didn't move her head from Ranka's shins. It couldn't have possibly been comfortable. "For what it's worth, you're strong enough to conquer it. You always have been."

Ranka said nothing, and Aramis didn't push further. She fell asleep to the soft whistle of Aramis's breath. She feared nightmares of Yeva, Vivna, or the winalin witches—but instead she fell into a deep, dark sleep, the first she'd had in ages, and dreamed of nothing at all.

When night faded into the pale blue of early dawn, Ranka woke to find Aramis beside her, curled in a ball on top of the sheets, dark hair fanned across the pillow. Galen dozed on the other cot. Percy sprawled facedown on the floor.

Ranka pulled a blanket over Aramis, tracking the worry lines that etched her face, the frown that creased her brows, the exhaustion curling her shoulders even in sleep.

Ranka pressed a kiss to the top of her head and made a promise in the dark.

"I failed them," she whispered. "I will not fail you."

48

THE WITCHES ARRIVED WITH THE DAWN.

The Murknen came first, dour and scowling, with moss woven through their wild hair. Ongrum had always said the Murknen hailed from a territory of swamps and little sunlight—and they had the personalities to match. The Arlani came second, flouncing through in their white robes, their haughty gazes carrying an air of superiority. Then the guards sent up a cry—except instead of pointing to the city, they pointed to the ocean.

There, across the reach of the Broken Sea, still little more than smudges against the waves, sails blossomed against the horizon.

The Oori.

Their ships drew closer. Individual witches could be made out, moving across the decks with effortless grace. There were hundreds of them, all linked by a single cause, a single name. It made the Skra look like they were only playacting at what it meant to be a coven. The Oori were the unknowns. The Murknen's distaste for the Sunras was well known; the Arlani favored the treaty because both previous Bloodwinns had come from their camp. The Kerth had been broken entirely, thanks to the Hands. But these witches, made of salt and spray—which side did they favor?

And if it came to a fight—whom would they choose?

The four of them had done everything they could to prepare. Every guard was on duty, armed with tranquilizers and instant-click torches. Major roads in and out of the city were closed to delay movement, and Aramis's workshop had been outfitted with rations in the event the twins needed to shelter in place. They could also flee through the mines—though troubling reports of strange, bloody attacks had increased further. Galen had promoted a temporary captain—Damon, a young, nervous man who'd been Foldrey's second—who'd seized the role with surprising efficiency and handpicked a small unit of several soldiers to brief about the Hands.

Aramis, Galen, and Percy would spend tonight swaying powerful nobles to their side, while Ranka tried to ensure the commitment of the covens to following her as Bloodwinn. The morning of the coronation, the palace would be so heavily guarded, the Hands would have to be suicidal to attempt anything.

And if it still went south, two rowboats had been anchored within a cove beyond the cliffs. Just in case a pair of royals had to abandon their home in a hurry.

"We won't need them," Percy assured. "We're so close to a cure. The humans want to support the twins, and the witches will too, once we make winalin a temporary nuisance instead of a world-ending threat. We can win this."

It was a good plan, a solid plan, and yet Ranka was still afraid. Because what they didn't know—what she couldn't tell them—was that it wasn't just a coup from the Hands they had to fear.

A whistle cut through the air, and finally, the Skra arrived.

Sixty-seven witches poured through the gate, cloaked in Northlander furs despite the heat, bearing weapons and stone faces as they entered the palace. They looked small compared to the ranks of the Oori, but there was a ferocity to the northern war band that made Ranka's heart ache to join them. She should have been down there, chin high and proud, instead of watching from the palace steps like a stranger.

At their lead, steady as always, was Ongrum. The sight of her made Ranka's knees buckle. She needed to talk to Ongrum immediately, explain the new plan, make her see reason, before it was too late. With Ongrum as the twins' ally, the Hands wouldn't stand a chance.

Percy angled his head to the side, his silver-ringed fingers flashing in the morning light. "You know, my family loved me until their last breaths. I'd rather they'd despised me and lived."

Ranka's heart skipped a beat. "I'm not sure what you mean."

Percy gave her a long, sad look, until she was forced to turn away.

"Why help Isodal?" she asked, eager to talk about anything else. "Why come here and put yourself at risk? Why not just leave the continent to burn?"

"You know why. You more than anyone." He frowned. "I have . . . so much to amend. Someday I'll have to go home. Find a way to fix what my father helped break. But it starts here, with winalin. It always did."

Ranka looked at him, at the way the sunlight cast his face into sharp, beautiful lines. Again she recalled the rumors she'd heard about the Star Isles, about the people who were tied to that land because of the impossible magic it lent them. The rumors that they'd never really been people at all.

"Besides," Percy tacked on cheerfully, breaking the spell, "I really *do* hate Ilia. Gods, what I wouldn't give to see her face when she realizes she's lost." He held up an imaginary glass, toasting only empty air. "To betrayal."

Ranka patted his shoulder affectionately. "You are completely and utterly unhinged."

"Entirely." Percy shrugged. "It's how I've survived."

Where is she?

Navy tile gleamed across the western ballroom floor, a stain of ink against golden Sunra banners. A sound mage stood in the corner, fingers hooked as she wove gentle melodies from nothing. Visitors packed the room, nobles and wealthy merchants, travelers from king-doms over, all of them nervously mingling with the Arlani, Murknen, Oori, and Skra.

Most of the Skra.

Ranka could not find Ongrum.

She'd searched for her for the better part of an hour, but the Skra leader was nowhere to be found. When Ranka questioned her coven mates, they'd simply shrugged and said something about her having business to attend to. They were lying, and it stung. She'd asked them as a Skra—and they'd responded as strangers. Even the witches she knew well—Tafa, Sigrid, Nadya, and so many she'd trained alongside, gave her the cold shoulder.

You are not one of us, their eyes said. *We do not recognize you. You will have to earn us back.*

Ranka's fingers drifted self-consciously to her own clothing. Black trousers showed off her muscled legs, vanishing neatly into sturdy boots embellished with gold buckles. The Sunra emblem of an explod-ing sun shimmered in pale gold across her shoulders. Threads of deep, bloody red and gusts of silver wind swept down her sides, weaving together into a single, unified pattern. The tailors had opted to leave her scarred, muscled arms bare, burn marks and all, but now her old wounds looked like marks of power instead of shame. She'd nearly wept over the clothes. They fit perfectly, finer than anything she'd worn before. Instead of boorish and out of place, she looked power-ful, brilliant, and *strong.*

And . . . human.

Ranka's fingers went nervously to her bracelet and found only skin.

A hush fell across the room, and every eye turned to the gilded doors from the private wing as they swept open.

Ranka's world went quiet.

Tonight the Sunra twins were not children. They were power.

They were ethereal in blue military dress, complete with gold-embellished decorative knives and shoulder armor. Galen's fingers dripped with signet rings; his gold circlet shone from his brow. Delicate silver thread depicted the gale winds he always wore, but now lightning swept over his chest in vibrant gold. Storm clouds gleamed across his shoulders. The message was clear: gone was the boy prince, the wind mage, the weakling of his line.

Galen Sunra was a Skybreaker now, and he'd dressed in a storm.

Aramis looked sharp and dangerous in the neatly cut military clothes. Her mass of curls had been left free, framing her face and bobbing above her shoulders. But it was her clothing that drew murmurs. As the magicless heir, her clothes should have been plain. Instead, stark white thread depicting healers' herbs flowered up her sides, and odd, sharp symbols cascaded down her arms. *Molecule chains*, she and Percy had explained, though it meant nothing to Ranka. The Hands had called the practice of science heretical. Now Aramis wore it proudly and claimed it as her own.

They stood side by side, the boy with a power born, the girl with a power made, united only by their twin gold circlets, and Ranka knew that no matter what happened tonight, this country would never be the same.

Galen cleared his throat. He was the kind of person whose smile radiated something infectious even when it meant nothing. "Tonight we celebrate the Bloodwinn treaty. We celebrate three generations of peace." How many others who knew him looked at that smile and saw how hollow it was? "All right, then—enough formality. Enjoy!"

Music jumped into the air. The revelers turned back to their dances. None of them knew the twins well enough to recognize the grim light in Aramis's eyes, the way she stepped into the ballroom as if preparing for battle. The twins separated, Aramis flashing a honey-sweet smile and wielding a light touch to the arm like a weapon, Galen greeting people with a forced formality.

Ranka steeled her nerves and stepped into the crowd.

It was time to stop a coup.

49

RANKA COULDN'T FIND ONGRUM.

She'd banked everything on tonight, on making Ongrum see reason and swaying her to their side.

How could she do that if Ongrum was nowhere to be found?

To her left, Aramis and Galen danced with Murknen witches, smiling easily and chatting through the music. Percy twirled with a beautiful human noblewoman whose pink gown made her brown skin glow. He met Ranka's eyes over her shoulder, scowled, and mouthed, *dance.*

She glared back at him.

He took a hand from the woman's waist and drew a line across his throat.

Ranka turned to the witch behind her. "Will you dance with me before my friend has a heart attack?"

The leader of the Oori coven gave her a smile that was all teeth. "Nice to meet you, too, little Bloodwinn."

Oh, sweet Goddess, kill me now.

Ranka may have been the Butcher of Belren, but Ursay Whitehook had long earned the title of Demon of the Seas and embraced it.

They were taller than Ranka, sharp faced and lean, their ears and fingers adorned with pale gold jewelry. Tattoos wrapped their limbs, but the one that marked them as a witch worthy of legends was the shark's teeth tattooed around the column of their brown throat, carefully inked so it appeared the teeth closed in from each side. Nearly meeting but never quite. Ursay was older than Ongrum, but not by much. And they carried a power even Ranka couldn't match—not the raw power of blood-magic, but the unshakable confidence of a leader who knew they were the most dangerous one in every room they entered.

Ursay was the longest-ruling coven leader in recent history. They'd overtaken the Oori at only fifteen and had spent forty years swelling their ranks to nearly three hundred witches. Though the palace would never confirm it, rumor had it even the last Skybreaker king had been forced to bend to the Oori's incredible power and had delegated funds off the books to bribe safe passage for Isodolian cargo ships that were desperate to ferry goods to the many nations waiting across the Broken Sea and the ocean beyond.

Tafa liked to say Ursay wasn't a blood-witch because they were already too deadly. Any more magic would have tipped the balance too far.

Ranka regarded Ursay, and was inclined to agree.

"Would you like to dance," Ursay purred, "or stare?"

They held out a dark-nailed hand, and Ranka took it. A shiver rolled through her. Ursay's nails were the darkest she'd ever seen for a witch who didn't carry blood-magic in their veins.

The Oori leader swept her into a spinning, twirling set of fast-paced steps with surprising grace and fixed Ranka with a humorless smile, as though she were a particularly cute child showing off a party trick rather than a girl about to lead a nation. "All right, give me the speech."

Ranka stumbled. "My speech?"

"Your plea, your call to action. Come on, that adorable little princess already tried. Give it to me. Tell me about the good of the kingdom, the world witches deserve, yada yada yada." A bored smile curled their lips. "I'm all ears, Bloodwinn."

The room turned, and Ranka caught Percy gaping at her, white faced. They'd agreed Aramis alone would handle Ursay. The Oori had nothing to lose by leaving them all to rot, and everything to gain by staying to fight the Hands. This would be a negotiation that required the utmost care and decorum.

But now, spinning hand in hand, as Ursay watched her with a languid smile, anger spiked in Ranka. Ursay had agreed to dance only to mock her. They didn't believe in Ranka or the treaty. This was a game to them, one they thought they were immune to, because they'd escaped winalin mostly unscathed.

Ursay wanted her to talk? She'd talk. Screw decorum. Screw every rule she'd learned from humans—this was a conversation between witches. And it was a conversation between killers.

"You're confident," Ranka observed. "Your reputation precedes you. Even the Sunras owe you their deference, which is something my coven has never received."

"Flattery? That's your route?"

"Your ships have been spending a lot of time in the north. Early fall is usually when you dock in the south, though, is it not?"

"We prefer the sea, and the cold is good for the lungs." Ursay yawned. "You're beginning to bore me, little witch."

Ranka pictured Aramis's steel calm, Percy's polished charm, and Galen's disarming kindness. "How long have you been running from the sickness?"

Ursay missed a step.

"How long," Ranka added carefully, "have you been mourning your lost warrior?"

The noise of the room faded away. Now it was only her and Ursay, Skra and Oori, gripping each other's hands so tightly, their bones ground. Rage lined every muscle in Ursay's body. Good. Ranka could work with rage.

"Explain," Ursay warned. *"Quickly."*

"She was young," Ranka continued. "Tan and pretty, with kraken tattoos. We couldn't save her. There was another with her—a Kerth. Most of the victims have been Kerth—but you already knew about that, didn't you? You know they've been wiped out, and that's why you've been hiding in the north, because your newest recruits told you exactly what to run from."

The last claim was a shot in the dark. She'd noticed some of the Oori's tattoos were fresh, the skin around them raw, the new ink carefully bandaged. All their ears were lined with old puncture wounds—as if they'd spent their lives wearing wooden beads. From the fury rippling off Ursay, she was right on the mark.

They only stared.

"Whatever horror stories the Kerth told you about the plague are true. But there's something they don't know." Ranka steeled herself. "There's a cure."

"Impossible." All of Ursay's lazy bravado dropped away. Now a real leader gripped her hands. She could practically hear Ursay's mind whirring, calculating how the odds might have just shifted. "The blood plague is incurable."

"It was," Ranka corrected. "The Kerth they injected—we found her before the winalin managed to kill her. And she's still alive." Ursay said nothing as Ranka plunged forward. "The Hands of Solomei intend to weaponize winalin and infect every witch alive. That princess over there? She and the Star Isles ambassador have nearly cracked the cure. We are *close*, Ursay. So painfully, blessedly close. But if the Hands attack tomorrow and kill Galen, every witch is as good as dead."

The music shifted to a faster tempo. All around them, couples laughed and twirled. Ursay's dark eyes were unreadable. "You want my warriors."

"I want your promise you won't pick up anchor, head out to sea, and leave us all to rot." Her palms were lined with sweat. "I want your commitment to the Bloodwinn treaty—because without it, without those twins, it doesn't matter where you sail. Winalin will find you eventually. And with no cure, your fate will be the same as the warrior you already lost."

The music faded and slowed. It was time to switch partners. Still Ursay gripped Ranka's hands so hard it hurt, breathing unevenly through their nose to try to calm their fury. "My girl, Soma. Did she suffer?"

Ranka hesitated. She saw it in her mind's eye—the sores, the agony, the blood spilling over the floorboards, but instead of Soma it was Talis who died in that tavern. It was Yeva. It was the nameless witch wearing her bracelet in the morgue and the one who'd fled north only to die beneath foreign pines.

Did she suffer?

How could they not, in this world? A treaty strangled them, humans burned them. Now a foreign queen had taken the one thing that gave witches an edge and perverted it into a horror, and the humans sought to use it as a tool of extinction.

"Not long." She couldn't lie to Ursay. "But any moment with winalin inside you is a lifetime of torture."

Their nostrils flared. "And just how close are you to a cure?"

"Painfully close. The Kerth has been in a coma, but she's alive. The winalin hasn't gotten better—but it hasn't gotten worse, either. We've subdued it for now." Ranka's throat bobbed. "If we have a cure, we can inoculate healthy witches against the plague and save those already sick. But we need the Sunra twins alive to do it."

Ursay released Ranka at last, their lean body uncoiling as they stepped back. Ranka's heart hammered so hard, she thought she might pass out. The Oori leader looked her over, and a humorless smile twisted their lips. "The Oori will never support the current treaty."

"But—"

"Let me finish, little one."

Ranka's mouth clicked shut.

"We do not support the Bloodwinn treaty," Ursay continued, "for the same reasons as your coven. It's killing us all, strangling us year after year. The treaty was a mistake, signed out of desperation. But"—they lifted a tattooed brow—"we will support *you*."

Ranka hesitated, feeling more than a little foolish. "I don't understand."

Ursay looked right through her. "I know the rumors about you, Ranka of the Skra. I have my suspicions of why you came here out of the blue after months of running. Truly, I'm impressed by your restraint. I thought he'd be dead by now."

"That's not—"

"Shhh. I've just begun to like you. Don't ruin it by lying." Ursay stepped back, considering Ranka, and nodded. "Our interests are aligned for now. Make no mistake—the lives of the Sunra twins mean nothing to me. But the lives of my coven mean *everything*. You're in a position to rewrite the future here, little girl. When winalin is no longer a threat, I expect you to do it."

They turned away then, leaving Ranka rooted in place. A merchant tapped her shoulder and asked her to dance, and Ranka let him spin her away, reeling from Ursay's words. The hour dragged on. Ranka danced with other witches, with nobles and merchants and even a wealthy cattle farmer who supplied the military with leather armor. Ursay didn't come near her again, and she saw nothing of Ongrum. Where *was* she?

The merchant Ranka had been half-heartedly chatting with balked and stepped away. Ranka stumbled and turned to see who had stepped up behind her.

Aramis tilted her head to the side. "You're not that bad of a dancer."

"You're usually a better liar."

The smile that split Aramis's face made every nerve in her come alive. It was impossible not to remember their fight, or last night, the way they'd crowded together on the palace roof, and the promise she'd made in the dark.

I will not fail you.

They both stood stock-still, immobile in a sea of twirling witches and humans.

"You're neglecting your guests," Ranka said.

Aramis closed the space between them. "Dance with me, witch girl."

"Here?" Ranka's voice faltered. "In front of all these people?"

Aramis held out her hand.

Every nerve screamed for Ranka to bolt, but she took it. The princess's fingers felt cool and right against her own.

Together they moved to the center of the room.

50

ARAMIS DANCED AS THOUGH HER FEET DIDN'T TOUCH the floor. They turned slowly, swaying to the music as couples twirled around them in flashes of color and wafts of perfume. They turned and Ranka caught a glimpse of Tafa, watching them through narrowed eyes. Nobles slowed in their own dances, pausing to watch.

"People are staring."

"Let them."

"I've been thinking," Ranka breathed. "About tomorrow. And . . . what follows."

"Don't," Aramis said, her voice soft. "Let me have one moment. Just one, where we're not at war." She laid her head on Ranka's shoulder. Some of the pale gold glitter dusted across her cheekbones rubbed off onto Ranka, winking like stars. "Tell me about our cabin. The one you're going to build in the woods."

Ranka's eyes stung. Everyone was staring, but Ranka had spent so much of her life twisting herself into odd shapes to soften the gazes of others. She had sacrificed, lost, and grieved. There was no guarantee of what tomorrow would bring—but this moment, this she could have. So instead of pulling away, Ranka settled a hand on Aramis's waist and held her close.

"The cabin," Ranka said, her voice barely above a whisper, only for her ears even with the eyes of the world on them, "will be cut from cedar and built along a river."

Aramis relaxed. Ranka held her close and let the room fade away.

Ranka whispered to Aramis about the way the moss would grow up to the windows, the elk that would graze in the meadow over the hill, the berry-bright cardinals they'd lure in with sunflower seeds. She told her of the snows that would come so swiftly, so heavily, it would startle her. She told her of raw red sunsets and evening skies that deepened like a bruise, of the blush-chested robins that were the first homecoming of spring, the other covens whose witches would venture through their land in pursuit of a stray deer, the fangwolves that would slink down from the mountains when the herds ran thin. She told her of their mornings—how they'd wake to nothing but golden light and birdsong to eat from a garden that grew rich and wild off dark mountain-fed soil, and she told her of their nights, of the velvet blackness that would blanket the sky and wrap around them so thoroughly, it would feel like they were the only ones left alive in this world.

She told her about how no one would ever find them. Not unless they wanted them to. How for the first time in her life, Aramis Sunra would be away from the eyes of the world, and she could be wholly, entirely herself.

And finally, they would rest.

"I hope we get to build it," Aramis said, her voice far away. The scent of slow-spun sugar filled the air. Not the saccharine, fake sugar that was pumped into candy or pastries—she smelled of the soft tang of thistle flowers and the warm sweetness of honey, wrapped in a whisper of mint.

Ranka's knees buckled. Sometimes the people Ranka had stolen moments with had bubbled with the sharp ripple of lust, the overwhelming candy-reek of infatuation, but no one had ever looked at her and smelled of sugar.

Aramis stretched up on her toes and kissed Ranka on the cheek. "No matter what happens, Ranka—I'm glad you're here. I'm glad you chose us."

The kiss burned her skin, pleasantly warm, and for the first time, Ranka wouldn't have minded if the touch of another left a scar on her. Aramis stepped away, and Ranka understood why Ongrum had always said love was nothing but a weakness.

"I'm going to go check on our patient," Aramis said, the warmth fading as her regular mask slid back into place. Her eyes darted around, as if seeming to finally care that some were openly gawking, and she moved farther away, smoothing out the folds of her uniform.

Suddenly Ranka couldn't bear for Aramis to be anywhere she wasn't. "Do you want me to go with you?"

"Some quiet will do me good. Besides, someone ought to keep an eye on Galen."

Ranka stood there, lost and a little limp, watching the sleek line of Aramis's back disappear into the crowd. Her cheek burned where Aramis had kissed it. A beautiful Arlani witch extended a brown hand and asked Ranka to dance, but she politely declined, retreating to the back of the room, her head spinning. A newfound determination settled in her.

She would do everything in her power to protect that girl, no matter the cost.

And that meant finding Ongrum.

Ranka cut her way through the crowd, beelining toward a familiar, slender back and twin red braids. She clapped her hand on Tafa's shoulder, and the Skra girl she'd once loved spun around so fast, her braids snapped against her shoulder.

For the briefest flicker, Ranka saw it—guilt and anger intertwined, cascading across Tafa's sharp, beautiful face before smoothing into false indifference.

"Ranka," Tafa said awkwardly. "Hi, I meant to find you sooner— this place is pretty overwhelming, huh?"

From the sidelines, Sigrid, Nadya, and two other Skra watched. They'd shut her down when she'd pressed about Ongrum, but she and Tafa were *friends*. Had been more, once. Tafa would tell the truth. Ranka shook off their glares, took Tafa by the elbow, and steered her toward the corner of the room.

"Why are you treating me like the enemy?" Ranka demanded.

"I have no idea what you mean."

"Yes, you do. I've been trying to talk to the Skra all night—and you keep skittering away from me like scared little ants. Even you look terrified of me. What's going on, Tafa? Where is Ongrum?"

There it was again—that odd flash of anger mixed with guilt. "She's here."

"But where is *here*? I've been looking for her for an hour and . . ."

Several heads turned. Ranka lowered her voice.

"I need to talk to her, Tafa. It's about tomorrow's coup. It's important—so important that whatever Ongrum is doing can wait, because the very future of our coven is at risk."

"Our future," Tafa said flatly. "Right. I'm sure you're real concerned about the Skra's future."

"What is that supposed to mean?"

"Do you think we're stupid?" Tafa snapped. "I just saw you dancing, Ranka—what are you doing, making moon eyes over *Aramis Sunra*? Following her and her brother around like some loyal puppy? We sent you here to do a *job*."

"And I'm doing it," Ranka snapped back. She'd never been anything but loyal to the Skra—why were they acting like she'd already betrayed them?

She's trying to rile you up. Breathe, you big oaf, a familiar voice reminded her. *And look closely.*

The room faded away. Tafa remained where she was, her face drawn and frustrated, but there was no actual bite to her words. She was just trying to distract Ranka—to drag out time.

Why?

Once, Tafa might have gotten under her skin with ease, might have soothed her screaming instincts with a few well-placed lies. But Ranka had spent weeks under Isodal's sun, fighting against and then alongside two children raised in a court where the only weapons were their words. No Skra held a candle to them.

Ranka made her tone go carefully neutral. "Tafa, where's Asyil?"

The color drained from Tafa's face. "What?"

"Asyil," Ranka said slowly. "I didn't see her walk in with the Skra—but everyone else is here."

Tafa wouldn't meet her eyes. "She's . . . waiting in the city."

"With Ongrum?"

"What? No—"

"So she's alone?"

"No," Tafa snarled. "She's just waiting, okay? With the others who can't come in yet."

"What others?" Ranka's heart started beating harder. "If Ongrum is here, then who else is with Asyil in the city?"

Horror washed across Tafa's face. Her pupils shrank to two tiny, dark points. The whispers of fear that had been building in Ranka all night evolved into full-blown screams.

"Tafa," Ranka asked slowly, her hand drifting to her hip, where her axe typically sat, and finding only leather. "What's going on? What aren't you telling me?"

Tafa's mouth opened and closed like a fish gasping for air. Her eyes darted frantically across Ranka's face, and she took the slightest step backward, as if to bolt. The hair on Ranka's arms stood on end.

A whistle split the air.

It was a sharp, earsplitting sound—two long blasts, one short, two more long. She'd heard that whistle a dozen times over—it was the first signal a new Skra learned when they joined the coven.

It meant: *Get ready to fight.*

Ranka turned.

A pale-skinned noblewoman stood in the middle of the ballroom, obliviously adjusting an emerald brooch in her hair. Behind her, Nadya stood immobile, looking rough and out of place amid the glittering silk and perfumed bodies that swirled over the dark-tiled ballroom floor.

Nadya was smiling at Ranka.

And Nadya was holding a knife.

The Skra raised her fingers and whistled again. Time slowed. Gold flashed in Ranka's periphery as several guards drew pins depicting a fist wrapped in flame from their pockets and donned them. The noble-woman gasped. Red bloomed at her ribs, flowering across her lilac gown. The woman raised a hand toward Ranka—and collapsed.

Behind Ranka came the soft click of the ballroom doors being locked.

And then the screaming began.

51

THE TILES SHIFTED FROM BLUE TO RED AS THE REVEL-
ers died.

All around Ranka, Skra, Murknen, and humans wearing Hands
pins pulled their weapons free, cutting down anyone who was within
their immediate circle. Screams of terror spiked in the air, mixing with
the coppery tang of blood.

It's too soon.

I had until tomorrow.

Guests rushed past her to yank at the locked ballroom doors. They
clawed at the wood with their fingernails, pounding on them, begging
to be let out. The ballroom was a menagerie of chaos. Witches turned
to one another, expecting to find allies, only to have their throats slit.
Humans who had danced with one another only moments before now
drove knives through the ribs of their partners.

The Hands of Solomei had arrived—but instead of fighting the
Skra, they were fighting *with* them.

The Skra lied to me. The thought sliced through Ranka with blistering clarity. *They knew this was going to happen, and they lied.*

Behind her, Ursay fought in a whirlwind, their face a thing of cold
rage as they wrestled an axe away from a hapless Murknen. They cut

the witch down, pressed two bloody fingers to their lips, and let loose a piercing whistle. Every Oori in the room turned and lunged toward their leader, forming a wedge as they forced their way toward the door.

A familiar voice broke the air, and Ranka's focus narrowed as she spun to see Galen Sunra cowering against the wall.

"Please," he begged a Murknen witch approaching him with a bloody dagger. "Please, you're making a mistake, I mean no *harm*—"

Ranka threw herself forward.

Bone crunched against bone. It stunned her, how weak she was without her blood-magic, how mortal. Her fingers knotted in the Murknen's filthy hair, and Ranka jerked her backward, slamming her to the tiles. Ranka swallowed her guilt, spinning to face Galen. "Are you all right?"

"Ranka, what's happening?"

"I don't know. We have to get you out of here—"

"My sister—"

"Not here."

"Percy?"

"Not sure." A Murknen hurtled toward them. Ranka dropped, twisted, and punched her in the throat. The witch collapsed, clawing at her windpipe, tears leaking from her eyes. Ranka cringed. Violence felt more personal without her blood-magic's giddy rush. Her knuckles throbbed with an unfamiliar ache.

Ranka angled herself in front of Galen. Now wasn't the time for questions and confusion. All she knew was that until she spoke to Ongrum, protecting the twins was her priority. Ranka pointed to the second set of ballroom doors. "Take them out."

"But there could be people on the other side—"

"Take them *out*!"

Galen flinched—and raised his hands.

A gale wind tore from his palms, roaring through the room, flinging witches and humans aside. The massive oak doors buckled, straining, and crashed into the hallway beyond. Someone screamed in the hall as they were crushed by the doors. Galen blanched. Ranka locked her fingers around his slender wrist and broke into a run.

People throttled one another on either side of them, guards disemboweling women in beautiful dresses, women in beautiful dresses choking out guards. If there was any time in her life she needed to be a monster, it was now. But she didn't know who to fight, didn't understand what was happening, why Hands and Skra seemed to be fighting side by side, painting this ballroom in death in a coordinated attack, when it should have been *each other* they fought.

A guard wearing a Hand pin swung for Galen. She recognized him—he was one of the guards who'd accompanied Foldrey to Bell's Corridor. Had risked his own life that day, to save his prince.

Now he sought to end him.

Please, Ranka begged her blood-magic, scraping mental claws against the kernel in her chest. *Please!*

Galen lurched in front of her, one hand flying up. Wind scooped up the guard and hurled him sideways. He hit the wall with a crack.

They spilled into the hallway. It was a mess of blood and death, too churned together for her to parse individual scents, to know which path was safe.

Four humans wearing pins skidded across the corner to their right. Three Murknen witches appeared in the hallway ahead.

Left it is.

Galen slid his hand into hers.

Together, fingers linked, they ran.

They sprinted together, dodging corpses, skirting unfortunate souls caught in the massacre. A serving boy whimpered, pawing half-heartedly at the spearhead protruding from his stomach. Around the corner an older merchant lay stretched across the tiles, throat slit, shuddering like a gutted fish as her last breaths left her.

Ranka could have screamed. It wasn't supposed to *be* like this. All her planning, all the *work* she'd done. It was all for nothing.

Tile shifted to old wood and drab walls as the sounds of fighting faded behind them. Ranka slowed, heart pounding, sweat dripping off her skin. Galen trembled beside her, his eyes dull with shock. In the back of Ranka's mind, all she saw was the flash of gold pins and Skra axes, slicing into the bodies of other witches as though they were nothing.

Ranka swallowed the bile rising in her throat.

"Okay," she breathed. "Okay, Galen, we need to get you out of here. I think we lost them for now—"

"Not quite."

Tafa stood at the end of the hall. Two more Skra flanked her.

Blood smeared Tafa's forearms, soaking the white tips of the furs she wore. She was always so vain about them. So careful. Now they were ruined; no matter how long she soaked them, no matter how hard she scrubbed, they'd always carry a blush of pink.

"Ranka." The wobble in Tafa's voice betrayed her. "Get out of the way."

Ranka stepped in front of Galen. "Tafa, listen to me, *please*. You're making a mistake. The twins are not our enemy, the Hands are."

It should have been enough. Tafa was Skra, after all. She and Ranka had grown up together, fought alongside each other, spent evenings whispering their dreams of the victories they'd win.

"Move," Tafa whispered. "Please."

But this felt wrong. And the memory of the Hands donning their pins—the way the Skra had cut down witches from the other covens, as if they were animals instead of their own—

"Galen Sunra is under my protection," Ranka said quietly. "No harm will come to him until I talk to Ongrum."

Tafa closed her eyes. For an agonizing moment Ranka thought she might see reason—that whatever had changed in her and the Skra in the months Ranka had been away wouldn't be enough to sour her so deeply.

Then Tafa nodded at the witch holding a bow to her far left. Ranka's stomach lurched. It was Yursi, who Ranka had taught to make rabbit snares just a year ago. She was only fourteen.

"Shoot the boy," Tafa said. "And if the Bloodwinn interferes, shoot her, too."

Yursi nocked an arrow, training the point at Galen's heart.

Please, Ranka begged the useless kernel lodged behind her heart.

It pulsed and did not open.

Ranka braced herself for the impact.

And fire lit up the world.

Galen threw his hands up. Wind spiraled, protecting them from the inferno. Another blast of flame came, and then another, burning hotter as Percy Stone stepped forward.

"You Skra and your lack of *manners,*" Percy said, "are *really* beginning to get on my nerves."

Percy had never looked less human. His eyes shone gold, and though flames danced across his skin, they did not burn him. His robes crumbled to ash, leaving only tatters where finery had been before. A sheen of pale scales flickered beneath his skin, shifting with his movements.

Percy spread his hands, looking more like a carnival barker than a boy carrying a forest fire inside him. "Now, now. Surely, even northern barbarians can be reasoned with. Can't we talk this out? Split a bottle of wine, eat some cheese, and whine at each other instead of resorting to this silly violence?"

"Shoot them!"

"Oh, fine," Percy sighed. "Violence it is."

The witch aimed her arrow—and Percy opened his mouth.

Fire roared from his parted lips, engulfing the nearest two witches. They collapsed, screaming, beating at their blackening skin. Percy didn't stop. The fire kept coming, an endless wall of roaring heat. Ranka cringed away. Even Galen looked horrified, but Percy's eyes were empty, his face serene, as if this inferno had spent months building under his skin and it was a relief to finally set it free.

Tafa screamed, ordering the Skra to move forward, to get to the prince. Percy kept his eyes on the witches and dropped his voice low. "Ranka, there are Skra in the tunnels."

Her legs buckled.

No.

"The vaccine," she whispered. "They're looking for the cure—and Aramis is down there. Someone else must have tipped them off."

Percy's eyes darted from her to Galen and hardened. "Go."

"But—"

"I can protect Galen. *Go*, Ranka."

Ranka took one last look at them—and then she was running. The roar of fire came again, followed by the screams of the witches who'd once been the only family she'd ever known. Ranka kept running.

All she could think of was Aramis. Aramis, who would sooner die than let the Skra destroy her work.

Aramis, alone.

52

THE SUNRA ESTATE HAD COLLAPSED INTO CHAOS.

Blood clouded everything as Ranka tore through the eastern wing. A woman screamed to her left, sobbing as a witch aimed a knife at her heart. Humans wearing gold pins lay dying in the hall, and witches wrestled with one another on the ground, screaming curses as they fought for their lives. Everywhere Ranka looked, she found death.

She kept running.

The stables reared up in front of her. Horses tugged at their reins, eyes rolling, whickering with panic at the stench of blood. They'd likely not survive on their own, but they had a better chance in Seaswept than with the Skra. The Skra had no use for horses. They'd sooner butcher them for their meat than let good animals go to waste.

Ranka sliced through their restraints, set the horses loose, and hit the tunnels at a sprint.

Please, please, please.

By now she'd memorized the intricate path to the workshop. Her feet pounded in time with her frantic heart.

Right, right, then left, right, then straight, left, right.

The tunnel walls flashed by. Roaches skittered out of her way. The stench of corpses wafted around her, coupled with that sour rot, that reek of horror that had never belonged in this world or the next, and Ranka tried not to think of the rumors of the hungry creatures beneath Seaswept's streets that grew more frequent each day. Was that a moan from somewhere down the tunnels—or just her fear-addled mind?

Again, Ranka reached for her blood-magic.

Again, nothing answered.

Without her magic pumping adrenaline through her, she was painfully slow. Her lungs burned, and her strides felt sloppy and weak. Still, she ran. The workshop reared ahead of her, and Ranka hurled her shoulder against the door. It flung open, and she exploded into the room, grasping for any kind of weapon—

"Ranka?"

Aramis stood in the center of the room, tears streaming down her face.

In front of her lay the Kerth they'd pinned all their hopes on.

She was dead.

The blisters had started to heal. There was a flush to her cheeks that hadn't been there prior. Even in death, she looked less monstrous, like a part of the girl she'd been before had returned, before winalin won its battle.

"I don't know what happened," Aramis whispered. "She was still comatose when I left for the party, but when I got here, she was just . . . gone."

Everything in Ranka threatened to crumble. The agony lining Aramis's face was so real, it cut her.

Aramis just stood there, her shoulders heaving as she fought back sobs.

"Aramis," Ranka said gently. "We'll figure it out, I promise—but right now I need you to listen to me very carefully."

Aramis raised her head to look at her, her tear-streaked cheeks glistening in the dim light of the mines, and froze. "Is that . . . blood?"

"We have to go," Ranka said. "We have to get you out of here. I—I messed up, okay? The Skra are attacking the palace and—"

"They're *what*?"

"I know, I'm sorry, I'll explain everything later, *please*, but I need you to trust me. We have to run, Princess, and we have to do it *now*."

"All my work," she whispered. Her eyes swept the room, taking in the leftover journals, the vials, the dishes she and Percy had spent months tweaking, testing, protecting. Her hands began to shake. "It was all for nothing."

"You can make a new cure. But you need to be alive to do it. Aramis, please. We have to *go*."

Aramis exploded into movement.

She scrambled around the room, flinging notebooks into bags, swiping at the chalked walls with the sleeve of her uniform. In seconds the workshop was in shambles. She hesitated, lingering over the Kerth witch, and then took a sample of her blood, gagging as she desecrated her body to give the still living a chance.

Vials of half-developed vaccines glinted on the tables and in a cabinet in the corner. Aramis drifted toward them, agony lining her face. "These ones—these are the most recent. They're the closest we've gotten." Her mouth trembled. "I can't carry them all."

"You don't need them all. Just a few, right?"

Aramis blinked rapidly and nodded. She pulled a vaccine down from the shelf and tucked it carefully into the bag. "We'll pack as many as we can, and then we can go—"

"Go?" a new voice said. "Go where, exactly?"

No.

Nadya lounged in the doorframe. Blood splattered her pale cheeks and matted her hair. She and her lover, Sigrid, had always been defiant of Ongrum—and only their seniority protected them. Two other Skra flanked her, features indistinguishable in the gloom.

Ranka's mind blanked. Her hand was a deadweight on Aramis's shoulder.

Nadya's attention skipped over Aramis to the worktable. "So this is it, then. The princess's magic potion, come to save us from the scary witch plague. It's so . . . underwhelming." She gave Ranka a long, dry smile. "How sweet of you to lead us here."

Aramis whipped to look at her, betrayal washing across her face as it dawned on her.

"I didn't—" Ranka sputtered. "I wouldn't have—"

Nadya dropped a vial. It shattered, shards of glass tinkling as the precious vaccine pooled on the floor. "Oops."

How would the Skra have known the location of the workshop? How had they known about the cure at all? Had she said something tonight without thinking?

Had *Ursay* betrayed her?

Nadya approached the second table and swept her arm across it. A dozen vials shattered on the salt floor. All the eyes in the room swung to the cabinet behind Ranka. The most recent batch of vaccines—the ones that had not quite saved the Kerth but had come far closer than anything before.

Ranka's mind whirred. All night she'd searched for Ongrum. All night the Skra had been standoffish and strange. But they'd always been cold to her. Only Ongrum's love had shielded Ranka. Had given her a home, when no one else would.

Nadya hadn't been the only Skra to make her displeasure with Ongrum known. What if she'd seized power somehow?

Ranka's heart did a panicked flip.

What if they'd betrayed her, and Ongrum was hurt somewhere?

Ranka forced herself to stand taller. "Stand down, all of you. No one makes a move until we have Ongrum's orders. I have information for her regarding our mission—and no one is to act until she's briefed."

At the word *mission* Aramis jerked to look at her. Ranka forced herself to stare straight ahead, her heart giving a painful squeeze.

Nadya gave her a funny look. "You really don't get it, do you?"

"Get what?" When Nadya said nothing, she looked to the other Skra. "What is she talking about?"

If they knew, they didn't say. These witches had made up their minds. That much was clear. Bloodlust had driven them to betray their coven's vision—and now they'd all pay the price if she couldn't sway them.

If appealing to their loyalty meant nothing, maybe she could appeal to their desire to save their own skins.

"Listen to me," Ranka said in a low voice. "None of you have been here in this city, haven't seen what I've seen. The Hands are not your allies. I serve the Skra. I have *only* ever served the Skra. So believe me when I say that whatever your feelings about the Sunra twins are, we *need* them. All of Witchik relies on that princess and the cure she's built. If you destroy those vials, you're killing us all."

Nadya gave her a sad, pitying look and pulled an axe from her hip. Ranka's legs tensed. But instead of attacking, the older witch offered the weapon to Ranka. It was an old, worn thing, with a nicked handle and a gleaming gray head. A woodcutter's axe instead of the ice axes the Skra favored, but a weapon still.

"I'm not going to destroy the vaccine, Ranka," said Nadya. "You are."

Ranka flinched involuntarily. Had Nadya lost her *mind?* Beside her, Aramis made a strangled noise of panic. But the Skra looked calm—as if they had expected this and knew how it would play out.

There would be no reasoning with them.

Now a question waited before Ranka, gleaming in the curve of the axe's blade.

Despair closed white-hot claws around her heart. None of this was right. The Skra and the twins were on the same side. If she could just talk to Ongrum—just make her *see*—

Except Ongrum wasn't coming.

If she were hurt, Ranka would have felt it. Would have known. It was *she* Ranka followed. It was *her* vision for the coven Ranka fought for. Not Nadya's or anyone else's.

Which meant anyone standing against Ongrum while she still

breathed was not Skra, but a traitor. And Ranka had long been trained that the Skra didn't believe in mercy when it came to those who betrayed their own.

Her vision narrowed.

Without her blood-magic, she would have to be precise, and fatal. She liked Nadya, truly, but what was a few witches, for the safety of her coven? Right now the vaccine was paramount. Without it, the covens were doomed. Ongrum would be aligned with her once Ranka found her. She might even be proud.

One swing to the throat. That's all it would take. Even without blood-magic, Ranka might be able to take the other two witches with the element of surprise on her side. Nadya was the only real threat. With her dead, Aramis would be safe. They would reconvene with Ongrum later and clean up the mess the rebel Skra had made.

She'd save the cure. Save Aramis. Find Ongrum, explain what had happened, and salvage what was left.

She could still do this—save nearly everyone, with a few painful casualties along the way.

Ranka took the weapon.

The axe yanked her arm down.

This was the right move. The right choice. The cure and the twins. The future of witches over the temporary dreams of her coven. The twins were their best chance. They were her new path, her new mission.

They were the family she chose.

And the Skra . . . they would see, someday, she'd done this for them. Even if they hated her for it.

Ranka raised her hand.

And Ongrum stepped through the door.

53

ONGRUM LOOKED WELL. THERE WAS A LIGHT TO HER
eyes, a fullness to her cheeks, and an electric energy that seemed to
ripple from her very pores. Even the silver in her hair seemed to shine
brighter than usual. She looked out of place in the workshop, her skin
streaked with ash, her clothes spattered with blood. Had she earned
new scars since Ranka had last seen her? Ranka couldn't tell. It was
strange, the space that existed between them now. Save for Belren,
Ranka had never gone more than a few weeks without seeing her.

Ranka's legs turned to water.

Ongrum had come here to kill a kingdom. Now Ranka had to convince her to save it instead.

There was so much she wanted to say. She wanted to know if
Ongrum had worried for her in the months she'd been away. If she
was surprised Ranka was still standing here, alive and well in a nest of
vipers. If she was proud of her.

She wanted to know if Ongrum had missed her at all.

In the end, all Ranka could do was swallow nervously and say, "Hi,
Ongrum."

Ongrum lifted a brow. "Hello, witchling." She paused, her calculating gaze taking in the room at a glance. "What's going on?"

Ranka's throat bobbed. Her hand was still on Aramis's shoulder. The princess was hardly breathing, every line of her body held rigid, her eyes darting frantically between Ranka and the rest of the Skra.

"I looked for you everywhere, and I couldn't find you, and they followed me here and . . ." Ranka's voice trailed away. Ongrum looked calm, too calm, for someone whose plans of a coup had just been upended. "You changed the plans without telling me."

Ongrum took a long look around the workshop. Her eyes went to Ranka's hand, still clasped protectively on Aramis's shoulder. "Yes. But you can still play your part, witchling."

"Your part?" Aramis echoed.

Shame wriggled deep in Ranka's core. She'd planned everything so carefully—every word she'd say to Ongrum, every reason to spare and side with the twins. She'd spent months waiting for a chance to talk to Ongrum. Dreaming of the day she'd be able to pass this burden to her.

Praying Ongrum would see reason and take their side.

"Ongrum," Ranka said dizzily. "Please just . . . listen to me, for one second. I don't know what the Hands told you, but *they're* the true enemy here."

She summarized, as quickly as she could, what she'd learned in Seaswept: the false blood-magic the Star Isles had developed, the way the Hands sought to use it, and the twins' role in trying to cure it. All the while the Skra watched her with neutral expressions, and Aramis with an increasingly devastated one.

The betrayal rippling off her threatened to cleave Ranka in two.

"You lied to me," Aramis whispered. "About all of it."

There was no use denying it, not when the evidence was unfolding before them in real time. Any apologies or softness shown now would only be confirmation of her weakness to the Skra.

Ranka looked to Ongrum.

"Look, I know how this sounds—but I have *only* ever cared about the Skra. Winalin will find us wherever we go, Ongrum. We *need* a cure. And to do that, we need the twins. Please, listen to me. *Trust me*. And stand down."

Ongrum closed her eyes. "I trained you to be better than this."

Ranka's knees buckled. "What?"

"Can you really not see it?" She laughed, the noise sharp, humorless, and wrought with disbelief. "They have been *lying* to you, child."

"That's not—"

"Everything you've told me—everything you so desperately want me to believe—it's all lies. From the moment you arrived here, the twins have been playing games with you, and you've been all too willing to dance along."

Ranka's head spun as though Ongrum had slapped her.

"The cure is a ruse," Ongrum said gently. "They have no interest in saving us, not when they can crush us beneath their heels instead. They just wanted you as their pawn. I mean, look at you, child. Standing against your own sisters. Fighting for a human's life instead of theirs."

"She's lying," Aramis said, her throat bobbing. "Ranka, don't listen to her—"

"Am I?" Ongrum switched her focus to Aramis, her smile cruel, and cold. "Ranka, did you tell the princess you were looking for Yeva?"

Aramis stiffened.

Bile rose in Ranka's throat. "Yes."

"Did they help you search for her? Did they permit you to look at all?"

"Well . . . no, but—"

"That's not fair," Aramis said desperately. "That was in the beginning, and—"

"Quiet," Nadya warned. "One more word out of you, and you get an arrow in the heart."

Aramis's mouth clicked shut. She looked desperately at Ranka, but now Ranka's eyes were only for Ongrum.

"Did they ever try to change the public outrage directed at you?"

Ongrum asked coldly. "Did they order you extra guards or do *anything* to ensure the violence increasing against witches didn't blow back on you?"

"No," Ranka said weakly.

"Yet you're alone here, so you try to do the right thing. You work with them. You give them your trust, your secrets, your blood." Ongrum's voice was an ocean, and Ranka was going to drown. "And at the same time, winalin is getting worse. But do they call in extra help? Do they involve the covens, or other provinces, to ensure that if something happens to you all, the work can continue?"

Ranka couldn't get words out. She shook her head.

"Of course not. Because they *want* this city to hate you. They *want* winalin to succeed." Ongrum's gaze pinned her to where she stood. "You say the Hands have your blood. That it was the key to making this horrific disease even more infectious and deadly. But who gave it to them?"

Ranka couldn't breathe.

They'd been so careful to conceal the actual lab. She doubted even Galen could find his way back. Foldrey was dead. Percy was too haunted by his role in winalin to jeopardize a cure.

That left only one.

"Ranka," Aramis said, horrified. "I would never—"

Ranka removed her hand from Aramis's shoulder.

"Oh, Ranka. My naive, lost girl," Ongrum said softly. Sadly. "You always want to believe the best in people. But look what it got you and Vivna back in Belren. Look what it's getting you *now*. Pleading for their lives. Fighting your own coven to protect the rulers who embolden their people to burn us alive."

Tears slipped down Ranka's cheeks. Aramis had hated her at first, she knew. But that night on the roof—the moments they had after—hadn't the twins and Percy become a kind of family? She had been so reluctant to trust them, and so glad when she did.

Could it all really have meant nothing?

Could it all have just been a lie?

Ongrum seemed to take up the entire room. The lines of her face were deeper, the hue of her hair shifting from gray to streaks of silver. Gone was her normally stoic expression, the harshness in her eyes. Her face was open, raw, and eager.

"Look at you—my little girl, all grown up, poised to end a kingdom or save it, with no clue what you should do." Ongrum pursed her lips. "We can fix this world together. You and I, Ranka, in your rightful place as my second. I know you're scared, child. I know you're confused. But you knew this day was coming. And you know who you belong to. Who your family is. You know I love you, don't you? You know you are the only daughter I've ever truly had."

Ranka swayed where she was. Ongrum said she loved her, but some of things she'd done hadn't felt like love. Thirteen years of memories flashed behind her eyes. Of Ongrum, teaching her to palm a knife, to start a fire, to track a deer by following star-bright flecks of blood on snow.

Of Ongrum, the day they met.

A house, a street in Belren, the echo of her sister's cries, and a witch.

Ongrum had been a force of nature even then—all pale skin and dark hair, with a lined face and scarred hands. She'd knelt in front of Ranka, those dark eyes bright and inquisitive. "And what's your name?"

"Ranka," she'd whispered.

"Ranka. A strong name for a strong girl." She'd offered her hatchet and laughed when it yanked Ranka's hand to the ground. "Heavy? No matter. You'll handle it in time."

Ranka's biological mother hadn't even bothered to change her clothes. Didn't even give her boots. She just gave up her daughters to the witches and shut the door. Ranka stood in her nightgown, braids fuzzy with sleep, shivering and barefoot in the snow as Vivna cried beside her.

Ongrum had picked Ranka up and carried her the whole way home.

Ranka blinked back tears. Ongrum closed the space between them now. She lifted a hand to cradle Ranka's cheek in her palm. It was so hard not to lean toward her. Not to collapse into Ongrum's familiar weight, her scent, the tenor of her voice.

"I never should have sent you here alone. Try as I may, I never hardened that soft heart of yours. You have always been so desperate to be loved." Ongrum softened. "You must be so tired."

Ranka blinked furiously, trying to will away the tears that wouldn't stop coming. Tired didn't even begin to touch it. She was exhausted. This was all so beyond anything she'd ever trained for or wanted. She wasn't smart enough for any of this. Wasn't strong enough. That's why she needed people like the twins, like Ongrum. People with answers and clear minds.

People to follow.

She didn't hide it well, she knew that. Ongrum, Vivna, even Yeva, had seen that in her.

Who was to say the twins and Percy hadn't either? They were the manipulators, trained to deceive. It would be so easy for them to trick her. To tug at her heartstrings and make her dance down whatever path they needed.

She'd thought herself smart. Had started to believe she could finally do good, instead of harm.

She'd thought they loved her.

"Fight with us, witchling. We can end this now. All of it—and then you can have your life back. The mountains, the Skra, the north. Isn't that want you want?" Ongrum's eyes never left hers. "Destroy the vaccine, child. Secure our victory. And all of this will finally be over."

"But people will die," Ranka protested weakly. "If winalin spreads, so many will get sick, and—"

"People always die," Ongrum said. "But they'll be dying for a better world. A *new* world."

There's never a new world, Ranka.

But what if Percy was wrong? What if there could be?

"Witchling," Ongrum said, her voice gentle. "I am not these twins, who used you. I am not Vivna, who left you. Remember why you came here. Remember what you fought for—and finish this."

It wasn't supposed to be this way. She never wanted to *choose*.

"Ranka," Aramis whispered. *"Please."*

Tears coursed down Ranka's cheeks.

Witchik or Isodal.

Her coven or the twins.

"Ranka," Ongrum murmured. "Come home to me."

Ongrum or Aramis.

Who was she kidding?

There'd only ever been one choice.

Ranka loosened her grip on the axe. In a wide, great arc, she sent the blade flying into the cabinet, and even Aramis's scream couldn't drown out the sound of the vials of the vaccine shattering against salt.

PART FOUR

BLOODWINN

COUP SUCCESSFUL

54

THE PALACE BURNED—AND THE WITCHES DRANK.

Ranka sat immobile and numb as witches celebrated around her. After she'd destroyed the vaccines, the Skra had made quick work of taking Aramis prisoner. Still, her screams lingered.

The witches had overtaken the Council room. They stumbled between the great, ancient chairs, cracking bottles of imported Star Isles wine open against the arms, laughing as they spilled Shiraz down the marble. A Murknen hurled her empty bottle through a stained-glass window overhead and whooped as the entire panel of glass shattered. A few Hands of Solomei had remained in the palace after the coup, but they'd largely extracted themselves from the celebrations. Ranka watched them with a churning stomach. It was clear the Hands had no love for the Skra—yet they'd allied with them in the end.

But why?

Glass shattered overhead. The witches kept celebrating, paying their silent, solemn Bloodwinn no mind. She'd barely spoken to anyone all night.

What was wrong with her?

She'd won. She'd accomplished her mission. She'd done what generations of witches could only dream of.

Yet she felt nothing but misery.

Outside, the gardens burned. Smoke billowed into the air in great black clouds, and patches of palace-bred lilies sizzled as they were charred down to their roots. There was so much smoke, the koi ponds were now shrouded from view. Once, Aramis had told Ranka of how she'd named every single one of them as a little girl. She'd bawled when the fish inevitably died of sickness or old age. Had blushed, lashes fluttering in that way that made Ranka's heart quicken, when she admitted that even now, balanced on that precipice between girl and woman, it brought her peace to watch the great, lazy fish float to the surface and beg for scraps.

They'd probably boil alive in the heat if they hadn't already been killed for sport.

The witches slowed only when Ongrum stepped forward. She moved deliberately, face set as she climbed atop the Council seat that had once been Galen's. Standing on the marble chair, clothes painted in blood, Ongrum looked every bit the conqueror.

Ranka was going to be ill.

"I want you all to take a moment," Ongrum said. Her voice was soft, but it carried through the great room as well as any shout. "And witness where we are. Witness what we've done. We stand in the heart of power—and now it's ours."

A few witches cheered. Ranka closed her eyes.

"Three generations of witches have suffered under the Bloodwinn treaty. Before that, centuries of witches suffered in their fight with Isodal. But no more. Tonight we celebrate. And in three days, we change the world."

Bile climbed Ranka's throat. In three days, it would be the seventieth anniversary of the first Bloodwinn treaty. Ongrum had decided it was a day as fitting as any for Galen to die.

More cheers. More wine bottles cracked open, the alcohol spilling onto the floor.

This was what she'd wanted—wasn't it? What she'd dreamed of?

This was why she'd headed south, axe in hand and a fire in her heart. To kill the prince. To end the treaty. To set Witchik free.

Except, Yeva's voice whispered, *you didn't come here for Galen, really. You came here for me.*

And she'd failed.

And now the prince wasn't just a prince. He had a name. He was a boy who'd stood by her when a witch turned to kill them, and when he'd thought they were facing their last moments, he'd held her hand.

"Please. The real hero is the Bloodwinn." Ongrum turned her dark eyes on Ranka. "Rise, witchling. Let them see the girl who defeated a dynasty."

Every eye in the room landed on her. Slowly, Ranka stood, her ears ringing, and did everything in her power not to vomit.

Wasn't this what she'd wanted? She stood before witches from all across Witchik, and they looked at her as though she were the hero. All her life she'd been ignored, feared, and blamed. Her own coven had scorned her. Now they beamed at her, these wild-hearted witches in their bloodstained clothes, their eyes glittering with reverence, hunger, even a hint of jealousy. They whooped and raised their bottles. Others pounded their fists on tables or cried out her name.

She'd earned all of this. She'd *won.*

So why did she feel so hollow?

Stop it. Ranka could have slapped herself. All of this—everything she'd done—was for the Skra. Once they left the palace behind, none of this would matter. She was just confused, like Ongrum had said. Tangled in the web of manipulation the twins had spun. Once she was back in the north, her head would clear. And eventually, the smirking boy from across the sea, the prince who called his wind to make music instead of storms, and the beautiful, brilliant, infuriating princess who was the bravest of the lot of them would be nothing but memories. In time, even those would fade.

She hoped.

Ongrum inclined her head toward Ranka. "Anything to say, Bloodwinn?"

Bloodwinn. A title she didn't deserve. A title that would no longer exist. She'd made certain of that. Maybe it was right that she had lost her blood-magic. She'd caused enough damage for one lifetime. Her fingers drifted self-consciously to her chest, where the kernel of locked-away power pulsed. She'd not yet told Ongrum she'd lost her magic. She'd learn soon enough.

"Witchling?"

Ranka swayed. She cleared her throat, cleared it again. How did Ongrum make this look so easy? So many eyes on her. So many waiting faces, ready for whatever left her lips. She hated all of them in that moment, and the realization made her ill. Sweat beaded her temples. "Thank you. I'm excited to go home."

She sat back down.

A few half-hearted cheers rose, though most of the witches looked puzzled. Ongrum looked faintly annoyed, but she stepped forward and took control of the room once more.

"I want to thank you for fighting with me," Ongrum said, her eyes sweeping over the crowd of witches before settling on the Murknen and the handful of Arlani who had sworn to their side. Not a single Oori was in sight. "For fighting with us. I know our histories have not been the most peaceful—but we have a common enemy now. One that goes beyond humans. By now all of you have learned of the Sunra-made disease they call winalin."

A hiss went up from the crowd.

The hair on Ranka's arms stood on end. The Star Isles had made winalin. Ongrum knew that.

"There's little we know about winalin—but we know it was created to kill us. To wipe out witches entirely."

Another lie.

"There is no cure—and if my sources are correct, the disease has begun to spread on its own."

More panicked murmurs among the witches. What was Ongrum doing? They'd already won. Why rile the witches further?

The rest of Ongrum's speech flowed over her like water. It was more familiar beats—the greatness of witches, how the covens had suffered, and what the path forward looked like. Yet strangely enough, at no point did she discuss returning home. And they would be returning home soon. In three days Galen would die. In three days there'd be nothing keeping them in Seaswept.

Right?

A commotion came at the back of the room. Someone shouted in the hallway outside, and two witches burst through the door.

"This one slipped free of his cell," Tafa called. "Killed two witches before we stopped him."

Stumbling between them, free of his rings and robes, bound like a stag to be roasted on a spit, was Percy Stone.

He'd been beaten, and badly. Blood dripped from his nose and ran from his ears. Bruises bloomed on his face, his neck, his arms. Ranka's heart sank.

I thought he escaped.

The witches held him by his biceps with iron grips, but from the way he sagged between them, it was plain they'd beaten him too severely for any proper escape.

Ongrum leaned forward, her dark eyes narrowing with dull amusement before she shrugged. "We have no use for him. Get rid of him."

"Wait," Ranka blurted.

Every eye in the room turned to her.

Ongrum's voice carried a warning note in it. "Yes, Bloodwinn?"

Sweat crawled down the back of Ranka's neck. She could let him die. It'd be so easy to say nothing at all. If Percy died, he'd take any answers about winalin with him. It would no longer be her problem—her burden. Her tie to Aramis would be severed further.

How much easier it would be if he were just another stranger, another life that didn't matter. But Percy had held her while another witch burned. Percy had been just as guilty as her, and he'd left it all behind—his home, his country, his people—to right the wrongs of his father. And what would he get for it now? An anonymous death in a cold cell. A miserable end to his short, brilliant life.

Ranka sank back in her seat and curled her fingers into fists. "He might have information we need."

Ongrum rolled her neck. "Does it really matter at this point?"

"It matters when he's the ambassador from the nation that created winalin."

Several witches cried out and leapt to their feet.

Ongrum's nostrils flared. Her gaze locked on Ranka, burning hotter than a forge.

What was she *doing*? Defying Ongrum—and for what? To gain some last bit of mercy for a boy who now rightfully hated her?

"An interesting theory," Ongrum said, her voice clipped, though her attention lingered on Ranka in a way that made her skin crawl. "We'll let him live—for now. Until he no longer proves useful."

Percy said nothing. He stared at the ground, blood dripping in a slow, sluggish stream from his recently broken nose. The witches hauled him up, and then Percy bucked away from them, half jerking forward. He was free for only a moment, but it should have been enough for him to escape. He was faster than any witch in this room.

Instead he came to stop in front of Ranka. "I thought you were better than this, Ranka. I thought you were braver."

Ranka didn't need a mirror to know the blood had drained from her face.

The witches took him down, and Percy let them. His jaw cracked against the floor, and blood spattered out, gleaming like a dozen tiny red jewels on the pale tile. When they hauled him back up, Percy lifted his head a fraction and met her eyes.

A thousand fires burned there—hatred, betrayal, and disgust, but brighter than all was grief.

Percy looked at her as someone to be mourned.

"You chose wrong," Percy whispered. "It should have been us. It always should have been us."

"Get him out of here," Ongrum snapped.

The Skra jerked Percy back. He twisted and spat as far as he could in her direction.

Ranka sat there for a long time after they dragged him out, staring at the blood mixed with saliva on the tile, Percy's words ringing in her ears.

I thought you were braver.

Every part of her ached.

"Pathetic," Ongrum snorted. The older witch turned away, completely unperturbed by Percy's outburst, either not noticing that Ranka sat frozen—or not caring.

The rest of the witches went back to their celebration, faces lit with gluttony and joy or so lost in a drunken stupor that they were blank entirely. Witches she'd never met came up to her to congratulate her, their breath hot and warm as they threw arms around her neck and kissed her cheeks.

Ranka drifted among them like a ghost. A witch toppled one of the great Council chairs and cackled as the marble cracked up the center. Ranka stared at it, struggling to remember the name of the Council member who had sat there. Why couldn't she remember? Why did that bother her?

It should have been us.

It always should have been us.

This was meant to be her night. Her shining moment. A nameless witch from the north, gifted with a terrible magic, had infiltrated the most powerful monarchy on this side of the world and brought it down in a matter of weeks. She'd been born no one, to nothing, but now when they sang the stories of history, her name would be the chorus.

In three days' time Galen would die, and a new world would be born.

So why, after everything she'd fought for—after everything she'd sacrificed—did it feel like she'd failed?

55

AFTER A FEW HOURS RANKA EXCUSED HERSELF. MOST of the witches were such a drunken mess, she could barely stand to be around them. She retreated from the Council room and was halfway to Galen's room before she realized where she was going. Her steps slowed. The last time she was there had been with Aramis curled at her side. Everything had felt like the most fragile kind of hope then.

"Stop it," Ranka hissed under her breath. *Pull. Yourself. Together.*

She was Skra. She was the Bloodwinn, the Butcher of Belren, the pride of Witchik, and the worst fear of every human. She'd come here to do a job and she had done it.

But this palace, these *people*, were addling her mind. She'd gone so deep into her deception that she'd fooled even herself. She should be back there, celebrating with her coven. Rejoicing over the fact that they'd won.

Instead she wanted to curl into a ball and disappear.

She wanted, more than anything, to see that goddess-cursed, infuriating, know-it-all princess one last time, even if it ended with Aramis spitting in her face.

Footsteps sounded behind her, and the scent of witch floated her way. Ranka tensed and then felt sick. What was wrong with her? Tensing at the presence of a witch? What had this place done to her?

An arm looped through hers. "There's the hero of the night."

Ranka grimaced. "Hi, Tafa."

Her longtime friend was horribly, terribly drunk. A deep blush colored her cheeks. Her clothes were covered in blood. "We won, Ranka. I can't believe we actually did it, but we won." Tafa threw an arm around Ranka's neck. It was strange, to be this close to her and feel nothing. Once, a glance or a touch from Tafa had filled Ranka with a rush. Now she felt like a stranger.

"Hey, remember when I ordered Yursi to shoot you? That was stressful. You should have seen your face. I can't believe it worked so perfectly. Ongrum had everything planned. She really is brilliant." Tafa took a long drink of wine. "Just *look* at this place, Ra! And now it's ours!"

"I mean, sure." Ranka walked a little faster. The garden fires crackled in her ears, coupled with the distant crashes of witches tearing the palace apart as they celebrated. "It doesn't matter, though. We'll be going home soon."

"Ongrum didn't tell you?" Tafa took another swig and grinned, her teeth stained dark with wine. "The city is too unstable. We have to stay and make sure no one else steps in to fill the throne."

Every part of Ranka went still. "That wasn't the plan."

"Plans change. I mean, are we going to give over the seat of power to those crazy Hands?"

"But we can't *stay* here. Who cares who rules Seaswept? It's not our home."

"Oh, relax." Tafa leaned against the wall, a sloppy smile curling her lips. The wine slipped from her fingers and cracked on the tiled floor. Tafa frowned. "Oops."

Ranka left her behind, her steps short and quick, and told herself the chill was just from the night air that was creeping in.

Why wouldn't Ongrum have told her she planned to stay in Seaswept longer?

It wasn't the plan. And Ongrum's not supposed to change the plan without telling me.

She didn't know where she was going, only that it mattered that she kept moving. Hysteria bubbled up through her. Cool air hit her face, and then she was outside, striding through the smoking, charred ashes of the palace gardens. She dug her fingernails into her temples. The pain was bright, and it lingered with an unfamiliar burn without her blood-magic to eat the sting away.

Every time she closed her eyes, she saw them—Aramis, Percy, Galen. How odd everything had been when they'd met, how quickly they'd aligned with a common goal. How easily she'd fit in among them, once she'd found her place. How quickly they'd become her family. She had liked them, and later, all too easily, thought she loved them.

No. They were just using her.

Except Percy had noticed that blood made her uneasy, had seen through her shield and recognized a part of himself. And Galen had noticed her discomfort from day one and extended kindness, even when he had no reason to at all.

And Aramis . . . Aramis had done everything she could and more. She'd seen every ugly part of Ranka, more clearly than anyone else, and she hadn't turned away. She'd looked right into her terrible soul and demanded she be better. Aramis had taunted her, threatened her, kissed her, trusted her, taught her, and protected her.

Aramis had started to feel like home.

Ranka was going to lose her mind.

Once she was back in Witchik, none of this would matter. Ranka pictured the north, the ancient pines, the forests wrapped in cool shadow, the mountains permanently capped with snow. The Skra would be safe. All the covens would. No humans would dare press north for decades. And once they did—once history had smoothed away the stain of the violence left here—she would be long gone. Let another witch stand and fight. She was done.

And Ongrum was finally proud of her. For the first time in Ranka's life, she'd done something right. Had made all of Ongrum's patience and training worth it. Ongrum wasn't perfect, no one was, but she always put the Skra first.

Except for Yeva, whom she barely mourned.

Except for Asyil, whose disappearance hardly seemed to concern her at all.

Ranka stopped walking. She sank to her knees and put a hand to her chest. It was getting harder to breathe. Dots swam in front of her eyes, and she forced herself to be calm, even as her head spun.

She needed to stop this. Needed to get her act together.

She would talk to Ongrum tomorrow. Even if Ongrum wanted to leave some Skra in place to watch over the capital, surely *she* could leave? With a good horse, and a few sleepless nights, she could be home in two weeks. One and a half if the weather held.

"Witchling?"

Ranka looked up.

Ongrum stood over her. Her lips were stained with wine, but her eyes were clear. She looked out of place here. Ongrum belonged in the north like Ranka, cloaked in furs, outlined against the shadows of pines. Seeing her like this, in southern robes and leather sandals, was disconcerting.

She looked far too comfortable.

"What are you doing?"

Ranka looked up at her. The truth burned on her tongue.

I'm confused.

I have everything I've ever wanted—and I'm miserable.

I achieved the Skra's greatest dream—and I feel like I've made the worst mistake of my life.

If she told Ongrum the truth, would she understand? Would she send her home at last? Back to the north—back where she belonged? Shadows wrapped around them, carrying the scent of smoke, of blood and death. Only hours before this palace had been blanketed in screams.

Now the celebrations of witches broke the air. And Ongrum—still bloody, bearing the signs of battle flecked on her skin and matted in her hair—looked like a ghost come to haunt her.

Ongrum crouched in front of Ranka and draped her arms over her knees with a sigh. "Tafa told you, didn't she? That we need to stay a little longer."

"I don't understand—"

Ongrum dragged her nail in the ashes, drawing one long spiral after another. "You were born with power, child. It erupted out of you. But I—and too many other witches—know what it is to have nothing. To be weak." Her hands shook. "They burned my sisters. My friends. They've never stopped, never gotten anything more than a slap on the wrist. To be born a witch is to be born afraid. When we came here to kill the prince, I thought ending the treaty would be enough. . . ."

Ranka swayed. Once, she'd have craved this admission from Ongrum, would have drunk in the private details of her life and been honored by the trust. Now she only wanted her to stop talking.

"Ongrum," Ranka begged. "Send me home. Tonight. I don't need to be here when Galen dies. I've done my part. We won. Send me back."

"Send you home? Witchling, if anyone must stay, it's you. We need you now more than ever."

Dread crept through Ranka. "Why?"

Ongrum smiled. "Why don't I show you?"

56

ONGRUM WOULDN'T TELL RANKA WHERE THEY WERE going.

The farther they walked, the fewer witches they saw, and soon the crashes of bottles breaking faded into the distance. The elaborate mosaics shifted to simple white tile as they moved to the older back end of the palace. Ongrum strode with purpose, as though she'd walked these halls a thousand times.

It wasn't until they were nearly in sight of the infirmary that Ranka scented witches again. Except—something was wrong. A shadow moved ahead. Ongrum's hand twitched to her hip, but it was just Sigrid. She strode forward, her face a careful, sober mask.

Ongrum eyed Sigrid. "How are they?"

Sigrid stared straight ahead, not meeting Ongrum's eyes. "Stable enough."

"Did you have any trouble bringing them in?"

"I didn't. But Nadya—they got away from her, in the tunnels."

"I warned her," Ongrum snapped. "They were going to need special handling. That woman never *listens*. When I see her—"

"Nadya is dead."

Ranka stiffened. Nadya was dead? She had seen her only hours ago.

The witch had been alive and well, healthy enough to launch a coup and bold enough to threaten Ranka's life. She couldn't be *dead*.

Ongrum closed her eyes and exhaled. There was no grief on her face—only irritation. It was unlike her not to grieve the death of a Skra. Ongrum had lived alongside Nadya for twenty years.

Ranka couldn't help herself. "What happened to her?"

Sigrid's eyes flew to her, but only for a second. And Ranka saw it: fear.

"Be more careful next time," Ongrum said slowly. "We still have more to bring in."

"I don't think that's—"

"Your job isn't to think, witchling." Ongrum waved a hand. "Find someone else and sober them up. Tafa, maybe? Get it done by tomorrow."

Sigrid's face twitched at being called a witchling at thirty-seven, but she nodded and said, her voice cool, "Yes, Ongrum."

Sigrid turned away then, her back a rigid line, careful not to meet Ranka's gaze. Right before she turned the corner, Sigrid stumbled and retched. She made a horrible choking noise, as if she was torn between sobbing and puking, and then she was gone.

Ongrum turned to Ranka, her eyes strangely alight. "Once you see what we've accomplished, you'll understand—"

"We don't belong here," Ranka burst out.

The smile slipped from Ongrum's face.

"What is the point of this? Of any of this? We should be going home, Ongrum. We should be packing. Nadya should be alive, not transporting political prisoners."

Ongrum snorted, as if Ranka had said something funny.

"We won. We can go back to the north and have this all be done with!"

"It'll never be done with." Ongrum's eyes flashed. "Don't you see, child? We're vulnerable. If some far-off island nation could make something so dangerous, who's to say something else won't land on our shores in a few years?"

"Ships can't land in Witchik," Ranka said numbly. "Our shores are safe. We have to go home. And even if you succeed—what will the world look like when you're done?" Ranka pressed, her heart pounding. "If everything goes perfectly—what do you want, Ongrum? What's your goal?"

Ongrum's mouth opened and closed again, her face open and raw. Ranka held her breath. Maybe she would realize how futile this was—how wildly unmatched for it they were. Maybe she would ask for help. Maybe there was hope.

And then Ongrum's face hardened. "The world will look however we build it to look."

"A country is not a coven," Ranka said slowly. "This is not a group of sixty witches in the woods. There are millions of people in Isodal, Ongrum. Entire districts, each led by their own Council member. Covens don't pass laws. We don't govern. We don't even know *how* to govern."

"Listen to you," Ongrum said, her voice rife with disgust. "You've always had it so easy—found by the Skra, gifted with blood-magic but too scared to use it. If it had been me, if *I* had your blood-magic—"

Ranka went cold. "You couldn't possibly understand."

"No, *you* don't understand! You don't understand what it means to be weak. The Skra were nothing before me. They were in danger of being wiped out. *I* fixed that. *I* saved them." Ongrum's nostrils flared. "Everything I have, I built myself. I have spent my entire life fighting for scraps—and now that we sit here, at the heart of a kingdom, you want us to—what? Walk away? Give them back their kingdom? Go home?"

"Yes," Ranka said softly. They were safe in the north. No one could land on their shores. No human could survive their winters. Their only weakness was the border. Let the next generation of witches suffer to protect what her misery had given them. "If the humans agree not to cross the border—"

"The humans don't get to decide anything anymore. Not with us at the helm."

Cold settled in Ranka.

Ongrum's entire life had been a scramble for power. She'd been born to nothing—no coven, no magic, no training. She'd fought, clawed, and killed her ways toward every scrap of influence she now wielded. In Ongrum's mind, to turn away a kingdom, to turn away any bit of leverage she might have, was weakness.

Ranka could almost see it in front of her—Ongrum, a witch who had never stepped foot in anything larger than a northern lumber town, finding herself in the largest city in the country. Ongrum, who'd never commanded more than a few dozen witches, suddenly poised over an entire kingdom.

It didn't matter that she didn't understand it. It didn't matter that she didn't have a plan.

Ongrum was dying of thirst and had stumbled across a spring, and she would drink until her stomach burst. She had spent her entire life prepared to die for power. Now that she had it, she would cling to it no matter the consequence, even if it ate her alive.

"Please," Ranka whispered. "Take us home. You won't survive this country. None of us will."

Doubt flashed in Ongrum's eyes, but only briefly.

"You still think us weak. Outnumbered. But let me show you why we get to rewrite history." She jerked her chin toward the infirmary door. "Let me show you our future."

The scent grew stronger, a rot like winalin, but not quite the same. This rot was newer, fresher, like a wound that'd just begun to turn.

"This, witchling. This is our future. And this is why we'll be untouchable."

Ongrum opened the door.

Filling the room, secured in makeshift cages, chained to the walls and tied to the infirmary beds, were dozens upon dozens of winalin witches.

57

THEY WERE ALL CHILDREN.

Some were close to Ranka's age, but some were far younger, all cycling through various states of decay as the disease coursed through their veins. Most were beyond saving—they slumped on the floor, secured by manacles and chains, snarling at the sight of Ranka, drool running down their chins. But a few weren't yet lost. Witches lounged on infirmary beds, hooked up to tubes similar to the ones Aramis had used to pull blood from Ranka's veins, watching as disease slid into their bodies. Hands of Solomei moved between the beds, checking their vitals, patiently administering more of the disease to the ones who were still lucid. Others sprawled unconscious, their wrists and ankles secured to the posts with leather straps while vomit crusted their chins, and sore after sore erupted on their skin.

Blue vials of tranquilizer sat on neat shelves against the wall. When one of the witches rose from her bed with a snarl, the nearest Hand injected her without blinking. She slumped back onto the sheets, unconscious before her head hit the filthy, sweat-stained pillow.

Close to Ranka, a witch who couldn't have been older than twelve sat down on a bed, her chin lifted stubbornly in the gesture of someone borrowing courage. A Skra held her unmarked, healthy arm up to the light, pulled a syringe of winalin down from the shelf, and pressed the plunger home.

"Stop!" Ranka blurted, surging forward. "What are you doing? You're going to die! *Stop!*"

A hand clamped around her wrist. Ongrum yanked her backward with an iron grip and spun her around. She slammed Ranka against the wall with ease, her eyes flashing. Only the fully corrupted witches paid them any mind, snarling at the noise.

"Be calm, witchling. We just got them settled."

Ranka's vision dimmed. There was one witch in the room who had caught her attention—and try as she might, Ranka couldn't tear her eyes away from her. She needed to understand what was happening here. And to do that, she needed Ongrum to leave.

Ranka took several panicked breaths, willing her frantic heart to slow, and pictured Aramis's steel calm.

When she spoke, it felt as though she were floating outside her body.

"This is impressive," she said hollowly. "I . . . never could have imagined something like this. Can you give me a moment to take it in? I'll rejoin you in the hall. I think I just need . . . to collect myself. And understand."

She barely registered what Ongrum said. Her eyes were only for the witch. The girl lay on her side, eyes closed, body so ravaged by disease that her ribs pressed against her skin.

But Ranka would have known her anywhere.

Ongrum left Ranka there, standing listlessly in the face of all the horror, drinking in the sight of what she'd wrought, and it was then a pit of despair opened up in Ranka—one so deep, it threatened to swallow her whole.

She wanted to turn and flee. To leave this nightmare behind, to let the palace and the ones she'd betrayed burn to the ground. But all she could see was the witch before her. All she heard was the echo of a thousand promises she'd never made right.

Ranka took one uneasy step forward, then another. The witch was either asleep or in a stupor. She lay with her arms bound to the bed with leather straps, her narrow chest rising and falling rapidly. If the attending Hands noticed Ranka approaching, they didn't care.

The witch stirred.

Ranka dropped to her knees beside her bed. "Hello, Asyil."

Asyil had decayed horrifically since Ranka had last seen her. Gone was her confident smirk, her lanky muscles, and her beautiful dark hair. Now she was a living corpse, panting in the musty air of the infirmary, waiting to die.

Ranka forced herself to remain calm, though she wanted to scream and rage, to flip the infirmary beds over and break them in half. Asyil panted, her skinny frame soaked with sweat. The sores on her skin were small—only the size of a fingernail. She was only in the early stages of infection, then, as Talis had been.

But her fate was sealed.

Asyil's fever-dull eyes searched Ranka's face. Her voice emerged in the barest croak. "Ranka?"

Everything in Ranka threatened to collapse. "Hi."

Asyil's gaunt face stretched into a weary, crooked smile. She was missing half of her teeth. "You look terrible." She hesitated, her smile faltering. "My sister?"

"She's gone," Ranka croaked. "I—I failed. I am so, so sorry. Yeva . . . I couldn't . . . she's . . ."

Asyil closed her eyes. "I knew. I woke up one morning, sweating half to death, and I just . . . knew." She struggled against the bed restraints and then slumped back down, defeated.

Ranka leaned her forehead against the bed. She trembled. None of this was right. Asyil should have been home, healthy, with Yeva at her side, not dying in some distant human city, ravaged by a man-made disease.

"How did you get sick?" Ranka asked faintly, though the dread filling her whispered the truth she already feared.

"She told us it would make us strong. That we could go anywhere and do anything." Asyil laughed bitterly. "Ongrum loves her lies."

"But the Hands were the ones that had it. They were the ones injecting them. They . . ."

They were the villains. We were the less-than-perfect heroes, but heroes nonetheless.

They were the killers. We were the monsters strong enough to stop them.

In the far corner a young witch howled and lurched forward. They'd penned her against the wall by twisting the metal legs of an old bed into a cage, but from the way she rattled the bars, they clearly wouldn't hold her for long. Her left arm dangled uselessly at her side, dislocated from throwing herself against the bars, but she was too far gone to register any proper pain. At this stage, she felt only hunger.

The room spun.

This was what Nadya and Sigrid had been transporting. *This* was what had killed Nadya in the tunnels. Which meant there were more winalin witches loose beneath the city, likely hunting humans at this exact moment. All along the Hands had sown stories of monsters lurking beneath their city, snatching their pets and children, feasting on their corpses in the night.

Now Ongrum had ensured it would be a reality.

How many of these witches had been promised glory, power, or freedom, only to be rewarded with disease instead? Treated as failed experiments, cast aside in search of a weapon that would stick.

Ongrum had crossed lines before. They all had. But that had been in the heat of battle. It had been necessary. This was anything but.

To their left, a newly sickened witch moaned, her body convulsing as new sores appeared on her skin.

"We all own this," Asyil said dully. "We watched her mold you. I suppose it's easier, to let the bad thing happen than stand against it. But she's a poison, Ranka. She always has been. If I could go back—Goddess, Ranka. If I could go back, I would have shot her through the heart. I would have gotten you and Yeva the hell out of there and never looked back."

It could have been the fever making Asyil speak gibberish, but something told Ranka that, at least right now, the witch's mind was clear.

"You should go."

"I can't leave you—"

"I'm dying," Asyil said bluntly. "And there is nothing you can do." She took a ragged breath. Sweat crawled a trail down her temple. "Do you remember what Ongrum said to you, the day you decided to go after Yeva?"

It felt like a lifetime ago, yet still she could see it. The coal-pits burning low, the Skra pressed close, and all the attention in the world on her as Ranka faced a decision that would change everything.

Is there a chance that I can save her?

Oh, witchling. You'll save them all.

"Ask Ongrum about the sick witches," Asyil whispered. "About the first ones that got sick. Ask her how they got them."

Ranka rose, her legs shaking so badly, she had to put a hand out for balance. She wished she could have offered Asyil more—a cure, a grain of hope, a promise that this would end in something besides a painful, wretched death.

But Asyil was out of time, and they both knew it.

"Ranka," Asyil whispered. "Send me home."

Tears flooded Ranka's eyes. Asyil didn't mean the north. It had never been her home, not truly. Her home had only ever been wherever Yeva was. The sisters were what Ranka had dreamed of for herself and Vivna, a dream Ranka was slowly beginning to suspect she never could have had.

Ranka pressed a kiss to Asyil's sweat-slick, burning forehead and ripped the tubing from the bag. A sigh of relief slipped out. Without the concoction of drugs feeding into her, she'd be gone in minutes. Free of the experiment they'd turned her into.

She looked down at Asyil, frail and gray, her skin covered in painful sores—but even now Asyil's feverish eyes were fierce.

"Tell Yeva I'm sorry," Ranka whispered, though she wasn't sure Asyil could hear her anymore. "Tell her I love her and I'm finally going to make it right."

Was it her imagination, or when the light left Asyil's eyes, did her mouth curve in a smile?

Ranka didn't know how long she stood there. Something in her was breaking open. She was lost, but Asyil's words were an anchor. An order. Something to fight for.

And Ranka had always been so very good at fighting.

58

RANKA BARELY REGISTERED THE CLICK OF THE INFIR-
mary door as it closed. All she could see were the witches in that
room. All she could hear was Asyil's voice winding around her. All she
could remember were the faces of the ones she had lost.

It still didn't make sense. Ongrum wasn't smart enough for this.
She was a conqueror, a warrior, not a biological-warfare-waging
mastermind. Why would the Hands just *give* her winalin when she was
what they hated most?

Ongrum leaned against the wall, her eyes closed. She stirred when
Ranka approached.

When she looked at Ranka, it was as though Ranka were some
prized calf. Not a girl she'd called a daughter.

Ranka approached, fighting the urge to vomit. Ongrum was distracted right now, too lost in the fantasy of her own conquest to curate
information like she normally would. Ranka needed to play this right,
to glean whatever answers she could.

But all she wanted to do was curl into a ball and scrub at her skin
until the stench of those rotting witches was nothing more than a
distant memory.

"So you're making them," Ranka said flatly. "You have winalin.
Now what?"

Ongrum smirked. "Now is where you come in."

Ranka struggled to keep her voice even. "Oh?"

"Isn't it obvious? The Star Isles were missing a key ingredient: a real, healthy blood-witch. With your biology we can refine winalin until it becomes stable. And a new generation of blood-witches will have the perfect teacher, ready and waiting to help them conquer their power."

Faces flashed behind her eyes. Yeva and Asyil, destroyed by a virus that ripped them apart from the inside. Talis, a girl barely over thirteen, cowering in her parents' house and whimpering as false blood-magic flickered in her veins.

"Have you ever seen anything like this before? Witches from every coven in the same room, coming together for the same goal. The same cause. And the cause is *you*, child." Ongrum squeezed her shoulder. "None of us will ever be weak again. Imagine a world where, instead of a handful of blood-witches every generation, we have hundreds. A world where *all* of us have that power."

Ranka backed away from her. Her spine collided with the wall, and she held up her hands as if to ward Ongrum off. "You mean to use me," Ranka realized. "As an experiment, until winalin works for real. To create the weapon the Star Isles always dreamed of."

"No, child. To create the weapon *we've* always dreamed of."

"Winalin has killed every witch it's infected—"

"So we keep practicing until we get it right." Ongrum shrugged. "And until then even the ones who don't survive it long-term will have their uses."

How could Ongrum ask this of her, after everything she'd done? She'd given up everything for her—first Vivna, then Yeva and Asyil.

She had given up Percy. Galen.

She'd given up *Aramis*.

And instead of earning Ongrum's approval, her love, or the trip back home she dreamed of, Ranka had merely cemented her future as an experiment instead.

A monster, destined to spend the rest of her days creating more.

"Ongrum, we have no idea if this will even work," Ranka said desperately. "No blood-witch on record has ever conquered their blood-magic. It's killed every single one of them—even the past Bloodwinns. My entire life has been a ticking clock for the day this power ruins me—and you want dozens of witches to take that on willingly?"

The kernel pulsed deep in her chest. Her senses had dulled when her blood-magic retreated, but now the vivid colors of the hallway, the delirious greed alighting Ongrum's face, and the blood on her clothes felt like some kind of sensory assault.

"The other Bloodwinns were weak. Eventually, something has to stick."

"The other Bloodwinns thought blood-magic had no chance of mastery," Ranka said. "They thought it was like a parasite, or a chronic infection, designed to kill the host. Ongrum, if that's true . . ."

Then Ongrum was ensuring they would have an entire generation of blood-witches who died a horrific, torturous death.

"Who told you that?" Ongrum sneered. "The princess?"

"Well, yes—"

"Don't you see she wants you weak? For all you know, the past Bloodwinn mastered her power, and her daughter is desperate to prevent you or anyone else from achieving the same thing."

A year ago, Ranka would have believed her readily. But Ranka had seen the pain in Aramis's eyes when she spoke of her mother, the fear as she recounted what blood-magic had done to every witch who inherited it. And hadn't Ranka's magic grown more volatile every year? Hadn't it demanded more death, stolen more of her life, stolen more of *her*, swelling in breadth the same way a disease overwhelmed its host?

Ongrum's lip curled. She lifted a hand as if to strike her—and then her expression smoothed out.

"Let me worry about the details. I know this is a lot, but you can do this, Ranka. You are so, so strong. And so brilliant. These witches believe in you. They see your power. They trust you to lead them."

Ranka's mind stuttered to a halt. It felt like she was in a long, unending nightmare. Why did it always happen like this? Ongrum would be so angry, so cruel, and then it was like something flipped in her and a different person emerged. A witch who was gentle, who looked at her like she was someone who mattered. A witch who loved her.

It felt so genuine.

And yet.

Percy's voice was there, digging at the back of her mind like a thorn. *You chose wrong.*

Percy, who looked at her with a quiet pity and called her a fool when she spoke of Ongrum's love. Percy, who had been through this before.

Ranka's stomach roiled. All her life she'd chased Ongrum's love. Starved for her approval. She'd thought herself inadequate, a failure, someone who just needed to work harder, faster, longer, to be worthy of Ongrum's praise.

There was still a piece she was missing. A piece she didn't understand. Why would the Hands know who Ongrum was to begin with? Why would someone from the palace know to go to *her* of all people?

"Ongrum," Ranka asked quietly, "what happened to Yeva?"

"Oh, her?" Ongrum snorted. "She probably just moved to a human village when they set her loose."

Ranka could hardly breathe. "When who set her loose?"

"How else was I going to get you south?" Ongrum flapped her hand, though she looked faintly troubled. "She looked so similar to you—I knew it'd be enough to fool them, at least temporarily. But once you turned yourself in, she never did come home. She probably defected to some ugly little town."

Ranka swayed. She could see it unfurling: Ongrum, thinking herself clever, towing Yeva south and turning her over to humans who were desperate to collect the Bloodwinn bounty, assuming they'd simply *let Yeva go.*

The Hands seeing an opportunity—seeing a power-hungry woman from the north who knew nothing of politics and games, who wanted only strength. A temporary deal with a demon, to purge the rest from existence.

Ongrum had doomed them all.

And she had started with Yeva.

A horrible suspicion bloomed in the back of Ranka's mind. The Kerth coven had been the first to be destroyed by the Hands—and their lands had shared a border with the Skra's. Ever since she'd arrived in Seaswept, the presence of winalin witches had increased tenfold. Which meant either the Hands had gotten particularly adept at catching them—or someone else was helping them.

Someone the witches were more inclined to trust.

Ask Ongrum, Asyil had rasped, *about the sick witches.*

"Here's what I don't understand," Ranka said slowly. "Why the Skra? Why would the Hands trust us with something as volatile as winalin? Why work with us to begin with?"

Ongrum looked puzzled, if not a little bored. "I mean really, Ranka. Who do you think supplied the Hands with witches to begin with?"

Ranka waited for Ongrum to laugh or backtrack, but instead she remained standing, her posture confident and relaxed.

Who do you think supplied the Hands with witches to begin with?

It was too far, even for her. Too horrific. And yet, painfully, horrifically, the pieces clicked together. The timeline was too perfect—of not just the missing witches, but the presence of more humans in the north.

Hunting not for any witch they could get their hands on—only one.

Ranka's knees buckled.

She'd long wondered who had given up her identity to the humans. Who had known her so well, so *intimately,* that they were able to describe her down to her scar.

It hadn't made sense for it to be a Skra before, because the Skra didn't benefit from everyone knowing the Bloodwinn was one of their own.

Unless they wanted to drive her south.

Unless they'd worked out a deal with the humans, and Ranka's identity was included in the price.

How many witches had died because of Ongrum's greed?

How many more would?

Ongrum was speaking again, talking about how foolish the Hands were, how greedy, didn't they realize they'd never be able to stand against the witches now that they held the capital?

Ongrum had orchestrated all of this. And she'd only been able to because of Ranka. Because Ranka had trusted her. Served her. Fought for her.

Now innocents would pay the price.

The panic swirling through Ranka went quiet. When she spoke, her voice came from far, far away. "I understand now."

Ongrum brightened. "Well, it's about time—"

"It's incredible, really. Even I couldn't have imagined something like this for you."

"I'm glad you're finally getting on board, witchling."

"Just one question—who in the Hands dreamed this up?" Her heart pounded. "Who knew so much about me, about you, about coven politics, that they could orchestrate this so well?"

Ongrum looked faintly annoyed. "I haven't a clue. It was a different messenger every time. Why?"

"No reason," Ranka said numbly.

And then she drew the tranquilizer from her pocket and stabbed Ongrum in the throat.

Ongrum made a horrible gurgle as her hand flew to her neck. Her fingers scrambled uselessly against the vial of tranquilizer Ranka had palmed on her way out of the infirmary. The Hands hadn't even noticed. She'd planned to use it on a winalin witch.

"You little *bitch* . . ." Ongrum stumbled. Ranka caught her, and it was then, finally, that the thing that had been building inside her broke, and she began to cry. *"Traitor."*

"I'm sorry," Ranka whispered. Tears streamed down her face as she lowered Ongrum to the floor. "I'm so, so sorry."

Ongrum kept grunting and gurgling, her eyes saying every cruel threat that her lips could no longer form. Ranka's vision burned, and snot dripped from her nose.

How had it come to this?

Ongrum's face contorted as the drug took hold. The tranquilizer wouldn't last long.

Ranka set her down gently. Ongrum twitched on the floor, shivering as the tranquilizer sank deeper and deeper, and Ranka turned her onto her side lest she choke on her own vomit. Every part of her threatened to break.

"I love you still, despite it all," Ranka said softly. "And that's why I can't let you do this."

Percy had spoken the truth. She'd chosen wrong.

This wasn't who she was—not anymore.

There would be no redemption for her. She had betrayed the twins, and there would be no coming back from that. There would be no north after this. No Skra.

There would be no place for her at all.

After everything she'd done, it was what she deserved.

In a different world, in a different time, Ongrum might have chosen her. Might have been the mother Ranka craved. In another life, Ranka would have been the perfect daughter in turn. They'd been that once, when Ranka was a little girl, barefoot in the snow, and Ongrum was simply the witch who carried her home.

Both of those people were gone now. Ongrum had chosen her path, had tried to reforge Ranka to walk it with her, and Ranka had tried. Had been ready and willing after the flames of Belren took everything from her.

But that was before the south. That was before a boy with storms in his blood, a gold-eyed ambassador, and a brilliant girl who had upended everything Ranka thought she knew about what it meant to love and be loved.

"I'm sorry," Ranka whispered. "Goodbye, Ongrum."

Ranka turned and left her behind.

For the first time in her life, she was making the right choice. The hard choice.

She just hoped she wasn't too late.

59

IT DIDN'T TAKE LONG FOR RANKA TO FIND THE SCENT she hunted. Though half of the palace had collapsed into smoke-streaked, wine-drenched ruins, she could have navigated it with her eyes closed. As a witchling, when her magnified sense manifested as scent instead of sight like Vivna's, she'd been so distraught. She'd always wanted to be a perfect copy of her sister.

But now the air told a story—one of smoke, blood, and ruin mostly, but beneath that swirled something more. A maid hiding in the kitchen, a drunk witch hopelessly in love with another, a guard bleeding in the corner.

And there, ahead, that familiar scent, the one she'd have known in any lifetime.

Ranka put on an extra burst of speed. As soon as Ongrum could muster even the barest grunt, she would send the witches after Ranka. And they would not be taking prisoners.

Ranka rounded the corner.

Two witches stood in the hall. Before them, kneeling on the floor, was Percy Stone.

They'd beaten him again. Percy sagged, blood trickling from both of his ears, his left eye swollen shut, lip split down the middle. Yet even now there was an edge to him, a whisper of something older and more powerful, from before witches had ever walked these lands.

"Not much of a smart mouth on you now, huh?" one of the witches taunted. Ranka's heart lurched. It was *Tafa*. Her knuckles were bloodied. She looked small and slight against Percy's long, lanky frame.

The other witch leaned against the wall—a Murknen, by her moss-pleated shirt. She reeked of red wine.

"You're lucky the Bloodwinn wants you alive," Tafa told Percy. "Or I'd cut your throat right here."

"Yes," Percy slurred. "I'd say this is the luckiest I've felt, ever, in my entire life."

Tafa hit him again. Percy reeled back, coughing up blood. He glanced at Tafa, and Ranka saw it—a flicker of gold, a pulse of scales. Then it was gone.

Percy was holding back. But why?

You know why.

Because Percy, unlike Ranka, had learned from his mistakes. Percy was loyal to Aramis even now. If there was even a sliver of a chance he could save her, he'd use it.

Tafa raised her hand—and Ranka stepped into the hall. "Having fun?"

Percy flinched at the sight of her.

I'm sorry, she wanted to say. *You were right. I'm going to fix it.* Instead, she barely looked at him, schooling her face into what she hoped was a mask of indifference. Her heart pounded as she strolled forward, the image of Ongrum frozen in her tranquilizer-induced stupor flashing behind her eyes.

They had ten minutes at best. Less if Ongrum's body processed it faster.

Tafa whirled and then immediately relaxed. *"Raaa."* She lurched forward, her breath so heavy with wine, it turned Ranka's stomach. *"Theeeere* you aaaare."

It took everything in Ranka not to flinch away from her. "Ongrum wants the ambassador moved to where the princess is being held."

Percy stiffened.

Tafa blinked. "Really? Why?"

"She knows the girl has a soft spot for him—figures it'd be best if we did our interrogation within her earshot."

"Smart." A wicked grin bloomed across Tafa's face. "Always more fun with an audience anyway."

Ranka forced herself to smile in return, though it felt like her lips were carved from stone. Had she never come here, she might have meant that smile, might have indulged in the eager light in Tafa's eyes. Now she felt only disgust.

The Murknen unfolded herself from the wall with a frown. She was older than Ranka, far shorter than her, with flaxen hair that had bits of moss woven through it. "Why is the Skra leader sending a pup to give us orders?"

A wave of panic prickled up Ranka's spine, but she forced herself to remain steady. She looked at the Murknen and pictured Aramis—the way the princess wielded her cool dismissal like a weapon, the way she remained steady with that disinterested light in her dark eyes and the curve to her lips that suggested anyone who questioned her was nothing but a fool.

"She didn't send a pup," Ranka said coldly. "She sent the Bloodwinn."

The Murknen glanced at Tafa, who nodded, and then dipped her head, though suspicion still shadowed her face. "My apologies."

They stood there for an awkward beat. *They expect me to lead.* Which would make sense if Ongrum actually had ordered her to do anything. Ranka gripped Percy by his collar.

"You lead," Ranka said. "I'll keep an eye on him."

"What an honor." There was an odd edge to his voice, and his tone was particularly wheedling. "Escorted by my very best friend, the Bloodwinn. How privileged I am."

"Quiet." Ranka's voice was flat. It took everything in her not to look down at him. If he saw her face, she'd betray them both, and then they'd be doomed. She glanced at Tafa and the Murknen, doing her best to look properly impatient. *How long has it been now? Three minutes? Five?* "Shall we?"

"Ranka," Percy whispered. "Please, if you ever cared about us at all—"

"Quiet."

The witches gave Percy and her an odd look.

He can't talk to me like this.

"If you have an ounce of decency left in you—"

"I said *quiet*."

They're going to figure it out if I let him talk to me like this.

"You can't let them near her—"

I'm sorry, Percy.

Ranka cracked a hand across his face.

She hit him harder than she needed to. Percy reeled backward, his cheek already beginning to redden in the faint outline of her hand. His eyes flicked over her several times, round with disbelief, and Ranka watched as the last bit of faith he'd had in her slowly shriveled and died.

Now Percy looked at her with nothing but loathing. Her enemy at last.

She might have laughed in any other circumstances. She had gotten terribly good at that lately, it seemed—making an enemy out of everyone around her.

Ranka fixed her attention ahead. "Let's go."

"They've got them in the dungeons." Tafa shuddered. "It's so creepy down there."

Ranka made a noncommittal noise and did everything to quell the relief pulsing through her. She hauled Percy upright and stepped after Tafa, ignoring the Murknen witch, who still eyed her warily. Once they found Aramis, Ranka would set both of them free, and then she could find Galen. She knew better than to hope they'd want her help after this, but so long as the three of them made it out, she'd gladly face Ongrum's wrath.

Footsteps sounded ahead. A Skra tore around the corner and paled at the sight of Ranka. *"You—"*

Ongrum was awake. She'd called her witches, and they were coming for blood.

Ranka's time was up.

60

RANKA LUNGED.

Without her blood-magic, she was so much slower. So much *weaker*. Only surprise gave her an edge. She brought the girl to the ground and cracked her head against the floor. Blood pooled from the witch's ear, and Ranka rose, her hands trembling. When her blood-magic made her hurt someone, it stole away the sounds, the feeling of them under her hand, the knowledge of what she'd done. But now this girl was bleeding—now she might not wake up—

"Ranka," a familiar voice behind her whispered. "What was that?"

Ranka turned, her ears ringing. She hesitated over the unconscious witch. Tafa and the Murknen witch stared at her, mouths hanging open in shock. Behind her, the faint sound of more feet pounding on tile came closer.

So much for a silent escape.

Ranka's hand inched toward the witch's belt.

Tafa's mouth trembled. "Ranka, what was that?"

"Listen to me," Ranka said, her heart in her throat. "Ongrum is lying to us."

"I knew something was off," the Murknen spat. She whipped a knife from her belt and brought two fingers to her lips. A piercing whistle ripped down the hall, and the Murknen stalked forward. "Pathetic."

Somewhere, in the distance, three whistles answered in turn.

Shit.

Ranka palmed the girl's knife. Percy sat up straighter, an interested light in his eyes, and Ranka gave him a hard stare, praying he understood.

Tafa looked between them. "You can't be serious, Ra."

"I'm sorry," Ranka said, her voice gentle. And she was. Even now she cared for Tafa. She wanted a better world for both of them.

"You are weak," the Murknen spat. "You are not worthy of your title, or the blood-magic in your veins."

Funny thing, that.

Ranka tensed. The Murknen took a step forward—and Ranka hurled the knife.

Both Tafa and the Murknen jumped sideways. The knife clattered to the floor at Percy's feet. Ranka hurtled forward, slamming into the Murknen's legs. They hit the ground, the Murknen screaming in fury as Ranka sank her teeth into her wrist to wrestle her dagger away from her. More whistles pierced the air. Fire ripped across Ranka's scalp as Tafa grabbed her by the hair and yanked her backward. Without her blood-magic, the pain left her breathless. Agony lanced down her leg as the Murknen bit her, and Ranka wrenched away, baring her teeth in frustration. She was so *weak* without her blood-magic. Was this how everyone else lived? How could anyone even fight like this?

Footsteps drew closer. Ranka twisted on the ground and slammed her elbow into the Murknen's temple. Pain crackled up her arm, and her hand went numb, but the witch crumpled.

Ranka turned and found herself staring at Tafa.

Had it really only been a day since they'd faced off like this as Ranka tried to ferry Galen to safety?

"Tafa," Ranka said softly. "What Ongrum is doing—"

"Don't." Tafa's hand trembled.

"Have you seen them, Tafa? The sick ones?"

Did you know? Did you help her?

Tafa looked away. "It's necessary."

"Tell that to Yeva and Asyil." Ranka swallowed. "What she's doing is wrong. I think you know that. I think you're scared too. If winalin gets out into the world, our entire coven is at risk."

"Don't talk about the coven. You have no right. You have no place—"

Tafa didn't get to finish her sentence. She gasped, and then her eyes rolled back in her head as she crumpled to the floor.

Percy stood behind her, holding the hilt of the knife he'd just slammed into the pressure point of her neck. The voices drew closer, coupled with the crackling of the fires that were only now beginning to sputter out in the garden.

"Percy—" Ranka started.

He pointed his knife at her. "Why did you change your mind?"

Her mouth open and closed. There were a thousand things she could have told him—that he was right, for starters. That she realized he'd been trying to warn her all along because he had made the same mistake as her once and was trying to spare her the horror of fighting for the wrong side. That she would fix everything or die trying because her entire life had been a series of terrible mistakes and she was *done* being a tool, a pawn, a monster on a leash for someone else.

That she loved them—him, Aramis, Galen—and it terrified her, because she'd already lost them.

But instead Ranka whispered, "She's making them, Percy. The winalin witches."

The color drained from Percy's face. "You're certain?"

She told him, quickly, of what Ongrum had been so proud of—the witches who had turned themselves over to become monsters and the ones taken against their will. Of Yeva, Asyil, Talis, and so many others who had been used as pawns in some terrible game by a woman who couldn't even handle the weight of the power she craved. Of the Hands, manipulating Ongrum—and the missing piece she still couldn't figure out, because how had a bunch of ragtag, witch-hating rebels been directed so well?

The witches drew closer. Percy had a choice to make. If he rejected her, Ranka would accept it. She would understand.

"I know better than to ask you for trust or forgiveness. I'm—"

"Save the poetics for your girlfriend. I'm too pretty to die." Percy cast a nervous glance over his shoulder and pointed the knife at her again. "One slipup, Ranka, and I won't hesitate. This doesn't mean we want you back—that *she'll* want you back."

"I know," Ranka said all too quickly. "I just want to help. Please, Percy."

Another whistle cut through the air. On the floor to their left, the Murknen witch moaned and brought a hand to her bloody ear.

Percy looked down at Ranka and then rolled his eyes.

"Oh, all right." He held out a hand. "Try not to screw us all over a second time, will you?"

When Ranka first started working with Aramis and Percy on winalin, she'd wondered why they opted for the old salt mines instead of the palace dungeons. Surely, dungeons were more secure. She'd chalked it up to anonymity at the time. It'd be easier to lie, to pretend they had nothing to do with it, if a workshop were discovered.

Now, as the dungeons unfolded around her, she understood why.

Damp limestone stretched around them—not the beautiful, curated sheets of white rock that built the palace, but uncut, uncured stone carrying an almost orange hue, as if lit from within by fire. The dungeons smelled of death. Water puddled along the floor. Roaches skittered at her feet, shiny carapaces winking. How lucky the first Sunras must have thought themselves, to land on these shores and find a natural-made prison that had been built layer over patient layer within the cliffs.

How many had died here? How many had been witches like her, left to rot with no recourse?

Percy was silent. If he was having mixed feelings about agreeing to let Ranka help, he didn't show it. His expression was focused as he followed close on her heels.

"Percy," Ranka whispered at one point. "Thank you."

He poked her in the back with the knife handle. "Quiet."

A single word, loaded with so much.

I don't trust you. I don't forgive you. I am beyond angry with you. But I do need your help.

That would have to be enough.

The scents of pain drew her like a moth to flame. And there, cutting through decades of ruin, was something familiar. A spark of new amid the old. Nerves swirled through Ranka. The twins were here. She'd help Percy get them out—and then she would face Ongrum.

Her stomach twisted itself into knots at the thought. *What is wrong with me?* Ongrum had betrayed her, the entire coven, and every witch in Witchik. Ongrum had shown herself to be a far worse monster than Ranka.

So why do I still want to save her?

"They're here," Ranka whispered, her heart beating harder. Tafa's hatchet burned in her hand. It was too light for her, but it still felt like a piece of home. Behind her, Percy wielded the Murknen's knife.

Ranka's head spun. She wasn't ready to face them yet. Wasn't ready to meet their eyes and admit she had betrayed them when she needed them most, that she had been too weak to protect the ones who mattered yet again.

"Percy," Ranka whispered. "A little light?"

He hesitated, and sighed. "Oh, all right. It's not like anyone in possession of a single brain cell wouldn't have caught on yet."

The ambassador brought two fingers to his lips and blew.

A flame flared to life in the dark. It was no bigger than a robin's egg, burning just as blue. Heat pulsed against Ranka's skin. Percy watched her with narrowed eyes, as if daring her to comment, but she said nothing.

He could keep his secrets. Goddess knew she had plenty of her own.

With the flame at his fingers, Percy took the lead. He turned the corner, casting warm blue firelight all around them, and Ranka followed him with her heart in her throat.

"Oh no," Percy whispered.

Two cells waited for them.

One held Aramis. She'd not fared well in the hours since Ranka's betrayal—her hair was a mess, her dress torn, and blood ran sluggishly from her nose. The skin on her wrists was rubbed raw from chains, and the princess was slumped sideways, her eyes closed and her mouth parted. For a moment panic flashed through Ranka, until she saw the gentle rise and fall of Aramis's chest. The princess was alive—just unconscious.

But the cell beside hers was empty.

Galen was gone.

61

"*NO,*" PERCY WHISPERED. "HE WAS SUPPOSED TO BE here."

Ranka put a hand on Percy's shoulder and breathed in. Scents swirled over her tongue: old water and worn rock, pain and grief, and there, the scent of metal polish, of windy days and old ink. Galen had definitely been here, but there was no sting of death.

"He's still alive," Ranka said quietly. "Or at least—he didn't die here."

For all they knew, the Skra could have dragged the prince out of the dungeons and killed him in the gardens. Percy swung toward Aramis's cell and whispered her name, but she didn't stir. She lay painfully still, left hand splayed open as though she'd reached for something right before slipping into a drugged stupor.

"Shit. Shit, shit, *shit.*" Percy pressed his knuckles into his eyes as he paced back and forth. "They had to have known. Where would they have moved him? Where could he have *gone?*"

"We can keep looking," Ranka said, her voice low. "I can search the rest of the dungeons—"

Behind her came a light.

It was faint, no bigger than a pinprick, but someone was definitely coming. And with the light came a familiar scent—old leather, wood-smoke, and a lifetime of disapproval.

Terror opened a well in Ranka's stomach.

"It's her," Ranka said weakly.

"I can't just leave him," Percy said, his voice cracking. "He won't last here alone, Ranka. I told him I wouldn't leave him—I told him . . ."

She'd never seen him like this before. For all his pomp and arrogance, Percy was just a boy. A child, caught up in some great and terrible game. And Percy was not well. His breathing was labored, and he leaned against the wall to support himself, his left eye swollen shut from Tafa's beating as the bruise overtook the left half of his face. It would be a miracle if he got Aramis out of here on his own, and he seemed to know it.

He needed her. They both did.

And when they no longer need me?

No matter. She'd chosen this path, and she would walk it until its end.

Her eyes swept the dungeon, noting the insects scuttling along the floor, the old lichen dried on the ceiling, the salt stains above her head from when the dungeons were entirely submerged. The first Sunras hadn't been stupid; they'd have known someday they might need to make a hasty escape. They'd have left themselves with multiple exits.

Ranka stepped forward and breathed.

The dungeons were a map of history. Even here, hundreds of feet beneath the earth, buried between layers of salt and rock and old bones, there was a current, a draft fed by sea air. Ranka went deeper, pulling the scents over her tongue, past the smoke of Percy's fire, the old ghosts of witches long dead and humans who had suffered here, past the scent of wet limestone, of torches guttering in sconces and blood on the walls. And there—a whisper of salt, a hint of the sea. Deep, deep below the dungeons, the old salt mines still ran; the original Sunras had opted to build directly on top of them. That was their way out, if they could make it in time.

But there was something else, too. Something alive and rotting, moving in the dark, waiting for them. Winalin witches—packs of them, judging by the scents.

"The salt mines are below us," Ranka said. "We can get out that way, make it into the city. I can get us to the surface." Even if they were in total darkness—even without her blood-magic—that was one thing she was confident of.

Scent had always guided her home when nothing else could.

"And where would we even go?" Percy demanded. Had he always been this frightened, and only now it was slipping through? Or had Galen's disappearance truly undone something in him?

But he had a point. Most of Seaswept was in shambles or occupied by the Hands. Surely, there had to be somewhere they could hide. Foldrey's home was an option, but she wouldn't know how to find the address from the mines—

Lanna, Ranka realized. "She knows Aramis, cares about her. She'll hide us."

Percy's eyes lingered on Aramis. "When she wakes . . ."

When she wakes, she'll never want to see you again.

When she wakes, she'll kill you.

Ranka was ready for that. She'd betrayed them, but she'd betrayed Aramis the worst. The princess was entitled to every ounce of rage she would feel.

Another whistle pierced the air. Behind her, the lantern light grew brighter. They had two, maybe three minutes before the Skra were upon them. A scout would appear first—Ranka could take them with the element of surprise, but more witches would be only a few minutes on their heels.

"I know you don't trust me. But if Galen—"

She couldn't finish the words.

If Galen dies, Aramis is the last living Sunra in this world.

Ranka stepped past Percy and examined the lock. It was simple iron craft, worn from centuries of use. If she'd had her blood-magic, she might have been able to break the lock. But without it, she was mortal. Just another witch who'd made too many mistakes. "Percy, could you melt this?"

"What am I, a walking torch?"

Ranka fixed him with a hard look.

Still he hesitated. Only a day ago she had been on his side. Now they were on uneven footing again, the weight of Ranka's betrayal hanging heavy between them.

"Why?" Percy looked exhausted. "Why not run? The Skra are against you, we're against you. You are alone, Ranka. You have no allies, no friends. Why are you still helping us? Why are you still here?"

It was a fair question. A smarter witch would have betrayed Ongrum and run. "I wish I could tell you it was just about winalin—that I couldn't live with myself if I let it burn through the country. But the truth is that I am not that noble and I am not that brave. I'm still here not because of winalin." The next words felt like they might choke her. "I'm still here because of her."

In her cell, Aramis Sunra did not stir. A small blessing.

"You love her," said Percy. It wasn't a question.

Was a handful of months even long enough to go from hating a girl to loving her? Was she even old enough—healed enough—to know what love was?

Ranka didn't know. It would never matter. Girls like her didn't get happy endings.

But she could still make it right.

"I am tired of fighting for the wrong person," Ranka said finally. "Let me do this one thing, Percy. Let me help you save her. And then if she wants to be rid of me—if you both want me to leave this city and never return—I won't protest. I'll go."

The lantern light bobbed closer.

"I have nothing left," Ranka said quietly. "No friends, no family, no coven. But I am still a weapon. I am still a girl groomed for a cause. Let me have this one."

Percy looked down the tunnels. "When I realized what Ilia had done with winalin, I panicked. I tried to return to my old mentor, and he cast me out. I lost everything—my family, my true magic, my home. And I deserved it. I came here, expecting nothing, and found . . . everything." He laughed, the noise quiet and surprised. "Those twins . . . this place. Sometimes I wonder if the gods brought all my painful mistakes early in life, so I might spend the rest of my days earning the life that followed. I'd like to think I have earned my second chance. I'd like to think I'm better now." He looked at her. "I serve the twins. If Aramis wants you gone . . ."

Ranka nodded. "I understand."

Still he watched her, as if in Ranka he saw an old memory he couldn't quite shake. "You are not done with her. Ongrum."

Ranka began to shake her head, but Percy held up a hand.

"You think you are—but trust me. This is how it works, with people who wield abuse like a knife and convince us they're cutting us with love. There will come a moment more dire than the one you faced last night. A moment you can't come back from, and everything in you, everything you've been conditioned for, every fear and hurt and hope and dream, will scream for you to choose Ongrum again."

Ranka's breath hitched. "I'll choose Aramis this time."

"No." Percy shook his head. "No, that's not the answer. That's not how you heal. It's time for you to be your own person, Ranka. We're not responsible for the wounds we suffer—but we *are* responsible for healing them. So when the moment comes, and when that choice is in front of you—I'm begging you to choose yourself. That's the only way you heal. It's the only way you can be free."

"I—" Her voice faltered. All her life she'd looked for someone to follow. Someone to believe in. A person, a mission, a cause. And

Percy was telling her that was a *bad* thing? "I don't know if I can do that."

"You have to," the boy said, his voice soft. "The only way out of this is to choose yourself, again and again, even when it's hard. Even when it's terrifying. Even when you feel like the most broken, unworthy, worthless person in the world."

It was asking too much of her. She had always been a follower, a fighter to be directed toward the next target. And Percy was asking her to choose *herself*? It was laughable. It was terrifying. And it was impossible. Couldn't choosing Aramis be enough?

"Okay," Ranka lied. "I will."

Percy watched her, a quiet sorrow lining his face—and then he put his lips against the lock and blew.

Fire flared. The lock glowed and melted away entirely, sliding to the floor. Scales shimmered on Percy's jaw where the flames touched him and then faded, vanishing as his skin cooled.

The door swung open. Aramis looked so small, unconscious and crumpled into a heap. Ranka lifted her with ease. Her head lolled, lips half-parted. Aramis would not forgive her as quickly as Percy had, if she did at all.

It wouldn't matter. Their quiet, gentle days were behind them. They were at war now, and Ranka was a soldier fighting for Aramis's cause. No more, no less.

It was all she should have been from the beginning.

I'll choose her, she told herself. *It will be enough. She'll be enough, this time.*

Percy turned to her. "You sure you can get us out of here?"

Ranka nodded, holding Aramis close to her chest. Of all the things she was uncertain of, this she was confident in, because this had nothing to do with her head, her heart, or the blood-magic dormant in her chest.

This relied only on her status as a witch. And that part of Ranka had never faltered.

Her black nails gleamed in the light.

"Burn the lichen on the walls—the fire will slow them down."

She didn't wait to see if Percy listened.

With the princess she'd betrayed wrapped in her arms, Ranka took a breath and stepped into the endless dark.

62

RANKA LED THEM DOWN.

Here, where even the first Sunras had stretched their influence, only the whims of water and time molded the rock, carving through the layers of sediment and salt, leaving natural tunnels that were small, sloping, and uneven. Ranka and Percy were forced to walk with their heads bowed, shoulders scraping the walls.

Down they went, deeper and deeper, until the air ran so cold and dark, Ranka finally relented and let Percy lead the way with flames glowing at his fingertips. Seawater dripped all around them.

They didn't speak. Didn't dare, not here, where the smallest sound carried and tunnels yawned on either side of them, containing nothing but endless dark. Every scurry of a roach or hiss from a rat made Ranka jump out of her skin. Every few steps she caught a whiff of old blood and rot. Twice the scent grew so strong that they doubled back.

After three hours Percy began to stumble. He was exhausted and had lost too much blood. Ranka was too tired to speak. She shifted Aramis to her left shoulder and pulled Percy's arm around her neck to take his weight. He didn't protest, didn't even offer a quip—the only indication of what bad shape he must have been in. Ranka's limbs trembled, and her back ached.

What she wouldn't have given for the rush of her blood-magic, if only so it could eat away her fatigue and propel her through. It had been so long since she'd slept—since she'd rested at all. She wasn't going to be able to make it much farther. Still, Ranka hauled them forward, carrying Aramis, half dragging Percy.

Finally the acrid scent of the city swirled around them as the watery light of dawn leaked into the tunnels.

And from ahead, came a snarl.

All of Ranka went cold.

No, please.

She was so tired. So *weak*.

And so she could only watch as a winalin witch stepped from the tunnel ahead, followed by another, and another.

They were so young. That was the cruelest piece of it all. They'd been children so recently, with dreams and hopes of their own, lured into this nightmare by a glittering lie.

The first winalin witch gurgled low in her throat. She limped forward, her ankle dragging awkwardly. Blood painted her lips, and bits of flesh were visible beneath her nails. They had killed recently, then.

Were these the witches who had killed Nadya? Or were they just a few of many, now loose in the mine, set free to terrorize a city unequipped to fight them?

"Please," Ranka whispered. "Don't."

From the dark came a flash of gold.

She could not defend Aramis and Percy. She could hardly defend herself. After everything, it seemed she'd dragged them down here to die.

The first witch hissed.

Ranka braced herself—and then the tunnels were ablaze.

One moment they were alone. The next, the Hands of Solomei surrounded them, pouring into the tunnels, gold pins on their chests gleaming like beacons of hope as they waved torches at the winalin witches and drove them back.

"Secure the princess!" Was it Ranka's addled mind, or was that the echo of a ghost? *"Protect her, above all."*

The Hands were the enemy. She should flee. Should fight them off.

Instead, Ranka sank to her knees.

Someone struck her in the temple, and the world went dark.

Ranka awoke to gloom. She groaned, tilting forward from where she leaned against the wall. Despite her best efforts, she'd fallen asleep. Judging from the golden hue of the sunlight that crept in watery strands through a gap in the boards, it was late afternoon, nearly evening. They'd slept all day.

Where am I?

Memories came back in broken fragments—winalin witches, attacking them in the dark.

And the Hands, cutting through the mines with their fire and swords, fighting off the witches. Saving them—and then taking them prisoner.

In the corner, Percy and Aramis began to stir. They'd been settled on a narrow, single-person bed. Percy's eyes fluttered open first. He blinked down at the bandages that now swathed his limbs. He looked around, plainly confused, and sagged backward.

"We're alive," he croaked. "What a shame."

If Percy could be annoying, then he was all right.

Aramis's eyes flew open.

"Galen," she cried. *"No!"*

Aramis pitched forward and Percy caught her. Aramis scrambled against him, and then her eyes cleared as she took in the room, her look of horror replaced by one of confusion as she registered unfamiliar walls—and the witch who sat across from them.

"You," Aramis snarled. "What is this? Where's my brother?"

Percy put a hand on her knee. "Hey—"

"Percy? Why are you all bruised? Are you all right?"

"Aramis." Percy gripped her by the shoulders. "Calm down.

Breathe. We're not in the palace, we're in Seaswept. Ranka broke us out."

Aramis watched him with wild eyes, her chest heaving, and Ranka didn't dare move. Maybe Aramis would forgive her—maybe she'd see clearly the position Ranka had been in. Maybe—

"*She* broke us out?" Aramis's laugh was sharp and cruel. She eyed Ranka with a look that could have wilted grass. "How convenient. Where are we, then? Are the Skra waiting on the other side of this door to kill us?"

Ranka frowned.

"What, nothing else to say now, witch girl? You got what you wanted, didn't you? Let me guess—you're here to force me to unlock your blood-magic for you. Or you want information about Galen. Or . . ." Her voice faltered, and Aramis's eyes flashed. "*Say* something, you massive coward."

Ranka's eyes stung, and she hoped against hope that the dim light concealed the wetness in them. When she spoke, her voice was rough and shaking. "I'm sorry."

"You're *sorry*? You've doomed us all and you're *sorry*?" Aramis waved a hand. "Well, how lovely. Ranka is sorry, everyone! Even though she destroyed the vaccine, turned the palace over to an enemy coup, probably got my brother killed, kidnapped us, and dragged us to some random hellhole in the middle of Seaswept, she's *sorry*."

Ranka sat there, took every bit of it. She deserved it. But her mind spun. Something about this wasn't right. The Hands had had every reason to leave them for dead—instead they'd saved them. Bandaged and cleaned them up with expert hands.

"Ranka?" Percy asked. "Where are we? Who saved us in the mines?"

"I don't know," Ranka said faintly. She chewed on her knuckles. "I was so tired. And I caught a familiar scent that didn't make sense, but I could have sworn—I thought I saw—I don't know. . . ."

The Hands had saved them. Healed them. Which meant, for now, they wanted them alive.

Why?

Ranka crawled forward on her knees, feeling along the walls, pressing her ear to them. Boots clacked in the street outside, and somewhere a stray dog barked. Ranka peered through the gap and saw no one—only a fluffy black cat nosing at some trash and a street sign that read FELLHAVEN.

The feeling drained from her.

"In the mines," Ranka said numbly. "I thought I saw a ghost."

The door creaked open.

"Not a ghost," an all-too-familiar voice said. "Though I do *feel* like one these days."

Foldrey Wolfe leaned against the frame, a golden pin gleaming on his chest, and gave them a humorless smile. "Hello, children. I suppose we have a lot to discuss."

63

ARAMIS AND PERCY STARED AT FOLDREY. THEIR BODIES were rigid, their lips half-parted in shock. Above Aramis's head, a single beetle scurried up the wall, its black carapace winking in a beam of sunlight. For a long, terrible moment no one spoke. Ranka blinked several times, but the ghost in front of her did not evaporate.

"Foldrey," Aramis whispered. "You're alive?"

Foldrey watched them wearily. "I know you must have many questions—"

"It was you," Aramis said thickly. "All along, guiding the Hands. Sabotaging my work. Ensuring it was only ever dead winalin witches we found—it was *you*."

Foldrey watched her, and in that precious beat of silence Ranka willed for him to say something, anything, besides what they all now knew to be true.

But Foldrey simply nodded. "Yes."

"How?" Aramis whispered. The agony in her voice was palpable. "*Why?* You—you lied to us. All this time? You were supposed to protect us. We trusted you, Foldrey. We trusted you with our lives. Mother and Father trusted you. You were family—you were—you *bastard*."

Foldrey remained quiet as Aramis unraveled, the shadows beneath

his eyes more pronounced than usual. How many men had he lost to Ongrum's cause? How many had been loyal and died? How many others had gleefully switched sides?

Foldrey did not gloat. But he did not seem particularly sorry, either. Only tired. The man waited for them to be quiet, and his eyes flickered. "I never intended for you to know," he said, his voice soft. "I never thought you'd get so close with winalin—not until *she* arrived. Not until a cure became possible."

Every missing piece clicked together with terrible clarity: Foldrey, urging her to leave. The way the public opinion had turned against *Ranka* when she wouldn't flee.

Foldrey, intending to lead her into the city to kill her, insisting they leave him behind to die when the Hands swooped in to save him from the winalin witches he'd used as bait.

The Hands, manipulating Ongrum so easily, as if whoever led them was knowledgeable enough of the northernmost covens to know who was most likely to betray their fellow witch.

Ranka went cold.

"My blood," Ranka whispered. She was going to vomit. "You stole my blood and gave it to the Hands."

Foldrey had been with them every step of the way. Foldrey had been there, in the workshop, watching as Aramis worked tirelessly for a way to neutralize a virus that turned witches' bodies against themselves.

And Foldrey had been working against them this entire time.

"I did." Foldrey dipped his head, and this time he spoke only to Aramis. "I know you won't believe me, but I am doing this for you and Galen both. For all of Isodal."

Aramis laughed bitterly. "By helping the witches launch a coup?"

Foldrey's lips thinned.

"The Hands split," Ranka guessed. The anger on his face confirmed it. "You were never going to aid Ongrum. You were going to pin the coup, winalin, *all* of it, on her—but some of your men broke from the plan."

It was too perfect. Draw the witches in with the temptation of winalin. Promise them the world, an equal split of power—and when they launched a horrifying loose massacre on the palace and turned winalin witches into the streets, pin the entire plague on them. It would have been neat. Easy.

It would have ensured the Bloodwinn treaty could never exist again—and that any witch in Isodal would be burned alive the day their nails turned.

But he didn't account for Ongrum. For all her faults, all her greed, Ongrum was a leader who knew how to inspire. She'd taken scared children and molded them into warriors. Could rally a band of bleeding, broken witches into believing sacrificing themselves was a glorious, noble pursuit, if it meant retaining a piece of territory.

There would have been Hands who resented Foldrey's careful protection of the twins, humans who wanted them to burn along with the witches. It would have been all too easy for Ongrum to appeal to their bloodlust, to steal them to her side, both parties plotting to betray each other once Galen was dead.

"So why are you here?" Aramis snapped. "To gloat? To kill me yourself?"

Foldrey's pale eyes flickered with something like grief. "I am here to help."

"Right," Aramis laughed. "And then you're going to—what? Expect us to forgive you, expect us to trust you again?"

"No," Foldrey said softly. "I offer you my help, but I have chosen my side. I am not your ally when this ends. And when it does, I will reshape Isodal. I will seal Witchik off, as intended. And you and your brother will live your days in the Sun Keys, guarded and protected."

"As prisoners," Aramis said bitterly.

"At least you'll be *alive*," Foldrey snapped, showing a rare flash of temper. "You were set up to fail, both of you. I'll ensure you're protected. Free to live out your days unburdened by rule. *Safe*, finally, for the first time in your young lives."

"Galen—"

"Would be eaten alive by the throne, and you know it." Pain warped Foldrey's face, but it was brief. He continued, his voice softer, more determined. "Trust me when I say this is not what I wanted. But after I'm done, we'll have a new world. A *just* world. We'll have trade regulations that make sense, an education system that serves everyone, not just the privileged. And finally, we will have peace." He held her stare. "What are the lives of the few for the future of the many?"

And for the first time Ranka understood.

Here was a boy raised in northern Isodal, who'd watched witches hunt humans and humans hunt witches, all fighting over the same resources, the same scraps of land, tearing themselves to pieces. So he'd made his way south, to serve a king and make a difference, only to be a tool of war. He had loved the king's children and sheltered them and protected them, even as he understood that their lives ensured a broken treaty would continue the cycle again and again. The Bloodwinn treaty had merely been a bandage on an already-rotting wound.

And then along had come winalin, and Ongrum with it. The perfect weapon, and the perfect fool. She'd never stood a chance against him— not Foldrey, with his uniform and ideals and polished words. Foldrey with his promises, his ability to make you feel like he understood.

But that had been his mistake. Foldrey had forgotten Ongrum was a witch. He'd viewed Ongrum as nothing more than an uneducated woman from the north who he could manipulate as he pleased. Foldrey had expected Ongrum to follow his rules—*human* rules—not understanding Ongrum would set herself on fire, if only to ensure her enemies ended up ablaze too.

There was no logic with her—only a relentless, brutal battle for every scrap of power she could find.

And even now, he didn't regret it.

Foldrey was going to burn it all down—the treaty, the Council, the country—to protect the twins and the land they ruled over. Ranka had ruined his plans for the twins never to know of his involvement. Now this was his only option. So he'd ship them away and attempt to pick up the pieces of the country he'd broken.

Save them, though they'd hate him. Take the reins Galen could never bear, to ensure the violence he'd known as a child wasn't repeated.

Is it worth it?

There'd be no changing Foldrey's mind, she realized.

I have loved them, more than I ever had a right to.

To him, it was. It always would be.

What could she say to that? Hadn't she been willing to burn down the world to protect the ones she loved? Wasn't she still?

Silence filled the room. They stared at each other—Foldrey exhausted, Aramis furious. They had never looked more like father and daughter. Even now there was love between them, shimmering in Foldrey's weary resignation, in Aramis's hurt.

The sunlight outside was beginning to fade. They were edging into evening now and losing time. Ranka ghosted her fingers over her chest. No one in the room looked at her. She was no longer an asset; she was an afterthought. Just another witch, as mortal as the rest of them. It was an odd feeling, to be useless. And strangely welcome.

Ranka found her voice. "Foldrey, how many men do you still have?"

Foldrey lifted a brow. "And who is to say I want to help you, Bloodwinn?"

"If you didn't want to help us," Ranka said slowly, "your men would have left us to die in the mines."

The corner of his mouth twitched. She'd called his bluff perfectly. A part of her ached. Foldrey, more than anyone, understood her—a northerner born to nothing, a warrior self-made. He was the mentor she'd always wanted.

And she had no doubt that as soon as he got the chance, he'd put a knife in her heart.

Aramis looked between them. "You've got to be kidding me."

"Look around, Princess," Ranka said flatly. "You are alone. You have no allies, no army, no money, and no power. Your brother is imprisoned by a madwoman, and your people are burning in the streets. Beneath your city, monsters roam, picking off innocents at night. You have *lost*, Aramis."

Aramis watched her, her very being vibrating with fury. Foldrey held painfully, carefully still.

"We all have a common goal," Ranka said softly. "Stop Ongrum and save Galen. The rest doesn't matter if he dies."

They all stared at her. Aramis looked like she wanted to say something cruel, but she closed her eyes and nodded. Percy was watching Ranka with that knowing, soft-eyed look of his, as if he saw himself in her and he was sorry for her. It had always pissed her off when he looked at her like that, but right now it just made her more tired.

Aramis leaned forward. Her voice was still cold, but a spark had entered her eyes that reminded Ranka of the girl she had fallen in love with in the workshop beneath the mines. "The Bloodwinn is right."

Ranka flinched. *The Bloodwinn*. Not *Ranka*. Not *witch girl* said with a smirk. It was the biggest distance Aramis could put between them without physically leaving the room.

"Ongrum means to execute Galen on the anniversary of the Bloodwinn treaty," Ranka supplied quietly.

"Very dramatic," Percy said. "Maybe next time she'll consider theater instead of genocide."

Aramis looked exhausted. "That's in two days. Foldrey—how many provinces could we call upon in that time?"

"At least half."

"Would it be enough?"

"It would be close. But with fresh soldiers and weapons, we would be able to secure the city, so that even if . . ." His voice caught.

Even if we fail.

Even if Ongrum murders Galen for the whole world to see.

"Even if we have to establish control in a less neat manner," Foldrey finished tightly, "then at least we'll have the weapons and soldiers."

Soldiers who would follow every command Foldrey gave them when he finished the coup Ongrum had started, and seized control in the name of preserving Isodal and the lives of the twins he'd deemed unfit to rule it.

Dread rose in Ranka. It was too easy, and too neat.

"I don't like it," Ranka said. "I'm sorry, but—a bunch of humans showing up to the palace to fight Ongrum? It only compels the witches further to her side."

"And what do you suggest?" Aramis fired back. "Since you *started* the coup, I suppose you might be the one to ask."

Ranka hesitated. This part wasn't her specialty. She was a soldier made to follow orders, not a leader trained to give them. Did she even have a right to question Aramis and Foldrey, after what she'd done?

"Never mind," Ranka said softly. "Just let me know how I can help."

They turned away from her, and that was answer enough.

On the other side of the wall, a dog barked in the street, followed by the shriek of a child and a mother's hurried *shhh*. Panic seeped from every pore of this city—the Hands, and then the Skra, had made certain of that.

The shadows in the room lengthened. All of them were exhausted, whittled out. It was a blessing, oddly enough, that the anniversary was two days away. It gave them time to recover and plan.

"Very well, then," Foldrey said. "I'll send messengers out and bring news in the morning."

It was be a relief when Foldrey left. It was too confusing with him here, too painful to see his face and recall he'd been plotting against them from the beginning. The faces of the winalin witches flashed through Ranka's memory. How many had he let die?

How many had he injected personally, knowing he was dooming them to torture?

"Aramis," Percy murmured. "I won't let him ship you both off. You know that, right? Even if we have to run—I wouldn't abandon you two. Not now, not ever."

Aramis blinked several times and squeezed his hand. "I know."

An awkward beat passed between them as they seemed to remember Ranka was there.

Aramis glanced at Ranka, her eyes cold. "And what about you? You've been awfully quiet. Where will you go after?"

Ranka looked at her hands. She had no lands, no people, no country. Neither Witchik nor Isodal would welcome her, and unlike Percy, she did not have a heroic cause to pull her abroad, nor did she want one.

"Ongrum will not be easy to beat, especially without blood-magic," Ranka said softly. "I do not expect there to be an after for me."

Finally, the truth she'd been carrying all this time, spoken aloud. It lifted a weight off her. Ranka's ending had never been destined for anything but a knife in the heart.

They knew it, and so did she.

Was it Ranka's imagination, or did grief flash briefly in Aramis's eyes?

"Well," Aramis said, still trying to sound snappish but less certain than before. "Now you're just being dramatic."

"Taking a cue from Percy. Trying to keep it interesting."

"Take better cues," Percy muttered.

Ranka said nothing. She watched the space Foldrey had occupied long after he'd left, turning the names of the ones she'd lost over in her mind and the faces of the ones she'd never learned the names of.

Ally or not, former friend or not—Foldrey Wolfe would pay for his hand in winalin.

Ranka would make certain of it.

64

DUSK CREPT UPON THEM. FOLDREY RETURNED A FEW
hours later bearing food and left again. It was simple fare—salted fish,
dry cheese, waterskins, and berries gone soft and warm from sitting
too long in the sun. It wasn't until the food was gone and silence
flooded the room that the reality of their situation seemed to settle in
the air. They were trapped here for the next two days, holding out thin
hope Foldrey would keep his word.

Ranka pressed herself into a corner. Finally, when Aramis and Percy
had looked at her before glancing away for what felt like the hun-
dredth time, she blurted, "Foldrey's going to be gone all night. Probably not wise for the three of us to hang out in here like sitting fowl.
I'll take first watch."

Ranka pulled the door closed behind her and stepped into the hall.
The floorboards creaked pitifully. The home was tiny, little more
than a front room offering a small table and a paltry kitchen. The
table stood alone, its chairs propped against the front door to slow
anyone trying to break in. A few toys were scattered across the floor,
which was covered in a thin coat of dust. Ranka lifted a portrait from
the wall. Foldrey stared back at her, his face younger and less heavy,
his arm around a small, brunette woman who held a red-haired baby.

A single window lit the front room. The blinds had been drawn, but Ranka drifted forward, peering through the crack that let in moonlight. A stray dog nosed trash in the gutter outside, flea-bitten ears twitching as drainage pipes dripped onto its back, but the city was deserted. Every home on the street had dark windows.

How many more days could these people hide inside all day? How much more horror could this city sustain?

Voices drifted down the hall, and Ranka inched backward, rolling the weight of her foot from heel to ball to keep the floorboards from creaking. Ranka drew to the door and listened.

"You should have seen her face. When she turned the corner, Aramis—I don't know. She looked like a scared little kid. And even before that, in the hall, when they'd caught me—I think she knew she'd made a mistake. I think she regretted it right away."

"That doesn't make up for what she did."

"It doesn't," Percy agreed. "But I've met a lot of villains, Aramis. And I've met good people who made bad choices because they didn't know what else to do. Ranka's a lot of things—but a master manipulator isn't one of them."

"She *betrayed* us," Aramis spat. "She's a monster—"

"As am I," Percy said quietly. "There are no heroes here, Aramis. No villains. There are only monsters—the ones we need, the ones we spare, and the ones we burn. Which of those do you think Ranka is? Which do you want her to become?"

Another lapse of quiet. Ranka reeled in the dark. Images of witches burned alive flashed behind her eyes, of the humans who burned them but the humans that had healed her too. Of a child's bloody shoe in the street, a village reduced to ash, a healer's weary smile, and a mother's clever, cruel lies.

She saw Yeva, rotted to nothing—and Asyil, dying by Ranka's hand, because Ranka had been too late to save her, too.

You'll be the monster, Galen had said. There had been so much faith in her then. Hope that Ranka might be the terrible thing they needed.

She had almost let herself believe it—that she could be the monster, the knife in the dark, staining her soul to protect those who deserved it. And she had failed.

Aramis finally spoke, her voice barely audible. "Is it true, then? Her leader is . . . making them? Was supplying the Hands with witches this whole time? And she didn't know? You believe her?"

"I do. I'm so sorry, Aramis. I never imagined . . ."

"You don't have to—"

"But I do. This is my fault—more than Ranka's, or Foldrey's, or anyone's."

"You were a child. *Are* a child." Aramis laughed bitterly. "We all are."

"I'll have you know I am *very* mature for my age."

Aramis snorted and said something too soft for Ranka to make out. She forced herself to draw away, Percy's words still churning through her mind.

It was nearly midnight when the door creaked open and Percy stepped out. "Need a break?"

Ranka shrugged. She'd spent entire nights like this, sitting in silence somewhere in Skra territory, eyes on the horizon. "Not really."

"Let's try that again—you need to sleep." When Ranka didn't move, he crossed his arms and glared. "I don't know if you've forgotten, but we have to try to uncoup a coup in two days. This is the last break we're going to get."

"I can sleep out here—"

"Oh, for the love of—she's not going to *bite* you. Go get some rest, you useless oaf."

"Watch who you're calling oaf, oaf."

"I am not an oaf," Percy said primly. "I am *annoying*."

Ranka glared at him but rose all the same.

He waved dismissively at her and settled himself on the kitchen table, eyes trained on the door. Reluctantly Ranka turned away, and she made her way into the back room, where Aramis waited.

65

THE PRINCESS WAS ASLEEP.

If Percy thought Ranka was going to sleep next to Aramis, she had an icehouse in the desert to sell to him. She crept into the room and lay down on the floor, as far away from Aramis as she could manage.

"Comfortable?"

Ranka went rigid. "I've slept in worse places."

Aramis sat up, barely visible in the gloom.

Ranka cleared her throat. "I can sleep outside—"

"I'm not going to make you sleep in the street like a rat," Aramis snapped. "Here." She snatched a threadbare blanket from the bed and tossed it at her. Ranka shrugged it around her shoulders. It was warm from Aramis's touch. Ranka tried not to think about why it made her dizzy.

A few days ago things had finally been easy between them, had been gentle and warm and *good*.

Now Aramis could barely stand to speak to her.

And could she blame her? After what Ranka had done, it was a miracle Aramis hadn't tried to strangle her yet.

They stared at each other. If the gods were real, then they were particularly cruel, because even exhausted, even bloodied and bruised,

Aramis Sunra was still the most magnetic person Ranka had ever laid eyes on.

Ranka wanted to say she was sorry. She wanted to know if she died tomorrow if any of this would matter at all. But she was beyond deserving any answers from Aramis, so instead she lay back down.

But Aramis didn't.

"What you said earlier," Aramis said. "About not expecting there to be an after for you—you meant that?"

"Ongrum is a skilled warrior, and without my blood-magic . . . I don't know."

"How can you say that so calmly?"

"This isn't my first time facing death." Ranka closed her eyes. "And I am tired of fighting."

If the princess wanted a fight, Ranka was too exhausted to give one to her. Somewhere in the front room, the floorboards creaked as Percy adjusted his position. An owl hooted outside. Ranka thought maybe Aramis had fallen back asleep, and then, so soft Ranka could barely hear her:

"Foldrey." Aramis's voice trembled. She locked her arms around her knees. "He's . . . leading . . . the . . ."

"Princess," Ranka said gently. "Breathe."

But Aramis's gasps only increased in violence. She rocked back and forth, her breath hitching higher, higher, higher. Ranka knew what was coming next.

Aramis bit her fist—and *screamed*.

For the first time since Ranka had met her, after months of hunting winalin witches, creeping through tunnels, and facing down death, the princess of Isodal finally, entirely unraveled.

The tears came quickly. Aramis's entire body shook with great, terrible sobs as everything finally hit her in full force. Ranka watched her, dimly reminded of a different day, five years ago, when she'd woken in Belren and realized Vivna had left her behind. She recalled the terror that had sunk into her bones, sharper than a knife, colder than the deepest trenches of the Kithraki rivers. She recalled anger.

And above all, she remembered betrayal.

The way it had burned her throat, stolen her breath, carved out her chest, and collapsed her ribs. The way it had made her want to plunge into denial and break everything around her. The way it had shaken her to her core—this new, unrelenting belief she was not worth loving.

That she was not worth anything at all.

There would be no tempering this pain for Aramis. So instead of whispering her hollow reassurances, Ranka did the only thing she could.

She stood in witness of Aramis's fury and grief, and she stayed.

After several minutes, Aramis's sobs slowed. She picked her head up, her eyes red and raw. Snot dripped from her nose and crusted her chin. Deep, angry half-moons winked from her palms where she'd dug her fingernails so hard into her skin, she'd drawn blood.

"My parents loved us, but they had a kingdom to run. But Foldrey . . . Foldrey always had time for us. It was Foldrey who taught us how to read." She laughed, low and sad. "Can you imagine? A guard teaching his charges to read, instead of the tutors. Mother used to joke that they couldn't pry him away from us. From the time Galen and I were born, he was there, and he never left. He was supposed to protect us."

"I know, Princess," Ranka said softly. Ongrum's face flashed through her mind's eye. "I know."

"I thought . . ." Aramis shook her head. "We grew up with power. With everything we could have ever wanted. We were spoiled as children—but Foldrey never treated us as special. I hated him for it sometimes, truly. He could have been fired, or worse, for the way he spoke to us sometimes. But he was always honest." She wrapped her arms around her knees. "He always loved us, in the end."

A lump formed in Ranka's throat. Somewhere overhead, seabirds cried. This land, this people, this girl, they were all so different from what she'd always known—but the pain was familiar. Ranka didn't know why that was a comfort—that she could cross the continent, could leave behind everything she knew, and their hearts still broke the same.

"Sometimes," Ranka said slowly, her words coming from far away. "The people we love aren't worthy of it. They betray our history, take away hope for any future that might have been. But it doesn't change what they gave us. Not if we don't want it to. And the knowing—the truth of it, that they weren't who you thought? That you didn't know *sooner*? It doesn't make it any more our fault."

Tears dripped from Aramis's chin.

"It's not worth torturing yourself over why you loved them, why you love them still," Ranka murmured. She looked away, and when she spoke, it was not a princess in a sun-soaked land she saw, but a girl in the north, a girl among the trees, a coven beyond the mountains, a sister, a mother, a family. The words kept coming.

"Why do we love anyone?" Ranka whispered. "It usually isn't logical, and it's not always right. But I don't think we're usually given a choice. Love doesn't just disappear. Even if you want it to. Even if it would be easier for everyone involved."

"I am so angry," Aramis whispered. "I am so, *so* angry at you. At *both* of you."

"I know."

"I don't want to be, and that makes it worse. He was my family. You were my *friend*, Ranka."

"You were mine."

"You were my friend, and then you—we—I thought . . ."

Neither could give air to what both were thinking: that *friend* didn't even come close to describing what they'd dared to feel, knowing the impossibility of it all. Knowing the cost.

"You love her," Percy had said, so simply, as though he'd been noting the color of the sky.

She did.

It was terrifying. It should never have happened.

But she did.

"I don't expect your forgiveness." Ranka pushed herself into a sitting position, the blanket scratching at her skin, and now it was her turn to hold back tears. "Or your trust. I am owed neither. I deserve neither. But I want you to know, Aramis—I have never regretted anything in my life more than I regret betraying you. I should have buried that axe in Ongrum's heart, but I wasn't strong enough. And for that I am so, so sorry. Truly. I have made many mistakes in my life—I have done so many wrongs, have hurt so many people. This was the worst of them. This, more than anything, is what I wish I could take back."

Aramis's lips began to tremble.

"But I can't." Ranka's voice broke, and she dug her fingernails into her thigh. "I . . . have spent so much of my life lost. I've always been a weapon, a monster, a threat. And I have never felt worth anything, to anyone. I'm realizing now . . . some of that was by design. I have lived my life as a girl living lost." Ranka swallowed. "But I didn't feel lost with you. I ruined that. And I will never forgive myself."

Now Aramis was crying, and Ranka was crying too. How badly Ranka wanted to hold her then. How much it stung to know she couldn't. They remained like that for a long time—wiping furiously at their eyes, Aramis telling Ranka over and over again how angry she was, and Ranka only saying *I know*, because she did, truly, and she loved Aramis too much to do anything but take every ounce of anger she'd earned.

It was a long time before they quieted. It wasn't anything like before. They felt like strangers, but the crackling fury had eased. Aramis wiped some of the snot from her nose and looked at the ceiling.

Ranka stood. She took a step forward, and it was more terrifying than any of the steps that had led her through the mines. Slowly, she sat on the edge of the bed.

Aramis scooted back so Ranka had room to sit.

"I loved her," Ranka said softly. "I know that doesn't change anything. But the woman you met that night, she is—was—my mother, in every way but blood."

"Will you be able to do it this time?" Aramis whispered. "Stand up to her?"

I'm begging you to choose yourself.

Even now Percy's words struck a chord of fear in her. Ongrum had always had a grip on Ranka, had always known how to reel her back in. But that was before the winalin witches. That was before Ongrum had taken dozens of innocent girls and turned them into monsters.

Ranka was learning that even love had its limits.

"Yes," she whispered. "Yes, Princess. This time, I will."

There was a chance—a slim one—that Ranka could beat Ongrum. She didn't have to kill her. She only needed to distract and subdue her long enough for Galen to get away. Once he was safe, nothing else mattered.

"It's Volst," Ranka said suddenly.

Aramis turned to her. "I'm sorry?"

"You asked me once, about my name. My real name, before the Skra took me in." Ranka closed her eyes and leaned back in the dark. "It's Volst. Ranka Volst."

She had never told anyone. It didn't feel like a thing that ought to matter. That name, this old piece of her, an echo of a little girl born to a village that no longer was. She'd told herself Ranka Volst had died in Belren, but it felt like it mattered now, that someone knew who she'd been.

Felt like it mattered even more that that someone was Aramis.

Aramis didn't say anything. Just nodded. Her lips formed the name, as if testing it out, rolling it over her tongue, this new piece of the girl who'd betrayed her.

Ranka leaned her back against the wall and closed her eyes. She would move, soon. It was improper for her to sit up here. But she would take just a moment to rest, in this fragile calm.

"Maybe we'll win," Aramis breathed finally. "And maybe . . . I don't know, Ranka. I need . . . I don't know." Her voice quivered. "Maybe we'll get a second chance to start over, without some plague, a war, or meddling covens."

Pain blossomed in Ranka's heart. This was as close as Aramis would come to admitting that some of Ranka's feelings were returned. That she regretted what had happened. That she, too, wished they could return to the girls who'd danced in that ballroom without a care, dreaming of a cabin they'd never build, in a life they'd never have.

Ranka remained on the bed, painfully aware of every inch between them. She needed to get up soon. But she was so tired.

"Maybe we will, Princess," Ranka whispered. "Maybe we will."

66

SUNLIGHT WOKE HER.

Golden rays lanced across Ranka's skin. Someone warm nestled against her, legs tangled with hers, arm draped over her hip. Touch had always been what made Ranka feel loved. She'd forgotten how badly she'd starved for it. Ranka rolled over, still half-asleep, and the person stirred. Brown eyes fluttered open, only a few inches from Ranka's own.

For a lovely, muddled moment, caught between the realm of sleep and waking, Ranka had no idea who this girl was, but Goddess above, she was gorgeous.

Reality returned.

She was in Seaswept. This girl was the princess of Isodal.

And they were hardly on cuddling terms.

Aramis seemed to have this same realization, because she tried to jerk backward—which was a bit hard because her arms were around Ranka's waist, and their legs were tangled together.

Voices came down the hall.

The door flung open. Percy paused in the doorway. A brief, goofy smile lit up his face. "Well, isn't this sweet."

Ranka practically tumbled out of the bed, and she didn't need a mirror to know her face was bright red. She smoothed her clothes as quickly as she could and staggered into a standing position just in time for Foldrey to barge into the room too.

Percy's smile fell. Aramis looked between them, her eyes still foggy with sleep but already beginning to brighten with worry. "What is it?"

"The witches have changed their mind," he said. "Galen dies at sunset."

The palace announcement was brief: Galen Sunra would be executed at sunset to answer for his forefathers' crimes against Witchik.

Aramis paced the room. "Have we heard back from any of the provinces?"

Foldrey shook his head. "The messengers will be getting there today. And even if they leap into action, soldiers will never arrive in time."

No one dared speak. Aramis was silent for a long, slow beat, and then she shook her head. "Very well. Then we rescue him now."

"Princess, we can't possibly—"

"You had your own small army of Hands and loyal guards prepared to launch a coup, did you not?" Aramis asked coldly.

Foldrey glared back at her. "I did, until half of them defected and another quarter were murdered." He passed a hand over his face. "I have a handful of men in the city. The rest—if they're even alive—are probably in the dungeons."

An idea sparked in Ranka's mind. She looked up. "A few loyal men won't be enough—but a whole coven might. Ongrum never won the favor of all the witches, correct? Her grip on power is tenuous at best. That was why she needed me."

Percy sat up straight. "If we can upstage Galen's assassination and sway at least one coven to our side . . ."

"The rest may follow." Ranka's heart began to beat faster. "I talked to Ursay, the Oori leader, at the ball. They know about winalin, and they don't like Ongrum. They fled when the attack started, but if we could get the Oori to take our side and make a stand, the Arlani may switch loyalties too. Then it would only be the Murknen and the Skra. They wouldn't have the numbers."

Foldrey looked up. "I can send a messenger to the Oori."

Ranka shook her head, remembering the dark intelligence in Ursay's eyes, the fury that sparked there when Ranka had told them of the plague. "One of us will have to go. Ursay's too smart to risk their coven's life without promises from someone close to power."

"I'll go."

Everyone turned.

Gone was Percy's mocking smile, his airy humor. The boy stood quietly, his face grim.

"I'll go," Percy repeated. "I met Ursay at the ball—and I know more than anyone the cost of letting winalin rage free. I can convince them."

He needed this. Winalin haunted him, would always haunt him, if Percy didn't do everything in his power to undo the damage it had wrought. He rose, pulled Aramis into a tight hug, and made for the door.

"Percy," Ranka said suddenly. "Tell Ursay—tell them I won't waste my chance. Tell Ursay the Bloodwinn intends to keep her promise."

He held her stare, a question in his eyes, and nodded. Ranka had the uncanny sense she was looking into a mirror of what her life might have looked like had she made different choices.

I thought you were braver.

Maybe she could be yet.

"All right," Aramis said quietly, her eyes burning. "Now how do we get my brother back?"

67

THE TUNNELS WERE CRAMPED.

It was strange how familiar they'd become. The long, sloping caverns of dried salt might have been a comfort were it not for the stench
of death that permeated them.

Ranka led the way. Foldrey and Aramis both bore torches, as did two
men who brought up the rear. They wore no gold pins, but from the
loathing in their eyes when they regarded Ranka, they were clearly Hands.

They'd been walking for an hour when the screaming began.

It was far away, but unmistakable. At least five voices, pitched in
horror, cut short as soon as they'd started. Ranka's skin crawled.
Aramis looked to her with a question in her eyes, as if expecting her to
want to run to their aid, but Ranka turned away. It could have been
anyone in those tunnels—but it was no question what had killed them.

A small, dark fire sparked to life in her heart.

Ongrum had done this—and Foldrey had helped. They'd both
unleashed this terror on the world, turned witches' bodies into weapons, turning them against their own.

It would end today, one way or another.

Ranka drew a prayer sigil on her chest and kept walking.

She recited the plan in her head. Aramis and Foldrey would free the

Hands who were imprisoned and rally the rest serving in the palace. Meanwhile, Ranka would approach the arena where Galen was likely to be executed and stall Ongrum by turning herself in.

The ground shifted under their feet. The air was warmer here, drier, as salt caverns shifted from rock to hand-laid stone. Foldrey and Aramis put out their torches. The weak light of the dungeons flickered ahead of them.

Ranka's heart quickened.

This was it. Even if things went well, she would likely not see tomorrow's sunrise. Ranka had spent her entire life preparing to die. To be born with blood-magic was to be born with a time bomb in your veins. She'd stopped fearing death long ago.

The question that lingered, then, was this: would she die righting the wrongs of her past or cementing them?

Together the three of them walked forward—the witch, the princess, the traitorous guard. It was ten minutes to sunset. The covens would be gathering now, eager to watch a prince die.

"This is where you leave us," Foldrey said softly, his voice startling Ranka. He nodded to a corridor to the left. "That way will take you to the arena. Exit the stairs, turn left, and you'll be there shortly." He paused, his eyes flicking over her. "Good luck, Bloodwinn."

She knew better than to think Foldrey wished for her health or safety. His work would be easier after this if she was dead. But a piece of her longed to ask if things might have been different—in another life, could he have been the mentor she'd thought she'd found in Ongrum?

Could he have loved her, the way he loved the twins?

A part of her thought he could. It changed nothing, but it hurt all the more.

Aramis nodded. "I'll walk you there."

Foldrey frowned. "I don't think that's—"

"I don't care. I have some things to say to the Bloodwinn. I'll be back shortly."

Aramis started off down the hall then. Ranka followed, and they left Foldrey behind.

The dungeons were too narrow to walk side by side, so instead Aramis led, Ranka trailing behind her. It felt too familiar—walking in the dark, the two of them headed toward uncertainty. For a moment Ranka thought only of that morning, how warm Aramis had been, legs tangled with hers, her skin sweet with the scent of sleep, eyes cloudy with lingering dreams.

In another life, they might have had a chance. They might have even been happy.

"We're here," Aramis said softly. The staircase loomed ahead of them.

Ranka hesitated.

Suddenly every word felt inadequate. What was she supposed to do? Apologize again? Say goodbye? All of it felt too watery, too weak. What do you say to a girl you'd hated, loved, and betrayed?

What do you say when you love her still?

They stared at each other, witch and princess, warrior and healer, each victims of a different fate.

The sun sank lower.

"I'll save him," Ranka blurted.

"Your blood-magic," Aramis said at the same time.

Ranka reeled back. "What?"

"You still don't have it." Panic fluttered in Aramis's eyes. "I know what you're doing, Ranka. You have no magic. You're injured. You didn't even bring a weapon with you."

Ranka kept her face blank. She didn't want to talk about this with her—not now, not in their last moments. "Aramis—"

"You're strong enough," Aramis said. "Have always been strong enough. You are not the worst thing that's ever happened to you. You are the girl who survived it." Aramis stepped forward, her face suddenly urgent. "Promise me you won't just give up. You won't just quit. You'll fight. Even if it comes to *that*."

Ranka's fingers strayed to her chest. There the kernel of power sat, still frozen and unreachable. "I . . ." Her throat closed. She would sooner die than return to Belren.

"Look at me, Ranka," Aramis whispered. "And promise me you're not heading out there to die."

"Princess," Ranka started, her voice soft.

"Promise."

"I don't—"

"Say it."

"I can't. . . ."

Aramis's eyes flashed. She stepped forward, grabbed a fistful of Ranka's shirt, and yanked Ranka's lips down to hers.

It was not like their kiss in the inn. This was not gentle and sweet, a timid gesture of a girl too nervous to act on feelings she wasn't allowed to have. This kiss was all urgency. It was anger and want and a demand wrapped in one. Ranka froze, but Aramis didn't pull away, only wound her arms around Ranka's neck and pulled her down, and then Ranka was kissing her back, and her lips said everything they couldn't before—that she was sorry, that she was ashamed, that she was terrified and she had wanted to be better, that in another life she would still try to be better, if only they had the time.

Percy was right—Ranka loved this girl. Would always love her.

Maybe, in the next life, she would make the right choice and be worthy of her.

Aramis took Ranka's face in her hands one last time.

"Promise me, Ranka Volst," Aramis whispered, her lips an inch from Ranka's. "Promise me you won't give up. That you'll show them what it means to be the Bloodwinn. Promise you'll fight your way back to me, or don't promise me anything at all."

Outside, the sun was setting. Each second wasted was a second that could cost them everything. Yet still Ranka hesitated, frozen in the intensity of Aramis's gaze, her lips swollen and her body aching for more. The look on Aramis's face—it wasn't forgiveness. Ranka's betrayal was too new for that, too raw. There was so much work needed to mend the wound she'd wrought between them, if it could be mended at all.

But Aramis wanted her to win this. That much was clear.

Aramis wanted her to come back.

And that was a gift far beyond anything Ranka deserved.

"Okay," Ranka whispered. "You win, Princess. I promise."

Aramis pulled away. She cleared her throat and leveled her gaze at Ranka. Only the quiver of her lips betrayed her. Even here, cloaked in the shadow of the dungeons, she wielded her calm like a weapon.

"Aramis," Ranka said, her voice soft. "For what it's worth—I am sorry. I will always be sorry."

Aramis closed her eyes. "I know."

Ranka climbed the stairs, and she did not look back.

68

LIGHT HIT HER FACE. THE DYING SUN CAST DEEP, bruised shadows across the palace grounds, rendering burned buildings into ghastly husks. Even if they won today, it'd take years to rebuild the Sunra estate, to erase the stain of violence her people had left here. Even then, the ghosts would linger. The air swirled with death. There would be more before she was done.

The witches were amassed at the cliffs—the same cliffs where Ranka had trained with Percy, had fought Galen. Now the Sunra prince knelt with his hands bound behind his back. Ongrum stood with her back to the sea, and she had a knife in her hand.

No one turned as Ranka trekked through the dust. All eyes were on the blade gleaming against Galen's skin and the witch who nearly had the throne.

Light glinted off Ongrum's knife, reflecting the scared eyes of a boy who should have never been given a crown. The crowd of witches seemed to inhale as one, their hunger crouched behind their teeth, coiling in their clenched fists. A new world was within their grasp. One cut of a slender throat was all it would take.

A falcon screamed, its wide, pale wings slicing through the endless blue that sprawled above them.

Ongrum raised her hand.

Galen closed his eyes.

And Ranka roared, *"Wait."*

Every eye in the arena turned to her.

I am the shield.

She had been silent after Belren. Passive when Ongrum burned and looted, complacent when the witches she loved crossed too many lines.

I am the monster.

She would not be silent now.

I am the knife in the dark.

"I am Ranka Volst. Butcher of Belren, and Bloodwinn named." Ranka raised her voice. "And I challenge Ongrum to trial by combat, for the right to lead the Skra."

Noise exploded from the crowd. Skra and Murknen leapt up, jeering and shouting. The Arlani stood off to the side, faces carefully blank, their eyes bright with interest. The Oori were nowhere to be seen. Below, Aramis and Foldrey would be at work freeing the imprisoned humans from their cells.

Ongrum paused, lowering the blade at Galen's throat, and cocked her head to the side in the movement reminiscent of an owl studying a mouse. "What do you think you're doing?"

Every instinct screamed for Ranka to run. She didn't stand a chance against Ongrum. She *couldn't* fight her. This woman had raised her, had *made* her.

Quietly, Ranka said, "Making the right choice."

A Murknen stepped forward. "Seize her—"

Ongrum held up a hand. "Wait."

The cliffs quieted. Ongrum stared at Ranka for a long, hard moment, thirteen years of memories crackling in the air between them. A cold smile lit Ongrum's face. "Very well, witchling. You want a fight? You'll have it."

Galen shouted through his gag. Ranka couldn't bring herself to meet his eyes.

Foldrey had asked Ranka to distract Ongrum.

She was about to give him the distraction of a lifetime.

Ongrum raised her voice. "In my three decades of leading the Skra, seventeen witches have challenged me for that right. Seventeen failed." She held Ranka's stare. "This will not be a fight of first blood, child. If you wish to take my coven, you'll also have to take my life."

Ranka palmed the blade she'd stolen. It was a blunt, worn thing, weighted awkwardly, better suited to sparring drills for new recruits than a proper fight. What she wouldn't have given for an axe.

"I know," Ranka said softly.

"Very well." Ongrum drew a short sword from her hip. "We fight, then."

A wave of calm settled over her.

It was always meant to end like this—her, and Ongrum.

Ranka turned the blade over in her hand and stepped forward to battle the woman who had raised her.

69

IT WAS RARE FOR A WITCH TO CHALLENGE THEIR leader.

Ongrum was reminding Ranka why.

The older witch fought like a whirlwind. She was constantly moving, ducking, weaving. Every time Ranka tried to earn space between them, Ongrum pressed closer. Every time Ranka struck a blow, Ongrum was ready. She fought with more brutality, more cruelty, and more efficiency than Ranka could ever dream of. Ongrum had three decades on her. And seventeen witches who'd thought themselves just as capable as Ranka.

Sweat covered Ranka's body. She staggered backward, and this time when Ongrum lunged for her, Ranka froze. Her knees locked, and Ongrum seized her. She raised her blade—and then pulled back a moment later, slamming the flat into Ranka's face. Ranka's nose broke with a crunch. She jerked backward, her ears ringing, blood dripping down her chin, swaying from the pain.

Ongrum stepped back, a cold smile on her face. She intended to draw this out, to make a lesson out of Ranka. "You disappoint me."

Ranka wiped the blood from her lips and leapt.

She tackled Ongrum and took her to the ground. Ongrum tore

at Ranka's face, dragged fiery lines down her arms with her finger-nails, and Ranka kept fighting. Ongrum placed a foot on her chest and kicked her away. A wild light gleamed in the older woman's eyes as she lunged for her blade.

I'm going to lose.

Sweat rolled down her forehead and burned her eyes. The circle of witches who surrounded them pressed closer, watching as mother and daughter danced in circles, drawing blood. Some Skra jeered in encouragement, others winced or cast their gaze away. The Arlani remained silent, their white robes snapping, their faces severe and blank, waiting to see who would rise from the dust and lay claim to a coven that sought to uproot the world.

The Oori were nowhere in sight. Neither were the Hands.

Ongrum stumbled. Ranka's sword snapped out, snaking in a butterfly cut over the older witch's thigh. Red sprayed the dust, and Ongrum's hip sagged as her leg buckled.

"Filthy trick," Ongrum spat, her nostrils flaring as she breathed through the pain.

"I learned from the best."

Ongrum grinned—and then the expression vanished as she remembered where they were. What they were doing.

Even now this felt like the dozens of trainings they'd done before—first with sharpened sticks when Ranka was only a witchling, learning to duel in hip-deep snow, practicing until her fingers were too frozen to feel anything at all. And years later as a girl, a teenager, a warrior, the weapons growing sharper and the scars thicker, but her battle part-ner always the same.

"Make me proud," Ongrum would say, and some days those words felt less like an order and more like the compelling of a priestess toward her disciples. Ranka had never felt the touch of the Goddess or the spirits. She'd never tasted the divine. She'd never needed to because where faith might have lived—where some deity might have cast their golden shadow—was first a sister with watery eyes and then

Ongrum was beginning to falter. She was still stronger, still better than Ranka, but even Ongrum was not infallible, and panic made her sloppy. She swung at Ranka in a clumsy, slow arc, and Ranka parried. The blade flew from Ongrum's hand. Victory pulsed through Ranka. She slashed at Ongrum, and the woman toppled backward.

Before she could rise, Ranka was upon her, one foot planted on her chest, sword aimed at her throat, a perfect reversal of the position they had been in only a moment before.

On the dais, Aramis cut Galen free.

Ranka looked down at Ongrum. "Yield."

"No."

Ranka pressed the blade until a droplet of ruby beaded on the edge of the metal. "*Yield*, Ongrum, and keep your life."

"*No.*" Ongrum's fingers scrabbled for purchase in the dust but found no weapon save for a few stray pebbles. She pushed herself into the earth as though she could sink away from Ranka's sword, but in the end, she was just a woman on the wrong end of a blade. "I do not yield."

Rot swirled in the air.

Ranka wouldn't kill her. Couldn't. But if she had to injure Ongrum or knock her out to keep the peace? She had the strength in her for that. Her leg ached, still bleeding into the dust from Ongrum's earlier cut, and her arms trembled with exhaustion.

"You will not take this from me." Ongrum's face changed. Instead of the frantic rage that had lit it before, peace softened her features. "I would have given you an easy death, witchling. But if this is how you want this to end—so be it."

"Enough, Ongrum. You lost."

"No," Ongrum said, shaking her head, digging Ranka's blade farther into her skin. "I've only just begun."

Her eyes darted past Ranka, locking on to someone beyond her— and then Ongrum bellowed: "*Let them out.*"

Ranka turned.

a witch reforged in fire who'd taken a band of witches and made them conquerors.

For the past thirteen years, Ongrum had been her prayer, her hope, the thing her heart spun around, whom she fought for and what she feared and why she loved.

And now Ranka was supposed to kill her.

Ongrum swung her blade in an arc toward Ranka's head. Ranka jerked sideways, her shoulder burning, and electric crackles of pain shot down her wrist.

"The worst thing," Ongrum panted, "is that after all this, you're still weak. You could have been a legend."

Belren flashed behind Ranka's eyes. *Blood and fire and bodies in the snow.* She already knew what it meant to live a legend. She had no interest in dipping deeper in legacy's bloody waters. The best gift this world could give her would be to forget her entirely.

Exhaustion thrummed through Ranka's muscles. Her eyes darted to the sea, hoping for a flash of white sails, but all she saw was endless blue. She needed to trip Ongrum up somehow. Stall her until Foldrey could free his men or Percy appeared with the Oori. If he appeared at all.

"I was just a girl," Ranka told Ongrum with more feeling than she expected. Words that were thirteen years building rushed out of her. "A *child*. You put the weapons in my hands, Ongrum, and ordered me to kill."

"You want the truth?" Ongrum stepped closer, her eyes bright with cruelty. "That monstrosity was already there. You have always been hateful, Ranka, and you have always been cruel. And then you *wasted it*!"

Ongrum sliced at Ranka, and this time her blade met its mark. Pain exploded across Ranka's thigh.

No.

Ranka's leg buckled. She sank to one knee, and Ongrum kicked her in the face. Ranka tipped backward. The world spun around her.

I'm going to die.

A foot connected with her ribs. Blood bubbled from her lips.

Everything burned.

Ongrum stood over her. Blood gleamed against the white expanse of her chest, and Ongrum dug the point of her sword into Ranka's throat.

"You disappoint me," Ongrum said softly. "You've always done nothing but disappoint me."

Where was Percy? Where were the Hands?

Time slowed. Dust caked Ranka's wounds, coated her lips. She was so tired—and she had lost. Behind Ongrum, the setting sun painted the sky in broad strokes of fire. And between Ranka's ribs, settled behind her heart, her blood-magic sat, cold and as unreachable as ever. Even on the brink of death, it did not want her, and Ranka was not strong enough to pull it free.

Ranka opened her eyes and met Ongrum's own.

"Just tell me this," she rasped. Sweat beaded on her lip. "Did you ever love me? Even a little?"

Ongrum's face contorted, and Ranka saw her for who she was—not just a woman hell-bent on raising a new world from the ashes of this one, but someone who had been a sister, a daughter, a mother by choice if not by blood. A woman who'd looked into the scared eyes of a four-year-old witch and carried her home.

"It doesn't matter," said Ongrum.

"It *does.*" Ranka's voice cracked. "You loved me. I know you did. This wasn't always about power. You were better than that. You cared. You called me your daughter once—and for a while I think you meant it."

"I should have left you in that village," Ongrum whispered. "I should have let the fires burn you alive."

Ranka braced herself. She reached for her blood-magic one last time, but it did not reach back. Her mind spun. There was nowhere else for her to run. At least she had bought them time.

Ongrum's grip tightened on the sword.

Ranka closed her eyes.

A horn blared.

Cries filled the air, sharpening to outrage, confusion, alarm, and then—pain. The coppery scent of blood spiked. The vibration of boots on packed dust rolled through the ground.

Ranka twisted.

The Hands of Solomei had arrived.

Foldrey's movements were those of a northerner through and through—brutish and quick, aiming for low, dirty jabs, instead of the rolling, graceful fighting style popular in the south. This wasn't the dance of someone who had learned swordplay to show off for nobles at the ball; it was the style of a boy who had grown up fighting for his life in the snow-swept woods of the wild, endless north, where the only art to a weapon was how to swing it in a way that ensured it cut through bone. A witch dove for Foldrey, and he spun, driving a knee into her stomach, and then slammed the hilt of his sword into her temple.

She crumpled, and he kept moving. "Secure the prince!"

Ongrum's eyes widened. *"No."*

Another horn blew, and there, on the horizon, came sails.

They were stark white against an endless blue, and they were the most beautiful thing Ranka had ever seen. Seventeen ships in all, bearing the largest coven in the world. They cut forward with impossible speed, bows breaking against the waves as they barreled toward the shore.

Behind Ongrum, a princess crept toward her brother, kneeling on the dais.

Ranka kicked up with her injured leg and slammed her heel into Ongrum's kneecap. A crunch sounded, followed by Ongrum howling. She staggered, sword slipping from her hand. Ranka turned sideways, twisting until she was on her knees.

Now Ranka fought with a new energy, a new urgency. She didn't need to kill Ongrum, just subdue her. Ranka drove Ongrum back.

a witch reforged in fire who'd taken a band of witches and made them conquerors.

For the past thirteen years, Ongrum had been her prayer, her hope, the thing her heart spun around, whom she fought for and what she feared and why she loved.

And now Ranka was supposed to kill her.

Ongrum swung her blade in an arc toward Ranka's head. Ranka jerked sideways, her shoulder burning, and electric crackles of pain shot down her wrist.

"The worst thing," Ongrum panted, "is that after all this, you're still weak. You could have been a legend."

Belren flashed behind Ranka's eyes. *Blood and fire and bodies in the snow.* She already knew what it meant to live a legend. She had no interest in dipping deeper in legacy's bloody waters. The best gift this world could give her would be to forget her entirely.

Exhaustion thrummed through Ranka's muscles. Her eyes darted to the sea, hoping for a flash of white sails, but all she saw was endless blue. She needed to trip Ongrum up somehow. Stall her until Foldrey could free his men or Percy appeared with the Oori. If he appeared at all.

"I was just a girl," Ranka told Ongrum with more feeling than she expected. Words that were thirteen years building rushed out of her. "A *child*. You put the weapons in my hands, Ongrum, and ordered me to kill."

"You want the truth?" Ongrum stepped closer, her eyes bright with cruelty. "That monstrosity was already there. You have always been hateful, Ranka, and you have always been cruel. And then you *wasted it*!"

Ongrum sliced at Ranka, and this time her blade met its mark. Pain exploded across Ranka's thigh.

No.

Ranka's leg buckled. She sank to one knee, and Ongrum kicked her in the face. Ranka tipped backward. The world spun around her.

I'm going to die.

A foot connected with her ribs. Blood bubbled from her lips. Everything burned.

Ongrum stood over her. Blood gleamed against the white expanse of her chest, and Ongrum dug the point of her sword into Ranka's throat.

"You disappoint me," Ongrum said softly. "You've always done nothing but disappoint me."

Where was Percy? Where were the Hands?

Time slowed. Dust caked Ranka's wounds, coated her lips. She was so tired—and she had lost. Behind Ongrum, the setting sun painted the sky in broad strokes of fire. And between Ranka's ribs, settled behind her heart, her blood-magic sat, cold and as unreachable as ever. Even on the brink of death, it did not want her, and Ranka was not strong enough to pull it free.

Ranka opened her eyes and met Ongrum's own.

"Just tell me this," she rasped. Sweat beaded on her lip. "Did you ever love me? Even a little?"

Ongrum's face contorted, and Ranka saw her for who she was— not just a woman hell-bent on raising a new world from the ashes of this one, but someone who had been a sister, a daughter, a mother by choice if not by blood. A woman who'd looked into the scared eyes of a four-year-old witch and carried her home.

"It doesn't matter," said Ongrum.

"It *does*." Ranka's voice cracked. "You loved me. I know you did. This wasn't always about power. You were better than that. You cared. You called me your daughter once—and for a while I think you meant it."

"I should have left you in that village," Ongrum whispered. "I should have let the fires burn you alive."

Ranka braced herself. She reached for her blood-magic one last time, but it did not reach back. Her mind spun. There was nowhere else for her to run. At least she had bought them time.

Ongrum's grip tightened on the sword.

Ranka closed her eyes.

A horn blared.

Cries filled the air, sharpening to outrage, confusion, alarm, and then—pain. The coppery scent of blood spiked. The vibration of boots on packed dust rolled through the ground.

Ranka twisted.

The Hands of Solomei had arrived.

Foldrey's movements were those of a northerner through and through—brutish and quick, aiming for low, dirty jabs, instead of the rolling, graceful fighting style popular in the south. This wasn't the dance of someone who had learned swordplay to show off for nobles at the ball; it was the style of a boy who had grown up fighting for his life in the snow-swept woods of the wild, endless north, where the only art to a weapon was how to swing it in a way that ensured it cut through bone. A witch dove for Foldrey, and he spun, driving a knee into her stomach, and then slammed the hilt of his sword into her temple.

She crumpled, and he kept moving. "Secure the prince!"

Ongrum's eyes widened. *"No."*

Another horn blew, and there, on the horizon, came sails.

They were stark white against an endless blue, and they were the most beautiful thing Ranka had ever seen. Seventeen ships in all, bearing the largest coven in the world. They cut forward with impossible speed, bows breaking against the waves as they barreled toward the shore.

Behind Ongrum, a princess crept toward her brother, kneeling on the dais.

Ranka kicked up with her injured leg and slammed her heel into Ongrum's kneecap. A crunch sounded, followed by Ongrum howling. She staggered, sword slipping from her hand. Ranka turned sideways, twisting until she was on her knees.

Now Ranka fought with a new energy, a new urgency. She didn't need to kill Ongrum, just subdue her. Ranka drove Ongrum back.

Ongrum was beginning to falter. She was still stronger, still better than Ranka, but even Ongrum was not infallible, and panic made her sloppy. She swung at Ranka in a clumsy, slow arc, and Ranka parried. The blade flew from Ongrum's hand. Victory pulsed through Ranka. She slashed at Ongrum, and the woman toppled backward.

Before she could rise, Ranka was upon her, one foot planted on her chest, sword aimed at her throat, a perfect reversal of the position they had been in only a moment before.

On the dais, Aramis cut Galen free.

Ranka looked down at Ongrum. "Yield."

"No."

Ranka pressed the blade until a droplet of ruby beaded on the edge of the metal. "*Yield*, Ongrum, and keep your life."

"*No.*" Ongrum's fingers scrabbled for purchase in the dust but found no weapon save for a few stray pebbles. She pushed herself into the earth as though she could sink away from Ranka's sword, but in the end, she was just a woman on the wrong end of a blade. "I do not yield."

Rot swirled in the air.

Ranka wouldn't kill her. Couldn't. But if she had to injure Ongrum or knock her out to keep the peace? She had the strength in her for that. Her leg ached, still bleeding into the dust from Ongrum's earlier cut, and her arms trembled with exhaustion.

"You will not take this from me." Ongrum's face changed. Instead of the frantic rage that had lit it before, peace softened her features. "I would have given you an easy death, witchling. But if this is how you want this to end—so be it."

"Enough, Ongrum. You lost."

"No," Ongrum said, shaking her head, digging Ranka's blade farther into her skin. "I've only just begun."

Her eyes darted past Ranka, locking on to someone beyond her—and then Ongrum bellowed: *"Let them out."*

Ranka turned.

Sigrid stood frozen, disbelief clouding her face as she stared at Ongrum. Blood slicked down the Skra warrior's front.

"Let them all out."

Sigrid shook herself as though Ongrum had slapped her. She cast her eyes to the sky—and then drew a prayer sigil on her chest. The woman ran for the guard barracks.

"Traitor," Ongrum snarled, drawing Ranka's attention back to her. Her chest heaved. "It's like I've always said, child. You were never strong enough to wield true power. But *I* am."

Ongrum twisted suddenly, but instead of reaching for a weapon, she shoved her fist into her pocket, hand shaking but mouth set. She looked up and met Ranka's eyes. The scent of rot spiked.

Ranka realized what Ongrum intended a moment too late.

She lunged—but she was too slow. Her injured leg buckled. Ranka crashed to her knees, and she could only watch as Ongrum drove a full syringe of winalin into her own thigh and pressed the plunger home.

70

NO.

The arena vanished, and with it the Hands, the witches, even the boy on the dais and the girl who had just cut him free. There was only Ranka, the woman in front of her, and the plunger in her thigh, emptying all too fast. A horrible scream split the air—not the cry of the enraged or the howl of a warrior plunging into battle, but the plea of a child, of a scared little girl caught in a nightmare—and it wasn't until Ranka's throat burned that she realized the scream was coming from her.

Ongrum stumbled, and Ranka rushed forward to catch her. "What have you done? Ongrum, what have you *done?*"

"Don't touch me—get *off* me." Ongrum shoved her away. She fell to her knees.

All around Ranka, people were dying—humans cut into witches, and witches cut into humans and one another. The Arlani were beginning to set down their weapons, uncertainty clouding their faces as blood speckled their pristine white robes, but it was too late. It wasn't enough. The Skra and the Murknen were still fighting, and Ongrum—Ongrum had injected herself. Ongrum was going to die.

Tears slid down Ranka's cheeks. "You horrible fool."

On the ground, Ongrum curled into a ball and spasmed. Her

veins bulged, and her fingers hooked into claws. She pitched forward, retching until nothing came up but bile and blood.

Ranka knelt beside her. "We have to get you out of here—we might be able to stop it—"

Ongrum swatted at her, but her touch was feeble, no stronger than the half-hearted bat of a kitten. "Don't *touch* me."

"You're doing to *die*. You're going to—"

"I said don't touch me." Ongrum's eyes flashed white. Her nails had always been a mellow rabbit-fur gray. Now they flickered to black.

And all Ranka could do was watch.

She had not wanted this for her worst enemy, let alone Ongrum.

Let alone someone she loved.

Ongrum's nails flashed to black and remained. She pushed herself upright, trembling, her all-white eyes surveying the surrounding chaos with awe.

"It's gray," Ongrum whispered. "It's all gray."

Could she feel it? The power inside her that hungered for death? That strength that should only ever have belonged to the gods?

Ongrum turned to Ranka and flexed her hands, looking down at her clawed fingertips with awe, and laughed.

"You are so weak," Ongrum said, "to have *wasted* this."

Ranka took a step backward. A scream split the air, and with it came the scent of putrid, rotting flesh.

Ranka turned. The door Sigrid had vanished behind remained closed. But from it came that unmistakable stench of a body turned septic, of wrongness and death, of a decay not meant for this world. It was getting stronger by the second, swelling in the air.

Blood seeped from under the door.

Something slammed against the other side of it. The knob rattled—and the door swung open.

Sigrid staggered out, clutching at her stomach. She was missing most of her fingers; someone had taken a bite out of her shoulder. She whimpered, limping forward.

The rot scent grew stronger.

She didn't. She couldn't have.

A winalin witch limped into the light.

She was young, delicate, and frail, but her eyes were an empty, dead white. It was the twelve-year-old Ranka had seen only two nights ago, but now she was changed, her skin covered in hundreds of thumbnail-sized blisters. She panted with her mouth open, scenting the air.

A Murknen witch staggered past, clutching her bleeding arm.

The winalin witch leapt.

She was on the Murknen in a moment, sinking her teeth into her, digging her claws in for purchase. The Murknen screamed, scrabbling at her with her hands, crying, *please, no, I'm on your side*, but the winalin witch didn't care, didn't even register the words.

The winalin witch hauled the Murknen to the ground and ate her alive, and Ranka could only watch in horror as another winalin witch appeared, and another, and another.

They filed out of the guard barracks one after the other, drawn by the blood, all of them in various states of decay, all of them scenting the air. Soon there were ten, twenty, *thirty* of them in the arena. They outnumbered the Hands Foldrey had mustered. They nearly outnumbered the remaining Skra.

All of them were hungry, and all of them were unchained.

The fighting slowed. Bodies lay all around, dead or dying, but in the face of those monsters the arbitrary lines between the factions vanished.

There were only the living, and the living dead.

Predator, and prey.

Ranka turned then, not to Ongrum but to every other soul gathered there, and bellowed, *"Run! Run for your lives!"*

There was a moment before the change was complete—when Ongrum stood there, the image of a blood-witch in power, of a woman with the deadliest magic on the continent in her veins eating any scrap of pain—when her eyes cleared. The white vanished, restored to that gentle winter-sky gray.

Reality finally seemed to hit her in full. She looked at Ranka then, and in her eyes Ranka saw it: terror.

And then the sores appeared.

They burst from her skin in massive, tangerine-sized purple cysts that cracked in the center and spilled pus down her limbs. Her teeth elongated into fangs; her gums split open. The hair dropped from her head in clumps as sores erupted across her scalp. The stench of decay gushed from Ongrum's mouth. Ongrum moaned, and the last bit of humanity in her eyes winked out as they turned white again. She swayed, panting, her clawed hands hanging loosely at her sides. She was a mistake, a horror of science and magic that never should have existed, a caution against what it meant to push the limits of power too far.

And she was hungry.

Ranka took a shaky step backward.

The woman's head swiveled at an unnatural speed, her chin tilting upward as she scented the air in two long, slow pants—and licked her lips.

"Ongrum," Ranka pleaded. *"Mama—"*

The creature that had once been Ongrum gurgled—and lunged.

71

RANKA WAS GOING TO DIE.

Ongrum hurtled toward her, spittle flying from her lips, teeth bared as the sores on her skin pulsed.

Ongrum collided with Ranka and hurled her to the ground, clambering on top of her, and wrapped a hand around Ranka's throat. Ranka gagged, fighting against the pressure, spots swimming in front of her eyes. Suddenly she was back in the forest, watching a sick witch barrel toward her with a gold pin in her fist.

"Ongrum," Ranka wheezed, clawing at the woman's hand. *"Please."*

Ongrum squeezed harder. There was no recognition in her wild stare, only an animal hunger. She bared her teeth and leaned forward to bite down—and wind cleaved the sky.

It came with the force of a gale, roaring so fiercely that Ranka's ears popped. Ongrum went flying off her. The winalin witches bounced off one another and fell in heaps, scrambling for purchase.

On the dais, blood dripping from his lips, Galen stood.

"Do it," Foldrey roared. "Blow them back, Galen!"

The Sunra prince raised his hands—and the sky answered.

Storm clouds appeared from nothing. The air dropped ten degrees and the sun vanished, concealed by the thick swaths of deep hurricane gray that now swirled in the sky. Lightning flashed overhead and Galen's hands trembled, but still he kept them raised, lips moving silently as he called forth the storms that his forefathers had once used to wreck this wretched, sun-soaked land.

Behind him, Aramis knelt. She'd procured a crossbow from somewhere. A winalin witch snarled and hurtled toward them. Aramis barely flinched. An iron-tipped dart snapped forward and slammed into the witch's eye. A second one followed, hitting her in the jugular. The winalin witch gurgled, scrabbling at her throat, and collapsed, dead.

To Ranka's left, two winalin witches cornered Tafa, who held up her hands in appeal.

"I'm one of you!" Tafa cried. "I'm on your side!"

The witches limped forward, licking their lips.

Ranka pointed. "Galen!"

Wind took them down. But for every winalin witch Galen felled, another picked themselves back up. Witches and humans were falling one by one, and others were casting down their weapons and fleeing. What should have been a battle was now a bloodbath.

The cliffs had become a feeding frenzy.

Something slammed into Ranka's side. She twisted, fearing Ongrum, but it was just some nameless winalin witch. Ranka bit back a sob and scrambled backward. The witch clawed at her, her mouth parted in hunger, and raked her nails down Ranka's thigh. She raised a hand to strike her—and blood blossomed across her chest.

Foldrey stood behind her, a thunderous expression on his face as he drew his sword from the witch's back and drove it into her again.

The winalin witch died with a whimper and fell at his feet.

The guard wiped the blood from his face and offered Ranka a hand.

Behind them, Ongrum fought three Hands at once. She was a nightmare, her natural abilities as a fighter aided by the animal hunger in her veins. Ranka swayed. She picked up a sword someone had dropped and turned the blood-slick weapon over in her hand, but it felt pointless.

A winalin witch hurtled toward them. Foldrey cut him down.

He turned to Ranka. "We're going to lose, Bloodwinn."

All around them, people were dying. Another winalin witch shot toward Galen and Aramis. It took four iron-tipped darts to stop her in her tracks, and she collapsed only a few feet from them.

Blood soaked Galen's chest. If he kept summoning at this rate, he would die.

Foldrey locked eyes with her. "Do you remember what I said to you?"

"What?"

"The role of the guard." He held her stare. "To protect, at all costs."

"I'm not—"

"It's time, Bloodwinn."

From his pocket Foldrey drew a vial.

Ranka stared at him. The sounds of the arena faded away. Now it was just the two of them, standing in the mud, panting and bloody as the tiny syringe that threatened the world glinted between them.

Ranka began to shake. "You can't be serious."

You have it in you to make the right choice. I see it, even if you can't.

Foldrey tossed the winalin to her. Ranka caught it. Her skin crawled. It was so small—just a harmless vial, with only a few ounces of liquid sloshing in the glass casing. At a glance, it seemed impossible this tiny quantity had created the chaos around them.

Ranka swayed.

From the poison comes the cure.

You're not strong enough, that voice that had haunted her for five years whispered. *You've never been strong enough. You can't handle the truth, little sister. And you can't let me go.*

A winalin witch made it to the dais. Aramis screamed, scrambling backward and tugging Galen with her. The witch sank her teeth into Galen's ankle before the prince blasted her away.

Ongrum killed the three humans she had been battling and turned, her attention locking on to the twins.

What did you expect? Did you think you could save them? You can't even save yourself. It's no wonder that no one wants you. No one loves you.

No, that wasn't true. The twins had wanted her, briefly. Vivna had loved her, at least before Belren. Ongrum had tried to love her, in her own way.

You are too weak, even now. You're nothing, to no one. Did you honestly think you could save anyone?

But she had tried. Why wasn't that enough?

You're a monster. That's all you are. It's all you'll ever be.

No, she'd been more—she'd been a warrior, a sister, a friend. That meant something. Even if she died in disgrace, it had to mean something.

The kernel pulsed in her chest, a cold, useless bead. She'd promised she'd never go back into Belren. Had sworn she'd sooner die. She would never be strong enough to face it alone—but her blood-magic was a parasite, designed to keep her alive until it had chewed up every part of her.

What better way to wake a parasite than to sicken the host?

Ranka swayed.

She had come here to die, hadn't she? She'd thought it would be by Ongrum's blade. But so long as she didn't have to live with these memories—so long as she could save the twins—she would accept her end, however it came.

I'm sorry, Aramis. It seems I have to break one last promise.

"Foldrey," Ranka called.

He twisted. His face was awash with blood. All around them the grounds had become a theater of death.

"If it doesn't work—if I turn . . ." She swallowed. "End it, while I'm still here."

He held her gaze and nodded.

Ranka was no fool. He would not mourn her death. Winalin or not, she couldn't occupy the world he wanted to build. But she trusted his love for the twins. Trusted he would do what they could not.

Ranka sat and closed her eyes. The chaos faded away, even as blood spiked in the air, as the screams of the dying swelled to a fever pitch. Foldrey circled her, leaving his men to die as he protected the Bloodwinn.

She wasn't ready, would never *be* ready.

But it was time.

The kernel pulsed.

Yeva. Asyil. So many others.

They had died, burned up by this nightmare of a disease, for her to make it right.

Ranka stretched mental fingers toward that memory, the truth she'd spent half a decade running from.

From the poison, comes the cure.

She took a breath—and slammed the winalin into her thigh.

And there, in the arena, Ranka faced Belren.

72

ALL OF BELREN BURNED.

Smoke writhed in the air. The ground was a churned mess of half-melted snow and blood. The fire spread to the last of the houses, trapping its occupants inside, and Ranka didn't—couldn't—care. Nearly everyone had fled by now. Even the farm hounds slunk away into the woods.

The worst part was that it felt good to kill. It made sense. Like it was something she'd been built for. Had it been horrifying—had she not wanted this—maybe she could have turned around. But every time someone died, a jolt of euphoria slid through her veins. Her magic numbed her wounds, whispered for her to ignore the blood she was losing.

A man and a woman lay dead at her feet, their eyes stretched wide, faces frozen in masks of horror. Some part of her knew them.

Belren kept burning. What had been a village echoing with screams only minutes ago was now permeated with eerie silence broken only by the crackling of flames, the popping of burning wood, the groans of houses collapsing in on themselves. All of Belren's residents had died or fled, and now she was just a witch, standing among the wreckage.

The fires raged. Her blood-magic faltered in its presence, weakening, and for the first time Ranka felt the pain in her hands, her arms, her legs. People were strewn across the snow like broken dolls.

I . . . did this?

From behind her came a faint keening.

Vivna knelt by their parents.

Her hair fell across her face as she shook their mother, digging her fingernails into the soft flesh of her limp forearms. "Mama? Mama, no. Wake up. *Wake up!*"

Ranka's legs buckled. "Vivna."

Her sister jerked backward. Panic flared in her eyes, and she cringed away from Ranka, her fingers still on their dead mother's arms. "What have you done?"

"It was an accident. I didn't mean to—I was trying to protect you—"

"What have you done?"

Ranka started to cry. "I'm sorry!" She tried to push her matted hair out of her face, but blood soaked her clothes and her skin. "They were going to kill you—"

"You should have let me die."

"No, Vivna, please." Something inside her was collapsing. "I'm sorry."

Her older sister stared at her, and then her expression morphed, cold and strange. She stood, hands trembling, and smoothed down the front of her ruined dress. "It's okay," she said, her voice carefully neutral. "Come here, Ranka. It's okay."

She held out her arms.

"Come here."

Ranka jerked out of the memory. Her head pounded. Lines of fire shot through her chest, lighting up her arms. Bile rose in her throat and she vomited, pitching forward. The memory was already slipping away, the kernel hardening, but she was so close, so close.

In her body, something foreign, twisted, and rotting was taking root. It raced through her in a tidal wave, sliding through her veins, attacking her cells. Tiny, fingernail-sized blisters appeared on her palms. Belren flickered.

Blood gushed from Ranka's nose.

From the poison.

She was done hiding. Done running.

Comes the cure.

Ranka sank claws into Belren and tore it open.

"Come here, little sister."

Ranka inched forward, shaking. She folded herself into her sister's arms. The sobs came fully as it hit her what she'd done. What she was now, what she could never be again.

Vivna's hands ran over the back of her head. "I'll fix this."

"I'm sorry." Ranka sobbed harder. There was blood in her mouth, her hair, her eyes. She wanted to peel away her own skin. "I didn't mean to. I'm sorry, *I didn't mean to.*"

"I know," Vivna said. "I know. I'll fix it."

And then Vivna took their mother's butcher knife and stabbed Ranka in the stomach.

Pain flared, and her blood-magic rose in a roar, but it was exhausted past its limits, and in the presence of so much fire it was little more than a flicker. Ranka screamed and fell backward. Vivna kept coming, her movements frantic, her eyes wild. Ranka's entire world was a haze of pain, and all the while her mind reeled with shock. What was Vivna doing? Vivna was her sister; Vivna *loved* her. Why was she hurting her? The sisters sank into the snow. Vivna stabbed Ranka over and over again, until the knife was slick with blood and Vivna could barely keep a grip on it.

"My responsibility," Vivna whispered, tears sliding down her cheeks. "Mine to fix."

The flames reached burning fingers toward Ranka. A pitiful croak left her. She was losing too much blood, too fast.

"I'm sorry," Vivna whispered. "I'm so, so sorry."

And then Ranka's only sister left her for dead, bleeding out among the flames of Belren.

73

Ranka screamed—and the kernel *burst*.

74

DYING WAS STRANGELY PEACEFUL.

After a lifetime of near brushes with death, the realization that her body had hit its limit was oddly calming. Every part of her burned. White-hot power flared in her veins, straining against her skin, stretching through her bones, battling for control against the winalin raging through her system. Two blood-magics, one born, one made, fighting for control of the host. She deserved this, didn't she? The monstrous witch, the Butcher of Belren, the girl who should have lain down and died five years ago but instead had kept living, kept hurting, kept *fighting*.

She should have been terrified, or angry. But instead, Ranka felt calm. It would be fitting if it was her blood-magic that killed her in the end. If, after everything, this power she'd never wanted swallowed her whole. It would end her life before it let winalin have her.

She had only ever been a host.

At least now she understood.

Monster, Butcher, murderer—they were all just names. She hadn't been born a monster—she'd become one to protect those she loved. Aramis had been right. At the end of the day, Ranka was the girl who survived.

She was the protector.

I'm sorry. Pain ate her up. Power burned her away. *I'm sorry for the lives I took, the terror I caused—but I don't regret it.*

I did it to protect her—to protect everyone I've ever loved.

I don't regret becoming the monster they needed.

I don't regret protecting them.

I don't.

I refuse.

I won't.

75

FRAGMENTS OF MEMORY CAME BACK IN FLASHES OF color and sound, pieces of history she'd locked away long ago in a bid to protect herself.

Vivna, turning away when Ongrum beat Ranka.

Ongrum, manipulating Ranka into believing she was nothing without her.

Vivna and Ongrum, Ongrum and Vivna, taking what should have been love and turning it into a weapon.

A memory, clear as day, splintered her mind: Vivna, shoving dirty fabric into Ranka's mouth to muffle her screams as she uncorked acid and poured it over a twelve-year-old girl's hands.

"Stop screaming," Vivna snarled. She slapped her. "I said stop *screaming*!" And then, as if remembering herself, her voice grew soft. Buttery. It soothed Ranka, set hooks in her heart, and drew her in. "If we don't fix your nails, we'll have to leave. If you love me, you have to do this. Don't you love me, Ranka? Won't you prove that you love me?"

It was no wonder it'd been so easy for Ongrum to fill the hole Vivna had left.

If Ranka could have stepped back in time, she would have seized the bleeding, blistering hands of her trembling twelve-year-old self and whispered with every ounce of fury in her heart, *This is not what love is.*

She would have told her love didn't demand *pain*.

And it certainly didn't require little girls to bleed in a snow-soaked field.

76

RANKA PITCHED FORWARD, RETCHING UNTIL HER
stomach cramped. Memories unlocked in a flood after she'd broken
the mental dam that was Belren. Blood trickled sluggishly over her
lips.

In her veins, swirling in her bones, was sheer, godly power. The
desire to flex that magic was still there, but now it was like a faint
pressure, a nudge of wanting. Gone was her hunger for death, her
insatiable itch to cause pain. Sores opened and closed on her skin as
the winalin tried to take hold. For now, her blood-magic kept it at
bay.

Belren flashed behind her eyes, and so did seventeen years of trauma
and pain and *lies*. What Ongrum and Vivna had felt for her had never
been love. It'd been control, and Ranka had been too wrapped in their
web of abuse to see otherwise.

Ranka saw their faces, and understood.

She had not been loved by these women. She had survived them.

It never should have happened. She'd been a child, a girl, a witch
desperate for a scrap of warmth. She had deserved better. She had
always deserved better.

Ranka opened her eyes.

All around her, lives winked out like candle flames. Witches fell on top of one another, crying out in horror as winalin witches sank their teeth into their flesh.

And Ongrum, at the center of it all, a hulking monstrosity of science and magic gone wrong, ruined by her own greed for power. She limped toward the twins, a low moan leaving her throat. Galen trembled, blood dripping from his nose, his lips, his ears. Aramis held his weight, using her free hand to fire iron-tipped darts into the witches who came toward them.

It was a such a waste. There would be no victory here today, not with the carnage on each side and the earth painted red.

Monster, the dust seemed to whisper, swirling at her feet. *Butcher.*

Yes, she *was* a monster.

She had done horrible, terrible things. Ranka would never be a hero—that shining title was for people like Galen and Aramis, the royal leaders, the golden twins. And so Ranka would be the shield, the knife, the thing in the shadows. Their secret weapon, and silent protector.

I am the monster.

She would stain her soul to keep theirs clean.

I am the shield.

And that would be enough.

I am the knife in the dark.

Ranka closed her eyes. She found the magic she'd never wanted. It had made her, earned her the title of Butcher, monster, pride of the Skra.

Ranka reached—and power ripped through her.

She staggered under the weight of it. The pain from her injuries faded. She was losing blood, but she could no longer feel her body dying. She would merely fight until her heart stopped. If she was lucky, she'd bleed out before the winalin took hold. Claws winked back at her from her hands, blacker than night and sharpened to fine, deadly points.

The world burned gray.

And finally, the Bloodwinn rose.

77

EVERY COLOR VANISHED, REPLACED BY THE WASH OF monotone that had haunted Ranka for five years.

Ranka looked down and flexed her hands. Instead of some lethal, starving force, this power felt like a friend, an ally, a weapon she could wield at will.

And wield it she would.

Ranka took a breath. She had only a few minutes before the winalin took hold. Foldrey would stay true to his word. The guard would take her out, even if she hadn't finished her duty.

Ranka began to walk.

A winalin witch hurtled toward her. Ranka could feel the vibration of the witch's footsteps, could hear the thrum of her breath. The witch leapt, and Ranka twisted, impossibly fast, and struck.

Ranka kept walking.

In the entire history of Witchik, only two blood-witches were rumored to have ever conquered their magic, eons before the first Sunra landed on Isodal's shores. The women had cemented themselves into legend, idolized as creatures that transcended the plane of mortals and stepped into the roles of gods. No one had ever rivaled them again. No one had come close, and the concept of conquering blood-magic had been chalked up to myth.

Now Ranka understood why.

"Ongrum," Ranka said, her voice quiet.

Ongrum turned.

The leader of the Skra was a wretched mess. Gone were most of her clothes and the hair on her head. Her entire body was a mess of blistering, bubbling sores, the result of taking a full injection of win-alin instead of administering it slowly, like the rest of the witches. Her left hand was nothing but a bleeding, bulbous mass. Were it not for Ongrum's eagerness to kill the twins, Ranka might have let her be. The disease was going to kill her on its own soon enough.

Ongrum barreled toward her.

The chaos sprawled to her right. To her left was nothing but the cliffs and the open, endless sea. There was no recognition in Ongrum's gaze. There was no one left at all. Ranka knelt, scooping up a spear. It was slick with blood along the handle. She wiped it on her pant leg.

"You were wrong about one thing," Ranka said softly. "I *am* a monster. I am wretched and twisted and cruel."

With each word Ranka saw them—every person she'd become ter-rible for. Every person who made it worth it.

"But I am not the same as you." Ranka met Ongrum's eyes. "I am *worse*."

Ongrum swung for her. Ranka knocked the sword from her hand with the ease of taking a toy from a child. She broke Ongrum's arm with her bare hands and drove her leader to the ground, pinning her flat. Her blood-magic rose in a wave, and Ranka's lungs expanded.

With this power, she could do anything.

With this power, she was inevitable.

Behind her, the Oori held their own. Only the Skra and the Murknen remained. The Arlani had abandoned the fight entirely, choosing to see where the cards fell instead of risking their lives. Percy was a whirl-wind of fire, scales flashing along his neck, his wrists.

Ongrum writhed on the earth, panting like an animal, scratching at Ranka's calf. Blood welled on her skin, but she felt no pain, not with her blood-magic raging in her veins.

Ranka stood above Ongrum.

And then the sores appeared.

She felt the shift happen—felt her blood-magic cower and retreat as winalin took hold at last. Her leg buckled. Her mind scattered, engulfed in momentary bloodlust, before Ranka was launched back to reality. *No.* It was too soon. She was so close. A sore burst open on her forearm, another on her chest.

I wanted to keep my promise.

Ranka swayed.

I wanted more time.

But she had done enough. Now there was only one matter left to resolve.

Ranka knelt.

"I am not weak because I loved you," she whispered to Ongrum. "I am strong because I survived you. I am strong because after all the hurt, still I love. Still I trust. My strength is not owed to the wounds you gave me, but my willingness to let them scar."

Ranka swayed as fire ripped through her, as blood-magic and winalin warred all at once.

"Now I am going to give you something you were never capable of. *Mercy.*"

And then Ranka pulled the woman who'd raised her against her chest and tipped over the cliff.

78

THEY FELL. THE WORLD FLASHED AROUND RANKA. Ongrum screamed, clawing at her, and Ranka pushed her away. Together they tumbled, hurtling through the air—and then they hit the sea.

Water poured into Ranka's lungs. The winalin in her body kept raging, fighting with her blood-magic, warping it into something new. Her lungs burned.

And finally, after seventeen years, Ranka stopped fighting.

She let herself sink. Let the ocean pour into her lungs and turn her body into a leaden, cold thing. She pictured the cabin in the woods, those moss-dusted walls, the river that would always run.

If there is a next life, she willed, *send me there.*

Something splashed overhead. Salt water stung Ranka's eyes, rendering the ocean around her a blur. A witch with sweeping tattoos and a brown neck ringed with shark's teeth dove toward her.

No, she wanted to say. *I'm done.*

It was someone else's turn to fight.

Let me go.

Blackness crept across her vision.

A hand closed around her hair and pulled her up.

Ranka was dying.

At least—she was trying to.

Voices cried out all around her. She coughed violently, seawater spilling from her lungs, and her power twisted, jerking out of her control as soon as she summoned it. Strength flooded her body—but so did illness. Her skin turned feverish, and sores opened up on her palms. Fire burned in her veins, and with it came an unnatural hunger, a desperate, crushing need to kill, like the demands of her blood-magic tenfold. Hands pinned her down.

They should have let me drown.

I was almost done—why couldn't they just let me drown?

Familiar voices wrapped around her, vying for her attention, and Ranka fought, unable to see, hear, or feel anything but the burning in her veins.

A voice cut through the fog.

Witch girl.

Look at me.

Ranka Volst, damn you, open your eyes.

Ranka opened her eyes. She was on a beach. Witches and humans alike pinned her down. Her body was a festering, rotting thing.

Above her stood a girl. *The* girl. The one she'd betrayed, the one she'd burn down the world for, even now.

The world burned black and white—but she was all screaming color.

Aramis was sobbing. From her pocket, she drew a vial. It was the sole survivor from her workshop, the almost-cure that had nearly saved the Kerth.

Ranka stared up at her, a strange peace sweeping over her. The vaccine would kill her, surely. It would put an end to it. Maybe her corpse would prove useful. Maybe, somewhere in her diseased, poisoned veins, lay the cure.

Aramis looked down at Ranka, her eyes wild, terrified, and *angry*.

You made a promise, those eyes said. *You broke it, again.*

There was so much Ranka wanted to say. That she was sorry. That she loved her. That she trusted her, more than anyone she'd ever known. That it was a gift, for Aramis's face to be the last one she saw before she took her final rest at last.

Instead, Ranka mouthed, "Do it."

Aramis slammed the syringe down.

The world went dark.

Overhead, the skies opened up, and the rain came down in one great sheet, putting out the fires at last.

79

IT WAS TWO WEEKS BEFORE RANKA LEFT THE HEALER'S
tent.

It was a miracle, the attending healers whispered. They'd all
heard the stories of the Bloodwinn falling to her death, the rumors
of the sore-covered, screaming creature Ursay had dragged from the
water, more monster than girl. When Aramis stabbed Ranka with the
vaccine, they'd thought the coma she plunged into would kill her.
Instead Ranka kept breathing, lost to the world as three separate pow-
ers warred inside her.

Instead, inexplicably, she survived.

She learned the rest in pieces. The healers injected her daily, whenever the sores surfaced, and now they surfaced less, and smaller each
day. From the antibodies found in Ranka's infected blood, Aramis and
Percy had synthesized the early test stages of a new vaccine, one that—
so far—seemed to be working on the winalin witches they'd captured.
Every day they injected Ranka and drew more blood. Every day the
winalin in her system dwindled—and with it, her blood-magic.

It was an irony of the cruelest sort. Winalin had been developed to
re-create blood-witches. And so it would be cured, by a blood-witch
it had sickened.

Aramis never visited her.

Piece by fragile piece, the survivors put the palace back together. The Sunra estate was like an ancient beast that had been left to rot. Now, hour by hour, the ants that had lived within and around it came to haul its flesh and bones away. None of the palace was livable. Army tents were erected amid the rubble. It would be years before the palace was restored to its previous splendor, if it ever was at all.

Galen spent his days on the grounds, calling wind to whip ash and wreckage far out to sea, stretching and testing the limits of his power. With one wave of his hand, he could clean away a mountain of debris that would have taken an entire team a full day to clear. Crowds started gathering to watch him work. His councilors didn't dare approach him, not with the palace in shambles.

He had never seemed happier.

At first Ranka had worried that the twins would send her away, but they were simply too exhausted and busy to care. When enough of her strength returned to walk, she floated between humans and witches, helping out where she could, hauling away debris some days, and doing her best to ignore their stares. Every time the Skra tried to corner her, she avoided them. They were hers by rights now, and even if they had mixed feelings, none dared to go against a blood-witch— or whatever Ranka had become.

Ranka didn't know how to tell them she wasn't sure that she *wanted* the Skra. That now, after everything, she didn't think she wanted the north, either.

The one thing she did want was impossible.

Three weeks after the coup, the Council called a meeting.

Because the Council room had been destroyed, they met instead in the ashes of the old gardens. No one summoned Ranka. The guards had been a mess ever since Foldrey was arrested and imprisoned, guarded not by humans, but by witches, to ensure he didn't have access to any loyal men.

Now witches stood among humans, arms crossed in challenge as though they expected to be kicked out. Ursay was among them, silent as everyone made awkward space around one another. Only Percy seemed at ease, drifting between groups with a languid smile, thriving on the obvious discomfort.

When he saw Ranka, his face lit up. "There's the witch of the hour."

He slung an arm around her shoulder, and Ranka half-heartedly batted at him but didn't move away. He'd worked alongside her several times in the past days when he wasn't with Aramis, silently hauling away burned timber, breaking ruined tiles with hammers, and burying the dead. His hands, like hers, were callused and torn. There was a smudge of ash on his temple he'd missed when he'd bathed that morning. Ranka licked her thumb and wiped it away, and he rolled his eyes.

He had forgiven her, in his own way, these past few days.

Ranka looked at him sidelong. "How goes the cure?"

"Surprisingly well." Percy scratched at his jaw. "Of course, our patients all want to *eat* us. But having live winalin witches to work with has been a gift. Aramis thinks we should have something in a few months and that we can keep the sick ones alive until then. If it works on these, we can take it wide."

More reports had come in of winalin witches roaming the countryside, as far north as Skra territory and every stretch of Isodal between. It would take time to catch—and cure—them all. But it would happen.

There was a restless energy to Percy. Something told her that when winalin finally vanished, Percy would too.

Percy tilted his head to the side. "You know—we might use your help."

Ranka hesitated. "Does she want my help?"

"She will." He gave her a tired smile. "Give her time."

Ranka nodded, her throat tight, and looked away.

Movement rippled ahead of them.

The Sunra twins had arrived.

They approached together, arms brushing, Galen in a plain shirt and breeches, Aramis in a loose, shapeless dress that hung from her shoulders in a single sheet of white cloth. There was no place to sit, so instead everyone dipped their heads as the royals took their place.

Galen's eyes crinkled. He looked calm. The most at ease Ranka had ever seen him, in fact. Instead of letting his sister take the lead, he stepped forward with an easy smile. "Thank you, all of you, for taking the time. There have been many questions about our path forward—and I thought it best to bring everyone together and discuss exactly that."

Everyone looked faintly surprised. It was like a totally different prince had entered that garden. Percy watched him with a soft light in his eyes.

Maybe there was something that could keep Percy in Isodal after all.

All the Council members began speaking at once.

"—a coronation as soon as possible—"

"—uniting the country—"

"—Isodal in need of leadership—"

Galen held up a hand, and the garden fell silent.

He looked too content. Too comfortable.

"I know you're all eager for a coronation. Isodal has been without a proper ruler for over a year. We need strong leadership now more than ever." His smile broadened. "So effective immediately, I'm abdicating my right to the throne."

Noise exploded in the clearing. Council members shouted over one another, and witches clamored for answers. Beside Galen, Aramis stood with her mouth hanging open, staring at her brother with pure, naked shock.

Sunras didn't just *resign*. To Ranka's knowledge, no one had ever turned down the throne before.

"Your Highness," one of the Council members blurted, dabbing frantically at a sweat-slick temple. "If I may. You cannot just *resign*."

"I can," Galen said pleasantly. "And I do."

Palace workers drifted closer, drawn by the clamor.

"But Isodal needs a ruler," someone sputtered. "It needs a leader. You are the heir."

Galen shrugged. "I am not the only heir."

Every eye in the garden went to Aramis. Aramis didn't seem to know what to do or where to look. Ranka had never seen her so stricken. Her entire history seemed to flash across her face—memories of being groomed for this title, when the world had thought she, too, would be a witch. The first true witch queen, the first Sunra queen, the girl king of Isodal. Poised to make history, only for it to be snatched away when she proved to be plainly, painfully human.

Galen's voice wrapped around them. "She has always been more suited for it. My parents saw it, we all did. We would thrive under her reign. We would struggle under mine." He paused and added wryly, "We already have."

"Your Grace," someone said. "I'm sorry, but your sister has no magic."

"So?"

"It is the *law*—"

"Then I will take the throne as king," Galen said, and for the first time his smile was cold. "I will *change* the law—and resign."

More shouting. More panicked voices climbing in the air, piling on top of one another, and through it all Aramis said nothing, frozen in place, her eyes wild and fixated on her brother.

He truly hadn't warned her, then.

Galen watched them with steel in his eyes. "You will have Aramis— or you will have no heir at all. It's your choice, really. And hers, if she wants it." He paused and turned to his sister, who stood as if in a trance. "You do want it, right?"

Aramis shook herself, looking like she'd never wanted to sink into the ground more. "Can I talk to you, Galen? In *private*?"

Galen shook his head. "You've spent your life protecting me, acting in my name, sacrificing to make things better for me—but it was never

what I wanted. It's time I make a choice on my own terms, and this it. You already govern better than I'd ever care to. You're what they deserve."

Aramis's mouth opened and closed like that of a fish cast upon dry land. "I don't know if I . . . I'm not . . ."

A new voice cut through the clamor. "Do you expect the witches to simply fall in line?"

Ursay stepped forward, their face neutral. They didn't flinch at the glares some of the human Council members leveled, nor did they preen at the satisfied nods of the witches.

"Ongrum's methods were wretched, but her concerns were real—and echoed by your own people." Their dark eyes gleamed. "Where is our say in which direction this country heads? Winalin is still at large. The monsters who created it and shipped it to our shores remain unscathed, and it is the covens that suffer. It is *our* lands the winalin witches now roam through. Why should we support either of you?"

Galen looked at Ursay, shrinking momentarily.

"You shouldn't."

Heads turned.

"I mean," Aramis continued. "Not without good reason."

Ursay's eyes narrowed.

Aramis looked squarely back at them. "The covens are right to be wary. The Council has always been a mess—and the witches have always been underrepresented. Someone else pointed that out to me once." Her eyes flicked briefly to Ranka. "The witches deserve a place on the Council—two seats for each coven, with the Bloodwinn in their own formal seat. Participating, voting, and proposing laws instead of sitting spectator."

More voices cried out. The witches looked stunned, although Ursay's face revealed nothing. Some of the Council members looked furious, but others, most of them northerners who had grown up in times when the covens and humans depended on each other, looked thoughtful.

"It all needs an overhaul," Aramis said softly. "This land, this country, was broken long before even my grandfather took the throne and tried to patch it with the Bloodwinn treaty. So you're right, Ursay. Ongrum's methods were wrong, but her reasons for wanting change were not. We cannot continue on as we have."

"Pretty words," Ursay said slowly. "But I have been given pretty words by humans—and they meant nothing when it mattered."

The witches rumbled. The covens had every right to mistrust the humans, but without their backing there would be no pressure on the Council to fold. To accept Aramis as their queen instead of Galen.

Before she knew what she was doing, Ranka stepped forward.

Every eye flew to her.

Her legs turned to jelly. It was funny, truly. She had battled half-dead witches and assassins deep below the earth, but it was public speaking that would be her undoing.

"When I was chosen as the next Bloodwinn, I saw it as a death sentence." She swallowed. "If the Bloodwinn treaty is to be rewritten, then I ask that the role no longer be forced—the covens will take turns selecting their own, choosing any witch they feel is suited to speak for them. Not just a blood-witch." She paused. "And that witch will not be required to marry the Sunra heir."

Ranka took another shaky step forward, and her eyes were solely for Aramis. Only a few feet separated them, yet it felt like an entire ocean.

"When a plague came to our shores that killed witches, it was Aramis—not the Council, not the prince, not the covens—who dove into the mines to stop it. It was Aramis who put her life at risk to make a cure. She saved us when our own betrayed us. When our own saw our bodies as nothing more than experiments."

Aramis held Ranka's stare, her lips trembling faintly. The evening sun sank lower in the sky behind them, gilding the gardens in a honey glow, illuminating her from behind. With the threads of warm light weaving through her dark curls and glancing off her skin, Aramis looked ethereal.

She looked like a queen.

"We could have no one better," Ranka said softly. "She is braver than the lot of us. Smarter, too. I am not sure that we deserve her. But we would be lucky with her at the helm."

Aramis's throat bobbed, and though her eyes glistened, she held carefully, regally still.

Before Ranka could think twice—before she could let fear sweep in, that whisper that Aramis would not want her vote of confidence or her apology or whatever else she had left to give—she gathered together the last scraps of her courage and sank to one knee.

The last time she had knelt like this, it had been before Ongrum, swearing her fealty to the Skra.

Ursay held Ranka's stare, and their jaw shifted in the barest of nods. The humans looked wary, but not opposed. The witches murmured among themselves.

Behind them, Percy's eyes shone brighter than stars, and Galen held back a smile.

Ranka's heart ached.

How had she ever chosen anyone but them?

Ranka's next words felt like she'd spent a lifetime waiting to say them. They were a question, an apology, a promise, all wrapped together—one she was finally ready to keep.

"I vow to serve the full lifetime term of Bloodwinn under Aramis Sunra," she said softly. "I revoke my coven, my land, my birthright, in service of the Sunra throne. But only if it is *this* Sunra who rules." Her voice softened. "And only if she'll have me."

The Skra hatchet at her hip, the totem she had carried for nearly a week, had never felt heavier. Ranka unbuckled it and laid it at Aramis's feet.

"I give everything I have, and everything I am, to Aramis Sunra," Ranka whispered. "First queen of Isodal and first of her name. Solomei bless her reign."

The small noise that came from Aramis nearly made Ranka fall to her other knee. There would be no going back now. Either the witches would follow, or they would be in defiance of their own Bloodwinn. Either the humans would follow, or they'd have no witch alliance at all.

A smile lit up Galen's face. "You all know my feelings on the matter." And then he knelt too.

An awkward beat passed through the glade.

Then Ursay stepped forward, the slightest hint of a smile on their lips. "If the Bloodwinn is willing to serve a human queen, then the Oori are as well—so long as the new terms are honored." Ursay knelt, a proud line to their back. The rest of the coven followed in a ripple of movement, and then the Arlani. Finally, only the Murknen and the Skra remained standing. They shifted their weight from foot to foot, their eyes on Ranka, and then slowly, begrudgingly, sank to one knee as well.

Through it all, Galen was completely at ease. Ranka nearly laughed.

For the first time in his life, Galen Sunra was going to get exactly what he wanted.

One by one the humans followed suit, until only a few remained standing—and Percy, looking out of place in his swirl of purple and silver robes.

"I don't think I get a vote," he said cheerfully. "But you'd all be fools to say no." He stepped back and leaned against the trunk of one of the few orange trees that had made it through the fire, plucked a fruit from a branch, and bit straight through the peel.

The last knelt. And then it was Aramis, standing alone.

Ranka remained where she was. Her heart beat so hard, she feared it was going to crack her ribs. When she spoke, her voice was only for Aramis. "Well, Princess?"

Her question carried a dozen others.

Will you have me?

Will you let me stay?

Will you give me another a chance—a chance I don't deserve but am desperate for all the same?

And Aramis looked at her and said, "Okay."

A startled laugh bubbled out of her. She wrung her hands together. "Okay, that's enough. All of you, please, stand back up, for the love of light, you're making me nervous." She cut a glare at Galen. "I am honored, truly. And *surprised*."

He beamed at her and winked.

The first and future queen of Isodal regarded them all with a weary smile. "Now I suppose we ought to get back to work."

80

EPILOGUE
Three months later

THE SHIP WAS READY TO LEAVE.

Ranka stood at the dock, a single bag at her feet. Her heart had never felt heavier.

This was the correct move. The smart one. The covens had accepted Ranka reprising her role—but there was still the question of the Skra. They'd asked her to come home, and under the new terms the Bloodwinn no longer had to *stay* in the palace. Not with the first batches of the winalin cure rolling out, its concentration so refined, so strong, Ranka herself now only requiring a monthly injection to keep her winalin-warped blood-magic at bay. It no longer made sense for her to remain here.

At least, that's what she told herself.

There'd been a question of who should ferry the Bloodwinn north. The Oori had offered, but Ranka preferred the anonymity of a merchant ship instead.

But now she only wanted to turn and run.

"Don't look so excited," Percy said dryly beside her. "You're getting on a boat, not climbing into your grave."

When Percy had announced he would travel with the Bloodwinn

and continue on after, no one had been surprised. Aramis and Galen cried when they hugged him, much to Percy's utter delight. They knew better than to ask him to stay. Percy's place in Isodal had only ever been temporary. The Star Isles was destined to draw him back one way or another.

Percy nudged her. "Looks like our welcome party is here."

Ranka turned, worried he meant the Council or the few Skra who'd remained in Isodal to follow her around like lost puppies, but it was the twins. They were in regular dress save for their circlets, winding their way down Seaswept's tilted streets. Seeing a Sunra in the city was no longer a shock. Aramis toured nearly every day, meeting with citizens, listening intently to their grievances, ideas, and needs. They'd come to know her face better in three months than they had her parents' in a lifetime.

And they seemed to *like* her. Whispers wound through the city that this was the girl who had healed them in a tiny, underfunded clinic. Rumors spun of a princess sneaking through Seaswept's streets to fight the Hands, braving winalin-witch-infested tunnels, putting herself in harm's way to save the people who had long rejected her. Some spun tales that *this* queen was the same vigilante who had burned an inn known for torturing witches to the ground. Aramis smiled politely through all of it and confirmed nothing.

True to her word, the queen had reformed the Council. Its size had nearly doubled, with two seats added for each coven, and a formal one for the Bloodwinn. New seats were added for Isodal, too, for smaller, previously unrepresented provinces. There were nobles, but there were common folk like Ranka—a dockworker from Truvil, a midwife from Orvist, a fishmonger, two farmers, two healers, and even a blacksmith. Humans with worn hands and long, tired lives now sat in the land's highest court, writing and passing laws, given their seats via local election instead of a family name. Aramis had stunned everyone by writing into law a check on royal power. No longer could a ruler declare war without the Council, condemn a village to die, raise taxes, or cease shipments of medicine. All now required a Council majority, including the buy-in of the witches now serving.

It still wasn't perfect—but it was change, coming inch by inch.

Now the twins drew closer, their faces lighting up with love and sorrow at the sight of Ranka and Percy at the docks. Gulls whirled overhead, clutching a stray fish or a piece of bread. Ranka had never been more filled with dread.

Percy elbowed her. "What are you doing?"

Ranka stared at him. "What?"

"I know why *I* have to leave Isodal. But why do you?"

"I—" Ranka sputtered. "I don't—"

"What, you and Aramis haven't kissed and made up yet?"

"What?"

"That's a no, then." Percy rolled his eyes. "You useless lesbian. Oh, don't glare at me like that—I'm just stating the obvious. Seems like a weird move, to leave your girlfriend here just because you have the communication skills of a dead fish."

Ranka stared at him, speechless. There had been moments, of course—tender looks and quiet discussions, glances in meetings and stares that lingered far too long. But Aramis was queen now, and Ranka the Bloodwinn who'd betrayed her only months prior. Both girls had been launched overnight into positions of power whose influence rippled around the world.

Ranka could not blame Aramis for being cautious, for being hesitant to rebuild their friendship or . . . whatever had existed before.

It did not make her any less sad, though.

Maybe if I leave, she'd told herself. *Maybe when I come back, she'll be ready.*

When she had told this to the healer she'd been seeing, the woman had laughed.

"That," she'd said, "sounds like a recipe for heartache."

She was an odd creature—a healer for the mind, she claimed, not the body. Ranka had gone there expecting spells and tinctures, but all they ever really did was *talk*. The woman helped Ranka probe through everything—Belren, her history with the Skra, Vivna, the events of the last six months, unwinding old wounds and working through them. It felt pointless, but it was a commitment all four of them had agreed to. And though Ranka hated to admit it, it *had* been helping, even if she did leave some sessions completely numb and others with snot dripping from her nose from crying so hard.

Her nightmares had eased, and thanks to Aramis's vaccine injections, her blood-magic seemed to wither more by the day. It took more and more effort to wake, like a candle slowly guttering out. Every day Ranka awoke to a world of color, and most mornings it brought surprised tears to her eyes to see how blue the sky burned when death no longer held the reins of her life.

Some nights Ranka dreamed she awoke to no magic at all. That her power had vanished over time piece by piece, withering away until one day it was gone entirely, leaving behind just a regular witch. Just Ranka.

Aramis drew nearer, and Ranka's mind blanked.

Percy rolled his eyes to the heavens. "Hey, remember the advice I gave you about choosing yourself? That's an ongoing thing. Not just a moment-of-severe-trauma thing."

"I am choosing myself."

"Uh-huh." He shook his head. "Ah, well. Plenty of time for me to talk sense into you. Just picture it, Ranka. Just you and your old pal Percy, trapped together in close quarters for weeks on end, with absolutely no escape." He hooked his arm through hers. "We're going to have *fun*."

Maybe she would be better off staying in Seaswept after all.

"What's the matter, Ranka?" Galen asked, finally within earshot. "Second-guessing your decision to be trapped on a boat with Percy for a month?"

"Yes," she and Percy chorused.

Aramis came to stand beside him. The queen was unusually silent, her hands clasped behind her back, her dress rippling around her legs.

On the ship, the last of the crates were loaded. One sailor raised an arm and shouted they'd be leaving soon. Ranka's stomach did a nervous flip.

"Well, then. I suppose this is goodbye." Aramis hugged Percy tightly before stepping back to grip his arms. She squinted at him and sighed. "Try to stay out of trouble."

Percy pressed a kiss to her forehead. "No."

Galen gave Ranka a hug, his chin bumping against her collarbone. He had forgiven her so easily, which only made her heart hurt more. But she supposed that was part of what made him a good prince—and an absolutely terrible king.

"Try not to kill Percy," he said.

"No promises," Ranka said dryly, and hugged him back.

Galen moved to say goodbye to Percy, and suddenly his posture grew shy. He cleared his throat. "Well. I, ah, I'll miss you, Percy."

"Oh, you *will*, won't you?" Percy laughed, and before Galen could react, he swooped Galen into a hug that lifted him clear off the ground. Galen yelped—but didn't protest. Something wry glittered in Percy's eyes as he set Galen down and bent to kiss him on the forehead. Galen squeaked, and Percy smirked, whispering something in his ear that made the prince blush furiously.

A throat cleared.

Aramis stood in front of Ranka.

All the courage Ranka had been trying to muster drained out of her.

"Hello, Princess," she said softly, and then winced. "I mean, my queen. I mean, Your Grace. I mean—"

"You can keep calling me Princess. I don't mind. I like how it sounds in your voice." Aramis looked to the sea, her expression faintly troubled. "So you're truly leaving, then?"

"Ah, yeah." Ranka rubbed the back of her neck. "Hence the boat."

"But *why?*" Aramis burst out. Her eyes widened. She clearly hadn't meant to ask it like that.

"After what happened . . . and you've been so busy . . . and we . . . I don't know," Ranka sputtered. She refused to look at the water. If she did, she was certain her face would be bright red. She hesitated, and added weakly, "I thought you'd be happier with me gone. I thought . . ." She swallowed. "I thought you wanted me to leave."

"You thought—oh, Ranka." Aramis looked up at Ranka through her lashes. Her voice came out soft and slow. "And if I wanted you to stay?"

"Oh." It had never occurred to Ranka that Aramis might want her here. That after all the pain Ranka had caused, the newly crowned Sunra queen would desire anything but distance.

"I thought you wanted to leave," Aramis admitted quietly. "There is . . . so much to rebuild. So much is broken. I am so terrified, all the time, that I won't be strong enough, wise enough, brave enough, for what they need. I know you've suffered. I know you've fought enough for a thousand lifetimes. A better person would tell you to go. To leave this city behind, disappear, and find the rest you crave. The anonymity you deserve." Aramis chewed her lip, her eyes searching Ranka's face. "But I am not a better person."

Ranka was fully going to pass out.

"I could never give you peace. And it would be no cabin in the woods." Every line of Aramis's face was open, hopeful, and raw. "But it would be something."

Ranka was conscious of the stares they were garnering. She knew the weight of what Aramis offered. To remain in Seaswept was to remain the Bloodwinn, the Butcher, the monstrous Skra. If Ranka stayed, she'd never be free of her old life, never slip into anonymity like she'd always dreamed.

But dreams were fickle, and prone to change.

The girl who'd entered Seaswept with rage in her heart and fear in her bones was still there, would always *be* there. But that girl had also found acceptance in a prince's gentle smile, understanding in an ambassador's golden eyes, and a home in a princess who was so much sharper than she had any right to be. They made her braver and kinder. They saw all of her, and in her they saw something better.

Maybe Ranka could become that still.

Aramis tilted her head to the side, those remarkable brown eyes of hers taking up the entire world. If there was one thing Ranka was grateful for about no longer seeing in grays, it was the color brown, the richness of new earth held in the gaze of this girl. "Well, witch girl?"

Ranka cleared her throat. "Would I be . . . useful . . . to you here?"

Was Aramis *blushing*? "I believe the Bloodwinn could be incredibly useful in Seaswept. It would be very easy, I think, for the queen to find many a reason to keep the Bloodwinn here." Her eyes darted back to Ranka. "That is, if the Bloodwinn wanted it."

"If the queen commanded it, I suppose it would be treason to refuse."

"It *would* be treason," Aramis said sagely. "Consider yourself commanded."

Every ounce of weight vanished from Ranka, replaced by a strange, bubbly giddiness. If this was a dream, she prayed to sleep forever. She and Aramis fell silent, both of them watching each other, speechless in this liminal stretch of wonderful new possibility. Ranka knew she had tears in her eyes, knew a strange, ridiculous smile was blooming on her face, matching Aramis's own. She couldn't find it in her to care.

"Well," Percy broke in, "this is very sweet, but we did pay for two tickets."

Aramis waved him away. "The Crown can afford one unused ticket."

"That's not very fiscally responsible of you."

"It's not fiscally responsible for me to have you executed, yet I consider it every day."

"All these threats to kill me, and you never follow through." Percy folded his arms. "They prepared the ship for two guests—would you like to tell a bunch of cranky sailors to go dump all their food and prep work, or shall I?"

Aramis glared at him, irritated, and Ranka was about to tell Percy to please be quiet and stop ruining the incredible warm and bubbly feeling currently rushing through her like wine, when Galen looked up. "I'll go."

"Right, and also, I don't want to travel alone. . . ." Percy's face went slack. "Huh?"

"I'll go," Galen said breathlessly. "I've never been on a boat before."

Aramis's eyebrows shot up her forehead. "Galen, you've never even left Seaswept before."

"Exactly." Galen bounced up on his toes. "Wasn't that the whole issue? Think, Aramis. Our family has been out of touch for centuries. When is the last time a Sunra went north, let alone to another nation?" He waved a hand, and wind danced around his fingers, bringing with it a warm swirl of dust. "What's keeping me here? You're queen now. Think of the good I could do, calling rain for parched villages and fending off storms. I spent my entire life trapped in this city. But I'm free from the crown now. I want to see this world. Who better to have with me than Percy?"

Behind Galen, Percy's cheeks had taken on a very interesting shade of pink. He stared at Galen. Something like terror glimmered there, but it was a sweeter fear. The fear of something recognized. Of a possibility one had never entertained before.

Of a new reality, suddenly within reach.

Ranka knew that fear all too well.

"You had me until you tried to sell Percy as a reason you'd be safe." Aramis's throat bobbed nervously. "Galen, you're still a prince. You'd be a target, you could be kidnapped—"

"I'll travel in disguise. Besides, I can call hurricanes, and Percy can breathe fire." He looped his arm through Percy's, who actually looked *shy*. "Isodal and Witchik are broken. Who better to repair them than one of the heirs?"

What could Aramis tell him? Galen had a point, and there were as many reasons for him to leave as there were for Ranka to stay. Yet from the way Aramis watched him, it was plain she wanted to tell him no. All her life she'd tried to protect her brother. Now, only months after Ongrum had held a blade to his throat, he wanted to walk onto a ship and disappear into the wide, cruel world.

Aramis closed her eyes. When she opened them again, they were bright with tears. "I suppose I can't stop you, can I?"

"Not really." Galen smiled warmly at her. "But I'd prefer to not have to sneak off."

Aramis drew in a shaky breath—and then yanked Galen into a hug. He winced, and hugged her back, burying his face in his sister's shoulder. With their twin circlets, they were mirror images of each other. They'd offered Aramis the original Skybreaker crown at her coronation—a monstrous, gaudy thing of terrible weight, constructed of solid gold waves. She'd politely declined, opting to keep the plain gold circlet she'd worn her entire life.

Aramis looked over Galen's shoulder at Percy and jabbed a threatening finger at him. "If *anything* happens to my baby brother . . ."

"I'm a minute older than you," Galen complained.

Percy's eyes were only on Galen. "I'll protect him." He cleared his throat. "I promise."

Ranka nudged him and muttered, "Useless."

He glared at her and batted her hand away.

Galen clapped his hands together, his entire face alight. "Well, that's it, then. Ranka stays, and I go with Percy. It works out perfectly."

Aramis edged closer to Ranka until their fingers were brushing. When Aramis looked at her, her eyes held a question, and Ranka wanted nothing more than to spend the rest of her days proving the depth of her yes.

"Yes," said Queen Aramis. "I suppose it does."

Aramis and Ranka followed the ship on foot, walking along the coast as wind carried the vessel toward the pale horizon. At first they could still make out Percy and Galen—one tall and lanky, the other short and stout, never leaving each other's side. The clouds churned over-head, twisting as if manipulated by a goddess's hand. Yet it was not some distant deity meddling with the sky, but a prince.

When they reached the beach and could follow the ship no farther, Ranka and Aramis kicked their sandals off and sat, burying their toes in the warm sand. Aramis watched the horizon with a quiet intensity, as though willing her brother back to shore.

"They're going to get in so much trouble," Aramis sighed, wring-ing her hands. "I wonder if Galen will be scared. Or bored. It's an awfully small ship."

"I think he'll be plenty distracted with Percy aboard. He likes him."

"So? Galen likes everyone."

Ranka turned to stare at her to see if she was kidding. "For a girl as sharp as you are, you are terribly dense."

"You can't possibly mean—Galen and *Percy*—you're *sure*?"

"Aramis," Ranka said slowly. "They are quite literally sailing off into the sunset together."

"That little *worm*. He didn't even *tell me*!"

On the horizon, the ship had shrunk to a smidge of color against an endless blue. It could have been a painting, the sails growing smaller, and the clouds settling as the winds resumed their normal paths.

"Do you envy them?" Ranka asked softly.

Do you wish you were leaving too?

Aramis paused and shook her head. "Do you?"

"No," Ranka said, and it was the truth. "I'm glad you asked me to stay."

"I didn't ask. I ordered it—remember?" Aramis gave her a wide, crooked grin. "It'd have been treason if you'd refused."

Ranka's heart fluttered. She ducked her head so Aramis couldn't see the warmth Ranka was certain was turning her cheeks pink.

She had made so many mistakes. She felt so unworthy of this place, this girl, this life. Ranka looked at Aramis, eyes tracing her lips, the slope of her shoulders, the delicate lines of her ink-stained hands.

Maybe Isodal wasn't home—and maybe that was all right. The Northlands would never be home again either. Maybe home was no longer a place, but a person, a feeling, a dream.

Maybe home was wherever her heart could finally rest.

"We should go back," Aramis said softly. "Before the new Council members get into a fistfight. Again."

Disappointment closed Ranka's throat. This was the first moment of quiet she'd had with Aramis in weeks. Soon they'd return to the palace, and they'd return to their roles of queen and Bloodwinn, pulled into a million different directions.

But for now they were just two girls, alone on a beach, the sun on their backs and the entire world at their feet. So she'd stretch this moment a little longer, if she could.

"Let's wait," Ranka said. "Just in case Percy has already set the ship on fire."

Aramis paused, a twinkle in her eye, and then nodded sagely. "Or pushed the captain overboard."

"Or made Galen cry."

"Galen wouldn't *cry*."

Ranka lifted a brow.

"Okay," Aramis admitted. "Galen would probably cry. Galen is probably already crying."

Ranka inched her hand sideways until their fingers touched. Aramis slid her hand in Ranka's and then, after a moment's hesitation, leaned her head on Ranka's shoulder. They relaxed, easing into the weight of each other.

"Ranka?" Aramis's voice was soft. "I'm glad you stayed."

Ranka squeezed her hand. "Me too."

How strange to think that a year ago they had been strangers— the disgraced princess, the Butcher of Belren. They had been enemies at their worst, reluctant allies at their best.

And now?

Take a girl, give her a kingdom, and see what she becomes. Take a witch, give her freedom, and see where she stays.

All they'd lost, all they'd suffered—it was moments like this, when it was them, and only them, that it felt like it might have been worth it. Their scars were still there, but even the newest wounds were covered in shiny tissue. Their future was not guaranteed—nothing precious ever was. But this chance was more than Ranka had ever hoped for.

It was certainly more than she deserved.

"I think we'll do good work here, Ranka," said Aramis. "I think we can make a difference."

There was still so much to change, so much to learn. But they had time. Ranka finally had nothing *but* time. Her entire life she had been counting on dying in her twenties, bleeding out on some distant, smoking battlefield.

But now, with her blood-magic dwindling more every day?

There was an entire life ahead of her, decades upon decades. If her luck held, she would see her hair turn gray, feel her limbs weaken, and watch her skin wrinkle. There would be more hard days, but the fact that she would *have* the days would be a miracle in and of itself.

And for this—this girl, this hope, this new life—she would take all the time she could get.

"I think we will, Princess," Ranka murmured. The word felt private now, a pet name instead of an honorific. Ranka relished the fact that she got to say it at all.

Seabirds cried overhead. Behind them, the voices of Council members lifted into the air, mixing with the thrum of the waves. They were definitely arguing again. Ranka didn't quite have it in her to care. Everything around her was rendered in sharp, brilliant hues of oversaturated color—the sand, the sea, the girl beside her. Ranka met Aramis's eyes, taking in the rich black of her lashes, the rose-gold blush dusted over her brown cheeks, the sky above her, and the golden rays of sunlight that fell across them like warm rain. So many hues, so many colors, and even now Ranka wanted to gather them in her palms and drink them until she burst.

The world had not been painted gray for three months now. Ranka hoped it never would again.

"The ship is gone, witch girl." Aramis traced a pattern on her arm. "We should head back."

"A little longer," Ranka whispered. "Rest with me, a moment more."

The queen smiled and put her head in Ranka's lap.

What a fool Ranka had been, to think she wanted the Skra, Ongrum's pride, or even Vivna's return. To believe she needed to meet the cruel conditions of someone else's love to be worth anything at all.

She had all she needed right here.

Ranka tilted her face to the sun.

The colors had never been brighter.

ACKNOWLEDGMENTS

ON NOVEMBER 12TH OF 2019, THREE YEARS INTO WORK-ing on this book, I slipped on ice getting out of my car. The first thing to hit the concrete was my temple.

I had no idea my author dreams were about to be put on hold; that what I would first pass off as a clumsy fall would evolve into a brain injury that would upend my entire world. I would quickly become homebound, unable to hold a regular conversation, read, write, work, or live any semblance of the "normal" life I'd taken for granted. It would be eight months before I could turn in a revision for *The Ones We Burn*—and it would be five months before I could write at all.

I'll be honest: it's a miracle this book made it into the world. I owe many, many thank-yous to many people—too many to recount here. But I'm certainly going to try.

I owe a massive debt of gratitude to Dr. Opada Alzohaili and the entire staff of the Metro Detroit Center for Endocrinology, who discovered after a year and a half of debilitating symptoms, that my concussion had damaged my pituitary gland to the point where it was no longer producing the growth hormone the brain requires to function. The injections I now take aren't the most fun, but they also saved my life. I am forever grateful.

To David, my best friend, my biggest supporter, and my whole heart. Thank you for always believing in me, my dreams, and my books, despite your complete inability to read. Thank you for the pep talks; reality checks; for holding my hand in doctor's appointments; tolerating my obsessive need to fit as many houseplants as possible in our home; and for the far too many, endless, "Oh my god it's 3pm and you haven't eaten" meal runs. Your love for our cats is borderline concerning and remains my favorite thing in the world. You make me kinder—and you make me braver. I love you so much.

I can never convey the depths of my *thank-you* to my editor, Alyza Liu, who waited with patience while I recovered to work on this book. Alyza saw the heart of Ranka's story from the beginning, and her incisive editorial eye helped me carve closer to the soul of this strange, messy book about a girl raised to see cruelty as love. Alyza, I appreciate you so damn much. Now please go take a nap.

Eli Baum worked an absolute miracle with this cover, and I don't think I'll ever cease to be amazed at the way he managed to create the cover of my absolute *dreams.* Karyn Lee—I literally owe you my life. I don't know *how* you designed a cover and jacket so perfect, but I remain perpetually in awe that you did. A massive thank-you to the rest of the brilliant minds at Simon & Schuster who this book would not exist without—managing editor Eugene Lee, production manager Elizabeth Blake-Linn, Justin Chanda, Karen Wojtyla, Erica Stahler, Wendy Rubin, Lisa Quach, Mitch Thorpe, Kaitlyn San Miguel, and Morgan York. My sincerest apologies to the Simonteen social media team. I am, unfortunately, not going to stop tagging you in memes.

An additional massive thank you to my incredible UK team over at Hoddar, particularly my wonderful editors Molly Powell and Natasha Qureshi, whose fierce love for this strange, feral book is a gift beyond my wildest dreams, and whose emails are always the highlight of my day. Thank you to Natalie Chen for designing such a gorgeous UK cover; Marcela Bolivar for the stunning art; and Kate Keehan, Callie Robertson, and Claudette Morris for championing this story. I am so, so grateful to you all.

Kiki Nguyen saw a spark in this story when it was just a messy garble of words back in 2018, and her love for Ranka gave me permission to hope and love for her too. This book wouldn't exist without her and I am forever grateful.

Jim McCarthy remains an absolute gift of an agent. I couldn't be more grateful to have found such an amazing advocate for the strange, eerie books I insist on writing. I appreciate you so much, Jim. Please see the above note about taking a nap.

To Andrea Hannah, the witchy, tarot-wielding big sister I never knew I needed; and to Aimée Carter, the publishing-badass big sister I always wanted. If fate is a thing, it definitely intervened by making me meet the two of you. I love you both beyond words, and I am so proud to know you. Thank you for being my best friends and my found family. And thank you for humbling me the day we met when I proudly announced I didn't outline books by politely saying, "It's a skill." This was the third book I ever wrote without an outline—and certainly the last. I will never do this to myself again. Lesson learned. I love you both so much. Remind me to listen to you, always. Kristin Lord, there aren't enough words to tell you how much I love you, how grateful I am for you, and how *proud* I am of you. I look up to you so much it's embarrassing and I can't wait to hold your book in my hands.

Grace Li read far too many drafts of this book, and loved it when it was an ugly, meandering mess, and endured the grueling process of learning how to actually *plot* a damn book with me. I love you dearly, and remain the ultimate fan of everything you write, forever. Achieving our publishing dreams together has been one of the greatest joys of this entire process for me. Sarah Underwood exploded into my life via Pitchwars and I feel like I honestly won the mentee lottery. You are a force, a talent, and a joy. I am deeply thrilled I tricked you into being my friend, and I am wildly, embarrassingly proud of you. Thank you for the encouragement, friendship, plant-pillows, surprise cupcakes, and for giving me a space in your lives. I love you both so damn much, and I feel like I won the lottery getting to call you my friends.

Katie Zhao & Amelie Wen Zhao saw this book in its earliest, ugliest, messiest forms, and believed in it anyways. I don't think I'd be writing books without either of you and I'm forever excited to read whatever you write next. Thank you to Hanna Alkaf for your warmth, kindness, internet mom-ing, and to Meryl Wilsner for your friendship, humor, and *excellent* taste in cheese. Thank you to Tess Sharpe for your wisdom, encouragement, brilliant shark advice, and for always giving me permission to dream a little bigger—and a little more ruthlessly.

There are so, so many brilliant minds in publishing I am forever grateful for, and while I know I am not going to be able to name them all, I'm going to try. SO! A massive thank-you to: Mara Delgado; Adrienne Tooley; Cam Montgomery; Adalyn Grace; Ruby Barrett; Alyssa Eatherly; Rosiee Thor; Roselle Lim; Francesca Flores; Alex Higgins; Ananya Devarajan; Sara Raasch; Anna Gracia; Andrea Tang; Peter Lopez; Ayana Gray; Ava Reid; and Suzie Sainwood; who have all been beyond generous with their encouragement, advice, friendship, and reality checks. You are all brilliant and I adore you. Thank you also to Kelly Van Sant and Laura Zats—the brilliant advice you've given me has been passed onto a-dozen-and-a-half other writers. I forever admire the hell out of the both of you. *The Pubcrawl Podcast* and *Print Run Podcast* are the only reasons I have made any smart publishing decisions ever, in my life.

Naseem, Victoria, Miriam, Skye, Brittany, Sierra—thank you for loving and believing in this book when I wanted to throw my computer into the sea. I love you guys. Layla Noor, Mike Lasagna, Rachel Stolle, Rhiannon, Cait Jacobs, Lizzy Smith, and Kaylie Steward, thank you for loving this book long after I'd stopped seeing the magic in it. Cristina—neither Ranka nor I deserve you, but I'm grateful for you every single day.

To Natasha Ngan, who is one of my favorite authors—and my first ever blurb. When I saw your email, I nearly passed out. Thank you, thank you, *thank you*. I will simply never recover. A massive thank you as well to Chloe Gong, Adrienne Tooley, Francesca May, Adalyn Grace, and Hannah Whitten for reading and for the lovely blurbs. I am so grateful to you all.

To my friends and family who loved this book in its messiest, ugliest form—Meagan Cotter, Natalie Noland, Sabrina Cotrell, Mara Bouvier-Schatz, Sarah Sprenger, Uncle Dusty & Aunt Diane—I can't believe you guys *read* this, let alone liked it, but your hope for this book when it was a sad, confusing mess carried me through endless revisions. Grandma, I wish you could have read this. It's nothing like the romance novels you loved, but you would have pretended to like it anyway. I miss you every day. Grandpa, I love you. Please do not read this. Mom, Dad, Hannah, I love you guys, thank you for letting me steal the family computer to spend all my time writing on Neopets instead of making friends like a normal kid should have. It paid off—I think.

Kristen Remenar is the reason I write and read fantasy. I was a reluctant reader when I wandered into her library, and it was through her recommendation I fell in love with magic (and . . . violence . . .?) through worlds built by Brian Jacques, Tamora Pierce, Suzanne Collins, and so many more. I blame you, Kristen, for all of this. I harbor the belief that all librarians are superheroes—but you are the Extra Super kind.

Vicky Stringer wasn't the first teacher to say I could write books, but she was the first that gave me the space and the time to do so. I don't know if my first (awful) book would have ever been written had she not somehow convinced my high school that letting a seventeen-year-old sit in the library every day and write was something that could count towards graduating . . . but she did, and that first, awful book led to many more slightly less awful books. Stringy, I wouldn't be an author without you; and I'm forever grateful to you. Thank you also to Jenna Bendle, Mary Moon, Jeff Chapman, and so many other wonderful teachers. I know you saw me secretly reading under the desk in class. Thank you for pretending not to notice anyway.

Kirsten Elliott and Tressa Mucci told their dorky, fresh-out-of-college coworker that yes, she could be an author and no, it was okay to go find a career that involved a little less math. You were right on both counts. I love you both dearly.

Thank you to my Patreon patrons, whose support keeps me writing, and keeps me dreaming. Thank you in particular to Krista, Hope, everyone in the Story Grove, and the entire Word Garden community—you guys are amazing, and I can't wait to see your books on the shelves. A special thank-you to my admin & mod team who diligently keep the discord from bursting into flames.

Can I put Taylor Swift and everyone who had a hand in *Avatar: The Last Airbender* in my acknowledgments? Because I'm going to. They'll never know who I am, yet their art remains the life rings I cling to when I have nothing else.

To the readers, book bloggers, librarians, and booksellers who have fiercely supported this book, and so many other sapphic books, with a staggering and almost terrifying passion—I am utterly verklempt at your support, and *eternally* grateful.

Ranka, I'm very sorry for literally everything that happens in this book. I didn't know it at the time, but when I was writing your path to healing, I was writing mine, too. You made my dreams come true. And I am so glad you are everyone else's problem now.

And lastly, to anyone who saw themselves in these pages, and to the kids who survived—this book is for you, first and always. Never let anyone tell you that you are unworthy of love.